Praise for
the action-adventure novels
by Captain David E. Meadows

"An absorbing, compelling look at America's future place in the world. It's visionary and scary."

—Joe Buff, author of *Seas of Crisis,*
Straits of Power, and *Tidal Rip*

"If you enjoy a well-told tale of action and adventure, you will love David Meadows's series, *The Sixth Fleet.* Not only does the author know his subject but [his] fiction could readily become fact. These books should be read by every senator and congressman in our government so that the scenarios therein do not become history."

—John Tegler, syndicated talk show
host of *Capital Conversation*

"Meadows will have you turning pages and thinking new thoughts."   —Newt Gingrich

"Meadows takes us right to the bridge, in the cockpit, and into the thick of battle. Meadows is a military adventure writer who's been there, done it all, and knows the territory. This is as real as it gets."   —Robert Gandt

"Meadows delivers one heck of a fast-paced, roller coaster ride with this exhilarating military thriller."

—*Midwest Book Review*

Berkley titles by David E. Meadows

FINAL RUN
ECHO CLASS

DARK PACIFIC
DARK PACIFIC: PACIFIC THREAT
DARK PACIFIC: FINAL FATHOM

JOINT TASK FORCE: LIBERIA
JOINT TASK FORCE: AMERICA
JOINT TASK FORCE: FRANCE
JOINT TASK FORCE: AFRICA

THE SIXTH FLEET
THE SIXTH FLEET: SEAWOLF
THE SIXTH FLEET: TOMCAT
THE SIXTH FLEET: COBRA

ECHO CLASS

DAVID E. MEADOWS

BERKLEY BOOKS, NEW YORK

THE BERKLEY PUBLISHING GROUP
Published by the Penguin Group
Penguin Group (USA) Inc.
375 Hudson Street, New York, New York 10014, USA
Penguin Group (Canada), 90 Eglinton Avenue East, Suite 700, Toronto, Ontario M4P 2Y3, Canada
(a division of Pearson Penguin Canada Inc.)
Penguin Books Ltd., 80 Strand, London WC2R 0RL, England
Penguin Group Ireland, 25 St. Stephen's Green, Dublin 2, Ireland (a division of Penguin Books Ltd.)
Penguin Group (Australia), 250 Camberwell Road, Camberwell, Victoria 3124, Australia
(a division of Pearson Australia Group Pty. Ltd.)
Penguin Books India Pvt. Ltd., 11 Community Centre, Panchsheel Park, New Delhi—110 017, India
Penguin Group (NZ), 67 Apollo Drive, Rosedale, North Shore 0632, New Zealand
(a division of Pearson New Zealand Ltd.)
Penguin Books (South Africa) (Pty.) Ltd., 24 Sturdee Avenue, Rosebank, Johannesburg 2196,
South Africa

Penguin Books Ltd., Registered Offices: 80 Strand, London WC2R 0RL, England

This is a work of fiction. Names, characters, places, and incidents either are the product of the author's imagination or are used fictitiously, and any resemblance to actual persons, living or dead, business establishments, events, or locales is entirely coincidental. The publisher does not have any control over and does not assume any responsibility for author or third-party websites or their content.

ECHO CLASS

A Berkley Book / published by arrangement with the author

PRINTING HISTORY
Berkley edition / February 2009

Copyright © 2009 by The Berkley Publishing Group.
Interior text design by Kristin del Rosario.

ISBN: 978-0-425-22631-5

BERKLEY®
Berkley Books are published by The Berkley Publishing Group,
a division of Penguin Group (USA) Inc.,
375 Hudson Street, New York, New York 10014.
BERKLEY® is a registered trademark of Penguin Group (USA) Inc.
The "B" design is a trademark of Penguin Group (USA) Inc.

PRINTED IN THE UNITED STATES OF AMERICA

10 9 8 7 6 5 4 3 2 1

Acknowledgments

My thanks to all of you who offered your Cold War experiences. It helped in my own recall to events at sea that never made the headlines ashore. A special thanks and acknowledgment to my editor, Tom Colgan, who came up with this idea to develop a Cold War series. These books bring back a nostalgia for the era when we had an enemy that was easy to find, but hard to kill. Today, with asymmetric warfare (Pentagon-speak for terrorism), we have an enemy that is hard to find, but easy to kill. It has been fun and exciting to write this series and I hope you enjoy it also. My thanks to my agent, John Talbot, who encouraged me in this endeavor and to Tom Colgan's right-hand person, Sandra Harding, who sends such encouraging notes and e-mails.

My deep respects and thanks go to the readers who enjoy these action-adventure novels. I read each and every one of your e-mails to the website www.sixthfleet.com and appreciate your comments, reviews, and critiques. All the best, shipmates.

Cheers,
David E. Meadows

Foreword

This is the second in a series of novels written to capture the Cold War at sea pitting the United States and its allies against the Soviet Union. The time is June 1967, a few days before the Israeli Air Force would wipe out the Syrian and Egyptian air forces as the Six-Day War erupted. But this is not a story about that Middle East war. The story I want to tell takes place in the Pacific Ocean, far from the events unfolding in the Middle East.

It was a watershed year for both navies, with America engaged in the unpopular Vietnam War and the Soviet Union pouring supplies and logistical support into North Vietnam. America had its advisors with the South Vietnamese military, and the Soviet Union had similar advisors with the North Vietnamese. The American Navy had decided that nuclear submarines would make up its submarine force. It still had diesel submarines, but they were on their way out. The Soviet Navy was building nuclear submarines as fast as their shipyards could turn them out, having decided to transition to a full nuclear submarine force. They were also building professional sailors as well trained and patriotic as those in the American, British, French, Italian, and other Allied navies.

By June 1967, the Soviet Navy was a global naval power that with the passing of each year further threatened the dominance of the Western navies. It had no aircraft carriers, but like other modern nations that aspire to dominance on the seas it had started with building a massive submarine force to lead the way. Germany did it in World War II. The United States did it when Pearl Harbor left us with only submarines and aircraft carriers at the beginning of the war. The Chinese are doing it today. Countries who believe they stand on the precipice of being a global naval power start with submarines. They don't build aircraft carriers and battleships in today's modern era. They build submarines capable of taking the battle away from their own shores. Submarines are the military canaries of world power.

Throughout the Cold War, both sides fought never-ending battles for political victory through brushfire wars. The Middle East became the proving ground for the superpower giants, where clashes between proxies forever drew them nearer to cataclysmic events that could have turned the Cold War into a hot one. Nineteen sixty-seven was such a year, and the actions in the pages to come take place as the Arab militaries of Syria and Egypt rattled their war drums and announced to the world that they intended to wipe Israel from the face of the earth, and Israel responded with the air attack of June 5. It was also a time when superpowers were shown that their proxies were not without their own nationalistic ideas, as the Israelis intentionally attacked the USS *Liberty* on June 8.

At-sea clashes, collisions, and events are always easier to hide from the public, and many things that occurred between the Soviet Navy and the United States Navy will be taken to the grave by the men and women who served "haze-gray under way" over the horizon from their homelands. During the Cold War, confrontations between the two great powers out of sight of the shore never stopped. Whether it was cutting across the bows of ships to make the skipper take emergency maneuvering actions, or the continuous tracking, targeting, and simulated sinking of each other's naval forces: Things happened.

The Cold War is filled with documented incidents of confrontations and events that occurred at sea. And there are many more sea tales and hints of conspiracy in both navies that never made the newspapers of the era. Things happened. Sometimes men died. Sometimes ships and submarines disappeared. The belief that what happened at sea stayed at sea was a half-truth of the Cold War. The seas were where the Soviet and Allied navies looked for ways to flex their navy muscle; where captains and crews thrilled to the race of adrenaline through their bodies, while wondering if this "might be the time," when an at-sea brushfire roiled across the oceans and trampled across the beaches, inciting a global conflagration. Every incident held that possibility, and it was only through the restraint of both navies' commanding officers and professional crews that this never happened.

But let me tell you a little bit about this story. It pits against each other two career navy captains, who must try to figure out what the other is about to do, execute the dangerous orders of their superiors, and complete their missions without starting World War III. The Soviet submarines in the story are the Echo I class K-122 and the Echo II class K-56. Both are real, both existed during this period, both are nuclear, and both have a "real" history you can find on the Internet. While I populate the two subs with characters, rest assured I have no idea who the professionals were who actually manned them.

The primary American ships in the story are the destroyers USS *Dale* and USS *Coghlan*. USS *Dale* is the protagonist for the story, and I used a real Forrest Sherman class destroyer of that period, the USS *Davis* (DD-973), as the model. Though I identify them as Forrest Sherman class destroyers, the names of my destroyers honor two of the three that made a suicide run against a superior Japanese fleet in the World War II engagement known as the Battle of the Komandorski Islands. USS *Dale* was DD-353 and USS *Coghlan* was DD-606; the third destroyer was USS *Monaghan* (DD-354), a survivor of Pearl Harbor. This Komandorski battle stopped the Japanese from landing troops in the Aleutians. The three destroyers survived because a lucky hit by one of them killed the Japanese admiral leading the enemy battle group. The destroyers had been considered expendable and the torpedo run against the Japanese suicidal, with full expectation by Rear Admiral Charles McMorris that the ships would be destroyed. This story could not have been written if the *Coghlan* had not survived. My father was a first class radioman on board that destroyer during that fateful run. Someday I may write the story of that battle. My father, like many others on those three ships, never forgave McMorris for abandoning them to their fate while he sailed away with his cruisers to "fight another day."

In this story, none of the personalities on the Soviet boats or the American warships are real. They are fabrications of my imagination, and as with all works of fiction, this one carries a disclaimer inside the cover. As for the Soviet submarines, I have no knowledge of who the skippers were, or the Navy souls who manned them. It has been my intention in writing this series to capture the professional life of both navies, the humanity of the characters, and the challenges of the Cold War that catapulted our forces against each other.

Some literary liberty is taken in the story. For example, throughout the book, local Subic Bay time is used for both navies even though the Soviet Union always used Moscow time for its fleet. Trying to coordinate two different time zones was too confusing for the writer to keep track. Both navies show knots for speed, but the Soviet Navy used the metric system while the U.S. Navy used the English system of inches, feet, yards, and nautical miles. A nautical mile is two thousand yards, for the landlubbers among you.

ONE

CAPTAIN Second Rank Kostenka Bocharkov spun the search periscope in a complete three-sixty circle. Not a damn thing in sight. An empty ocean stretched for at least fifteen miles in each direction. The Pacific waves were calm, barely lapping against the scope, but then the K-122 was barely making way at periscope depth. Too much speed at this depth created a wake behind them that the Americans could see.

Bocharkov released the handles for a moment and rubbed his thumb across his fingers before grabbing the handles again. The Soviet captain second rank stopped the scope· when it was aligned forward with the bow of the K-122. For nearly a minute he observed the direction of the swells.

"Course?" he shouted.

"One-one-zero, Captain!"

He squinted, watching the swell of the waves again. It was amazing how easy it was to determine wind direction with heavier waves—not sea state five and above. Those waves were too rough and would have kept him down a hundred meters in the relative calm of the seas beneath. The Pacific was a calm ocean in comparison to the violent North Atlantic where he started his career.

Finally satisfied, he took one last full-circle glance around the ocean before leaning away from the scope.

He looked around the control room. "All clear. Sea state is one. Wind is north by northeast. Report." He glanced at the navigator, who had leaned up from crouching over his charts. An unlit cigarette drooped from the man's lips. As if feeling Bocharkov's gaze, Tverdokhleb looked up at the skipper and pushed the heavy black-rimmed glasses up off the tip of his nose.

"Sonar reports passive detection," Lieutenant Commander Orlov, the operations officer, announced, bringing Bocharkov's attention away from the navigator.

"Comms, Comrade Orlov? We still have comms with the *Reshitelny*?"

Orlov looked at Chief Starshina Volkov. "Chief, hit *Boyevaya Chast'* 1 and ask the communicators the status of our secure communications with the Kashin class destroyer trailing the Americans." Internal communications within Soviet warships were the same, with BCh-1 allocated to the communicators, 2 for surface ships, 3 for sonar, and so on down the list.

Nearly thirty seconds passed before the officer of the deck, also the operations officer, replied to Bocharkov's question. "The destroyer is still with the American carrier *Kitty Hawk*, sir. We are receiving a constant stream of targeting data from it. It is being inputted into the firing panel."

Bocharkov looked at the panel located on the aft port side of the K-122. Chief Starshina Diemchuk stood near the panel. Red and green lights, some steady, most flickering, readily told any observer why submariners referred to the firing panel as the Christmas Tree.

Bocharkov brought his eyes back to the periscope and did another search. The Kashin class destroyer had been tailing the American aircraft carrier for two weeks—ever since the *Kitty Hawk* departed its homeport of Yokuska, Japan.

He leaned away from the periscope, looked at Diemchuk, but spoke to Orlov. "And what is Weapons doing with the targeting data?" He caught the sideways glance exchanged between the chief of the boat, Chief Ship Starshina Uvarova, and the planesman he was always hovering near. Bocharkov smiled. He had yet to meet a chief of the boat who did not believe he was the real owner of the submarine. That was what made the COB so almighty important.

"They are refining the firing solution, Captain. We will be prepared to surface and simulate firing at your command."

"Very well." He let out a deep sigh. "Continue with the exercise. Remind everyone that no missile doors are to be opened when we surface," he warned. There would be no accidental launch, and if the Americans did stumble across them, there must be no misinterpretation of the K-122 intentions.

The Americans knew that to fire the missile required the Echo I submarine to surface. The Americans called the missile Shaddock. He wondered why. The Soviet nomenclature for the missile was the P-5.

Surface he would do. Firing also required that they open the missile hatches. That he would not do. If the Americans spotted the K-122, the closed missile hatches would ensure they understood this was an exercise. If a war were to start between the imperialists and the great Soviet Union, let it begin elsewhere. Not here in the South China Sea between the Philippines and Vietnam.

He glanced at the clock on the aft bulkhead of the control room. It was always night in a submarine until the periscope broke water. Four o'clock in the afternoon and barely a cloud in the sky. Why could they not do their exercises at night? A surfaced submarine was anathema to everything a submariner trained to do, especially during daylight hours.

"Sir, we have the targeting data refined."

Soviet doctrine showed that the Americans never engaged in two wars simultaneously. They were a one-war nation. They had never had to fight a modern enemy on their own soil as the Soviet Union did during the Great Patriotic War. When the Great Patriotic War ended, the Americans started a war in Korea. When they had enough training there, they jumped into the war between the Vietnams. It was only a matter of time before they decided they were ready for the Soviet Union.

"Engine room reports reactor coolant pump number one is acting up again, Captain. They have shut it down for repairs," Chief Diemchuk, the chief of the watch, reported.

"Have the chief engineer report to me when repairs are

done," Bocharkov replied. If it wasn't the number one coolant pump, it would be something else. As long as one of the three coolant pumps functioned, the graphite-water reactor would keep its temperature within parameters.

"Aye, Skipper," Diemchuk acknowledged.

"Officer of the Deck, last chance: Ask Sonar if they have any contacts closing us."

Bocharkov left the periscope unmanned and walked over to the sonar area just as Diemchuk finished relaying his orders to the engineering room. "Chief Diemchuk, make sure you do not hit the firing mechanisms, okay?"

"No contacts closing us, sir," Orlov reported

Diemchuk straightened. "No, sir, Captain." Diemchuk reached up and tapped the clear plastic covering the red firing buttons. "I have no intentions of lifting these covers, sir."

Bocharkov stroked his chin for a moment, then chuckled. He looked around the control room. "Looks as if we may have a successful exercise, comrades."

They laughed with him.

"Remember," he told them, raising a finger, "we practice for the day when we may have to actually do this. We do not practice for the sake of practice." He gave a curt nod. "Right?"

"Right!" they replied in unison.

"Good. Let's do this right and then we can head for the deep Pacific and have some of the great chow the K-122 is famous for. Right?"

When no one immediately answered, Bocharkov continued, "Okay, at least the food is plentiful. Right?"

"Right!" they shouted in unison, laughing afterward.

The moment of levity made Bocharkov think of his family in Kamchatka, bringing a brief moment of longing washing across him. He shook it off, his mind back on the exercise as he returned to the periscope. The navy had rewarded his less than zealous Party affiliation by giving him the honor of serving his country as the commanding officer of one of its nuclear attack submarines. Few others could claim such an honor. A wave of patriotic ardor swept over him.

"High-value target bearing one-one-zero degrees, distance three hundred twenty kilometers. Target course remains zero-three-zero degrees, speed ten knots," Lieutenant Orlov announced.

"Very well. And its direction of travel?" Kostenka Bocharkov asked.

"The American carrier is on course one eight five degrees, Comrade Captain."

"How old is the information?"

"The surveillance ship reported this less than a minute ago, sir."

"Then it must be so," Bocharkov answered, his voice trailing off. "After all, sometimes we must trust our surface comrades, right?"

"Yes, Captain," Orlov replied.

"Of course, it is right. After all, the *Reshitelny* is sailing with them." Bocharkov paused. He motioned the operations officer to him. When Orlov reached the periscope, Bocharkov said in a low voice, "Well, *Reshitelny* is near them, so he is our eyes. So, now what would you do, Lieutenant Commander Orlov? When should we surface?"

"I would input three more targeting solutions, sir. I would refine the targeting solution as much as possible."

"Why?"

"Sir, because once we fire our missiles, the Americans will know where we are. We will have to go deep to evade. We may not know the success until we are able to successfully evade their attack. So, we must make our first punch hard." Orlov raised a fist and shook it. "And, it must be on target."

"How many missiles does doctrine call for in this situation?"

Bocharkov's mustache stretched slightly as his lips spread in a tight smile. He liked his operations officer. Lieutenant Commander Orlov would go far in the submarine service.

The young officer rocked on his feet for several seconds. Bocharkov was sure that if they had had the space in the control room, Orlov would have paced instead of rocked. He had the look of a pacer to him. Bocharkov knew what the operations officer was thinking—weighing the tactical picture only visible on the charts across the plotting table and within the minds of the men who would fight the boat.

"There will be few times in actual combat when you will have the time to ponder a solution, Commander Orlov."

Orlov nodded, but said nothing. Several seconds more passed before Orlov stopped and looked at Bocharkov. "I would recommend six cruise missiles fired one after the other."

"Two questions," Bocharkov replied. "One, tell me why? And, two, why did it take you nearly a minute to reach a decision that is doctrine?"

"Because six missiles coming at sea level toward the American battle group would keep their ships maneuvering to avoid. It would keep the aircraft carrier from launching until after our attack. And doctrine shows that at least fifty percent of the missiles will survive their NATO Seasparrow missile systems."

"And the number two?"

Orlov's forehead rose for a moment before relaxing. "Six is all we have."

Bocharkov grunted. "Six is all we have, Commander, but you knew the answer without having to give this an hour of thought," he exaggerated. He leaned his head down as if sharing a secret. "You must know it instinctively. You must have thought about it long before the time comes for making the decision. You must have given thought to anything that can happen to a submarine, whether it is planned, an exercise, or, worst case, an emergency that requires immediate decisions to save the ship. Regardless, your decision must be viewed by the men as the right decision even if you are unsure." He leaned away. "Plus, you've got to stop this rocking on your heels whenever you are weighing various options. It gives the impression of uncertainty."

"I am sorry, Captain. Was I rocking again?"

Bocharkov smiled. "I think it is only because you are unable to pace. You strike me as a pacer. Let's say you were twisting from right to left, then back again left to right—more a Cossack wedding dance than a pace. So now tell me, Burian. Tell me why we only have six missiles in this class of submarine.

"As the captain so rightly pointed out our limitations, six cruise missiles are what navy doctrine says are necessary to sink an American aircraft carrier. We fire all of them at the

American carrier and then, once the missiles are gone, we shift to our secondary mission as an anti-ship submarine until our torpedoes are gone."

Bocharkov waited, expressionless, for Orlov to finish.

A second, two, went by before the operations officer continued, "Most anything can survive the American point defense system." He held up a finger. "With six low-flying missiles arriving near simultaneously over the horizon, we would hit the American carrier."

Bocharkov smiled with a nod, his lower lip pushing the upper so the thin mustache crowded the nostrils. His eyebrows rose as he spoke. "And do you agree with our doctrine? Are six missiles enough to sink an aircraft carrier?"

"We have tested the doctrine, sir. We studied it in class," Orlov answered.

"That is good, but that is the book answer. It's an emotional answer that someone who never had been in battle came up with." He grunted. "That is not to say they are not right, but the truth is the odds are against us hitting that one vital spot where the carrier's own armament or fuel is exposed." He shook his head. "During World War II multiple kamikaze hits on carriers seldom sunk them. They are truly indefatigable. We would need a minimum of four, I believe, to sink her."

"Our training said two could sink her."

Bocharkov nodded. "Two would merely piss them off. Four would sting, but not stop an aircraft carrier, but if the six missiles hit along the line of the carrier from bow to stern, then it would either sink her or render her out of action. Sometimes just taking a warship out of action can change the course of a battle."

Orlov looked bemused. "But in tactical training we were taught that two could sink, four would sink, and six made sure nothing was left above the waterline."

Bocharkov grunted and then leaned forward as if sharing a conspiracy. "There is a saying that those who can, do; those who can't, teach. Fighting at sea is very different from fighting the battle from a desk with a ruler, a pencil, and a stack of books."

"Yes, Captain."

"So, how would you space the firing trajectory to increase the odds of us hitting the American carrier more than once?"

Orlov replied, his thin frame straightening, "Sir, I would also recommend a one-degree spread with each missile." He waved his hand in the air, twisting the spread fingers. "One would hit the target."

Bocharkov nodded. "Didn't you tell me two had to have hit the target?"

"The exercise only calls for disabling it. For stopping it from achieving its launch location." Orlov's eyes darted toward the XO, who had stepped through the forward hatch. "One hit would disable it. The other missiles would also achieve an extra goal of possibly hitting other ships in the battle group."

"Lieutenant Commander Orlov, you are good, very good," Bocharkov said with a smile. "The exercise does not call for disabling or sinking the aircraft carrier. It just calls for us to simulate launching our missiles. But, I have to admit that was a good, quick answer designed to steer me away."

"Sir, I would never . . ."

"The truth, as I see it, Burian . . . and I am in the same situation as you: I have never fired on an aircraft carrier or any enemy warship for that matter. But, as I see it, with that many missiles appearing suddenly over the horizon, there will be many American sailors hunting for clean underwear afterward."

Ignatova laughed from behind Orlov and slapped the lieutenant commander on his back. "Amazing sight, an American aircraft carrier, isn't it, Captain?"

Bocharkov grunted. "We will have our own someday." He turned to Orlov. "Bring me up-to-date on how the events will unfold."

"I'll go check a few other things," Ignatova said, nodding at Bocharkov before walking off toward the other side of the control room.

For the next few minutes Bocharkov and Orlov exchanged technical discussion, finally deciding on a half-degree separation between the missiles, with the second three firing along the same lines of bearing, with the same half-degree separation. Theoretically, if the two officers were right, by the time the first three had hit target, the *Kitty Hawk* would be drifting, so the second three would deliver the coup de grâce. Bocharkov enjoyed the discussion. He learned, and so did Orlov, from doing it. The rest of the officers and sailors in the control room also learned.

"That satisfies me, Lieutenant Commander Orlov," Bocharkov said, motioning the operations officer away. "Go ahead and finish the exercise."

"Let's hope it satisfies the Kashin," Ignatova said as he returned. "After all, they are the graders for this exercise."

"Nothing satisfies a surface sailor except more vodka and port calls."

Orlov crossed the small space to his position near the helmsman.

In a soft voice, the XO Vladmiri Ignatova whispered, "The communicators are reporting that an American destroyer has locked its fire control radar on the *Reshitelny*."

Borcharkov's heavy eyebrows arched. "Why would they do that?"

"I suspect they suspect our surviellance ship is targeting their carrier."

Bocharkov shook his head. "No way they could know. The *Reshitelny* is using encrypted communications."

Ignatova shrugged. "He must have done something to alert them. He says his electronic warfare suite is lighting up all over the place."

"Is he asking or telling us?"

"I think he is hoping you will tell him that we are finished with the exercise so he can put some over-the-horizon distance between him and the American battle group."

Bocharkov shook his head and grunted. "No, we cannot run every time we think the Americans are going to attack us. They have never attacked us yet, so why now?" His eyebrows lifted. "Besides, the *Reshitelny* is expendable. He knows that. That is his job when he is tailing the Americans. He is to fire his missiles and torpedoes simutaneously with our launch and then die in the name of the Soviet Union."

Ignatova's eyes shifted right and left.

Bocharkov leaned down and whispered, "The *zampolit* is in his stateroom preparing for tonight's Party-political work."

His eyes twinkled. "I hear it's going to cover the bravery of Khrushchev in exposing the evils of Stalin."

"Sir," Ignatova said softly, his head lowered. "You must be careful."

Bocharkov smiled, and changed the subject. "Have we attacked the Americans? No. Besides, these are international waters. We are exercising our international rights. And both our navies exercise how we are going to sink each other. They would be disappointed if we stopped our exercise now."

"I think the skipper of the *Reshitelny* wants to exercise his international rights elsewhere."

"Surface sailors," Bocharkov said with a mix of humor and disgust. "I guess if I had to stay in a two-dimensional world like them, I would want to have more fighting room."

"*Reshitelny* reports the American carrier is altering course. *Kitty Hawk* is in a right-hand turn."

Bocharkov and Ignatova looked at Orlov.

"Maybe turning into the wind to launch aircraft?"

Bocharkov nodded, his lower lip pushing against his upper. "Did *Reshitelny* report any American aircraft airborne?"

"Yes, sir. It is conducting flight operations." He turned to the sound-powered telephone talker. "Starshina, hit *Boyevaya Chast'* 4 and ask the communicators to find out how many aircraft the Americans have up." Ignatova turned back to Bocharkov. "It should be in the *Reshitelny*'s situation report."

"And the rest of the battle group? Are they turning also?"

"I don't know, sir, but I will find out." He added the order to the earlier request.

"XO, we are going to surface and go through the checklist of launching our anticarrier missiles. Once we have simulated the launch—*without opening the doors*—then we are going to submerge and do the evasive part of the exercise plan."

"Don't forget the Middle East," Ignatova cautioned. "The rhetoric between the Jews and the Arabs continues to ramp up, which means Moscow and Washington are having one of their cooler months."

"Better cooler than hotter," Bocharkov mumbled. He looked at Ignatova. "Do you think we should call the exercise off?"

He shook his head. "No, sir, Captain. I agree with you, but

as your executive officer it is my responsibility to identify other options for your consideration."

"Go ahead," Bocharkov said. *No, doubt, XO,* he said to himself, *if I had my way, I would want to do what you would. Stay hidden beneath the ocean waves. But K-122 would be useless to our fighting forces if we never practiced how we would fire our missiles.*

"The *Reshitelny* has not reported any aircraft in our vicinity. We could surface as you propose, do our simulated firing, and leave the area submerged and undetected—or we could simulate surfacing also."

Bocharkov grunted. "We can simulate too much, I think, XO. Do you want to sign your name to the rationale we would have to send to Admiral Nikolai Nikolayevich Amelko, commander of the Pacific Fleet?"

Ignatova shook his head. "I would like to defer such an honor to you, Comrade Captain," he said buoyantly. "I agree. Less than a month ago, the admiral relieved a destroyer captain for returning to port early because of the threat of a storm."

Bocharkov opened his mouth slightly, then sighed. "XO, you sometimes surprise me with your options." He nodded sharply. "We will continue."

Bocharkov turned back to the firing console. "Lieutenant Commander Orlov! Are we ready?"

"All compartments report ready, sir. We are ready to fire at your command."

Bocharkov looked at Chief Ship Starshina Uvarova. "Chief of the Boat, surface the boat."

Everyone glanced at the senior enlisted man on board the K-122 as he grabbed the hydraulic control handles. The sound of compressed air filled the control room. High-pressure air rushed into the ballasts, pushing tons of saltwater out. Buoyancy was the key to survival for a submarine. The bow tilted upward as the K-122 rose the final sixteen meters toward the surface.

Bocharkov glanced at the depth gauge. Then he turned to the periscope, twisting it three hundred sixty degrees, searching the open ocean. Nothing. Still clear as far as he could see. "Clear!" he shouted.

"Surfaced!" came Uvarova's voice.

The submarine rocked slightly from the wave motion of the surface.

Bocharkov stepped back. "Down periscope. Open the hatch." He watched as a starshina—a petty officer—hustled up the ladder toward the sail area, passing through the last watertight compartment. On the diesel submarines, this compartment was called the conning tower. Less than ten years ago, when the Soviet and American navies had mostly diesel submarines, the periscope and most of the controls of the submarine were in the conning tower. Atomic power had allowed them to consolidate into the control room the systems and controls to both maneuver and fight the boat.

Bocharkov climbed into the compartment. Though he had never been in an American submarine, he knew the configuration was similar in both navies. Neither navy had figured out what to do with the conning tower.

The starshina never stopped. He scurried up the ladder, spun the hatch, and threw it back. A breath of fresh, warm Pacific air filled the small compartment. Bocharkov took a deep breath. You never realized how stale submarine air could grow until you surfaced and the outside air washed across your body.

Bocharkov followed the sailor up the ladder. Behind him came his executive officer, Captain Second Rank Vladmiri Ignatova. Captain second rank was the equivalent to an American or British commander.

"Ready?"

"Ready," Ignatova replied.

Bocharkov grabbed the sides of the ladder and scrambled up it, his eyes blinking as he adjusted to the glare of the summer Pacific sun. A slight breeze blew from the northeast. He nodded toward the east. "Somewhere in that direction is the Philippines."

Without waiting for an acknowledgment, Bocharkov raised his binoculars and scanned the horizon in the direction of the American battle group.

"Last position we had on the Americans put them northeast of our position," Ignatova said as he flipped open the sound-powered tube. "Simulate opening missile hatches!"

Bocharkov put a hand into his pocket and pressed the button on the side of the stopwatch.

A reply echoed up from the tube. "Simulating opening missile doors!"

A spot of motion caught Bocharkov's attention. He shifted the binoculars to the left, scanning the horizon. There it was again. Not quite clear, but something caught his eye. Something several degrees above the horizon. On a clear day at sea, the horizon was always twenty-four kilometers from your vessel. Fifteen miles, the Americans would say in their ancient system of measurements. What stubborn people the Americans could be. The rest of the world says, "Okay, we'll all switch to metrics." Not the Americans. "Too much trouble, we'll stay with our English measurements."

"Captain," Ignatova said.

Even the British were changing to the European metric system.

"Captain," Ignatova said again.

Bocharkov lowered the binoculars. "What is it, XO?"

"The missile doors are simulated open."

Bocharkov glanced forward where the near-circular outline of the missile doors covered the cruise missiles. Real-time, it would take nearly five minutes to prepare for launch and another couple of minutes to actually launch the missiles. Seven minutes was a lot of time to be on the surface of the ocean in the daylight. He had only launched twice in his career. Both launches were off Kamchatka during a live fire exercise.

He pulled the stopwatch from his pocket. Two minutes had passed.

"Let's give it five more minutes, XO. Two minutes is a little too much to expect, don't you think?"

The P-5 cruise missile was a magnificent missile, specifically designed to take out American aircraft carriers. It had a range of over three hundred fifty kilometers. Someday the Soviet Navy would be able to confront the Americans ship-to-ship, but in the meantime cruise missiles and the Soviet Naval Air Force would level the playing field. A massive number of cruise missiles arriving nearly simulateously from over the horizon—coordinated through command, control, and communications with everyone to create an ocean Armageddon of missiles fired by submarines, surface ships, and aircraft operating at staggered distances. Everything designed for the missiles to arrive at an American battle group simultaneously.

Bocharkov took a deep breath of patriotic pride over Admiral Gorshkov's strategic plan for winning the war at sea. Overwhelming might could be defeated by overwhelming fast and deadly weapons. And it was submarines that would make the difference. The Americans learned it during the Great Patriotic War. The Germans tried it in World War I and the Great Patriotic War. The Great Patriotic War forced the Soviet Union to start growing a submarine force.

Once launched, the wings of a P-5 cruise missile would unfold and it would zoom off toward the horizon at subsonic speed, leaving a spiraling contrail behind it as it sped toward its target. Bocharkov had six to fire and each had to be released separately. Once the first was fired, the others could be launched quickly, one after the other. Still, throughout the launching and the flight of the P-5 missiles, the submarine would remain on the surface—vulnerable to attack.

"Sir, I have an aircraft bearing three-three-zero relative off the bow!" shouted the starboard starshina, his finger pointing toward the horizon.

He was pointing to where Bocharkov had thought he detected motion a few moments earlier. Borcharkov glanced up at the periscope to see if the radar was active. It was open and turning, but he felt none of the static electricity associated with what the NATO countries called the Snoop Tray radar. He had not given permission to activate it. Electronic warfare being what it was in this age of electronics, they would have been detected almost immediately.

Definitely, he never had intention of activating the Front Door missile tracking radar during the exercise, for the same reason he had mandated the six missile doors be kept shut: an American misinterpretation. Americans were a dangerous lot. They were cowboys. They would fire first and with massive retaliation, then look at the damage, blow the smoke away from their barrels, and talk about what a fine fellow the victim used to be.

Bocharkov raised his binoculars, scanning in the direction of the starshina's finger. A flash of sunlight caught his attention. He pulled the glasses back toward it and a dark object filled the lens. He twisted the focus knob and quickly the vision of a four-engine propeller-driven plane with a bulbous bubble beneath its fuselage filled his eyesight. The three upright fins on the rear of the aircraft identified it as . . .

"It is an American reconnaissance plane," Ignatova said.

Bocharkov moved the glasses slightly, keeping them pointing at the aircraft, while he glanced to his side. His XO had his own glasses focused on the bogie. "It is an American Super Constellation," Bocharkov added. "An EC-121, they call them."

"Fleet Air Reconnassiance?"

"One. Fleet Air Reconnassiance One. Either flying out of the Philippines or out of Guam," Bocharkov added, dropping his binoculars.

"I think they are heading toward us."

Bocharkov grunted. "I think you are correct, XO." He put a hand over the binoculars to keep them from swaying as he turned. "Cancel the exercise, clear the bridge, and take the boat down," he said, his voice calm. Things like this happen at sea.

"Sir, I have bogies bearing zero-nine-zero relative!" the topside watch on the starboard side shouted.

Bocharkov looked to the right. Several aircraft were visible. Long white contrails marked their path like arrows pointed at the K-122. "Phantoms! They're fighter-bomber aircraft!" He looked at the sailors, all staring at the subsonic fighters heading toward them. "Clear the bridge!" he shouted, motioning with his hand. "Get below." Reconnaissance aircraft had no firepower, but those F-4 fighter-bombers could sink the boat, and you never knew what the Americans were going to do. They were mercurial in their tactics.

Bocharkov flipped open the brass cover of the sound-powered internal communications device. "Dive, dive! Take the boat down!"

As he shouted his command, the four topside watches scurried through the hatch and dropped onto the deck of the conning tower compartment below.

"XO, get below!"

Ignatova scrambled down the ladder.

Bocharkov took a last look around, ensuring no one was topside and making a visual inspection of the openings. Water rushed over the bow of the Echo. The angle of the bridge tilted forward as the boat sought solace beneath the surface. Once again his anticarrier warfare exercise had been disrupted by the Americans. What were they doing that allowed the Americans to find him so easily?

He took a last, quick look to the starboard side, the fighter aircraft now easily visible to the naked eye. Four, he counted. He looked forward and the "Willy Victor," as the Americans called the flying pig of an aircraft, must have vectored off its course, for he could make out the windows along the right side of the plane. They were probably photographing the K-122.

Then he turned, holding his glasses tight against his chest, and scrambled through the hatch. He stopped at the fourth rung to reach up and turn the wheel, securing the watertight hatch. Bocharkov gripped the sides of the ladder and slid the last few feet to the conning tower deck, stopping himself with his feet for a second before he continued to slide down toward the control room. As Bocharkov slid past, the senior starshina from the topside watches scurried up the ladder and double-checked the hatch.

"Take her down to one hundred meters, come to course two-two-zero. Increase speed to fifteen knots!" Bocharkov shouted as his feet hit the deck of the control room.

The Echo I submarine cut through the waters as an aircraft did the sky, heading downward while in a sharp right-hand turn, increasing speed.

Above the K-122, out of sight, American warplanes circled the area, radioing back to the battle group the exact location of the Soviet submarine.

Bocharkov imagined the scene above his boat, the Americans trying to pinpoint him, but he had seen no antisubmarine warfare aircraft capable of detecting and tracking him. He had several hours before the Americans could get their ASW forces arraigned against the K-122. By then, he would be lost in the Pacific, a notation on the intelligence sheets of the

Americans, but lost as each passing hour widened the search area in which they would have to look for him.

Bocharkov smiled and looked around the control room. Every sailor was bent forward over his position, focused on consoles or hands gripping levers and brass wheels as the boat sought safety in depth and evasion. He was under no delusion.

"Was that fun, Lieutenant Commander Orlov?"

The man's face seemed white in the red light of the control room. "It was exhilarating, Captain," Orlov replied, an audible exhalation following.

Bochavkov looked at Ignatova. "I believe we can do without the exhilaration, don't you think, XO?"

Ignatova nodded, his head turning to Orlov. "Officer of the Deck, report."

"Sir, steady on course two-two-zero, passing depth sixty meters, heading to one hundred meters. Speed fifteen knots."

"Very well," Ignatova acknowledged. The XO looked at Bocharkov. "Sir?"

"I heard, XO. Once we reach one hundred meters, we will do a left-hand turn to zero-seven-zero."

"Zero-seven-zero?"

Bocharkov grinned. "Zero-seven-zero. Most likely the reconnaissance aircraft caught our sharp turn to port. At one hundred meters only the fish will know when we turn. Our mission in this exercise is to simulate sinking the *Kitty Hawk*. Hard to do it if we are running away, so we'll turn back toward them."

"Yes, sir, Captain. But, most likely they are going to throw what antisubmarine forces they have against us . . ."

"You are right, Commander. Let's hope those forces pass right over us and search the area where we've been and not where we're going to be. Now it's time for the cat-and-mouse play where the ASW forces of our enemy seek out the evading target. We are their target."

Bocharkov was not worried. Seldom did either nation succeed in finding the other's submarine. When they did, it was a boasting accomplishment for the winner and a series of butt-tightening standing-tall explanations before their admirals for the loser.

"Looks as if we won this one," Orlov offered.

Bocharkov's forehead wrinkled as his smile faded. "I would say they accomplished their mission."

"But, we escaped," Orlov retorted too quickly. His eyes widened. "Pardon me, Comrade Captain."

Bocharkov motioned the apology away with a grunt. He looked at the XO. "Commander, would you enlighten our operations officer," he said good-naturedly.

"Of course, sir," Ignatova replied, with a slight smile. "The Americans were not after sinking us. They wanted us to submerge. What we witnessed with the F-4 Phantoms coming at us was the American tactic of disrupting us firing our missiles. They were successful"—he paused—"this time."

"Next time, they may not be successful, and when they let their guard down, that is when we will wipe a battle group from the face of the ocean," Bocharkov said. He remembered his stopwatch and pulled it from his pocket. Seven minutes had passed.

"How did they know where we were?" Orlov asked.

"I can only think the American reconnaissance aircraft in the vicinity detected us."

"But we did not have our radar operating. All we had was a broadcast link from the *Reshitelny*. We never acknowledged any of the transmissions."

Bocharkov's forehead wrinkled further. "I don't know, Lieutenant Commander Orlov." After a couple of seconds, he mumbled, "I just don't know."

"Steadying up on course two-two-zero."

"Final trim—one-zero-zero meters!" Uvarova announced from his position, looking over the shoulder of the planesman.

"Slow speed to eight knots," Bocharkov ordered and almost immediately felt the forward momentum taper off. "Come left to course zero-seven-zero."

He and Ignatova listened as Orlov turned his orders into actions. Bocharkov watched without comment as the helmsman turned the submarine. The planesman watched the angles of the bow planes as the boat turned. He glanced at the annunciator as the speed eased to eight knots. Everything running smoothly. For the next few minutes they would be going through the area where they had submerged.

In the background of voices within the control room, Bocharkov heard the starshina manning the sound-powered internal communications system call to the officer of the deck.

"What do you think?" Ignatova asked Bocharkov.

"I think they stopped us from simulating the launch of our missiles. In a real-world attack, we would have gotten one off, maybe more—but they would have sunk us during the targeting tracking phase, so the missiles would have been 'deadheads' heading toward targets that would turn away, jam them, or shoot them down."

"We have done successful anticarrier exercises, Captain."

"Of course we have," Bocharkov snapped. "We have studied the one we did last year in the North Atlantic."

Neither said anything, both of them realizing that the exercise Bocharkov referenced was a massive one involving Tupelov bombers, surface ships, and many submarines. Additionally, the American carrier battle group had been simulated. Both knew something was creating discord in the Soviet war-at-sea doctrine. Senior admirals knew it, too, but no one wanted to discuss it for fear they would be marked as anti-Party-political.

Orlov crossed the control room to where Bocharkov and Ignatova stood. "Just got word from the communciators, sir, on *Boyevaya Chast'* 4. They are reporting receipt of a high-priority message from Commander Pacific Fleet, sir."

"Tell the communications officer to bring it to me."

"Apparently, it is top secret code word, sir."

Bocharkov grunted. "Okay. XO, I will be in radio."

As he turned to go, a slight clang vibrated through the hull of the boat, drawing everyone's attention upward.

"What in the hell was—?" Bocharkov had started to ask, when a steady clanging started vibrating through the ship.

"Clappers," Uvarova said. "Damn them."

All eyes in the control room turned toward him. He had heard of these. Clappers. Hundreds of little magnetic noise-makers dropped by the Americans over a large area of the ocean, searching for something metal upon which to latch.

"Bring the boat to all stop." As the speed dropped off, the clacking sound created by water moving through the cheap mechanical devices diminished.

"What do we do?"

"Officer of the Deck, ask Sonar what is the layer depth," Bocharkov ordered.

A few seconds later, Orlov said, "Sonar reports layer depth at seventy-five meters, sir."

"Then let's hope the Americans cannot hear them," Ignatova said.

"I don't think they did, XO."

"Sir?"

The clappers continued to vibrate, with the intensity lessening as the boat slowed toward all stop.

"They have no ASW forces within a hundred miles of us. This was pure dumb luck. What they did was fire in the blind with their devices, putting noise in the water, hoping that we would continue away, and when their P-3 ASW Orion aircraft showed up, it would drop a few sonobuoys, detect the clapping, and ergo simulate a sinking."

Everyone looked at Bocharkov.

"We will use established Soviet Navy doctrine," he said.

Ignatova and Orlov looked questioningly at him.

"We stay put until nightfall, then we surface, rush out on deck, pull the little *zasranecs* off," he announced, using the colloquial expression for "asshole," "and then we continue our closure of the American battle group."

Laughter filled the compartment

"Toss them overboard," Orlov added to the humor.

Ignatova shook his head. "No, we bring them aboard for our scientists to assess." He looked at the captain.

"Probably a good idea. I suspect they already have a pot of them, but I would like to see what they look like also."

He turned at the sound of someone opening the aft watertight hatch to the control room. Lieutenant Motka Gromeko stepped into the compartment, wearing his dark Spetsnaz utilities. For the last six months, submarines heading to the waters of Vietnam had begun carrying a team of Soviet Naval Special Forces. Bocharkov nodded at the lieutenant, who stepped away from the hatch and pressed himself against the nearby bulkhead, away from the ongoing activity.

Five minutes later, after Bocharkov finished giving further instructions on what to do if American forces were detected in the area, he departed through the aft hatch, toward the radio shack. Gromeko followed him, causing Ignatova to scratch his head, wondering what was going on. An XO should always know before the skipper what was happening with the boat.

Bocharkov wondered what type of super-secret message Pacific Fleet would have sent for his eyes only. His mission was to track the *Kitty Hawk* until the carrier reached the Vietnamese waters, then they could return to Kamchatka.

Minutes later, Bocharkov discovered how wrong he was.

TWO

"CAPTAIN on the bridge!" the boatswain mate of the watch shouted as MacDonald walked through the port inside hatch that led from the combat information center.

At the navigator table directly ahead of him, the signalman on duty made a notation in the ship's log.

"What you got?" MacDonald asked, looking at the officer of the deck, Lieutenant Sam Goldstein, who was looking over the shoulder of the quartermaster, making sure the petty officer was making the proper notation. Goldstein was the *Dale*'s administrative officer and navigator.

Goldstein smiled. "Sir, Admiral Green wants you to contact him. He intends to detach us from the battle group to lead an antisubmarine surface action group."

MacDonald nodded, crossed the bridge, and crawled up in his chair on the starboard side. "I know," he replied. The combat information center watch officer told me on the way to the bridge." From the darkness lit by blue light in Combat to the bright sunlight of the bridge. Enough to ruin your eyes. He crossed his legs. Give him the bridge any day to fight his ship, rather than this high-brow concept of where the captain hides in the darkness to launch his weapons.

"Lieutenant Burnham has the watch," MacDonald said, his voice slow and methodical.

"Aye, sir. Does the captain want to go to general quarters?"

MacDonald shook his head. "No, the captain does not want to go to general quarters. If we have a submarine out there two hundred miles from us, it will be tomorrow morning before we reach the vicinity of last sighting. What would our condition be if we kept the men at GQ for . . ." He looked at Goldstein. "Quick! Tell me how long we would have to keep the ship at GQ before we reached the area." He put both hands on his hips. "Well, anytime this afternoon would be fine, Mr. Goldstein."

"Twelve hours, sir."

"Twelve hours is wrong," MacDonald said calmly. "But it would bring us to within the horizon of where the suspected submarine was last seen."

"I was told the reconnaissance aircraft out of Guam saw it."

"Airdales see what they want to see. They have been known to be wrong, but don't ever try to get one to admit it; it is like pulling teeth. Did I ever tell you about my niece who had a blind date with one?"

"No, sir."

"Unfortunately, I lined it up. She came back from the date just shaking her head. Brenda met her at the door, wanting to know how it went. My niece said the first half of the date all the airdale did was talk about himself. Then, about halfway through dinner he said, 'Well, enough about me, let's talk about flying.' "

Goldstein chuckled. "Aye, sir."

"Did we get any intelligence from the VQ-1 Willy Victor that overflew the submarine?"

"Not much, sir. They sent an operational report, but the OpRep only gave the coordinates of the submarine with the direction in which it dived."

"We can expect the submarine came to a different course as soon as it was out of sight."

"They dropped some clappers."

"Useless piece of shit those clappers. I don't think any

submarine has ever been tracked or detected because of those cheap things. We drop them and somewhere on the bottom of the ocean are growing beds of clappers, clapping away as the current swifts through them. Keep this up, by the time you and I have grandchildren, we'll have an ocean that's transmitting a continuous cacophony of clapper symphony.

"As for GQ, Mr. Goldstein, you keep offering advice when I ask it. If you don't and I make a wrong decision and you knew the correct answer, then you will have let me and the ship down. Meanwhile, let's keep the crew doing the day's work." He leaned forward, out of the shadow offered by the forward top bridge structure, letting the sun hit his face. "Might even be able to have the movie topside tonight if this weather holds," he said, leaning back into the shadow.

"Some new ones came aboard during the under-way replenishment yesterday, Skipper."

MacDonald pointed at the navigation table. "You need to have your watch work us a path out of the battle group. We're going to be heading southwest toward the datum."

"Datum" was the naval term commonly used to identify the last known location of a submarine. Whatever happened to the good old terms such as "enemy," "submarine," "contact," or even "sneaky bastard"? No. Somewhere there was an academic think tank laughing, drinking their martinis, and throwing all the dollars they'd made into the air, to let them rain down upon them because they came up with this new way of sinking subs. MacDonald sighed.

"Sir?"

He shook his head. "Nothing, Mr. Goldstein."

"Sir, the admiral?"

"Did you talk with him?"

Goldstein's eyes widened. "Yes, sir. He asked for you, and then asked for the officer of the deck."

MacDonald smiled. Green and he were old navy. When they wanted to talk with the senior officers, it was to the bridge they deferred.

The assistant boatswain mate of the watch brought him his first afternoon cup of coffee. MacDonald grunted as he took it, sipped, and calculated the coffee was leftover in the urn from this morning. He grimaced as the tannic acid burned when he swallowed. He put the cup in the nearby holder. It would remain there until the watch changed and the BMOW tossed the coffee out—if it hadn't eaten through the cup by then.

"Did he say how many ships he intended to put into this surface action group?" Before Goldstein could answer, MacDonald raised the palm of his hand at the officer. "And did he say who would be in charge of the SAG?"

"No, sir. He did not. He just asked to have you call him and for us to prepare to go after a submarine."

"Submarine? He called it a submarine?" MacDonald chuckled, his breath coming out more as a guffaw. It was nice working with Green again.

"Yes, sir. He said probably submarine. Said the—pardon me, sir—he said, 'the son of a bitch was targeting him.' "

"Well, he is on the carrier. Can't see a Forrest Sherman class destroyer like the *Dale* being the sub's high-valued target."

One moment he was grabbing forty winks and the next he was going after submarines. If the ocean had as many submarines as Green thought it did, then the marines could walk to Vietnam across their backs instead of sailing there.

He took a deep breath and let out an audible sigh. He knew Goldstein and the others on the bridge were wondering why he was waiting to return the admiral's call, but it was good for the crew to see the "Old Man" act as if events of a non-routine nature were normal. He believed strongly that to act otherwise promoted a condition much like Pavlov's dogs, where no one knew what to expect. It created a bedlam of confusion when your skipper was mercurial and unpredictable. He knew. He had served under such a man on his first ship as an ensign.

Besides, when all was said and done, it was his goddamn ship and not anyone else's. Might be his first. Might even be his last, if he screwed up this first command, but god damn it, it was his ship. He smiled.

The Navy Red secure communications squawked overhead; the bagpipe sound of the cipher keys synchronizing screamed for a couple of seconds before the normal white noise of the radio band filled the speaker. Then the call sign for Commander Task Force Seventy came from the voice on the speaker to every ship in the battle group, cautioning them that the *Kitty Hawk* was changing course.

Sailing with a carrier was dangerous. One wrong maneuver, one navigational error, and one ship's engineering casualty became another ship's navigational hazard, and a warship like the *Dale* would become fodder for the largest warship in the world—the American aircraft carrier.

The navigational rules of the road on the open ocean seldom applied to an aircraft carrier. The unwritten rule was that when an aircraft carrier was maneuvering, all others stood clear. It was the law of gross tonnage, and MacDonald did not want his last sight in life being the bow of an aircraft carrier hitting the *Dale* as those aboard the carrier wondered what that slight bump was they'd sailed over.

"How far are we from the *Kitty Hawk*?"

"Sir?"

"I said, Mr. Goldstein, how far are we from the *Kitty Hawk*?" he asked again, enunciating each word loudly and carefully. "A captain should not have to repeat himself."

"Aye, sir."

"Then how far are we?"

The quartermaster leaned toward Goldstein and whispered something.

"We are five miles, sir?"

"We are not five miles, Officer of the Deck. We are ten thousand yards. Not five miles," MacDonald rebutted. "Besides," he added, "it's five nautical miles, not five miles."

"Yes, sir."

MacDonald motioned Goldstein to him. When the young officer reached his chair, MacDonald leaned over toward him, putting his weight on his left elbow, resting on the arm of the captain's chair. "If you want to be a good officer of the deck, then you must own the bridge. Not depend on your sailors to cover your ass, Sam." He shook his head, his voice rising slightly. "Lieutenants should know the language of the bridge. Shit! I expect them to know the language of the navy. You should know . . . No—you *must* know everything about the condition of the *Dale*, and you must know every navigational detail about our destroyer and the ships surrounding it. Not wait until I ask you. Everything must be on the tip of your tongue. Understand?"

"Yes, sir," Goldstein answered, his voice shaken.

MacDonald saw the sweat inching down the junior officer's face, tracing a path across sunburn earned from standing the grueling four-hours-on, four-hours-off watches on the bridge. Shit! Couldn't any of these new officers take a little criticism? "You're doing well, Sam. You're going to be one of my best. Not your fault you were a supply officer for a few years before seeing the error of your ways and switching to the surface warfare navy. But that also means you're behind others of your year group in learning how to do battle group steaming."

"I am standing double OOD shifts, sir."

"I know. I think that is admirable and can only lead to improvements. Now, go back and get us a course safely out of this battle group toward the submarine's last location and a course that will ensure we don't get run over by the *Kitty Hawk*. Can you do that for the old man?" Thirty-seven and he was calling himself the "old man."

"Yes, sir."

MacDonald picked up the red handset in front of him. He looked at Goldstein, who seemed riveted in place beside his chair.

"Go," he motioned away, and watched Goldstein hurry back to the navigation table. MacDonald turned his attention forward, leaning back in his chair, failing to scc the silent glances exchanged among the sailors of the bridge.

Maybe he was too rough on his wardroom. But at the academy they taught you that command was a lonely position. Better he train them while they had some modicum of peace with the Soviets, before the eventuality of having to fight them occurred. Who knew when and where the at-sea battle would begin with the Soviet Navy, but when it did he wanted his ship battle-ready.

MacDonald pushed the small button in the center of the handset and listened to the cryptographic keys bagpipe synchronization with the secure network between the battle group ships. He glanced through the open hatch to the port wing. The USS *Kitty Hawk* was visible.

Automatically, his nautical mind took in the angle of the carrier. The stern of the *Kitty Hawk* was only partially visible. He could see more of the bow. That angle meant the carrier was closing the distance to the *Dale*, if only at a slow approach. Another F-4 Phantom catapulted off the carrier, the loud noise of its jet engines filling the bridge. Meant the wind was blowing toward them from the *Kitty Hawk*. Launching aircraft also meant the carrier had steadied up on its new course.

MacDonald glanced at the compass. Wind was coming from the north-northeast.

"Mr. Goldstein! Has the carrier completed its course change?"

Navy Red mounted over the angled windows of the bridge burst into life. "All ships, this is Alpha Xray; Corpen Romeo two-zero-zero."

Instinctively, MacDonald translated the broadcast. It was the *Kitty Hawk* announcing a course change—"Corpen Romeo" to two-zero-zero true.

"Belay my last, Mr. Goldstein."

He looked at the compass on the stand near his seat. *Dale* was on course two-one-zero. They should be safe, unless Goldstein screwed up and did a port turn.

"Make sure she isn't going to run us over, please, Mr. Goldstein. And I'm still waiting for a course to get us out of here." Then he mumbled, "And that course should take us away from this decreasing range to the *Kitty Hawk*."

The synchronization stopped and was replaced by a steady static, punctuated with a clear voice when someone on the other end pressed the "push to talk" button. Then several voices exchanged communication checks with one another. *God,* MacDonald thought, *grant me the serenity to understand why radiomen believe they have to check every circuit just when everyone needs to use it.* Nearly a minute passed before the ships, including the *Dale*, finished with the communication checks.

When the circuit seemed to pause between transmissions, MacDonald pressed the "push to talk" button on the red handset and called for Admiral Green. Several seconds passed before the admiral came on the circuit. His deep New Hampshire accent, ending even statements as if they were questions, identified the man without Green ever having to say his name.

MacDonald smiled when he heard the accent. Worst kept secret in the fleet was Green's nighttime attempts to find watches less than alert. The admiral would call a ship and pretend to be someone else. Green confided to MacDonald that this was the way to truly discover how ready a battle group was. A little operational deception, a feint here and jab there, and you had a real picture of battle group preparedness.

It also only takes a strong accent to identify who's on the other line, regardless of what he calls himself. So everyone played along, but called their skipper as soon as the admiral's voice was recognized.

Yesterday, his XO, Joe Tucker, had told him of a radio transmission to the CIC watch officer by Green pretending to be a chief petty officer. "Joe Tucker," MacDonald said aloud. The name "Joe Tucker" rolled easily off his tongue. Few ever called the XO "Joe." Peers and seniors alike referred to him as "Joe Tucker," as if it was one word. MacDonald chuckled over the thought.

"Skipper, this is Admiral Green. You got my orders, why haven't you changed course?"

"Sir, we were waiting for assignment of the other units to the SAG."

"What other units, Commander MacDonald? There are no other units. You are a one-ship SAG. Your job is to get out there and keep that goddamn Soviet submarine submerged and away from my battle group."

MacDonald reached down and pushed the mute button. Green's voice was still in his ear, but the admiral could not hear him. "Officer of the Deck, bring us onto course two-two-zero and bring our speed up to twelve knots."

"Aye, sir," Goldstein replied.

Behind him, MacDonald heard the scurry of activity as Goldstein relayed the commands to change course and speed and the navigation team started recalculating the distances to the other ships.

MacDonald returned to the voice on the other end.

"You got all that?" Green asked.

MacDonald unlocked the mute button. "Aye, sir. We are heading toward the datum, even as we speak."

"Don't kid me, Danny. If I hadn't chewed your ass, you'd still be steaming along placidly like another sheep in the herd waiting for someone to tell you to do it. You haven't become one of those rear-echelon desk jockeys, have you? So cautious you're waiting for your navi-guessers to come up with a safe course out of the battle group. I thought by now I would have taught you to act first and worry about the ankle biters—"

"Like safety?"

"Danny, don't get smart-ass with me," Green replied with a chuckle. "Don't forget I'm the admiral and I know what is going on. You're just a kid-commander listening at the knee of your mentor—that's me"

MacDonald smiled. Even when Green was chewing your ass, you had to remember that he was one of the few officers still on active duty wearing World War II ribbons and medals. "Aye, sir. And I appreciate your direction."

"Danny, one day someone is going to gangster-slap the shit out of you."

MacDonald nodded and felt his face blush. "Sorry, Admiral."

Green laughed. "It's too late, Danny me boy. If you want to get off my shit list, bring me the side number of that Soviet submarine. I've always wanted a photograph of one of these Soviet nukes for my office wall."

"I will try my best, sir. But if I follow your orders to keep it submerged, that's going to be hard to do."

"Skipper, that's not my worry."

"Are we sure it's a Soviet submarine?"

"Well, here's the reasoning of an old sailor, Danny. First, the tattletale has to be targeting. Second, the tattletale is Soviet. Third, there are no threat surface units in the area. And, fourth, we'd already know if Soviet Bears were airborne and heading this way. Fifth, the Chinese submarines are afraid to leave the shadow of their coast. And, most important, the Willy Victor has a visual on her. Ergo . . ."

MacDonald imagined the admiral raising a slim finger into the air when he wanted to make a point. He had seen that finger raised too many times to count, when Green was the chief of staff for Commander in Chief U.S. Pacific Fleet back in Pearl. Only a couple of years ago, but it seemed as if it was only yesterday.

". . . It is a Soviet submarine."

"Are we sure going southwest is the right direction?"

"Soviet tactics is for the tattletale to be aligned with the inbound missiles. If they fly over the head of that fucking Kashin, then they'll hit the *Kitty Hawk*. Do you know how pissed off I'm going to be if I have my afternoon coffee upset by a missile hit?"

Not too much, if your coffee is like the cup sitting here. "Very much so, sir."

"Of course you do, Skipper. Besides, I'm sending the *Gearing* out on a reciprocal course to the northwest just in case the Soviets start doing something unusual like being innovative."

The USS *Dale* tilted slightly as the destroyer turned starboard off the base course to the new one. MacDonald looked up at the OOD, raised his finger, and made circles in the air.

"If he's out there, we'll find him."

"There is no doubt in my military mind that you will, Danny. So go get the son of a bitch and scare the shit out of him. And, Danny . . . stay with him until you can force him up or you lose him."

"If he's out there, we'll find him," MacDonald repeated.

"Sounds to me like déjà vu, Danny. Listen! I'm going to let you go. Don't let an old sailor down."

"Aye, aye, sir," MacDonald replied, knowing Green would stay on the line longer, hoping to hear some inadvertent comment.

"Right full rudder!" Goldstein shouted.

"The *Dale* never loses a contact."

There was slight laughter on the other end. "Just like you to never put me on mute and order a course change, Skipper. What was that? The OOD not put enough rudder on?"

"Sir, you are a psychic."

"No, I'm just a destroyer sailor who has been there, done that, and envies you this opportunity."

"We'll get him, if he's still out there."

"That's the spirit. Wish I could afford another ship or two to help, but our mission is to get the *Kitty Hawk* off Vietnam as soon as possible. We still have a port call in Olongapo for a brief fueling stop and to pick up the *Tripoli* and her cargo of angry, fire-breathing marines. Operation Beacon Torch could be the turning point in this war."

"I know the crew is looking forward to the port call." Every Pacific Fleet sailor knew the joys of this Philippine town where the U.S. Navy had its largest Asian port.

"My EA has just handed me a note. Seems you're at twelve knots. Isn't that a little fast for the sonar to work?" the admiral asked, referring the capability of the sonar to work passively in detecting noise in the water.

"We'll slow down a couple of knots once we are over the horizon."

"Probably one of these Echo class submarines."

"Shaddock missile," MacDonald offered.

"Shaddock missile," Green concurred. "Wait one!"

A few seconds later, Green was back on the circuit. "VQ-1's visual on the submarine identified it as an Echo class. A formation of Phantoms on combat air-patrol point overflew the submarine. I am sending them back to orbit the area on the off chance the clappers the Willy Victor dropped worked. If I were a submarine skipper, I'd want to surface as soon as I could and pull them off my hull."

The ship's intercom blasted across the bridge. "OOD, is the skipper up there?"

"Admiral, we are getting the data over NTDS, sir," MacDonald continued, ignoring the voice box.

"I'm letting you go, Danny. Go get the bastard."

"We will."

"One last thing: Don't fire on him. We don't want a war started out here with the Soviets. Let's finish one war at a time."

MacDonald slipped the handset into the cradle after bidding Green good-bye. He should have an hour or so before the old man called back wanting to know his status. He leaned forward, pushed the CIC button on the 12MC console. "Combat, Skipper."

"Combat here, Skipper."

"Have you set the blue gold watch?"

"We have the gold antisubmarine team on their way to station, sir."

"Good. Does Sonar have any contact-convergence zone, etc.?"

"No, sir. Too much noise from our battle group."

"Repeat the contact information for the bridge, if you would, Lieutenant Burnham."

"VQ-1 reports its visual as an Echo class submarine on the surface. Bears two-one-zero degrees distance, two hundred nautical miles."

"OOD, you get that?" MacDonald asked.

"Aye, sir. Right ten-degree rudder, steady up on course two-one-zero," Lieutenant Goldstein sang out.

"Keep me appraised," MacDonald said, leaning back in his chair, watching the bow of the *Dale* cut through the light waves of the South China Sea, listening to the repeats from the helm as Mr. Goldstein attempted to steady up on the new course. Two hundred nautical miles. Good thing they had topped off from the *Mispillion* yesterday. He looked out the port-side door. The *Kitty Hawk* was sliding left. Meant they were opening up distance between them.

"Steady on course two-one-zero!" the helmsman reported.

MacDonald felt the tilt of the ship right itself. Two hundred miles meant the *Dale* would be late in arriving in Olongapo. That was enough for his crew to want to sink the submarine; a day lost in Olongapo was a day lost in paradise.

One day the United States and the Soviets were going to stare each other eyeball-to-eyeball and neither was going to blink. What would happen then? he wondered.

Since 1962, when America backed them down over the missiles in Cuba, the Soviet Navy had become more and more confrontational. Cutting across their bows to force American ships to maneuver and avoid collisions had been a common theme when the *Dale* was in the Mediterranean last year. Yeah, no doubt about it. One of these days there was going to be an incident at sea, and then America was going to have to kick some serious Soviet Navy butt. The sooner they did it, the better the outcome would be. MacDonald wanted to fight them now instead of leaving it to his children or his children's children to have to do it.

"LIEUTENANT," Chief Caldwell said, handing a message board to Burnham.

Burnham glanced at the radar repeater, then at the naval tactical data system screen, double-checking how the blips on the radar compared with the NTDS. The ship had been outfitted with NTDS during the last upkeep period. There was something about those comfortable with the old technology that made them suspect of the new.

"What is it, Chief?" Burnham asked as he took the board.

"Sir! Do you want us to set up a time-motion analysis—?"

"What do you think, Ensign?" Burnham said over his shoulder to young Hatfield, his voice betraying the boredom he'd found after joining the navy to avoid the draft. "Are you going to wait until the team is set and then prepare for it? Probably a good idea, but we can't do a damn thing until Sonar has contact, and we won't have that until we slow down to under twelve knots."

"The EC-121 reconnaissance aircraft gave us a datum on the submarine," Hatfield replied enthusiastically.

Burnham ignored the reply. Why in God's name did they have to send him an ensign who wanted to do everything at once at the speed of sound?

"Would you keep still, Peppercorn? You move around the place like someone with a nervous twitch. It gives *me* a nervous twitch."

"Sorry, Lieutenant. Just that we have a lot to do to get the chart table set up for doing TMA."

"A second of standing in one place when you're talking to me would help."

Burnham turned to the radioman chief. "Did you say something, Chief?" Burnham asked.

"No, sir. I was waiting for a moment to tell you the communications officer sent this," Caldwell replied.

Burnham flipped up the metal cover of the message board and scanned the machine-typed message. He pulled a pen from his pocket and initialed the red router stamped haphazardly on the front of the message. It was God's way of making sure everyone who ever read the damn thing was marked for life. He had lost count over the two years on the *Dale* of the number of messages he had initialed. Being the operations officer was supposed to be more fun than this. He had yet to see a message that was worth his time to read, much less initial, but with only fourteen months, two weeks, and three days left in the navy, he'd do it the navy way.

"Anything to take back to Mr. Taylor?"

He shook his head. "No, Chief. It's just a message from CINCPAC Fleet telling us the *Tripoli* has arrived in Olongapo. We'll join her for Operation Beacon Torch."

"Beacon Torch?"

Burnham motioned Chief Caldwell away. "You probably know more about it than I do, Chief. Ask the good communications officer. He reads all this stuff."

Caldwell laughed. "He used to, sir. Then a slew of supply messages arrived the other weekend and I think he got a migraine trying to decipher the national stock numbering system."

"NSN gives me a migraine."

The two men laughed. Caldwell took the message board and quickly departed the small CIC.

Burnham sauntered over to the plotting table. Ensign Hatfield, his tongue between his teeth, was busy taping down a see-through sheet of white trace paper over the navigational chart of the area.

"You're going to bite your tongue off one day, Peppercorn."

Hatfield looked up, smiling. "This is exciting, Lieutenant."

"Then you haven't been to Olongapo, my young virgin friend."

Hatfield looked around to see if anyone heard that. "Lieutenant!" he whispered.

Burnham laughed. "Just kidding, Peppercorn."

A sailor walked up to the two officers. "Sir, I'm a member of the Gold Team."

"Well, well, well, if it isn't Petty Officer Banks from the great state of Tennessee," Burnham said, slapping Banks on the back. He was one of the few on board who knew that this young man held a bachelor's degree from Duke University and was one year away from his master's in English literature. Unfortunately, when old Uncle Sam invited Banks to learn the ways of the infantryman, taking time off for the navy seemed the right thing to do.

The army's loss had been Burnham's gain. The two had found a harmony in intellectual discourse that only those with superior degrees could understand. At least, that was Burnham's opinion. He enjoyed the arguments with Banks, who was a dyed-in-the-wool Democrat to his Republican.

"There," Hatfield said, stepping back. "What do you think, Petty Officer Banks? Think we can use this for tracking our bearings?"

The unassuming Banks bent over the plotting table and ran his hands over the top. "That's a good job, Mr. Hatfield. We should be able to use this without the paper bunching or pulling away."

Hatfield smiled.

Another member of the Gold ASW Team had arrived silently and started sharpening pencils. Pencils would be used to mark off the lines of bearing to the contact once they had it on sonar.

Led by the versatility and "deep experience" in passive tracking of Ensign Hatfield, a couple of operations technicians such as Banks could calculate the submarine's course and speed based on common distances between several lines of bearing. It was easier than it looked, and it was definitely easier than trying to explain or describe how "target motion analysis" was done. Even he, the one and only "Great Burnham," had been amazed how simple he found TMA to be while others thought it was hard. Let the others discover it like he did. He saw no reason to share his insight. If the did, the others would never learn it.

"I'll get the clappers and compass, Mr. Hatfield," Banks said, reaching up and pushing several long strands of black hair off his forehead.

"Good idea, Petty Officer Banks," Hatfield said.

Burnham crossed his arms, rolling his eyes upward when Hatfield ran his hand across the top of the trace paper, almost a loving gesture.

TMA was something Burnham appreciated. No one could fail to watch a good ASW team whip out a submarine course and speed in minutes based only on lines of bearing taken from the sound the submarine had generated in the water. Of course, those minutes could turn into hours, if the submarine decided to do a lot of course and speed changes. The key was to sneak up on those sons of a bitches who hid beneath the waves, locate them, drop a grenade over the side to scare the shit out of them, and then—*head for Olongapo.*

Or, most likely, the *Dale* would follow the sub forever, or until eventually they lost it. Submarine skippers knew about the layer where the warmer waters of the surface and the cooler waters below clashed. That layer was like a curtain blocking off direct noise. Made it harder to locate and track a damn submarine.

"'Bout got it, Lieutenant," Hatfield said, interrupting Burnham's thoughts.

Burnham glanced at Hatfield as the ensign rubbed the tape edges down again.

"There, sir. That should do it."

Burnham grunted. Fourteen months, two weeks, three days, and he would be home in Crewe, Virginia. Whatever had caused him to join the navy? *Vietnam did, you asshole. Men your size are too big to hide; they become targets.* He'd already be back in Virginia, only he would have returned in the belly of a plane with tens of others.

"How long do you think until we reach the datum? Think we'll detect the datum once we get there?"

Burnham rolled his eyes again. "Ensign Hatfield, when are you going to learn the proper terminology of your navy?" He leaned down, his face inches from the young ensign. "Tell me the truth, Peppercorn. You're not going to make the navy a career, are you?" It would not surprise him if Hatfield ironed his Skivvies; he was so damn navy-fied.

"I don't know, Lieutenant. I hadn't thought of it. Are you?"

Burnham rolled his eyes again. "Please. Give me a break."

Banks leaned forward with his pencil and made a small circle in the center of the trace paper. "Last known location." Then the petty officer glanced at the navy twelve-hour clock on the bulkhead and wrote in the time. "Time—seventeen twelve hours."

"There's our datum," Hatfield said, a hint of excitement in the comment.

"Look, datum is where the submarine was last located. Datum isn't the submarine, Mr. Hatfield. Datum is just the original point of detection."

"Sorry, sir. I knew that," Hatfield explained, his face blushing in the blue light of Combat. "I was talking about the location, not the submarine."

This Hatfield had a lot to offer. Why would he want to make the navy a career? Burnham asked himself. He reached up and tweaked his nose, letting a huge sigh escape. Maybe because it was so easy? Maybe it was because the man was a shithead lifer seed and didn't even know it yet. Maybe it was because he—Burnham—was a shithead and just hated to see someone enjoying the navy?

A couple of sailors who'd heard the exchange between Burnham and Hatfield glanced at each other, their lips turning up as they moved away from the plotting table.

"Good. My mistake, Peppercorn." He motioned downward at the ensign, reaching up with his other hand and tweaking his nose again. "Don't mind me, Peppercorn. It's been a rough day." He picked up the clipboard with the graph paper on it. "Have you ever done a live TMA or ASW before?"

Hatfield shook his head. "Only at ASW School at Fleet Training Command." He rubbed his hands together. "This will be my first one."

"Doing it ashore in San Diego isn't the same thing as doing it live." He looked at the ensign. Brown hair, closely cropped, tapered in the back. Sideburns even with the top of the inner ear. No mustache and he doubted Hatfield's razor blade had even been dulled during these four months at sea. If the son-of-a-bitch momma's boy was a virgin, he wouldn't be after Olongapo. Now, there was a city where anything goes and usually did. Burnham reached up and rubbed his chin, pondering if there was anyplace in the United States similar to Olongapo; then he decided that the religious holy rollers would have long ago shut a "wonder of the world" like that down.

"Peppercorn, is this your first visit to Olongapo?"

Hatfield nodded. "I'm looking forward to it."

"Aren't we all," Burnham replied, then softly said it again, "Aren't we all. Maybe I'll take you with me into town."

Hatfield's smile broadened. "I would like that, sir."

Master Chief Turnbull walked up to Burnham. "Afternoon, sir."

Burnham grinned. He truly liked Turnbull. It was hard to believe the man was a lifer, unlike himself forced into the navy because of the draft. "What brings the mighty command master chief of the USS *Dale* up into the dark, blue-lighted cavern of CIC?"

"I'm headed to the bridge. Felt the ship turn and steady up on a new course. My compass . . ."

"Compass? You were on the signal bridge?"

"No, sir. I have a compass in my office. I saw us swinging off the base course of the battle group. Means either the battle group has shifted course, which means it's heading away from Olongapo, or the *Dale* is taking up a new position." Turnbull nodded at the plotting table. "But I suspect we have a submarine contact."

Burnham shrugged. "Not yet, we don't. Skipper said the tattletale—"

"The small Kashin destroyer that's been with us since Guam?"

"Same and very one. For us it means either they are going to sink the *Kitty Hawk*," Burnham said with irony, "or they are doing another anticarrier firing exercise."

Turnbull waved two fingers in the air. "So, it means the old man thinks the Kashin is the eyes of the submarine cruise missiles."

Burnham shook his head as Hatfield walked around the table to the end of the plotting table.

"Afternoon, Mr. Hatfield."

"Hi, Master Chief. You going to help us with the TMA once we get on station?"

Turnbull's eyes narrowed and he smiled that "you don't really expect me to do that" grin. "Most likely the skipper is going to want me nearby, sir. Though the offer is tempting."

Burnham shook his head slightly. At that moment, he came to the conclusion that Hatfield was dangerous. Having the crew like an officer too much was bad for good order and discipline, he decided.

The rough-hewn face of the senior enlisted man on board the destroyer eased down toward the plotting table, his visage coming into the brighter red light highlighting the table. The forehead scar over his left eye seemed to glow in the cross lighting of red and blue.

Once of these days Burnham was going to find out the story of the scar. No one seemed to know, but he was going to find out.

"One of the EC-121 reconnaissance planes out of Guam spotted an Echo on the surface," Hatfield said. "We are headed there to find her."

"They have to surface to fire their six missiles," Turnbull said, leaning away from the lighting. From the neck up, his body disappeared into the shadows above the plotting table. It made Burnham think of "The Legend of Sleepy Hollow."

"And we have to find him and make his life miserable for as long as we can," Burnham finally answered after a few seconds' pause. "As miserable as we can."

"Sounds like fun."

"Sounds like we might be late for Olongapo."

"Maybe we'll be lucky and the Soviet skipper will be one smart cookie and lose us fast."

"I hope not," Hatfield interjected. "This is a great opportunity for us."

"So is Olongapo," Burnham said. He turned to Turnbull. "Master Chief, anything new on our mad groper?"

Turnbull leaned down, putting both hands on the end of the plotting paper, his face coming back into view. Hatfield's eyes widened as he stared at the hands gripping his nicely laid trace paper.

"Not yet, Lieutenant. One day someone is going to catch him."

"I heard there was another incident."

"During the wee hours of the morning. Seaman Johnson woke to find a hand under the covers stroking him. By the time he came fully awake, the hand had gone and the sailor with it." Without waiting for further questions, Master Chief Turnbull nodded at Burnham and then at Hatfield. "You two officers have fun with the ASW exercise." He sighed. "Well, guess I better get topside and see if the skipper has any orders for me."

"CICWO! *Dale* coming to course two-zero-zero. Speed twelve knots." CICWO was the acronym for the combat information center watch officer.

"Very well!" Burnham acknowledged and meandered back toward the captain's chair in the center of Combat. He could sit in it, if he wanted. He did during the mid watches. He doubted the old man would say anything, but then the other CICWOs would start sitting in it.

Almost immediately, the ship tilted to port as the rudders lay over full for a few seconds. Then Burnham shifted his weight on his spread legs as the ship shifted rudders, straightening slightly as the OOD began steadying up on the new course. *What the hell does Goldstein think he's doing? We aren't dodging torpedoes—yet.*

He imagined the sharp comments from the skipper. Goldstein was the OOD. Good thing the man had a family business to which he could return, because he was a shitty officer of the deck. He's lucky the old man hasn't thrown him overboard yet.

Turnbull disappeared in the shadows, heading forward toward the bridge. The master chief was to be admired for the way he hiked up his pants and sauntered forward to do battle. Personally, Burnham would rather steer clear of the old man as much as possible, but as long as he was the operations officer, there was little possibility of avoiding MacDonald.

THREE

BOCHARKOV sipped his tea, the small porcelain cup engulfed in his large hand. With the other hand, he held a small black contraption. "It's heavier than I expected," he said.

Ignatova slid into the wardroom booth, setting his cup down on the table. "We found four of them."

Bocharkov looked at Ignatova. "Go ahead and say it, XO."

"Say what, sir?"

"That I should never have turned the K-122 back through our submerging area."

Ignatova's eyebrows rose. "I had not thought of it, Captain."

Bocharkov grunted. "It was the first thing I thought of." He set the clapper on the table. "These damn fifty-ruble cheap American things cost us nearly a half day. A half day—twelve hours—until we could surface safely, in the dark, and clear them. Thankfully only four stuck to our hulls."

"You think they dropped more than four?"

Bocharkov grunted. "The Americans never do anything that is simple. They always go for overkill." He glanced at

Ignatova and let out a sigh. "You think overkill is the right word?" Without waiting for Ignatova to answer, Bocharkov continued, "They saturate everything they touch with magnitude over simplicity. The Americans never do anything with simplicity, from their food supply to their economy to their massive military might."

"So, more than four."

Bocharkov grunted with a slight chuckle afterward. "They are not one society, you know? They are descendants of outcast religious nutters that other countries threw out. They had little choice but to come to America. Those choices centuries ago give us an enemy we chase for parity before their gods decide they should try to destroy us."

Ignatova said nothing. Bocharkov knew they would have to fight the Americans one day. Even the American Navy knew that one day the growing might of the Soviet Navy would demand an accounting. Life was a series of clashes in trying to determine who was the most powerful. Adversaries at sea were no different.

If he and Ignatova and millions like them did not fight the Americans now, one day their children or their grandchildren would have to fight them. He grunted.

"Sir?"

"Nothing." He smiled at his XO. "Should never have come back through the area from whence we submerged."

"Do you think the layer would have protected us if we had kept on going?"

Bocharkov chuckled. "Probably would have masked the sound from the Americans, but it would have driven us crazy with the continuous cacophony of clacking and clapping as we drove off, a constant changing of pitch and intensity as we altered speed and depth. It would have convinced us eventually—probably in minutes—that everyone in the world knew where we were located." He shrugged. "We would have been a submarine filled with paranoia until we had our own little war going inside here." He thought of the political officer—the *zampolit*. As if they weren't paranoid already.

"I did not think of that."

"Our scientists believe the clappers are part of a Western

psychological warfare initiative." He took a sip of tea, grinned, and held up his index finger. "But we, through our superior Russian—I mean Soviet—tactics have beaten back the American ASW attack on our submarine by keeping our sanity," he said with a smile.

"Let's hope that these are the worst they throw at us." Ignatova lifted one from the wardroom table and tossed it a few inches into the air. He looked at Bocharkov. "They are heavy, aren't they?"

Bocharkov set his cup down. "Our goal in the Soviet Navy should be to reach a point where the Americans worry about us; not we them. I think there is no better way to achieve that than through success. Success with our exercises; success with our missions; success by showing the flag around the world. If we and our men believe in ourselves, the Party, and our nation, we will push them and their allies away from our borders. Then it will be only time until we transform the world into a workers' paradise."

The curtain to the wardroom jerked back and Lieutenant Gromeko stepped into the small area, straightening at the sight of the two senior officers. He snapped a salute. "Captain, XO!" he said in a loud voice.

Bocharkov smiled. "We know who we are, Motka." He pointed to a chair against the forward bulkhead. The man licked his lips once. "Grab a chair and sit with Commander Ignatova and me." Bocharkov slid the message on the table toward Gromeko.

The Spetsnaz officer glanced at the message and frowned. He had already shared the message earlier with the head of the four-man team aboard the K-122.

Bocharkov let out a deep breath. *Marx protect me from young officers.* He reached out and flipped over the message, hiding the "TOP SECRET" stamped across the face of it. It was not as if someone was going to grab it and run off. Even if someone did, he would not get far on a boat only 111 meters in length.

Gromeko licked his lips as his eyes glanced at the hidden message.

Bocharkov's smile widened. "Not to worry, Lieutenant. While submerged this is a classified wardroom." He glanced at Ignatova. "Right, XO? You think the Americans use their wardroom the same way?"

Ignatova nodded. "Of course, but on a Soviet submarine everyone is of utmost loyalty—handpicked by Admiral Gorshkov himself."

"By the admiral himself?" Bocharkov asked, his face widening in feigned amazement. "I did not know that," he added looking down to hide the slight grin.

"Additionally, our special security officer at Kamchatka has assured that when a submarine is submerged, the entire length of it is a classified space where any topic regardless of its subject or classification can be discussed."

Gromeko let out a deep breath. "Pardon me, Captain. I did not know." He turned to grab the chair behind him.

Bocharkov leaned his head at an angle toward Ignatova, grimaced, and with an ironic smile asked, "The entire length? Gorshkov?"

"The entire length," Ignatova answered. "I, too, found that information amazing. I am sure the admiral would also," he added angelically.

Gromeko turned, holding the back of the chair with both hands. "I did not know," he said seriously.

"I was not sure myself," Bocharkov added, "but the XO knows these things. That is why he is the XO."

Gromeko set the chair near the table, sat down, and pulled it forward slightly. "I have been reading and leaving my messages in the communications compartment. Now that I know this, I can pick them up and read them in my stateroom?"

Ignatova clasped his hands in front, on top of the table. "That regulation only applies to the captain and the XO."

Gromeko nodded. "That explains why Lieutenant Vyshinsky never told me of this."

"Yes, it probably does, Motka. There are some things the communications officer is specifically forbidden to share," Bocharkov mumbled, noticing the discomfort on the face of the Spetsnaz officer. He picked up the folded message and handed it to Ignatova. "You should read this, XO, so you will know what we are here to discuss."

Bocharkov and Gromeko remained silent as Ignatova read the directive. When the XO finished, he folded it quietly and laid it on the table. "Is this real?" he asked quietly. "Do they expect us to do this, or is this another exercise by the Party to test our loyalty?"

"I had a similar disbelief when I first saw it," Bocharkov answered, absentmindedly stroking his chin a couple of times. "I thought maybe our fine Spetsnaz friends were playing a joke on us—maybe even Motka was responsible for this."

"No, sir! I would never—"

"Relax, Lieutenant. I know you wouldn't. Submarines can be very boring boats when you're a Spetsnaz and only have friends available to kill."

"I would never do something like that," Gromeko protested. "Never, sir."

Bocharkov motioned downward. "Okay, Lieutenant Gromeko. We also know you Spetsnaz have a very low tolerance for humor."

Gromeko's face reddened.

"Enough of that," Bocharkov said. "This is your chance to put that Special Forces training to use, don't you think?"

"Says in the message that we are to rendezvous with the K-56 in seven hours—early morning. It does not tell us what to do with our original mission of tracking the *Kitty Hawk* battle group as it heads toward Vietnam," Ignatova said.

"No, it does not, XO. But I am not too concerned with that. According to this, we are going to pick up some special equipment from the K-56 this evening." Bocharkov looked at Gromeko. "Then our fine fighting team under Lieutenant Gromeko will be equipped for their assignment."

"This is very dangerous, you know," Ignatova said, his voice serious and his gaze focused on the captain.

"Going to sea in a boat that deliberately sinks itself is not dangerous?" Bocharkov asked, his tone rising.

"But—"

"I know." He motioned downward. "I do not think any Soviet submarine has ever done this before."

"Neither has a surface ship," Gromeko added.

Both officers stared at the Spetsnaz lieutenant for several seconds, then looked at each other and ignored the comment.

"I mean, if a surface ship *could* do it," Gromeko offered.

Ignatova looked at Bocharkov. "The K-56 has only been with the Pacific Fleet a few months. I understand you know its skipper," Ignatova said, changing the subject.

"Captain Second Rank Fedor Gerasimovich and I were students together undergoing senior officer training at the Grechko Naval Academy. We were both lieutenant commanders at the time." He paused pensively. "He and I had a reunion of sorts before we sailed from Kamchatka." He looked at both officers. "He and his wife are true Soviet patriots that Elga and I grew to enjoy. I am sure Elga and Larisa are enjoying the great summer days of Kamchatka Oblast."

"You are senior to him," Ignatova said.

Bocharkov nodded. "Only by one rank, XO." He thought of the incident at Grechko that might still haunt his fellow submarine captain.

"The K-56 is a newer version of this class of submarine," Gromeko said.

"It is nearly the same. We are class six fifty-nine. He is commanding the newer six seventy-five class. Biggest difference is the six seventy-fives are about four meters longer and carry eight to our six cruise missiles," Ignatova offered. "Other than that we have the same basic reactor."

Bocharkov held up his hand. "Back to the message." He looked at Gromeko. "You have anyone who speaks American English?"

Gromeko's eyebrows furrowed. "Yes, sir. Starshina Malenkov studied at the foreign language school and spent a year in New York at the mission. I am told he is fluent in American."

"Told? By whom?"

"By him, sir."

"And his records?"

"I will check them."

"Do so. The last thing we need is for him to be boasting and you find yourselves guests of the Americans."

Gromeko straightened. "That will never happen, sir."

"Never say never, Lieutenant. It is a hard word to take back."

"But—"

"Don't argue with the captain," Ignatova interrupted.

"Lieutenant," Bocharkov continued, "according to this message we are going to do something that may sink this boat, at the worst embarrassing our nation if we are caught, and possibly resulting in the death of every officer and sailor on board the K-122."

"Yes, sir," Gromeko said softly.

"I do not intend for the K-122 to be captured. You understand?"

"Yes, sir."

"Of the three of us who are going to be responsible for none of this happening, you are going to be the most important. You understand?"

Gromeko nodded.

"Good. You and your mission ashore will be the most dangerous. I expect you to get in, do it, and get back to the boat as soon as possible. You understand?"

"Yes, sir."

Bocharkov looked at Ignatova. He looked at his watch. "This thing never works," he said, shaking his wrist. He took it off and started winding it, glancing up at the clock above the serving line. "It's eighteen thirty hours. XO, work with our esteemed navigator for a rendezvous solution with the K-56. I want no communications until an hour before the rendezvous. We'll come to the surface then. We are barely an hour away from where we submerged this afternoon, so if American ASW forces are not in the vicinity by now, they will be scouring the ocean for some time tonight."

"Captain, we will be doing the rendezvous in the dawn light. If the Americans are around, there is a good chance they will see us."

"Then Lieutenant Gromeko is going to have to do the transfer as fast as possible." Bocharkov looked at the Spetsnaz officer. "Lieutenant, when we rendezvous, you will be going across to the K-56 to bring the special equipment back. It will give you a chance to discuss this mission with your counterpart. Find out what he knows. In a mission such as this—or any mission one is assigned to do—the more you know, the more you are able to calculate the odds against you."

"I think the odds are quite significant," Ignatova said.

"Odds are always significant against a submarine."

"But, where we are being ordered . . ." Ignatova's voice trailed off.

MACDONALD stepped down from the captain's chair in Combat. "I'm going to Sonar and see what they have," he said, jerking his thumb toward the aft section of Combat.

"Aye, sir," Lieutenant Kelly replied.

"How far are we from the datum?"

"About ten miles, sir."

He looked at the standard navy-issued clock someone had mounted on a beam above the radar repeaters and the navy tactical data system that were aligned along the centerline of the ship. The hands showed zero four thirty. Another hour and a half to reveille.

"If the sub is anywhere around, we should have it by now."

"If we don't find it, sir, I recommend we take an intercept course with the battle group afterward. Good chance the Soviet skipper isn't going to give up so easily and we might run—"

"Straight up his butt without him ever seeing us."

"That was what I was thinking, sir."

MacDonald nodded. "Get me a navigation picture, Tom. Most likely you're right and the sub has fled the area. Maybe he is the backup for the Kashin. In which case, he'll be heading back to within firing distance of the *Kitty Hawk*."

"Sir, did you have time to approve the watch bill?"

MacDonald and Kelly discussed the coming week's officer watch bill for a couple of minutes. Lieutenant Thomas P. Kelly from Boston was Macdonald's Weapons department officer, and as well the young officer held the collateral duties of watch and training officer. On most ships the operations officer held the watch bill duties, but MacDonald had taken the job from Burnham after the longtime OPSO delayed in generating it on time.

MacDonald thought of Burnham as his "draftee" officer, a navy officer who never would have joined if Vietnam had not herded him into the safer arms of Mother Navy.

Having promised to sign the watch bill later in the morning,

MacDonald threaded his way in the tight confines of the combat information center to where the sonar compartment was located near the aft hatch. He avoided two sailors as he wove his way through the small, equipment-jammed compartment. One sailor had the sound-powered phone apparatus draped over his shoulders and on his head, making him look like some giant soldier ant guarding Combat. The other sailor squeezed himself against one of the radar repeaters, relaying to the sailor near the contact board the course and speed of the lone surface contact to the their north. The Willy Victor had earlier overflown the merchant vessel, identifying it as from Taiwan, one of their major allies in Southeast Asia.

MacDonald walked by the plotting table installed beneath a blue fluourescent light against the port bulkhead. The blue sleeves slipped over the two fluourescent tubes helped preserve the Combat watch team's night vision.

Ensign Hatfield stood between three sailors to his right and one wedged between the plotting table and a rack of equipment behind him. That sailor wore the sound-powered telephone gear. All four sailors and the ensign leaned downward, watching the motionless trace paper. All five were talking, pointing, making imaginary lines with their fingers on the paper. Hatfield was biting his lower lip as the sailors talked and he listened.

As he approached, MacDonald saw the penciled circles marked on the trace paper, each circle growing bigger as it moved outward from where the submarine was last seen. He caught the last few words of Hatfield's question: ". . . you think so?"

"Yes, sir. Why else would it be out here?" Petty Officer Oliver asked, looking up. MacDonald's and Oliver's eyes met. The sailor elbowed Hatfield and nodded toward MacDonald. Everyone straightened as he approached.

"Well, Peppercorn, doesn't look as if you and your team are getting much of a workout," MacDonald said when he reached the table, bending over slightly as he spoke because of an overhead cold water pipe that ran through Combat.

"No, sir, but when Sonar detects the submarine we'll know how far away he is," Hatfield replied, his words running together in excitement. Hatfield leaned down and placed his finger on the outmost circle drawn on the thin sheet of plotting paper. "Look here, Captain. We've been adding a 'farthest-on circle' every thirty minutes. This way, when Sonar does have a contact, we'll know what's the farthest it can be from us."

MacDonald's right lip lifted in a sort of forced grin. He knew, and the sailors knew, that Hatfield was repeating what the sailors were teaching the new ensign. "That's good, Ensign Hatfield. One thing to remember is that we are estimating the speed of the submarine. Therefore the submarine could be anywhere along the line of bearing when we get him. But good work. I am impressed."

"It's not me, sir, as much as it is the sailors here. Petty Officers Banks, Edgars, and Cleary are old pros. Petty Officer Cleary is our sound-powered-phone talker while Banks is leading our TMA effort," Hatfield bragged. He nodded toward the fourth sailor. "Petty Officer Oliver has been sharing some of his sonar knowledge about the Soviet submarines. It definitely helps when we get all this talent in one place."

MacDonald's forced grin turned real. He looked at the four petty officers. "Good job, sailors. So, Petty Officers Cleary and Oliver, why do we have you two on the target motion analysis team? We barely have enough sonarmen for twenty-four-hour watches."

"I'm not, Skipper," Oliver answered. "I'm about to go on watch in Sonar." With that, Oliver turned and headed aft away from the group.

Cleary looked down, hoping the skipper couldn't see the damage to his face. "The chief thought it would be . . ."

"Petty Officer, you'll have to speak up," MacDonald said, noticing the bruise, cut eyebrow, and—was that a growing fat lip on the left side of the mouth?

"The chief wants me to learn it, sir."

MacDonald's lower lip pushed against the upper one as he nodded. "Then let's hope you learn it." He looked at the three men. "Keep up the good work."

"Thank you, sir," they replied. Cleary eased the sound-powered headset back down on his ears, pulling the helmet forward slightly, hoping to hide his face and escape questions.

MacDonald eased aft a couple of steps so he could straighten up. "Mr. Hatfield, you and your team keep doing the good job you are, but be ready when we locate the contact. If anyone can find the Echo, it'll be the *Dale* team." He nodded at the second-class petty officer. "Banks, good work, right?"

"We'll try, Captain."

"Yes, sir, we're Gold. Right, team!" Hatfield added.

MacDonald saw the quick wide-eyed glances between the four sailors as they mumbled, "Gold."

"I like good esprit de corps among a team," MacDonald added. Then he patted Hatfield on the shoulder as he eased past, heading aft toward the small side compartment where Sonar manned its console. He chuckled.

Officers like Hatfield did well in the navy. Sailors adopted officers when they actively sought knowledge. On the other hand, those with arrogant infatuation with their rank, or with themselves such as Burnham, woke up one day to discover the meaning of "falling on one's sword." The navy would become more a memory for reminiscence than a career worthy of recognition.

The sonar compartment was separated by a heavy curtain that parted down the middle. The newer destroyers being designed, like the DD-963 class, had doors—a true physical barrier that separated the sonarmen from the rest of Combat. But it would be 1972 before they sailed out of the shipyard.

Once the *Dale* returned for its five-year yard period, it would have a true sonar compartment installed, like some of the other Forrest Sherman class destroyers.

MacDonald pulled the curtain back. Oliver was leaned back in his chair, feet crossed at the ankles and propped up on the narrow ledge in front of the sonar display. He jerked his feet down, nearly turning the chair over, before he sat up straight. "Morning, Captain. I wasn't aware you were—"

"Morning, Oliver," MacDonald said. "Doesn't take you long to get comfortable." He looked around the small area, then pulled his head back into Combat and glanced around. "Where are Mr. Burkeet and Chief Stalzer?"

"Sir, they stepped outside for a smoke."

"You got ashtrays in here, don't you?"

The sailor stood as if he had finally made up his mind on

whether to remain sitting or not. "Sorry, sir. Yes, sir, but they know I don't smoke so they decided to step out on the main deck," Oliver stuttered.

"You got anything?" MacDonald asked. "This SQS-26 living up to its expectations?" The SQS-26 was the newest sonar in the fleet.

Oliver let out a deep breath. His hand shook slightly as he touched the controls of the AN/SQS-26 sonar. "It's performing to specs, sir. I did the preventive maintenance check on it yesterday when we were diverted against the Echo class submarine."

MacDonald's right lip arched up. "That's good, Oliver. Was the PMS due, overdue, or not due at all?"

The sailor shook his head. "No, sir. I just thought it would be a good thing to do." The sailor smiled. "I wanted to make sure everything was working when we got on station."

MacDonald nodded. "You did well, sailor. I don't think most would have thought to do it." He uncrossed his arms and pointed at the console. "You got any indications of anything out there?"

"No, sir, but that was over fourteen hours ago when the reconnaissance aircraft spotted the Echo class submarine."

"You never know what a bubblehead is thinking, Oliver. Sometimes they screw up and decide to hide where they were last seen."

MacDonald turned at the sound of voices behind him. Chief Stalzer and Lieutenant Junior Grade Burkeet stepped through the hatch from the main passageway, into the darkened spaces of CIC. The conversation stopped abruptly when they saw MacDonald's frame blocking the curtained opening to Sonar.

"Skipper, we were just—"

"I know, Mr. Burkeet. Petty Officer Oliver told me you and the chief had taken a cigarette break. He and I have had a good conversation."

"Yes, sir. Last chance before we reach the datum."

MacDonald scratched his chin. "I agree, Mr. Burkeet. It was your last chance for that quick smoke. I'm impressed with what Petty Officer Oliver told me, but we can't have him manning the sonar alone. He needs some help, and I want some senior leadership down here as we take up the chase. I would like you or the chief down here with the watch at all times." His eyebrows lifted.

"Yes, sir."

"Good. Work with Lieutenant Kelly so he can make sure you and Chief Stalzer are on port and starboard down here at Sonar without having to give up your other watches. I think that's a good idea, don't you?" He saw Stalzer's Adam's apple rise and fall. It never hurts every once in a while to let a chief know whose ship he rides on.

"Yes, sir. I was thinking the same thing," Burkeet said.

MacDonald grunted. "I'm sure you were. By the way, Chief, you've done a good job training Oliver here. I was impressed he had taken the initiative to do the preventive maintenance earler to ensure everything was shipshape on the SQS-26. Ensign Hatfield told me about how Oliver had been sharing his knowledge of the Echo class submarine with the TMA team."

"Thank you, Skipper."

MacDonald turned away and started forward again. Time for him to pay a visit to the bridge. The bridge was where a skipper should spend most of his time, regardless of this new fad of fighting the ship from Combat. He opened the forward hatch and stepped out.

OLIVER sat down as soon as the skipper turned away and the curtain fell back in place.

The curtain came apart and Chief Stalzer slapped him lightly against the back of the head. "What did you tell the skipper, dickhead?"

Oliver leaned toward the sonar console, away from the chief, rubbing his head. "I didn't tell him nothing, Chief, he didn't already know."

Stalzer put his hands on his hips and looked at Burkeet, who stood outside the curtains. "He must have told him something for the old man to put us on port-starboard."

Burkeet shook his head as he crossed his arms. "Not Oliver's fault, Chief. Besides, this isn't punishment because we took a smoke break. It makes sense to have one of us two down here while we have the ASW condition set. I should have thought of it earlier." He sighed heavily as he dropped his arms. "I'm going to see Lieutenant Kelly. You, on the other hand, Chief, have the first watch." And, before Stalzer could say anything, the junior officer walked off.

Stalzer and Oliver watched him weave his way through Combat before Stalzer pulled the curtain shut. He turned to the sailor and lightly slapped him upside the head again, causing the headset to slide sideways off his ears. "What did you tell the old man?"

Oliver rubbed his head, taking the headset off. "I told him nothing. I told him you two had just stepped outside for a smoke because you both knew it bothered me."

"Oh, gee, Oliver. That's just what captains like: sympathetic officers and chiefs. Jesu-Christ. Lord, protect me from naïve sailors and know-it-all officers."

Oliver slipped the headset back over his ears.

"What else?"

"What else what?"

"What did you tell him about the PMS you did yesterday?"

"I didn't tell him nothing."

"Oliver, don't make me go back to old navy and beat the shit out of you. What did you tell him?"

"I told him that you had me do the PMS," Oliver lied, "because you wanted to ensure that everything was working when we reached the submarine search area."

Stalzer grinned and leaned back. Maybe that senior chief star was in sight after all. "Go ahead," he snapped. "Put your sound-powered headset back on and do a communications check with the topside and bridge watches. If they see anything, you tell them to make sure we hear about it. You got that?"

"Yeah, I got it, Chief."

"Good. And don't forget it. It's almost daylight. Can see the horizon already. We'll have sun by six thirty. I'm going to step down to the goat locker and get me a fresh cup of coffee since I've got to stay up here and babysit you."

"What if the skipper comes back?"

"What if the skipper comes back?" Stalzer mimicked.

"What are you, my mother? Tell him Mr. Burkeet is in Combat, checking on the weapons status."

"But, Mr. Burkeet said for you—"

"Oliver, shut your trap and do what I tell you. You argue too much. The navy was a nicer place before you draft dodgers showed up in it. You ought to be in Vietnam wearing army green."

"I tried, Chief, but they told me—"

"I know, Oliver, you keep telling me. Your brother is in the army and they refused to station you two together so you joined the navy. Do you realize how ridiculous that sounds? You think the navy and the army are going to sit down and put you two together?"

"No, Chief, but eventually the *Dale* will pull into Vietnam."

"Oliver, I hope for your sake this is youth and not stupidity talking."

Oliver pulled the headset down over his ears.

"You just remember: When I have the watch, you have the watch."

Oliver lifted up one side of the headset, uncovering his left ear. "But, Chief, I have other things I have to do also. Other things you've assigned me. My watch bill also has me doing a topside watch," he whined.

"Then I guess you better bring whatever it is you gotta do down here to do it because if I have to do port-starboard watches, you're gonna do them with me."

IT was nice watching the sun breach the horizon. It was always a beautiful sight from the bridge to watch the light speed across the ocean top as daylight surfaced. He licked his teeth. The strong tannic acid from that cup of coffee on the bridge had left its taste.

"Captain off the bridge!" came the shout as he stepped into Combat.

MacDonald weaved through the crowded area with sailors squeezing out of the way as he continued aft. He stepped through the knee-knocker separating Combat from the passageway, turning to secure the hatch before continuing aft through the main passageway.

A few steps and he stood in front of the radio shack. He pressed the buzzer.

Almost immediately the locked door opened. Petty Officer Williams appeared, his every-which-way oily hair looking as if a mighty wind was blowing in from the passageway. "Attention on deck!" the sailor shouted, stepping back, holding the door open.

"Carry on," MacDonald said as he stepped into the cramped square communications compartment, commonly referred to on every ship as the radio shack. He pulled up the stool from in front of the R-390 high-frequency radio. Nodding at the radio, he looked back at Williams. "Well, Sparks, have you found something to keep the crew entertained after breakfast?"

"Not yet, sir," Williams replied in a loud voice, rubbing his hands together, "but I had just got started." Williams's eyes seemed to glance beyond MacDonald.

"I won't be long, Sparks, just want—"

"No, sir, that's not what I meant, Captain."

MacDonald laughed. "I know, Sparks. Just thought I would read the morning message board. Save Mr. Taylor the effort of bringing it to the bridge."

Williams grabbed the letter-size metal clipboard off the hanger and handed it to MacDonald. "Skipper, we are still ripping the zero six hundred broadcast, but all the messages to the *Dale* since taps last night are on it."

"Uh-huh," MacDonald said as he took it, glancing at the clock on the nearby bulkhead. Zero six forty-five. He had been up all morning. He stifled a yawn as he looked around the spaces. "Aren't you supposed to have two people on watch here at all times?"

Seaman Korun stepped from behind the rack of receivers arrayed across the aft bulkhead of the compartment. "I'm here, Skipper. I was just checking the wiring." Korun yawned, then realized what he had done and slapped his hand across his mouth.

MacDonald looked back at Williams, frowned, and narrowed his eyes. He looked down at the message board and lifted the metal cover. "I hope the wiring is functioning properly, Sparks."

"I may have to double-check it myself, sir."

Without speaking, MacDonald flipped back the top of the read-board and began reading. Every message that came into the *Dale* was on the board. Copies of specific messages like those for Supply, with their legends of naval stock numbers that seemed as cryptic to most sailors as the Japanese ULTRA code of World War II, were the only messages MacDonald banned from the read-board. Otherwise he would have been forced to wade through a roller-coaster series of undecipherable stock numbers with something readable every tenth or twelfth message.

"Looks as if we're getting another radioman on board, Sparks," MacDonald said, holding one of the messages between his fingers.

"Out of 'A' school, Skipper. It'll take me months to retrain him to how the navy really operates."

"As long as he doesn't find himself checking the wiring during the mid-watches."

MacDonald smiled, surprised to see a slight blush on Williams's face. He flipped the message over the two-hole metal brackets at the top and continued reading. Thirty minutes later, he finished the board. He took his pen and initialed the space beside his name on the top sheet before handing it back to Williams.

"Sir, when do we get to Olongapo?" Williams asked.

MacDonald shrugged. "Depends on when we find the submarine and scare him away from the battle group."

Williams nodded. "Thanks, sir." The leading petty officer of the radio shack hung the metal board on the bulletin board beneath the word "TODAY." Another metal board hung under the word "YESTERDAY." A third empty hanger was beneath the word "TOMORROW."

In a few days, when the *Dale* tied up pierside at Olongapo, the liberty parties would fight their way down the gangway to the huge cement piers, bolting for the front gate and the sins of the city lying across bridge over Shit River—*American name*.

Williams was a one-port one-drunk sailor.

MacDonald already knew that once they arrived in Olongapo, Williams would amble down the same gangway, make his way to the on-base club, watch the strippers to the wee hours of the morning, and then someone would find his body between the club and the ship and bring him back. For the remainder of the port stay, Williams would remain on board except for a trip or two to the base exchange. Most sailors liked to entertain one another with their "girl in every port" stories, but they also entertained one another with their "one-port one-drunk" stories about guys like Williams. Try as they might—and MacDonald had stood on the bridge wing of the *Dale* and watched them—no one had yet been able to get Williams into Olongapo.

He automatically looked up at the 1MC speaker on the bulkhead when he heard the familiar click of someone hitting the "push to talk" microphone. "Captain to Combat." He glanced at the clock. MacDonald stepped hurriedly through the hatch, hunched over to avoid the low overhead of the passageway, as he headed toward Combat.

"Captain in Combat!" someone shouted as MacDonald stepped through the watertight hatch. A nearby sailor secured the hatch behind him. He moved hurriedly through the tight maze of equipment, noticing the activity around the target motion analysis table.

"What you got?" he asked as he neared.

"Sonar has a contact, sir," Lieutenant Kelly replied.

The two officers stood there, watching the TMA team plot the second line of bearing from the plotted location of the *Dale*. The line crossed the farthest-on circle.

"Soviet?"

"Not American."

"How far out?"

Ensign Hatfield answered. "Can't be more than one hundred twenty-eight nautical miles from us, sir."

"One hundred twenty-eight?" MacDonald asked.

"Yes, sir. We are estimating max speed of eight knots for the submarine. Any faster he'd be blind. His passive sonar would be unable to detect any signals. Ergo, one hundred twenty-eight nautical miles since the reconnaissance aircraft picked him up."

"We've had two lines of bearing?"

"Yes, sir. Just two."

MacDonald turned toward Sonar, stopped, and turned back to Kelly. "What is our course and speed?"

"Sir, we are still on two-two-zero, but speed is eight knots."

He had ordered the speed reduction a couple of hours ago to increase detection ability. "Well, we can't have this, can we? If the submarine is doing eight and we are doing eight, then we'll never close."

"No, sir, but if we increase speed, we'll have to restart our time motion analysis."

MacDonald shrugged. "We only have two lines of bearing. Bring the speed up to twelve knots, so we have some closure rate on the contact."

Kelly acknowledged the order, and as MacDonald walked toward Sonar, he heard the Combat watch officer pass his instructions to the bridge.

"What you got?" MacDonald asked as soon as his head parted the curtains.

Lieutenant Junior Grade Burkeet was hunched over the shoulders of Petty Officer Matthew Oliver. The two men were watching the display console as sound in the water bounced across the sensisive hydrophones within the bubble bow of the *Dale*. He straightened, but his eyes never left the display. "Oliver has a weak signal directly in front of us, sir. Very weak, but every now and again it grows stronger."

MacDonald pulled himself all the way into Sonar. He touched the sailor on the shoulder. "Does the signal fade in and out, or does it seem you have two signals: One that is faint but constant and then one that startles you as it overrides the faint one?"

Oliver's forehead wrinkled. "I don't know, sir. I haven't given it thought. I think it is a convergence zone signal. Would mean the contact is at least fifty-six miles from us." The petty officer ran his hand through his hair. "I think you're right, Captain. Every now and again it grows in strength. That's when I've gotten two good bearings on it."

MacDonald looked at Burkeet. "How far apart are the bearings?"

Burkeet seemed puzzled.

"Time, man? How many minutes apart between the signals?"

His eyes seemed to light up. "Five minutes—maybe six."

"Aren't you keeping track?" MacDonald asked sharply.

"Sir, the Gold Team is keeping track of the times."

"You keep track also," MacDonald ordered.

"Means we have both a convergence and a direct zone, doesn't it, Captain?" Burkeet replied.

MacDonald nodded. "Most likely. If we do, then the submarine is closer than fifty miles. Most likely not that far if we're getting both signal bounce off the layer and a direct path to the *Dale*. I doubt we have two submarines out here. The TMA team says we are within one hundred twenty-eight miles of it. I don't believe we are that far."

"I've got another one!" Oliver said, holding his headset tight against his ears as he glanced at MacDonald and Burkeet. "This one is real strong." Oliver shut his eyes. "Seems almost as if I have two signals instead of one."

"Convergence zone," both officers said together. Both officers were wrong. It would take time to reach the contact, but he had a line of bearing regardless of how the signal arrived at the hydrophones located in the bulbous sonar nose on the bow of the destroyer.

FOUR

"SKIPPER."

MacDonald heard the voice along the outer rim of his doze, pulling him back from the comfort of a near-dream of him home with his wife, Brenda, the joyful sounds of Rachel, twelve, and Danny Junior, eight, in the background. A comforting vision that had accompanied him on this voyage.

Without opening his eyes, he shifted in his chair on the bridge. "What is it, Lieutenant Goldstein?" The warmth of the early morning sun on his face disappeared.

"Sir, radar is showing a couple of contacts that are going to pass close to us—well, at least one of them. Combat recommends we alter course to open up our passage."

He opened his eyes. Goldstein stood between him and the Pacific sun. "You're blocking my morning sun, Mr. Goldstein."

The officer shifted quickly to the side. "Sir, Combat—"

"I heard you the first time." He pushed himself completely upright. The boatswain mate of the watch handed him his cup filled with hot coffee. "Thanks, Boats." He yawned.

"How close are they going to pass and how long until we reach the point where we see them?"

"One is going to pass about two thousand yards off our bow. Unless the second one changes its speed or course, it will be a CBDR."

CBDR stood for "constant bearing, decreasing range." A ship said to be CBDR was one you would collide with somewhere along the way, as the range between the two of you decreased and neither of you changed your course or speed.

"Time?"

Goldstein cleared his throat. "Sir, we can see the closest one. He's about twenty thousand yards off our port bow. The second one radar has just over the horizon, about twenty nautical miles out."

MacDonald stepped down from the chair and strolled to the port bridge wing. Goldstein trailed along the left side of him a couple of paces behind.

MacDonald stepped through the opened hatch into the glare of the sun, realizing he'd left his cap beside his chair. His wife had warned him to keep his face covered because of his proclivity to sunburn. It was that Irish-Scot pigment, she kept telling him.

"Merchant," MacDonald mumbled.

"Yes, sir. Out of Hong Kong."

"British."

"Flying the British Hong Kong flag, sir."

"How much will it upset our ASW team if we turn or change speed?" MacDonald asked.

"Mr. Burnham didn't say, sir."

"Mr. Burnham has the watch?"

Goldstein nodded.

"Have you tried bridge-to-bridge with the merchant?"

"No, sir. You said radio silence."

"What's your recommendation?"

"I recommend we alter course twenty degrees to starboard, sir. It'll open up our passing range to eight thousand yards, then once passed, we can return to base course of two-two-zero."

"When?"

"When?"

"Yes, Mr. Goldstein. When should we turn?"

"Captain, as soon as possible."

"Tell Combat what we are doing, then do it."

Goldstein disappeared back into the bridge. MacDonald stood alone, watching the merchant vessel, scanning the empty ocean surface. He was more surprised over the lone merchant occupying their space than over the closeness of approach. In this part of the China Sea merchant traffic was usually heavy. But nothing was as heavy as ships transiting the Strait of Gibraltar.

He had made the mistake once of transiting the mouth to the Mediterranean during the evening, figuring the traffic would be lighter. It was worse. And it was at night. During the night, the Moroccan drug runners joined the fray in their dash to the Spanish coast with hashish. Two ships in the middle of the morning in the middle of the China Sea were barely worth bothering about.

"Combat concurs, Skipper."

MacDonald turned. Goldstein stood straddled-legged across the hatchway, one leg on the bridge wing and the other inside the bridge. MacDonald realized how thin Goldstein was as the man stood there, his long neck giving him a flamingo appearance. Like those pink flamingos MacDonald's mom thought looked so attractive in her flower beds back in Middletown, New Jersey, home of AT&T. "Then let's do it."

He turned back to the merchant. Inside, Goldstein issued orders for a ten-degree rudder to port.

MacDonald gripped the railing lightly as the *Dale* tilted slightly to the left and changed course. Ten degrees wasn't much, but changing course and speed was the easy way to ensure distance between the two vessels increased. Two thousand yards was a nautical mile, which for a landlubber might seem a lot, but at sea two thousand yards was a small distance that disappeared rapidly if two ships discovered themselves suddenly on a collision course. More distance meant more time to react.

"Distance to contact?"

Goldstein shouted from his position behind the navigation plotting table, where the quartermaster of the watch was taking bearings from the radar repeater, "We show sixteen thousand yards."

MacDonald glanced inside the bridge. The second-class quartermaster was doing a quick maneuvering board calculation to see how the course change would affect their distance. Quartermaster was one of the oldest ratings in the navy. That and boatswain mate. Quartermasters served the navigators, ensuring the ship arrived at the right port at the right time, while the boatswain mates did the work of keeping the ship shipshape. Ratings from the days of sail that kept the navy moving, through the decades of coal, to today's modern steam-driven plants and growing number of nuclear-powered ships.

MacDonald's forehead wrinkled. He looked at his wristwatch. An Omega his wife gave him on their tenth wedding anniversary five years ago. At the time, they could not afford it and he wanted to return it, but she insisted. "Fifteen to eight," he mumbled quietly. Her pert smile. The twinkle in her eyes when she was happy. She had been right about how every time he looked at the expensive watch he would remember her. If Goldstein had left him alone in his chair, he could have visited longer with her.

"I thought you said twenty thousand yards?"

"Yes, sir, but . . ."

"But what?" he asked sharply when Goldstein failed to finish his sentence.

"Sir, I think it has changed course also."

MacDonald turned his attention back to the merchant. "Bring me my binoculars!"

A few seconds later the boatswain mate of the watch handed them to MacDonald. He quickly raised them, spotted the merchant in his lens, and swept the glasses to the stern of the ship. The wake came into view. He followed the wake. "The merchant is turning to starboard!"

"Sir, it's turning into us!" Goldstein said.

"Distance?"

"Twelve thousand yards."

Six nautical miles. Still plenty of maneuvering room.

"Sir, we have CBDR!" the quartermaster shouted to Goldstein, the words reaching MacDonald.

MacDonald kept telling himself, *Plenty of time, plenty of time. Give Goldstein a chance.*

"Captain, recommend increase speed to twenty knots, maintain course."

"Solution?"

"Merchant will pass astern of us."

MacDonald lifted his glasses and looked at the wake again. The merchant was still turning. He dropped the binoculars and looked at the midships bridge of the merchant. He could see the starboard side of the ship, angling its bow as it turned. He looked at the wake again. No sign the ship had quit turning, then the wake was blocked by the port bow.

"The merchant is still turning, Mr. Goldstein, and he is turning so his direction will take him toward us."

"Yes, sir, but his speed is about eight knots. If we kick her up to twenty for about ten minutes, then . . ."

"You're assuming she is going to retain constant speed."

"No, sir," Goldstein answered.

MacDonald detected confidence in the officer of the deck's reply. "Why?"

"Distance eleven thousand yards, slight right-bearing drift," the quartermaster of the watch announced. "Will cross in front of us, less than one thousand yards!"

Still too close.

Still closing, but the bearing drift meant they were no longer on a collision course, unless the merchant took the bow of the *Dale* off.

MacDonald raised his glasses. The wake was visible again and now it was twisting left behind the merchant. So the merchant captain had realized the dilemma both ships had placed themselves in in their efforts to avoid each other and had shifted his rudder. The merchant was tilting left as it came about smartly to port. This would open the separation even farther. Even as he watched, MacDonald saw the left-bearing drift of the merchant begin, meaning that even at this speed the merchant would pass close down the port side of the *Dale*.

"Twenty knots is going to cause our ASW teams to have to start over," MacDonald said, his voice raised.

"Yes, sir, but it's either restart TMA in a few minutes or find ourselves changing course again, and the TMA solution will be even more garbled."

He was impressed. Goldstein had stood up to him, even if he did detect a slight tremor in the voice.

"Mr. Goldstein, seems to me you have the deck."

"Helmsman, ring up bells for twenty knots!" Goldstein shouted. "Ten-degree starboard rudder."

Several seconds passed before MacDonald felt the power of the *Dale*'s steam engines as they kicked in. The destroyer seemed to leap out of the water. The motion drift to port of the merchant ship increased. MacDonald smiled. Another officer had passed his standards. Goldstein was still a little rough around the edges for his liking, but with the trait of self-confidence combined with more time on the bridge, the junior officer might turn into a good officer of the deck.

Below in Combat, the Blue ASW Team were ripping the edges of the trace paper away from the tape, folding the penciled calculations to one side, and putting on new paper. At twenty knots, they would have to start over.

BOCHARKOV hiccupped.

"It's the cabbage," Ignatova offered.

"If it was the cabbage, I'd be farting like the rest of the crew," he whispered back, waving his hand in front of his face.

They laughed.

"Passing one hundred meters!" Lieutenant Yakovitch, the officer of the deck, shouted.

"I think with Yakovitch on duty, the noise of the sump pump below will be the second thing the Americans detect."

Bocharkov grunted. "Noise in the water is the curse of submariners. How else would we be so successful against the American submarines?"

"Give them our cabbage."

"Passing ninety meters!"

"Lieutenant Yakovitch!" the XO called. "Could you lower it a little? That operatic bass voice of yours is shaking the bulkheads."

Yakovitch smiled. He was proud of his amateur opera career. He cleared his throat to the amusement of the men in the control room.

Chief Ship Starshina Uvarova turned from his position of hovering over the helmsman, rolled his eyes, and nodded at Bocharkov.

"Even my senior enlisted man approves of your command, Vladmiri," Bocharkov added softly.

"Aye, sir!" Yakovitch replied, his booming voice not one octave lower.

Bocharkov smiled, the right side of his lip turning upward. "XO, I haven't heard a report from *Boyevaya Chast'* 4 in a few minutes. Hit them and see if our communicators still have underwater communications with the K-56."

Ignatova nodded and stepped to the sound-powered phone talker. "Give Communications a check and tell the communications officer to give me a call."

Almost immediately the internal communications box squawked. Ignatova looked down at the buttons and pushed in BCh-4. Across the small control room compartment, Bocharkov listened as the XO chewed the communications officer's butt about not keeping the control room informed on the communications ongoing between the K-122 and K-56 Echo submarines. Here they were surfacing simultaneously with another submarine—neither quite sure where the other was— and Bocharkov needed to know exactly what was happening around them. Oceans were so big that seldom did submarines collide with other ships and subs, but every so often, it did happen.

One of the sound-powered phone talkers pressed his headset to his ear, acknowledged the unseen talker on the other end, and then lifted the right side off his ear.

"Lieutenant Yakovitch, Bch-3 reports they believe they have faint noise of an American warship."

BCh-3 was the communications channel for Sonar and the torpedo rooms.

Bocharkov straightened off the bulkhead and walked toward the far end of the control room, where Sonar was located.

"Sir! K-56 is surfacing. The K-56 has us located off their starboard side."

"Starboard side?" Uvarova said briskly. "What does that mean? Starboard side—how far starboard side?"

Bocharkov had been going to ask the same thing, but his senior enlisted sailor had beat him to it. Ignatova looked at him. Bocharkov nodded. It was the right question, but one the chief ship starshina should have known the answer to.

"If they can hear us, then we have to be a couple hundred yards minimum, Chief Ship Starshina Uvarova," Ignatova answered. "How else would his sonar array be able to pick up a directional noise?"

Bocharkov reached up and grabbed a handhold as the K-122 continued upward toward the surface.

"Sorry, XO!"

"An American destroyer, Captain," Yakovitch said as he walked uphill toward Bocharkov. "Sonar is sure now. They have an American destroyer making high speeds, sir."

"I'm heading to Sonar now. What direction? Range?"

"Bearing is zero-four-zero, sir. Range unknown."

"It's coming from the direction of the American carrier battle group. Means the Americans have not given up on us," Ignatova added.

"Also means we need to know how far away they are. If we are picking them up now, then they cannot be too far from us," Bocharkov said, stroking his chin. "Have we set the anti–surface warfare team, XO?"

"With your permission, sir?"

Bocharkov grunted without answering. He continued to-ward Sonar. Behind him, Ignatova gave the orders bringing the submarine to general quarters. Neither officer expected the Americans to attack them, but if they had to make emergency maneuvers, they would need the crew prepared to react im-mediately. Bocharkov did not want to surface if they were detecting enemy presence, but his orders were explicit and they would not be on the surface long.

"XO, make sure the K-56 knows about the contact."

"If he didn't grunt, we wouldn't know he was listening," one of the sailors on the plane whispered to the other.

A slap hit him upside the head. Uvarova leaned down. "Shut up, comrade, and keep your eyes on your job. He is the captain. He can grunt. He can fart if he wants to. You on the other hand are barely a starshina and had better not fart or grunt when I tell you to do something."

The sailor rubbed his head. "Yes, Chief Ship Starshina Uvarova."

MACDONALD watched the merchant pass harmlessly down their port side, quickly exposing its stern as it maneuvered farther to port, opening even more distance between the two ships.

"Now, Mr. Goldstein, tell me about the other contact you had."

"It's opening, sir. It has changed to a more southerly direction."

"Let's bring her back down to eight knots so the ASW team can clear up their picture and bring her back onto base course two-two-zero."

"Captain!" the boatswain mate of the watch shouted from next to the 1MC speaker mounted near the captain's chair.

"What is it, Lowe?"

"Combat requests your presence, sir."

MacDonald looked at Goldstein. "Good job, Mr. Goldstein." He walked past the OOD, hearing the quartermaster announce, "Captain off the bridge," as he passed through the hatch leading to the combat information center.

"Captain in Combat" came the mirror-image announcement as he walked into the darkened space. The combat information center watch officer met him near the doorway.

"What you got, Lieutenant Burnham?"

"Sir, Sonar is getting some unusual noise on our contact and I thought you should know."

MacDonald was a step behind Burnham as the two officers hurried aft to the sonar portion of Combat.

Burnham jerked the curtain apart. "Captain's here," the combat watch officer said, making MacDonald think of it as more a warning than an announcement.

"Skipper, we have an anomaly here, sir," Lieutenant Junior Grade Burkeet said.

"An anomaly? I like anomalies, Mr. Burkeet."

"Yes, sir," Burkeet answered warily. The ASW officer touched Oliver. "You tell him."

Petty Officer Oliver pulled the left side of the headset away from his ear. "Sir, for the last seven to ten minutes I've been listening to the contact noise as it cycled up and down from faint to loud." The sonar technician glanced up at MacDonald. "Made me think of what you said about convergence and direct zones. But if it was direct, then we should be within several miles of them." He paused.

"Go ahead, Oliver," MacDonald encouraged.

"Well, sir, I think we have two submarines out there. I don't think we've been tracking one submarine, but two."

"Do you have two different lines of bearing?"

"No, sir, but what if the two submarines are traveling together? One nearer to us, which would explain the louder sounds, and one farther away, which would explain the fainter one."

"I think it makes sense, Skipper," Burkeet said.

MacDonald's lower lip pushed upward for a few seconds as he thought about it. They had had the same line of bearings on a contact since they first detected it several hours ago. The VQ-1 reconnaissance aircraft had visually sighted only one. The airdales had even identified the class as an Echo I before scooting back to Guam for their cold beer. His forehead wrinkled, his eyes narrowed. "Okay, Mr. Burkeet, why does it make sense?"

The ASW officer smiled. "It would explain why we are not getting any direct passive noise in the water, Skipper. We are listening to two convergence zone noises. Both submarines are over the horizon out of direct noise contact, but the noises of both are bouncing off the thermocline layer below and the surface of the water. They are both traveling at slightly different speeds, but the contacts are so close that their noises merge, making them seem like one contact."

When MacDonald nodded, Burkeet continued, confidence growing in his voice. "That explains why we sometimes hear the faint noise mixed with the stronger one."

"One of the submarines is closer," Burnham offered.

"How close?"

"Don't know, Captain."

"There is something else, Skipper," Oliver interrupted.

All three officers turned to the sonar technician.

"What's that?" MacDonald asked.

"Since we detected the noises, they have never been together. I mean you hear one, then the other would cycle through. That's because as we move through the water, our sonar is passing through the convergence-zone bounces of each of them. The sounds never really merged until the past half hour or so. That is why we thought we only had one." Oliver slipped his headset back on. "And these two are both Echo class submarines."

"That makes sense," Burkeet argued.

MacDonald grunted. "Okay, Oliver, let's say we buy this argument there are two of them. Are you telling me that we are going to run over one of them and if we keep going we'll come in contact with another one?"

Oliver shook his head sharply. "No, sir," he replied confidently. "These two submarines are together now. They are sailing side by side."

Several seconds of silence passed before Burnham asked, "How can you tell?"

"The noise synched in the last few minutes, sir." Oliver held his hands up side by side, palms down. "They have to be near each other because the faint noise and the louder noise are together now, riding the convergence zone bounces like a couple of lovers in a roller coaster." He waved his right hand. "This submarine's noise is arriving simultaneously with the louder noise of the other submarine." The sonar technician made a motion with his left hand, and then dropped them both, before turning back to the console. "No, sir, both of these submarines are together."

"Kind of a Soviet wolf pack," Burkeet offered.

MacDonald stroked his chin for a few seconds. "Okay, I'm not completely convinced, Petty Officer Oliver, but you make a good analytical argument." He looked at Lieutenant Burnham. "Tom, let's get a message off to Commander U.S. Seventh Fleet, Admiral Green on the *Kitty Hawk*, and to Commander Naval Intelligence telling them of the possibility that we have two submarines."

"Probability," Burkeet corrected.

MacDonald glared for a moment, then his face relaxed. He looked at Oliver. "You are sure we have two contacts and both are Echo class submarines?"

"Same sound signatures, Skipper," Oliver answered quickly. "And, Skipper, I'll stake my reputation that we have two submarines out here."

Burkeet smiled and nodded sharply at MacDonald.

MacDonald nodded, his lips clenched tight for a moment. "Petty Officer Oliver, I cannot ask for much more proof when you stake your reputation on it." He reached out and patted the sailor's shoulder twice. "But, even if you are wrong, you did right in bringing this to my attention."

"I'll get the message ready to go."

"Good, Mr. Burkeet. Oh! By the way, change possible to probable submarines."

Lieutenant Commander Joe Tucker, the executive officer of the USS *Dale*, walked through the open aft hatch. "Do submarines steam, or do they nuke when they move?"

"Morning, XO," Burnham acknowledged. "The Echo class submarines are all nuclear-powered."

"Echo class?"

MacDonald turned to his exec. "Morning, Joe. Seems our hot-running young sonar tech has gotten him two Echo class submarines ahead of us. Glad you're here."

Tucker nodded. "Just came from Radio, sir, reading the morning traffic, and did a quick tour through Engineering checking their logs."

MacDonald stepped out of the small sonar space. Burnham hurried toward the ASW plotting table along the port bulkhead of Combat. The curtain fell back in place as MacDonald and Joe Tucker walked toward the bridge. A minute later the two men were standing on the starboard bridge wing.

"Mornings like this make me glad I made the navy a career," MacDonald said, taking a deep breath.

"The Pacific is like a beautiful woman when she's calm, no clouds on the horizon, and the slight breeze makes you feel alive. A sight to behold and enjoy."

MacDonald chuckled. "Everything we do in the navy is feminine, with men running it. The ship is a 'she.' The oceans are 'her' and even the storms are named after women."

"Storms are named after women because when they arrive they are wild and wet, and when they leave they take everything with them."

"It's almost as if we men—we few brave men—did that because we miss them. Be good to get back to San Diego and the family for a few months," MacDonald added.

"You married guys are all alike. Now, for us certified bachelors, a six-month cruise is a chance to change the scenery at home port."

"I think I like coming home to the same woman, and one I love."

"Well, for me, I like coming home to different women, and I love them all."

"How did we get on this subject?"

"Something about oceans started it."

"What's the status report, XO?"

"We are going to have to refuel soon. I sent off a logistics request message to the USS *Mispillion*. She is headed toward Olongapo from Yankee Station. We can rendezvous with her in three days, if we are still out here. We should get a reply back to our logistics request sometime today."

"Let me know when the LOGREQ comes in, XO. Until we know for certain we can take on more fuel from the *Mispillion*, keep me apprised about it. It would be embarrassing to run out of fuel in the middle of the ocean."

"If we don't rendezvous with someone and get some fuel soon, we are going to be rigging sails in five days. We are under half now."

MacDonald nodded. "Should have topped off the other night when the rest of the battle group did."

"Wasn't our call, sir. Dawn was breaking and Admiral Green didn't want to conduct under-way replenishment during the daylight hours."

MacDonald's forehead wrinkled. "I wondered about that. That was unlike Green. I always wonder if he knows something we don't."

"Let's hope so. Otherwise why waste a lot of pay on admirals who only know as much as we do?"

Goldstein filled the hatchway. "Captain, Combat asks for your presence again. They think the submarine is surfacing."

"Submarines," MacDonald corrected. "They think we have two of them."

"Aye, sir," Goldstein acknowledged and quickly stepped back into the bridge.

MacDonald and Tucker hurried through the bridge to the acknowledgments of quartermasters. Opening the hatch separating the bridge from the darkened spaces of Combat, the two officers were quickly gone from the Pacific morning daylight.

Burnham met them at the hatch. "Skipper, Sonar believes either one or both of the submarines are surfacing."

The three worked their way aft toward Sonar. "Why?" MacDonald asked, but before Burnham could answer, he had already pulled the curtain apart. "What you got, Mr. Burkeet?"

"Petty Officer Oliver—"

"Sir, the submarine noises are increasing and at least one of them is now direct. I think they are above the layer."

"If we have direct noise, then they have to be no more than twenty . . . twenty-five . . . thirty nautical miles from us," Burkeet added.

MacDonald turned to Joe Tucker. "XO, take the bridge."

"We should see them on radar shortly," Burnham offered as Joe Tucker bumped by him on the way forward.

MacDonald's eyes widened. "Shut down the radar, Lieutenant."

"But, sir—"

"Shut it down. If they are surfacing, their electronic warfare gear will detect us." He looked down at Oliver. "Let's see our sonar expert here drive the *Dale* toward them."

From Combat came the shout of the electronic warfare operator. "I've got a snoop tray radar! Snoop tray!"

MacDonald's head shot up. "Snoop tray radar" was the NATO name for the surface search radar on the Echo class submarines. A thrill of excitement shot through him. Now he had both Sonar and EW confirming at least one submarine. He moved forward through Combat at a fast pace to where the EW operator manned his position. "Direction?"

"Bearing two one eight degrees, Skipper."

"Lieutenant Burnham! You got our radar secured?"

"Yes, sir," the combat information center watch officer acknowledged calmly.

MacDonald let out a sigh of relief. "Well, gentlemen," he said to the Combat watch standers. "Looks as if we have found one of our submarines."

"Second snoop tray radar active. Belay my last, sir! It just shut down."

"Then there are two of those sons of a bitches out here," MacDonald said, drawing a round of applause from the sailors. An applause more for the excitement of the moment than for the skipper. He motioned it quiet. "They're going to know they're being chased," he said in a loud voice. "We want to know why two submarines surfaced in the middle of the morning in the middle of the ocean. We don't want them to hear us before we see them." He looked at Burnham. "Make sure our message reflects current contact status."

MacDonald crawled up into his chair. The XO was on the bridge. They had three days of fuel and they had two submarines ahead of them. MacDonald mentally crossed his fingers, hoping he had shut down the *Dale* radar before the Soviets detected them. A two-submarine contact was unusual and, for a quick moment, he felt a slight chill. "Why have they surfaced?" he asked himself softly.

"Sir?" Burnham asked from in front of him, where he was gathering the data for the message.

"Nothing. Just thinking out loud." Around him the instincts of a well-trained warship took over. He felt the ship shift course slightly, knowing few others would have detected the movement, but over ten years at sea had given him nautical insight most would never realize and no one could ever explain except to other sailors.

THE K-122 broke surface. The bow shot upward a few feet before splashing down on the ocean, sending sprays of water upward ten meters or more. The rest of the light gray boat moved quickly forward.

The conning tower hatch clanged on the metal deck of the boat, with a starshina scrambling through the narrow opening onto the bridge, the young sailor never pausing as he hurried up the ladder to his watch station. The second man through the hatch was Bocharkov. His thin frame made his life within the strict confines of the K-122 better than most.

Bocharkov looked at the K-56 off his starboard side about three hundred meters. He lifted the cover of the sound tube. "Control room, this is the skipper. Right ten-degree rudder, speed two knots."

The speed quickly fell off as the engineering room responded to the command. Since the skipper of the K-56 was senior to Bocharkov, the Echo II submarine would maintain course and speed as the Echo I K-122 maneuvered closer.

The whistle of the tube drew Bocharkov's attention. "Captain here," he answered.

"Sir, Sonar reports the American warship slowed his speed then increased it again."

That could mean many things, he thought. "Line of bearing?"

"Zero-three-five, Captain."

"Signal strength?"

"Remaining about the same right now, sir."

He flipped the tube shut. The American warship was looking for him. He'd do the same if the roles were reversed.

"Sir, K-56 signals for one of us to turn off his surface search radar. They are interfering with each other."

"Turn ours off."

On the deck of the K-56, three sailors had inflated a small yellow rubber raft and were easing over the side of the submarine. Watching the sailors was an officer dressed in the darker uniform of a Spetsnaz.

Bocharkov lifted the tube covering. "Rudders amidships!"

From the control room came the answering acknowledgment. Bocharkov glanced aft and watched for several seconds, until he saw the change in the direction of the wake. Then he looked at the K-56. They were about one hundred meters apart. The wind against the sail of the K-56 and the wave action would push the other boat toward them, closing the gap, but he estimated they had nearly half an hour before he would have to maneuver to open distance again. In a half hour, he expected to be gone, back beneath the waves of the ocean where the world of the submariner operated.

"Control room, Skipper. Keep just enough revolutions on the shaft to keep us steady. I want to be under way without making way."

"Aye, sir," came the acknowledgment from below.

"And get our embarkation party topside. The K-56 nearly has its boat in the water and we don't have our sailors topside!"

As if responding to Bocharkov's command, sailors poured up through the aft escape hatch. He lifted his binoculars again and focused on the Spetsnaz. Maybe all submarines had the Special Forces on them now. Maybe they had special orders to protect against a defection or, worse, a Soviet commander who decided the time to fight the Americans was on his mission. Many, such as him, knew it was only a matter of time before the growing strength of the Soviet Navy rivaled, then passed the world giant. Giants did not appreciate being surpassed.

"Captain Bocharkov!" a bullhorn called from across the gap.

He dropped the binoculars, squinted as he raised his hands to shield his eyes, and looked at the conning tower of the other boat. He smiled when he recognized his comrade from Grechko Naval Academy and now neighbor in Kamchatka.

Captain Second Rank Fedor Gerasimovich stood on the bridge of the K-56. Gerasimovich raised his hand and waved when he saw Bocharkov looking in his direction.

Bocharkov waved before leaning down to the tube. "Have someone bring me the bullhorn." He looked over at Gerasimovich and raised his hand with his index finger extended.

"I understand, comrade. While you wait for your bullhorn, let me introduce Lieutenant Dolinski—Uri Dolinski."

The Spetsnaz officer on the main deck dropped his hands, came to attention, and saluted Bocharkov. Bocharkov returned the salute.

"He is transferring from me to you, my friend. He is the technical expert assigned for this strange mission no one will tell me about." The bullhorn squeaked like fingers down a chalkboard, causing everyone to wince. A couple of the sailors covered their ears.

From the hatch came Ignatova, a bullhorn tucked under his arm.

Bocharkov took it from him. "Any more news on the contact?"

Ignatova shook his head as he stood. "Same strength as passed along earlier, Captain. EW reports no radar of electronic intelligence contacts."

Electronic intelligence was the new buzzword of the fleet. Taken from the American publication *Proceedings*, it had quickly spread throughout the Soviet Navy. As much as they knew the Americans were the enemy, there was also a slight tinge of envy over their navy.

Envy of their strength, and their ability to sail anywhere in the world on a moment's notice, to have such allies who offered port facilities anywhere in the world.

"What's that?" Ignatova asked, nodding at the K-56.

From the bridge on the conning tower of the K-56, metal waterproof boxes were being handed down the narrow ladder from sailor to sailor. When the first one reached the deck, the sailors there set it at the feet of the Spetsnaz, who pulled a small notebook from his back pocket and checked something in it against the writing on the box.

"The Spetsnaz is Lieutenant Uri Dolinski. He is transferring from the K-56—"

"I am also transferring equipment you will need for your mission, Comrade Captain!" The bullhorn voice from the K-56 interrupted. "Only about seven thousand tons of it," Gerasimovich said, jokingly. "No, no, not that much, just five boxes. Should not be enough to change the trim of the K-122."

Bocharkov lifted the bullhorn. "Fedor, it is good to see you, comrade. I trust you have had a good voyage, and when you return to Kamchatka, please tell my wife and the wives of the other crew members of the K-122 that we are all well and are looking forward to our return."

"I will do that." Gerasimovich dropped the bullhorn, leaned over the bridge, and said something to Dolinski. The Spetsnaz officer saluted the captain second rank and then said something to the sailors. Soon the working party were moving the five boxes toward the deployed inflatable raft.

"I think the American is coming this way," Bocharkov said softly to Ignatova.

Ignatova glanced at him. "Sonar seems to think he is searching the area where we were sighted by the American reconnaissance aircraft, Captain."

Bocharkov nodded. "If the American captain is a novice, then that is what he is doing. If not, then he is headed this way."

"We will detect his radar before he detects us."

The Spetsnaz officer slid into the raft, where four sailors had already taken position. The boxes were carefully transferred from the main deck to the raft.

Bocharkov grunted. He glanced down at the bullhorn to make sure it was off. "How long have we had the American warship on sonar?"

"Nearly an hour."

"And has the bearing shifted significantly? One moment it is zero-four-zero, then the next a few degrees more, and now we have it bearing zero-three-five."

"But we detected it when it was moving at such a speed it could not possibly have detected our noise."

Bocharkov turned and studied Ignatova's face for moment, hoping his XO was joking, which would have been out of context for the serious officer. He believed those without humor lacked the intellectual flexibility to examine different perspectives of a complex situation. But then, of course, he was the captain and he could believe anything he wanted while on board the K-122, because whatever the captain believed became gospel for the crew. He sighed. With the exception of the *zampolit*. Party-political officers always believed everyone but themselves was bordering on a traitorous act.

The rubber raft pushed away from K-56; the *put-put* sound of the small engine rode the wind toward the K-122. The wave action was picking up a little, Bocharkov realized. Yesterday, when they were conducting the missile firing exercise, the waves barely lapped the sides. Now not even the faint wake behind the raft was discernible.

"It could have detected us before it increased speed, XO. It could have been following us without us knowing it, then for some reason increased speed, giving us an opportunity to know it was there."

"You are probably right, Captain," Ignatova responded, as he should to Bocharkov's statement.

"But you do not believe that idea, do you?" Before Ignatova could answer, Bocharkov set the bullhorn down on the deck and raised his binoculars to focus on the small raft headed his way. "There are many reasons ships at sea have to increase speed. Everything from avoiding other ships in the area to zooming after a contact so it can have better signal strength."

"Aye, Captain, you are probably right, but if I may offer a counterargument."

"You may."

"Maybe we picked up the warship as it was speeding to our last known location and slowing down when it reached it."

"Then we would have a spectacular sonar, XO. We would have picked up the warship over a hundred kilometers from here."

He dropped his binoculars and leaned over the aft portion of the bridge where the raft was making its approach.

"XO, after we are submerged, I want to meet with our Spetsnaz officers. I think there is more here than they are telling us."

"They are Spetsnaz, sir. There is always more to whatever they are doing than they tell those who do not wear the black. Fact is, I don't think they like telling each other what they are doing. One-way trips are their fantasy."

Bocharkov shook his head. "Hope you are wrong, Vladmiri. If it is a one-way trip, inside Subic Bay is not where they would want it to end."

Chief Starshina Trush, his face hidden by the heavy Cossack beard and hair, was shouting at the sailors on the stern, giving orders about casting lines. Before one of the sailors could toss a line to the raft, the chief had jerked it away and tossed it underhanded to one of the sailors on the raft. A few seconds later the raft was tight against the hull and the sailors were awkwardly moving the heavy boxes on board, to the profanity of Chief Starshina Trush.

Bocharkov grunted. "Get the lieutenant and his boxes aboard and down below. I want to get off the surface as soon as possible, XO. I dislike intensely being on the surface in daylight."

"CONTACT bearing three three five relative," cried the sound-powered phone talker on the bridge. On board ships there were two types of bearings. One was the normal compass bearing based on true north; the other was the relative bearing, which considered the bow as always pointing zero-zero-zero.

MacDonald stepped quickly into the bridge even as he looked toward the bow. "Who, where?" he shouted.

"Topside signal bridge watch reports two low contacts in the water off our port bow, Skipper."

MacDonald grabbed his binoculars. "Make sure Combat knows," he ordered, jerking his finger at Goldstein as he stepped back onto the port bridge wing.

"They know."

Dale *had them*, he told himself. Dead ahead practically. Two Soviet submarines. Had to be them. Nothing else in this direction. *Oliver, I could kiss you, you ugly sonarman son of a bitch. Just let them be our Echos.* Of course, they could be fishing vessels out of the Philippines.

"They know, sir," Goldstein repeated quietly to the hatchway.

"Very well, Sam. Tell them to keep piping up the contact information."

MacDonald lifted the glasses, focusing them as he scanned the horizon. There was nothing there. Where were the low-riders? He could not see anything, but then the signal bridge was another twenty to twenty-five feet higher. They had a higher height-of-eye. It also meant the *Dale* had to be about fifteen nautical miles from the contacts. *Let them be our Soviet submarines.* Only on the ocean could one truly tell the earth was round, and no matter where you sailed, the horizon was always fifteen nautical miles away.

He let out a deep breath. Decisions, decisions, decisions. What he decided now would determine how *Dale* would chase these submarines once they spotted him and submerged.

Submerging was a given. Submarines fought submerged, and once spotted, both would blow their ballasts—Sonar would hear them doing that—and they would drop like rocks into the abyss below. If warriors of the sea could earn points for "gotchas," then *Dale* would earn a bunch. . . .

What the hell are you doing? he asked himself. *You're acting like some junior officer about to lose his virginity after a long night of heavy dancing. Stop it, Danny,* he told himself. *This is just one more antisubmarine warfare operation and regardless of whether the contacts are fishing vessels or Soviet Echo submarines,* Dale *will follow protocol. Lord, just let them be those Soviet sons of bitches.*

The XO, Joe Tucker, stepped onto the bridge wing. MacDonald lowered his glasses for a second.

"Has to be the submarines," Tucker offered, raising his binoculars in tandem with MacDonald.

"I have my fingers crossed."

"Nothing else out in this direction according to Sonar." Tucker dropped his binoculars. "What now, Skipper?"

MacDonald dropped his glasses, letting them hang from the strap around his neck. "This is the tricky part, Joe Tucker," he said.

"What have you done before in a situation like this?"

MacDonald smiled, then laughed slightly. "Funny you should ask, XO. I don't think any American destroyer has ever sneaked up on two surfaced Soviet submarines."

"I don't expect they'll be surfaced once they see us."

"They have to know we are here. Or at least have a line of bearing on us," MacDonald opined softly. "This close, if their sonar team is worth a damn, they would have picked up our prop noise long ago."

Tucker shook his head slightly. "We're a pretty quiet ship."

"We are a surface ship putting noise in the water. Noise is a signature a good sonar team can interpret with ease. If they have picked us up—let's assume they have—then what are they thinking?"

"They are thinking we are after them?"

MacDonald nodded. "That's what you and I would think. But who knows what Crazy Ivan thinks. Maybe he gets his 'gotchas' from some other misguided tactic."

"Such as the closer we get before he pulls the plug the more points he gets?" Joe Tucker shook his head. "Kind of a crazy way to play the game."

"Yeah. His sonar team might believe they are picking up our noise from hundreds of miles away."

"I don't think they're as dumb as we would like to believe."

"I don't either, but when I was in Combat earlier, we still did not know if our contacts were twenty miles from us or a hundred. All we knew was which direction the noise was coming from. We have been on this base course of two-two-zero for over twelve hours. If they have a reciprocal contact on us, then they have to figure we are in pursuit."

MacDonald raised his glasses and looked in the direction of the contacts. From the bridge came another report of them lying motionless on a left-stern-to-left-bow angle.

"Why are they surfaced?" MacDonald lowered his binoculars.

"Skipper," Goldstein said from the hatchway. "Combat reports Snoop Tray radar still active."

"Don't know why they haven't picked us up yet?" Joe Tucker asked.

"They will shortly," MacDonald replied sharply. "So, XO, what do you recommend?"

"I recommend we come up to full speed, flip on the radar, put on face paint, run up the Jolly Roger, and see how close we can get to them." He shrugged. "We aren't going to sneak up on them, so the faster we go, the closer we'll get before they slam their foot on the gas and head for the deep." The XO braced both hands on the above-waist-high metal railing. "No reason to try to sneak up on them. Even the piss-poor Snoop Tray is going to hit us after we get about half our ship up over the horizon where it can paint us." Joe Tucker leaned forward and looked at the sea beneath the *Dale*. "The slight seas might be disrupting their video return a little, but any second now that Soviet piece-of-shit radar is going to detect us."

MacDonald nodded, his forehead wrinkling in concentration a few seconds before a broad grin spread beneath the pencil-thin mustache. "XO, let's do it. Tell Sonar they are about to lose contact, but be prepared to reengage. Once they submerge . . ."

"They're together. They'll remain together." Joe Tucker leaned away from the railing.

"I agree, XO." MacDonald stuck his head back into the bridge area. "Lieutenant Goldstein, bring us up to 'all ahead flank.' Tell Combat to prepare a submarine contact report for release at my order."

"Has to be them."

"Just want to make sure before I fire off a message to Seventh Fleet and get all those P-3 airdales wetting their pants with excitement."

He wondered if the *Dale* would really be the first destroyer to catch two Soviet submarines on the surface in the middle of the ocean. Might be another folktale, but one thing for sure: He was going to be sure the contacts were submarines before he sent the message.

"Skipper," Goldstein said from the hatchway. "Signal bridge watch reports the two contacts as submarines."

MacDonald let out a deep breath. "Is he sure?"

"I can ask him."

"Lieutenant, ask him to confirm the sighting and ask him to have the on-duty—"

"I'll go," Joe Tucker said, turning to the nearby ladder and sprinting up it to the signal bridge directly above them.

MacDonald watched the XO disappear across the deck. Less than a minute later Joe Tucker was leaning over the railing above him, a broad grin stretched from ear to ear. "You can release that message, Skipper. You got them!" Joe Tucker wet two fingers and dipped them as if scoring a dunk in basketball. *"Dos puntos!"*

The *Dale* engines kicked in and MacDonald grabbed the railing. A smile spread across his face as the destroyer leaped forward, heading toward the surfaced submarines.

"Officer of the deck! Activate the surface search radar!" No reason to try to hide now.

DOWN below, Oliver threw his headset down on the small shelf below the sonar console. "Damn it!" he shouted, rubbing his ears. He looked at Lieutenant Junior Grade Burkeet. Burkeet fell into Chief Stalzer as the *Dale* leaped forward, the propellers churning up the ocean behind the destroyer as the four steam-driven engines sped toward twenty-two knots.

"Sir, we are drowning out any passive noise from the contacts."

"Don't need sonar right now, Petty Officer Oliver," Chief Stalzer said. "We have them on visual." He reached forward and slapped the sonar technician on the shoulder. "Good job for a short-timer."

CAPTAIN Second Rank Fedor Gerasimovich lifted his bullhorn. "Captain Bocharkov! Our radar reports a contact bearing zero-four-zero degrees heading our way. Range . . ." The bullhorn squeaked, the noise causing Gerasimovich to lift it away from his lips. It stopped almost immediately and he quickly lifted the bullhorn back. "I said, comrade, the contact is horizon distance—about twenty-five kilometers!"

Bocharkov raised his glasses and trained them in the direction of the contact. He could see nothing. The voice tube whistled. He dropped his glasses and lifted the covering. "Go ahead."

"Sir, I have increased rotation on the American warship. He is increasing his speed."

"What is his bearing?"

"We hold him at zero-three-five with slight bearing drift to the right."

"Do you think it is the Americans?" Ignatova asked, nodding toward the horizon where K-56 had reported the contact.

Bocharkov grunted. He leaned over the railing. "Get that raft off my boat! And get those boxes belowdecks, Chief!"

Chief Trush held his hand to his ear. "What?" he mouthed.

Bocharkov lifted the bullhorn and repeated his instructions. Trush snapped a salute then scurried to carry them out. Trush's bass voice was easily heard above the ocean noise as he screamed, shouted, and pushed the sailors to action.

With the bullhorn near his lips, Bocharkov turned it toward Gerasimovich, who had heard the orders. "Fedor, it may be an American warship."

Gerasimovich nodded. "Here is what I recommend, Captain Bocharkov . . ." He briefly outlined his idea. And when he finished, he added, "You are the high-valued unit for this mission. If we do this, then I will pull him away from you. Once you're in his baffles, I recommend you turn toward the Philippines. By the time I lose him, you will be free."

Bocharkov looked at Ignatova. Ignatova had his glasses trained off the port side of the boat, scanning the horizon. "What do you think?"

"I think I can make out a mast clearing the horizon. It is American Navy dark gray."

Bocharkov lifted his glasses. Across the narrow strip of water separating the two powerful Soviet submarines Gerasimovich was doing the same thing. Motion was what usually identified a contact, so Bocharkov waited and a few seconds passed before a slight motion drew his attention. "Looks like the main mast."

"Looks like a main mast with an antenna that is turning."

Bocharkov lifted the voice tube covering. "Control room, Captain. Does the electronic warfare operator have anything in the direction of zero-four-zero true?"

Immediately, the voice of Lieutenant Commander Orlov, the operations officer, answered with a negative.

"It's turning but they have it turned off. Wait a minute, Skipper! Belay my last. Electronic warfare has a surface search radar in that direction. It is an American warship—probably destroyer!" Orlov shouted.

"Fast speed, radar on. What are they thinking?" Ignatova asked.

"He knows when we see him we will submerge. He wants to get as close to us as possible. He wants to see us. Photograph us. He knows we know he is coming."

"I would think he would try to sneak up on us."

Bocharkov grunted. "Most likely his EW detected the K-56's surface search radar. And, as we have with theirs, he would have know that our sonar operators had probably detected him." He laughed softly. "Smart captain. I would have done the same. Full speed ahead and see how close I can get before the submarines submerge. Being closer means being able to reestablish contact sooner."

The voice tube whistled again. "Skipper," Orlov said. "Sonar confirms the radar contact is the same as the sonar contact. It is the American destroyer cresting the horizon."

Bocharkov acknowledged Orlov's report. He lifted his bullhorn and quickly agreed to Gerasimovich's idea. Amidships of the K-122, the raft was released. The sailors cranked the small engine, and the raft started its slow transit toward the K-56. The two starshinas leaned forward as if urging the raft ahead.

Bocharkov looked down at the main deck. Trush was clearing the sailors off topside, urging them down the aft escape hatch into the aft torpedo room. What was so damn important that Soviet Pacific Fleet headquarters had risked two submarines by having them surface in the daylight? He'd know soon enough. And why in the hell did he have to have another Spetsnaz aboard his boat?

"Clear the decks, XO," Bocharkov said. He lifted the voice tube and told the control room to prepare to dive, but not to dive until he gave the order. He lifted his bullhorn, pointing it toward the K-56. "Fedor! I owe you a drink in Kamchatka."

"No, I owe you one, comrade. I have not had an opportunity to pit my wits against the Americans. You have had all the fun. If you get home before me, tell the wives I am not far behind."

Bocharkov handed the bullhorn to one of the topside watches. He turned to them. "You sailors, get belowdecks." Then he hit the dive button. The *ooga* noise common to both the Soviet and the American navies echoed across the open ocean. Bucharkov looked across the narrowing distance between the two submarines. The raft had bumped against the K-56 hull, and sailors were quickly pulling the two men out of it. The cap on the last sailor flew off, landing in the water near the raft.

Another sailor topside, a security expert, raised the AK-47 cradled in his arm, pointed it at the raft, and fired. The quick burst of the automatic weapon sent dozens of bullets into the inflated rim. Gerasimovich saluted Bocharkov, who returned the gesture. He did a quick look fore and aft, satisfying himself that both escape hatches were secured and no one other than him was above deck. Then he quickly scurried down the ladder, securing the hatch after him. In seconds he was in the control room.

"Orders?" Ignatova asked loudly.

"Take the boat to two hundred meters."

"Two hundred meters!" Ignatova relayed.

Across the control room the order was repeated by Lieutenant Commander Burian Orlov. Chief Ship Starshina Uvarova, chief of the boat, pulled the hydraulic levers back, his eyes locked on the meters above them as the ballasts filled.

"Passing fifty meters," Orlov said from his position halfway between the helmsman and the planesman. "Angle on the bow twenty degrees. Recommend speed eight knots."

Bocharkov said nothing. After a few seconds, Ignatova asked softly, "Sir, should we increase speed to eight knots?"

Bocharkov shook his head. "No, keep the speed to barely making way. Keep taking us down."

The sound of the ballasts filling on the K-56 as it submerged vibrated through the boat. Every person in the control room with the exception of Bocharkov glanced upward. There would be thoughts of the K-56 submerging faster than their submarine. Collisions at sea were terrible things, but none more terrible than two submarines colliding out of sight beneath the waves.

They had no way of knowing that the K-56 would remain on the surface until they were sure the Americans had seen them. Then like the wounded grouse on the plains drawing a predator away from its nest, Gerasimovich would lure the Americans northwest, away from the K-122.

"Passing seventy-five meters," Orlov said, his voice slightly louder than the last report.

"Continue to two hundred meters," Bocharkov said. "Maintain two knots speed."

More noise from the K-56 reached their ears as Bocharkov's comrade Gerasimovich engaged both propellers on the other submarine. The noise was the shafts increasing in rotation, the slight vibration of the props boring through the water overhead as the other submarine changed its direction away from the K-122.

If he were Fedor Gerasimovich, Bocharkcov thought, he would take the K-56 up to twenty knots. Twenty knots was not a tactically good move, but the noise would draw the

American to him and mask any noise K-122 was generating into the water.

"Passing one hundred meters."

"Very well," Ignatova answered.

"Angle on the bow twenty degrees. Speed remains two knots."

Two knots was just enough forward motion to keep the K-122 pointed in the same direction. When a submarine dropped through varying depths of temperature and currents, without some speed the ocean could gain control, twisting and turning the boat on its way downward. And if you hit a river current, you could find yourself ripped along with it until you put on a burst of speed to break through. Bocharkov let out a deep breath. With the K-56 whipping up knuckles in the water above them, he had little doubt the Americans would not hear the K-122. All he had to do was wait comfortably beneath the layer until the Americans and the K-56 disappeared northward.

"CAPTAIN, signal bridge lookout reports one of the submarines is submerging. The other one has a small boat tied up alongside."

"Thanks, Lieutenant Goldstein." MacDonald lifted his glasses. He wished he were up on the signal bridge instead of the XO, but his job was here or in Combat.

A sailor burst through the hatch, the ship's camera in his hand. When he saw the skipper, he stopped abruptly, snapped a salute. "Sorry, sir."

"Don't be." He pointed upward. "Get up there and get us some photographs."

He sighed. The sailor's boondockers clanged on the metal rungs as the young man ran up the ladder. He hoped the photographer was able to get a shot of both submarines together. It would be a nice memento to hang up in the wardroom. But if one was submerging, the sailor would have to act fast.

He lifted the binoculars again, training them off the port side of the bow. The submarines were in view down. He smiled. He had his two submarines, and as he watched, water washed over the bow and stern of the one on the left. Mac-Donald hummed. "Gotcha," he whispered. "More than *dos puntos* in any man's book."

The binoculars were not as powerful as the deck-mounted set being used on the signal bridge by the XO. The speck on the side of the other submarine must be the raft reported a moment ago. As MacDonald watched, the stick figures of the Soviet sailors started to disappear. The speck disappeared also. Then the control tower of the first submarine was gone. One below the waterline and one to go.

"Skipper!" Joe Tucker shouted from above.

Reluctantly he lowered his binoculars and shielded his eyes as he looked upward.

"They've cast off the raft." Joe Tucker laughed. "Man-oh-man, you should have seen them Soviet bastards scurrying for their lives. We have surprised the hell out of them!"

"You got that right, Joe Tucker." He lifted the binoculars again. Christ, he wanted to be on the signal bridge.

"And we may have a photograph of both submarines together. If we do, we only have the conning tower of the first submarine alongside the second."

MacDonald lowered the binoculars. "Give that sailor extra liberty in Olongapo, XO, if he caught both of them." Maybe this was going to be a winning day all around.

He had started to lift his binoculars again as Lieutenant Burnham stepped onto the bridge wing with his glasses strung around his neck. "Captain, I just got to see this, sir."

"Aren't you the CICWO?"

"Commander Stillman has it now, sir. I had the four-to-eight watch, but stayed for the fun."

Lieutenant Commander Stillman was the chief engineer and the third senior person on board the *Dale*.

"Very well." He discovered he liked the idea of having someone else enjoy this moment of nautical success with him—even if that someone was Burnham. *Dale* should get at least a "Bravo Zulu" from Seventh Fleet on this victory.

Water washed across the bow and stern of the second submarine. The submarine propellers churned a gigantic wake as the second Echo headed for the depths. Even with the bow underwater, the speed this skipper was kicking up to escape the "terrible, frightening Americans" gave MacDonald an extra burst of adrenaline. It was going to be easy to keep contact on that one.

When you're frightened or seeking an escape, it is amazing how even the most respected officer sometimes allows emotions to win over tactics. Whoever the skipper was of the second boat had to be a novice or lack self control, unlike the first submarine, which had just eased below the surface before taking off.

MacDonald lowered the binoculars and stepped inside the bridge. He flipped the 12MC button on the voice box. "Combat, Captain here. What is the distance to the contacts?"

"Nine miles, sir," Stillman replied, "and closing."

"Very well." He turned to Goldstein. "Officer of the Deck, bring us down to eight knots." MacDonald put both hands on the small shelf that ran the length of the bridge, beneath the forward windows. "You see that spot of water where we had those two submarines?"

"Yes, sir."

"Well, Mr. Goldstein, I want the *Dale* to sail right through it." Around the bridge everyone was smiling. They had rattled the Soviets. What a great way to start a navy day!

MacDonald went back out on the bridge wing. Burnham was grinning from ear to ear. The clanging of someone coming down from the signal bridge drew MacDonald's attention.

"Well, Joe Tucker," he said, a swagger in his voice. "Looks as if we had good—"

"Skipper, the Soviets left something in the water."

MacDonald faced the bow, shielding his eyes with his hand. "What?"

"I think it was the raft. We startled them so fast . . ."

Goldstein stuck his head outside the bridge. "Sir, Sonar has one of the submarines, tracking it on course three-three-zero."

"Tell them to continue tracking."

"Sir, should I change our course also?"

MacDonald shook his head. "Not yet, Lieutenant." He turned to Joe Tucker. "XO, let's see what they left behind."

THIRTY minutes later a bow hook pulled a sailor's hat onto the midships deck of the motionless *Dale*. Wind was pushing the half-sunken rubber raft toward the hull. Ten minutes more and the sailors had it on the main deck. MacDonald and Joe Tucker stood looking at it with arms folded.

Chief Warrant Officer Jimmy "Tiny" Smith handed the cap to MacDonald. "Sir, don't see any pants with it."

"Pants?" MacDonald asked.

"Yes, sir. If we scared him out of his hat, then maybe we scared him out of his pants, too," the first division officer said.

MacDonald turned the soaked hat over and over in his hand. The lettering across the brow was Cyrillic, but the number 56 was easily recognized. "Fifty-six?" he asked aloud. He looked at the XO. "Well, Joe Tucker, looks as if we have the identity of one of those submarines."

"Sir, what do you want me to do with this raft?" Smith asked.

"Warrant, have your boatswain mates wrap it up for Naval Intelligence. Those intel weenies enjoy having little things like this to add to their collection. Who knows? Someday they may have an entire submarine out at Northwest, Virginia, in that hangar."

"What hangar?" Tiny Smith asked.

Both officers laughed.

FIVE

MACDONALD rubbed his hand over his chin. His stomach churned, making him regret the last of too many coffees during the night. The gray of the mind from too little sleep clouded his thoughts. Any sleep in the last eighteen hours of pursuit had been a quick, few-minute doze in his chair on the bridge.

"It's been over three hours, sir," Joe Tucker repeated.

"I know," MacDonald replied, and a deep sigh followed. He gave a weak grin to the sonar team. "You sailors did great. Without you the *Dale* would never have followed them this long. We never would have caught them with their pants down on the surface. There is not a shred of doubt that if we had been told to sink them, we could have done so numerous times in the past two days."

Oliver looked up. The blue lights in Combat made the red in his eyes blend with wide pupils, creating an eerie appearance, as if solid fields of blackness filled the sonar technician's eyes. "I wish I hadn't lost him, sir."

"Petty Officer Oliver, we would never have kept track this long without you and your fellow sonar technicians." MacDonald's forehead wrinkled. "How long have you been on watch?"

"He refused to leave, sir. He's been the only sonar tech on watch for the past eighteen hours." Burkeet paused before adding, "Said it was his submarine and he'd stay with it as long as you did."

MacDonald touched the sailor's shoulder. Chief Sonar Technician Stalzer leaned into the small space between the sonar console and the forward bulkhead of the sonar compartment. "Chief, why don't you relieve Petty Officer Oliver so he can secure?" MacDonald pinched his nose for a moment. Christ! He had not realized how tired he was. "We're going to break off and rejoin the battle group in Olongapo." This would make the crew happy. Olongapo!

Stalzer uncrossed his arms and straightened. "Aye, sir. I was going to relieve Oliver as soon as I could." He reached over and touched the other sonar man's shoulder. "Petty Officer Oliver did an astounding job."

"That he did," MacDonald said. Stalzer was a "butt snorkler" extraordinaire. And he was as bad a butt snorkler as he was a chief, which was one reason the man would still be a chief when MacDonald left the *Dale* in a couple of more years. He had met others like Stalzer during his fifteen years of service. Most petered out soon, whether officer or enlisted.

"XO, how long you been up?"

"Not as long as you, sir."

"Good." He motioned Joe Tucker out of the small confines of the curtain-enclosed sonar compartment, into the main compartment of combat information center. "Let's move forward."

They walked together, inching through the equipment- and sailor-crowded Combat toward the hatch leading to the bridge. MacDonald touched Joe Tucker on the arm when they were in the one area of Combat where the two could whisper without being overhead. "XO, I'm going to hit the rack for a few winks. Would you see to it that we send an updated status report telling Seventh Fleet and Commander Naval Intelligence Command that we have lost contact? Tell them that 'unless otherwise directed' we are breaking off and rejoining the battle group."

"Will do, sir."

"If I recall correctly, XO, we are a couple hundred miles out, so bring the speed up to twenty knots. That should get us into Olongapo by nightfall. It'll make the crew happy if we can reward them with some liberty downtown tonight."

"Sounds like a great morale-building strategy."

"And, Joe Tucker, have the watch wake me at zero eight hundred hours. That will give me four or five hours' shut-eye. Then I'll return the favor."

Joe Tucker nodded.

"One other thing, Joe Tucker," MacDonald whispered, his head nearly touching the XO's. "We need to talk about the leadership in the ASW division. Not now. I never make decisions unless I have to when I'm this tired."

The XO nodded, his lips clenched tightly. "I know, sir. I made a mental note to myself on the same subject."

"Then you have a go at it first." MacDonald turned and headed aft. His in-port and at-sea staterooms were one and the same on the small Forrest Sherman class destroyer. The new Spruance class destroyer the navy was designing would be much bigger, and in the plans the skipper had both an in-port and an at-sea cabin. The in-port cabin even had a sitting room. Next thing you knew, destroyers would have bathtubs. What in the world were tin-can sailors coming to?

Five minutes later his shoes landed on top of each other. His khaki shirt he tossed on the nearby chair, and then MacDonald collapsed on his rack, still wearing his khaki pants. Sleep came almost instantly.

Two sailors ambled past his stateroom two hours later and smiled when they heard the loud snores coming from within, almost "rattling the passageway bulkhead," as one of them observed. From such inconspicuous moments come sea tales of the future.

"I know, Lieutenant Golovastov, and we will do the Party-political training we have missed," Bocharkov said with a sigh. "I recognize that we should have made time, but you have to admit that with the American destroyer breathing down our tail for the past two days . . ." His voice trailed off.

"A day and a half, Captain Bocharkov." The younger officer held up one finger. "Only a day and a half. A day and a half, we should have lost them, don't you think?"

Bocharkov shut his eyes for a minute and took a deep breath. Most *zampolits* were reasonable officers—men who took their jobs with the seriousness the Party required. But even they soon recognized the challenges of living in cramped quarters beneath tons of water.

"Excuse me, just one moment," Bocharkov mumbled. He turned to the sink, dipped his hands into it, and then splashed the cold water onto his face—making sure lots of it went over his shoulder, hitting Yasha Golovastov.

"Captain, you're getting more on me than you."

Bocharkov turned, grabbed his towel, and wiped his face. "Sorry about that, Lieutenant." He offered the towel to the officer. "It has been a long voyage."

Golovastov leaned away from the wet towel. "I have these movies that must be seen by everyone—including yourself." He pulled a handkerchief from his pocket and wiped his face. Then he lifted his notebook. "Here. I keep a record of attendance. It is something many of us *zampolits* are beginning to do. It helps us look at—"

Bocharkov interrupted. "There is not one officer or sailor on the K-122 who does not understand the importance of the Party-political work, Lieutenant, but sometimes the survival of the boat must come first." After three months on board the K-122, he had yet to penetrate the Communist zealotry of this Golovastov with the demands of the sea. Zealots such as Golovastov believed as fiercely in the tenants of communism as some Americans believed in the righteousness of God. Both ran with the yoke of servitude and both were pains in the butt for their countrymen.

"The Party demands we work to keep the spirit of Lenin alive. The Party-political work does that," Golovastov argued. "I think the survival of the boat is enhanced with the singularity of Party-political progress."

"You have a way of making me see the errors in my thinking, Lieutenant. We are truly lucky to have had you assigned to my boat." He wondered what Golovastov would do if he discovered the covert Christians who worshipped secretly in the forward torpedo room. If the man did not have a heart attack with the news, most of the crew—including Bocharkov—would be marched off for reindoctrination.

Golovastov nodded sharply. "This is my third ship . . ."

"Ship!" Bocharkov wanted to shout. "Submarines are not ships; they are boats!"

". . . and the other two captains said mostly the same thing." A tight smile appeared on Golovastov's face. "I am thankful you feel the same as they did, sir. When I arrived there was lack of unity in Party-political thought." A deep breath escaped him. "It took me lots of Party-political work—sometimes with the entire group before me, sometimes one-on-one, when I saw a comrade who wanted to travel the right path of the Party but lacked the tools to truly understand the way."

"Captain Demedewe . . ."

The tight smile disappeared. "Captain Demedewe had very little patience for the works of the *zampolit*, sir. Political officers were to be seen and not heard."

Bocharkov cocked his head to the side and nearly turned to the sink again. ". . . I think was very appreciative of your effort." He was walking on thin ice, but there was only so much bullshit any naval officer could take.

Golovastov's lips pursed as he seemed to weigh the comment. He opened his mouth to say something just as Ignatova stepped into the hatchway.

"Lieutenant Golovastov, am I glad I found you. I have assembled the off-duty watch in the crew's mess for your lecture and movie."

Golovastov turned, looking upward at Ignatova, who, like Bocharkov, towered nearly a head taller than the *zampolit*. His mouth dropped in his confusion. "I was unaware I had scheduled a Party-political time," he stuttered.

Ignatova grinned. "You told me last night that we were behind, Lieutenant. As the *zampolit*, I take your comments as orders of the Party."

"Yes . . . yes, my comments are orders of the Party," Golovastov replied, repeating Ignatova's words.

"Good." Ignatova looked at Bocharkov. "Captain, as you ordered, the men are assembled."

Golovastov straightened, his chin jutted out. "That is very good of you, Captain Second Rank Ignatova. Very good of you indeed. I will see that a comment is added in your Party record."

Ignatova nodded at Bocharkov. "Don't forget the captain. It was his orders to me and the officers that whatever the *zampolit* wants, make sure he gets it." He paused and took a deep breath. "Now, if you would hurry, Lieutenant. I am sure you will want to drill the crew while they are still alert and excited over the prospect of seeing the newest Party film from Moscow."

Golovastov nodded curtly, acknowledging both Bocharkov and Ignatova as he edged by the XO and hurried down the passageway.

"'Whatever the *zampolit* wants, make sure he gets it'?" Bocharkov asked with a smile.

Ignatova leaned into the passageway for a moment, seeing the forward hatch close as Golovastov disappeared behind it. He leaned back into the captain's stateroom. "I didn't say how he would get it."

"The men are in the mess hall waiting for him?"

"Chief Uvarova is finishing up training for the junior starshinas." Ignatova paused. "I think it is on the ballast tanks. Going over such minuscule details as to where they are located and how they operate."

Bocharkov laughed. "Zampolit *Meets Chief of the Boat*. Has the ring of a Japanese monster movie."

"What was that about?" Ignatova asked, nodding in the direction Golovastov had gone.

"Our *zampolit* wants the navigators to join the Party-political work just as he believes I am shirking my Party responsibilities by putting tactical stringencies like avoiding the American destroyer over seeing the latest Party movie."

Ignatova chuckled. "It is not the movies that are bad; it is that his lectures cure insomnia. Besides, the Americans are probably still chasing the K-56 thinking they have us in their sights."

Bocharkov put his finger to his mouth. "I admire Lieutenant Golovastov. He is truly a strong supporter of the Party and we can learn from him."

Ignatova nodded, an eyebrow raised. "I never meant to imply—"

"I know you did not, XO. So, shall we join the crew?"

"I will, sir. But you have a meeting scheduled with the Spetsnaz team in fifteen minutes to discuss the mission."

"How far away from Philippine waters are we?"

"We will be hitting the twelve-nautical-mile demarcation in four hours, sir."

"Speed?"

"Still at eight knots. We are about forty-five kilometers from their territorial waters."

"Do the Americans maintain a patrol of the harbor entrance?"

Ignatova leaned against the door facing. "No, sir. The Americans—as usual—are confident in their omnipotence."

"If only we should be that confident."

"The Americans have never learned from their history as we have been forced to learn from ours. They have never had their motherland invaded as we have."

"Not in this century, XO."

"This means to them that it is ancient history."

"So, XO, based on our lessons learned during the Great Patriotic War, you think we are better prepared to guard our ports?" Bocharkov teased.

"The difference is we know we have enemies on all sides of our borders. The Americans only have time for one enemy at a time, so they lump us and the Chinese together."

Bocharkov laughed. "Anyone who knows our history knows we and the Chinese aren't anything like friends."

"Not everyone. When they say 'the enemy,' they mean both of us."

"Then it is one of the few categories in which China and the Soviet Union are lumped together."

Ignatova nodded. "Guess we will be their enemy for at least this year."

Bocharkov sat down in the chair near his small desk. He waved Ignatova away. "Go have your Party-political discussions, XO. Tell the good lieutenant that I will be at the one this evening."

"By this evening, the tactical stringencies may once again distract from Golovastov's teachings."

"Let's hope not," Bocharkov said with a wink. "Where are our Spetsnaz heroes?"

Ignatova looked at his watch. "They should be waiting in Communications. I will join you after I have spoken to the crew about the importance of Party-political work. Once our *zampolit* gets started, he won't notice when I leave."

"Good. I'll see you in Communications in fifteen minutes."

"By the way, Captain, I told the lieutenant that transferred over to us . . ."

"Lieutenant Dolinski."

". . . Lieutenant Dolinski that I wanted to hear more about this plan of theirs. So far, it's been Spetsnaz secrets between the two officers."

"I am sure once they understand our lives are as much on the line as theirs, they will be more forthright in sharing their information."

"I would like to know which rear-echelon *zasranec*— 'asshole'—came up with this idea," Ignatova snapped.

"I want more than that. I want a detailed idea of what this Lieutenant Dolinski thinks they are going to do. We have not had much time to discuss the way ahead with this bunch of snake-eaters. It worries me. We are sailing forward without a clear picture from those who are to do it."

Ignatova nodded. "Spetsnaz would be just as happy to go in guns blazing doing what the Americans call a John Wayne."

"John Wayne always manages to get himself wounded or killed in his movies," Bocharkov added.

He sat down on the stool near the racks of cryptographic gear crammed along the starboard bulkhead. The communications personnel, with the exception of the boat's communicator—Lieutenant Junior Grade Vyshinsky—had been ordered out of the small compartment. The Spetsnaz lieutenants Gromeko and Dolinski squatted near the boxes transferred from the K-56.

"You have to wonder," Ignatova said from near the closed hatch to the compartment.

After a couple of seconds, Lieutenant Commander Orlov asked, "Wonder what?"

"Wonder who in the hell came up with this idea, OPSO."

Lieutenant Dolinski's eyes cut upward at the XO, and with an expressionless face he answered, "The *Glavnoe Razvedyvatel'noe Upravlenie*—the GRU—gave the orders, Captain."

Ignatova uncrossed his arms. He replied with a standard rote comment: "The GRU is known for its forward thinking in the world of naval intelligence. Tell me, Lieutenant Dolinski, are you GRU?"

The lieutenant stood holding an unidentified piece of electronic equipment in his hand. "Yes, sir, I am." He looked down at the box and dropped the piece back into it. "I am also a *zampolit*." The Spetsnaz's eyes narrowed as he looked up at Ignatova.

Ignatova uncrossed his arms and leaned forward. "Did you come up with this great idea of sneaking into Olongapo Harbor? Or was it some—"

"Where did this idea originate?" Bocharkov interjected.

"No, sir, I did not come up with this idea," Dolinski answered curtly. "I am not sure, sir, but I believe it came directly from Moscow."

"Lieutenant, I want to go over the mission again so we can best support you and make sure that we get in and out in one piece."

"Yes, sir, Captain."

Lieutenant Gromeko put a group of wires back into the box and flipped the flaps shut. Then he stood. "Lieutenant Dolinski and I have been discussing it, sir. Our thoughts are that once we are resting on the bottom, our team will—"

"Resting on the bottom?" Ignatova interrupted. "We are going to rest on the bottom?" he repeated with indignation. "How deep is the harbor?"

Gromeko shrugged. "I am not sure, sir."

"You are more than not sure, Lieutenant. You have no idea." He looked at Bocharkov. "This is ludicrous, Captain. It will embarrass our great nation if we fail, get caught, or find ourselves"—his eyes looked at Gromeko—"resting for eternity on the bottom of some foreign port."

Bocharkov grunted. "XO," he said with a downward hand motion, "let's hear what they have to say. Lieutenant Dolinski, why are we doing this mission? Do you know?"

"Yes, sir." The Spetsnaz officer stood.

Bocharkov took in the man standing before him. The young officer was a few inches taller than Gromeko. The exposed arms showed a tightness of muscle from exercise and training. He had short hair—almost more stubble than hair—covering his head; the high and tight style of the Spetsnaz. The officer stared directly into the eyes of Bocharkov for a few seconds before glancing away.

This man was not to be trifled with, Bocharkov realized. Men such as him, with their own sense of self-importance, had been the cause of more deaths in Russian history than even religion.

"Is this your first time on a submarine?" Bocharkov asked.

"I was on the K-56, Captain. This is my second."

"Then you have not operated from a submarine before now?" Ignatova asked sharply.

Dolinski shook his head. "No, sir, I did not say that. If I conveyed that, then I was misunderstood. I have done missions before now from submarines, but this is my first time in the Pacific."

"Could we go over the mission?" Bocharkov asked, crossing his arms.

Dolinski looked around the radio shack, eyeing each of the men in it. "It is very classified, sir," he said after several seconds.

"We promise to keep it inside this room. This is the most secure space we have on board the K-122."

Several seconds of awkward silence gripped the radio shack.

"Shit!" Ignatova said.

"Tell them," Gromeko said to Dolinski. "This is the captain; he has to know."

Dolinski looked at Gromeko for a few moments, and then nodded. "Sir, we believe the Americans are about to invade North Vietnam. My orders are to find out what they are going to do."

"So you think the answer is in Olongapo? The largest Asian port in the American Seventh Fleet?"

"Captain Second Rank Ignatova, an American amphibious task force was scheduled to arrive in the last forty-eight hours. The *Kitty Hawk* aircraft carrier and her forces should have arrived yesterday. These forces will sail sometime in the coming week for the Gulf of Tonkin—for Yankee Station, as their navy calls their operational area."

"Even if they are in Olongapo Harbor, there is not much we can do about it," Ignatova said.

Gromeko and Dolinski glanced at each other.

Dolinski spoke. "Captain, the Soviet Union has decided that we cannot allow the Americans to invade North Vietnam without doing something. If the Americans were to cross into North Vietnam, then the Chinese would come to their rescue."

"The Vietnamese hate the Chinese more than they do the Americans," Orlov said. "They have fought—"

"The Americans are already bombing the shit out of it," Ignatova said. "Their people will not support a new front in the quagmire the Americans have found themselves in."

"Maybe they are going elsewhere," Orlov volunteered.

"Where would they go?" Dolinski asked, the right side of his lips curling up. "This is their war. These are their warships. The only other thing going on now is in the Middle East, and the Fifth Eskandra is watching that."

"Even if the Soviet Fifth Fleet is watching those events, what is to keep the Americans from sneaking up through the Red Sea?" Orlov asked calmly. "It seems to me that this would be a good operational deception plan," he finished, looking at Bocharkov and Ignatova.

"I don't think the Americans will ever start a second war. Especially one to save their Jewish ally in the Middle East."

"I do not think that is—" Orlov started.

Bocharkov motioned Orlov quiet. "Excuse me, Lieutenant Commander Orlov." He turned to Dolinski and Gromeko. "The mission? How do you propose to discover if the Americans are planning on landing their Marines across the border—I mean how do you propose we stop them from invading our ally? Sink them?"

Neither Spetsnaz officer answered, then both shrugged simultaneously. "Don't know," Dolinski answered. "Ours is not to stop them, just find out what their intentions are."

Bocharkov uncrossed his arms. "Tell me what your plans are and tell me in excruciating detail."

For the next hour the officers of the K-122 listened as first Dolinski outlined his orders and mission, then the boat's Spetsnaz officer, Gromeko, reported on how the equipment they would need would be dispersed among the two officers and three enlisted Spetsnaz and how and where they would exit the boat. As the briefing continued, the two Spetsnaz officers seemed to loosen up in sharing details—proud of what they had planned, excited over the prospects of finally taking the battle to the Americans, and exuberant over the pride they had in being selected for this mission.

Bocharkov, Ignatova, and Orlov listened impassively, each aware of the dangers these Spetsnaz officers seemed unaware of in their planning. Lieutenant Vyshinsky stayed in the background at the briefing; Bocharkov was sure the shy Ukrainian was more afraid of being asked his opinion than he was of the mission on which they were embarked.

Each phase of the plan made sense from a logical sequence of events, but where they intended to do it, what they intended to do, how they intended to do it without alerting the Americans—all were fraught with danger.

There was a moment during the discussion where the two Spetsnaz officers stopped to straighten out a minute detail. During that lull, Bocharkov's thoughts turned to his junior officer years when he, too, had the enthusiasm and confidence these Spetsnaz officers had in their ability to do anything. It was an enthusiasm dampened by his age and tempered by wise confidence earned from experience.

He raised his hand when he realized the discussion had become more a jostle for leadership than a concrete assessment of operation. They stopped.

"Let me sum this up for everyone—and, XO, correct me if I am wrong." Bocharkov smiled at the Spetsnaz lieutenants. "Don't want to put either of you in the position of correcting me." Gromeko grinned. Dolinski's expression never changed. "We are going to sneak the K-122 into Subic Bay and park her on the bottom right up alongside the American warships. That your plan?"

"You can't be serious? Olongapo Harbor?" Orlov asked.

Both officers nodded.

"Gentlemen, that is the easy part," Dolinski said.

"About that, you are right, Lieutenant," Bocharkov agreed.

Vyshinsky seemed to meld into the bulkhead near the hatch.

"But where you are wrong is that we are not going to sit on the bottom—though I appreciate your initial idea. Bottoms are notorious for being unpredictable. You never truly know what is resting there—especially after this many centuries of use. Plus—and we will check—I don't know the depth, but if aircraft carriers can sail up and park alongside a pier then we will have plenty of depth beneath us."

"I understand there are lots of uncharted relics, sunk over the years, that dot the bottom of Subic Bay," Ignatova said. "And Olongapo Bay is nothing but muddy, shallow water. Only the local fishing fleet can use it."

"I believe the depth outside of Olongapo Bay is in excess of one hundred meters," Dolinski said.

"Then you would be unable to egress the boat at that depth."

Dolinski's lips tightened for a moment before he replied, "No, sir, Captain, it would be too deep."

"My thoughts, too," Bocharkov said. "We will have to go to periscope depth before you leave the K-122, Lieutenant. Sixteen meters. Two reasons for periscope depth: One, it allows me to see where we are inside the heart of the American fleet, which also means I can see where they are, and two, it will allow you easy egress and ingress to the K-122."

"Thank you, sir," Gromeko answered.

"And your mission will not be during daylight hours. I only say that in the event you may have thought differently."

"No, sir, Captain," Dolinski objected. "We would have to do it at night. Tonight would be excellent."

"Do you know where you are to go once you are ashore?"

"I have a map of the facilities, Captain, so regardless of where we are, we will be able to find the telecommunications facilities."

"I am sure you do, Lieutenant, but if you land ashore kilometers from the boat, you will not have time to accomplish your mission and return without being caught—or killed."

"But—"

"Let the Captain finish," Ignatova said.

Both Spetsnaz officers acknowledged the order with a curt nod.

"My intentions right now," Bocharkov said, "are to take some bearings to see where we are." He looked at Dolinski. "We also have a chart with the American facilities outlined on them. A navigation chart. An old one, I would think, but it will give us a more accurate idea of the depth beneath us. It may even show some landmarks on it. Will not know until I talk with our navigator, Lieutenant Tverdokhleb."

"Yes, sir."

"I want to get the boat as close to your objective as possible. I want you in the water as little time as possible. I want you ashore with as much night before you as possible. And I want you back aboard the submarine before dusk—if possible."

Bocharkov paused, and when no one said anything, he continued.

"You will exit the boat through the forward escape hatch, correct?"

"Correct, sir."

"Once you are out of the boat, we may take her down; we may not. I will decide once the mission begins. If I take her down, then I am in the dark as to what is happening above me. If I stay at periscope depth I can watch the Americans, but I also give their watches an opportunity to see the scope. That is a decision for later."

"Yes, sir," Gromeko said.

"I know you have thought of it and I may have failed to hear it, but when you go ashore, you are to mark the spot so you know where it is. If you have to make a run for it . . ."

Dolinski opened his mouth to say something, but Gromeko touched him on his arm.

"Around the time planned for your return, I will watch through the periscope until I see the infrared light telling me you are ashore, and I will blink back twice so you can take a bearing on the boat."

Gromeko started taking notes on his pocket notebook.

Bocharkov looked at the XO. "Captain Ignatova, we will stay deep—in the same location, coming up to periscope depth at twenty-five after the hour and five minutes to the hour to watch for an infrared signal." He turned back to the Spetsnaz officers. "You will have two minutes to signal us when you are heading back out."

"Yes, sir," Gromeko acknowledged. Dolinski nodded.

"Good. By the time you return, the K-122 will have turned its bow toward the harbor exit. When you are back on board, we are going to make quick work to get to the safety of the open ocean." He crossed his arms. "Does that agree with your plans?"

"With one exception, Captain," Dolinski said. "This is a GRU mission, and as a GRU mission, I need to weigh your plans with the guidance I received."

Blood rushed to Bocharkov's face. In the white light of the Communications Compartment it was not easy to hide his anger. "Lieutenant, you forget yourself. This is my boat. You are my passengers. The safety of the boat outweighs your concerns. Do we understand each other?" His arms dropped and he leaned forward, his face only inches from the Spetsnaz officer, who remained motionless.

Their eyes locked as Bocharkov continued, his voice dropping as he leaned away. "I will approve this mission, and I will stop it if I perceive it to endanger the survival of this boat and the crew who sail her. And when we return to Kamchatka, I have no doubt Admiral Amelko will stand by my decision. This is the submarine service—not the Special Forces service. I—and only I—make final decisions considering the ultimate safety of the K-122. Not you. Not the GRU. No one but me. Do I make myself clear?"

Dolinski stood to attention. "Yes, sir! Perfectly clear."

Bocharkov looked at Gromeko. "Lieutenant Gromeko, you are in charge of this mission. Not Lieutenant Dolinski. I hold you responsible for its flawless execution, and I am holding you responsible for doing it by the book—and getting back on the K-122 before daylight." He looked from one lieutenant to the other. "Do you both understand?"

"Yes, sir!" they both shouted in reply.

"Good. We are going to do this because we are ordered to do it. It is dangerous and we cannot have a Party caucus to determine what to do. There can only be one ultimate leader. I am it," Bocharkov said, emphasizing each word. "And, as it is, I will decide if the mission goes forward."

He saw Dolinski's urge to speak. "Lieutenant Dolinski, keep quiet. You have pissed me off and I hate to be pissed off. This is my boat. My submarine. If it fails to sail, it's my fault, not yours. If this mission fails, you can go home and tell them it was my responsibility and you'd be right. So forget what grandiose ideas someone put in your mind about leading this mission, all you are is the messenger. The mission is now mine to do."

"Yes, sir," Dolinski replied quietly.

"Good." Bocharkov looked at Ignatova. "XO, I think this briefing is over." He looked at Dolinski and Gromeko. "You two go with the XO and run over the details once again of your mission." Bocharkov glanced toward the hatchway. "Lieutenant Junior Grade Vyshinsky!"

The communications officer jumped as if he had been hit.

"Yes, sir!" he shrilled.

In a more normal situation, he and the XO would have laughed.

"Tell the control room to bring us up to communications depth. I want to check the broadcast before . . ." He stopped and looked at Ignatova. "XO, take these two officers with you and go over the mission. I want to stay here for a while."

Within seconds, their boxes still scattered on the deck, the two Spetsnaz officers were out the hatch, followed by Ignatova.

Vyshinsky was on the intercom and Bocharkov heard the acknowledgment from the officer of the deck. He recognized the voice as Lieutenant Yakovitch, the assistant weapons officer. His heart was pounding as he pulled one of the communications stools out and sat down on it. "Give me a message sheet," he ordered.

A moment later, the communicator gave a blank message sheet to Bocharkov, who sat at the small desk and starting writing. Several times, he scratched out a word and wrote a different one in its place. After several minutes he handed it to Vyshinsky. "Mr. Vyshinsky, I want you to send this to Pacific Fleet in Kamchatka. Only you," Bocharkov said, shaking his finger at the young officer. "Once they have receipted for it, you are to destroy this copy. Understand?"

"Yes, sir," Vyshinsky acknowledged.

The boat's sound-powered intercom beeped. Vyshinsky lifted the handset.

"Sir," Vyshinsky said, holding the handset out. "Lieutenant Yakovitch wants to talk with you."

"Put it on speaker. I can hear him from here."

"Sir, Officer of the Deck here. Sonar has picked up the American destroyer that we lost yesterday."

Things just keep getting better and better, Bocharkov thought. "Range and bearing?"

"Range unknown, but high revolutions indicate high speed. Bearing is two-zero-zero."

"Keep me informed."

"Sir, it appears to be a constant bearing."

Bocharkov nodded. "I'm on my way." He looked at Vyshinsky. "When the broadcast is finished, let Lieutenant Yakovitch know that I do not want to stay at periscope depth any longer than I have to."

Sweat beaded Vyshinsky's forehead.

"And, quit that sweating. You'll have me thinking it's because of me."

"Yes, sir—I mean no, sir."

Bocharkov slid off the stool and out the hatch. While the Spetsnaz "enjoyed" this mission, Bocharkov intended to have his own backup plan for escaping. For the safety of the boat, he'd leave the Spetsnaz in the middle of the harbor and in the arms of the Americans before he would surrender his submarine and crew. Death was better than dishonor.

SIX

Saturday, June 3, 1967

"MAKE our speed five knots," Bocharkov said. "Bearing?"

"Bearing two-zero-zero, increasing noise."

Bocharkov looked at Ignatova. "Seems this American never gives up."

"With due respect, Captain, I do not think at this speed the American sonar can pick us up."

Bocharkov grunted. "Maybe they put something on the hull of the boat other than those clappers. Something only they can pick up and track, something we do not know about."

"Depth one hundred meters, course zero-four-zero, speed five knots," Lieutenant Commander Orlov echoed from across the control room.

Ignatova leaned closer, nearly whispering. "While we have them at high speed now, this high speed disappears about every thirty minutes."

"Is it every thirty minutes at a certain time, or every thirty minutes the noise of his high-speed revolutions in the water are putting out?"

Ignatova took a few seconds to answer. "I would say the loss of contact with the high-speed noise the destroyer's screws are putting into the water seems to be timed."

"Then, they may well be tracking us, then leapfrogging ahead to try to catch up with us."

"If the Americans are tracking us, Captain, then to continue onward with this mission will be a one-way trip; it will be suicide," Ignatova cautioned in a low voice.

Bocharkov said nothing. Ignatova had only voiced what he was thinking. The question was, how was the American destroyer tracking them? It never occurred to Bocharkov, as it would never occur to MacDonald on the *Dale*, that serendipitous events centered on an Asian port would lead both captains to different interpretations.

MACDONALD ambled onto the bridge, passing through the hatch from the combat information center. He patted his pocket. He'd read the unclassified message again from his chair.

"Captain on the bridge!" the boatswain mate of the watch shouted.

The quartermaster of the watch grabbed his pencil and notated the time the skipper had arrived. So it had been done since the U.S. Navy was formally established in 1789 by an act of Congress.

"Carry on," MacDonald acknowledged as he crossed to the plotting table. "What time to Olongapo?" he asked.

"Sir, we are a few miles from Philippine national waters, then another hour to Subic Bay."

"That's good, Petty Officer Pratt. What time?"

"I have been doing dead reasoning based on radar fixes with the shore, sir, and I estimate we will be at the harbor entrance at this speed in less than an hour."

MacDonald grinned. "Pretty specific?"

Platt blushed and glanced at the black-rimmed navy clock mounted on the rear bulkhead. "Should be there by nineteen forty-five hours, sir."

MacDonald did not say anything. At twenty knots they should have been inside and tied up pierside by this time, but Lieutenant Junior Grade Burkeet had argued successfully for the *Dale* to slow to ten knots every thirty or so minutes. The young whippersnapper was determined to regain contact on the submarine, which, by now, was probably halfway to Kamchatka to explain why it had been caught on the surface. This leapfrogging speed had added time to their trip.

The hatch from Combat opened and Joe Tucker walked onto the bridge, carrying a metal message board in one hand. Unlike when MacDonald entered, no one announced his arrival.

"XO, we have an answer from Subic Operations Center yet?"

"Sent the logistic request when we turned off station, sir. We have not received an answer yet, but I'm confident they will have a pilot and tug ready for our arrival. I have Combat trying to raise Subic to confirm."

MacDonald nodded. Little was more frustrating to a sailor than to be able to see a liberty port and be unable to reach it because the logistics needed to tie up pierside were either late or nonexistent.

"We could take the *Dale* all the way pierside, Skipper. We've been in Olongapo before; isn't as if we're nicky new kids on the block."

"We'll see," he answered.

The boatswain mate walked up with MacDonald's cup filled with coffee. MacDonald's stomach rolled, but he took it with a thanks. He had been drinking coffee since five this morning.

"Have Burkeet and Oliver had any joy with their periodic searches?"

"Not yet, sir, but that does not keep them from searching."

"And Chief Stalzer?"

"He's down there with them."

MacDonald nodded.

"Officer of the Deck, let's bring the speed down to twelve knots when we cross into the territorial waters."

"Aye, sir," Lieutenant Goldstein replied.

"What do we have ahead of us?"

Goldstein shifted from near the hatch to the port-side bridge wing to the navigation table. "Bunch of fishing boats still out at sea, sir. Suspect most will start heading back soon, if they are not already. I show a couple of larger vessels northwest of the harbor entrance. The off-going watch reported them a few minutes before I relieved Lieutenant Kelly. Their course and speed indicate they are heading into Subic also."

"Probably merchants," Joe Tucker added. "OPSO has the harbor activity list and it shows a steady stream of Maritime Sealift ships coming into and out of the harbor for the remainder of the week."

MacDonald nodded. "What do you think the Tripoli Amphibious Task Group and our Carrier Battle Group are up to?"

"Whatever it is, sir, we both know it has to do with Vietnam."

MacDonald wanted to voice his misgivings about the war, but to express anything less than a positive result would almost seem traitorous. If the politicians would take the handcuffs off the military and let them fight, this war could be over within months. North Vietnam would be a U.S. territory or a parking lot.

"Skipper?"

"Uh?"

"Sorry, sir. I was saying that right now we do not have a set-sail date from Subic."

MacDonald pulled the message from his pocket and handed it to the XO. "Here. I'll trade you," he said, taking the message board from Joe Tucker's hand. "I'm sure we'll find out more once we arrive and get our telephone lines up. Anything else going on?"

Joe Tucker nodded at the metal message board as he unfolded the message in his hand. "Nasser continues to saber-rattle about pushing Israel off the face of the earth—push them into the Mediterranean."

MacDonald flipped open the metal cover. "Let's hope we stay out of this fight between the Jews and Arabs. Let them settle it among themselves."

The red stamp of "TOP SECRET" stared back at MacDonald. He scanned the message; it was a two-pager. When would intelligence weenies ever learn that no one reads more than the first paragraph in a message? He sighed before he started reading. He hated intelligence messages that were punctuated with "probables" and "possibles" as if they were covering their asses.

When he reached the final paragraph, he pulled the first

page back and read it fully. It was an encapsulation of the events up to yesterday: Egypt had closed the Straits of Tiran to Israeli shipping in May; the same month Gamal Abdel Nasser had ordered the United Nations peacekeepers out of the Sinai. In the last few weeks, the Egyptian Army had massed its armor along the Sinai border with Israel. This week the Syrian and Jordanian armies followed suit. He took a deep breath. As much as he disliked the idea of anything having to do with the Middle East, maybe this time the Arabs meant it. Maybe this time they truly would overrun a country with their combined military strength, which outnumbered the Israelis better than two to one.

He closed the message board. "Not much we can do," he said.

Joe Tucker had already finished the message MacDonald had handed him. The XO refolded it and traded it for the message board.

"We could do a lot if we had the political will and our people recognized that this is not the world of our fathers; it is a nuclear age where shifting of powers—" Joe Tucker stopped. "Sorry about that. Sometimes when I see a nation founded by the outcasts of the world, survivors of a Western civilization's attempt to eradicate them, it makes me think that everyone in the world has a responsibility to see it succeed. Instead, everything points to America standing back and letting the Arabs do what the Germans failed to finish."

There was silence on the bridge at the outburst. Joe Tucker was a man of strong opinions, so this was not unusual. The fact was no one really argued or debated with the XO. He usually won, and he had a way with words that left opponents mortally wounded and confused.

"You could be right, XO, but our job—*right now*—is on this side of the world with America's other war." Then he added somberly, "Let's hope they let us win this one before we jump into another one."

"Do we have any insight into 'Beacon Torch'?" Joe Tucker asked.

MacDonald shook his head. "They have a meeting tomorrow morning at Subic Operations Center. Guess while you are seeing to the refueling and replenishing of the ship, I'll be trying to keep my eyes open during a three-hour briefing."

"I see from the distribution on the message, you'll have plenty of company, to include Admiral Green." Joe Tucker smiled. "Knowing the admiral, he will want to know why you lost the submarine after tracking it only for a couple of days."

"That is his way of showering gratitude on his subordinates."

"Then I would hate to see him upset with them."

MacDonald chuckled. "It is not a pleasant sight."

"Any special instructions for tomorrow?"

"After we tie up, let's sit down and go over what we need to accomplish in the next few days while in-port Subic."

"Aye, sir."

Joe Tucker turned to go.

"Joe, will you check on the status of our LOGREQ again, please? I want that tugboat and pilot at the harbor when we arrive."

Joe Tucker saluted and was soon off the bridge. MacDonald looked up at Goldstein and saw the man staring at him. During the discussion, he had forgotten that the OOD was Jewish and his connection with events in the Middle East was probably stronger than that of a man named MacDonald. After all, England had given up trying to push Scotland into the ocean.

BOCHARKOV had remained in the control room as the K-122 sonar team tracked the American destroyer closing on them. Sound, or noise as sonarmen preferred to call it, was a strange character. Unlike in the air where most times sound travels in a straight line, in the water it moves in two paths. Straight—as in the air—but over shorter distances; and also like an oscillating wave riding a series of hills and crests for longer distances. You could only hear the oscillating sound wave when you were on a hill or crest that made the sound seem to be a straight line. Made it hard to know if the contact generating the noise was only a few miles from you, or hundreds of miles, its sound riding the roller coaster of hills and crests created by the properties of water.

"It's slowing again," Lieutenant Kalugin, the antisubmarine weapons officer, reported before pressing the intercom box and asking, "Signal strength?"

Bocharkov waited. On his left stood Ignatova, his XO's impatience nearly contagious. The K-122 had slowed to a crawl to reduce the chance of the Americans detecting him, but still the line of bearing remained constant. The increasing noise signature seemed to indicate a classic constant bearing, decreasing range situation. Everyone, including Bocharkov, was beginning to believe that something on the hull was giving away their position. He had gotten all the clappers, but what if the clappers were nothing more than a decoy from the real spy shit the Americans had put on the K-122?

"It is slowing down again, Captain," Lieutenant Alexander Kalugin said.

The lieutenant was covered in sweat. His collar was matted to his neck. Beads ran from the man's forehead. Bocharkov tried nonchalantly to touch his own forehead as if in a casual movement. No sweat on his brow. Sweat on a brow of a navy captain was a no-no.

He turned to Ignatova. "Status?"

Ignatova turned to Yakovitch. "Officer of the Deck— status?"

"Course zero-niner-zero, speed five knots. Depth one hundred meters."

Ignatova looked at Bocharkov.

"Distance to shore?"

Yakovitch heard Bocharkov's question and turned to the navigator sitting in the forward portion of the control room.

Uri Tverdokhleb raised his hand in acknowledgment before Yakovitch could ask him. He had heard the question through the unusual quiet of the compartment. Navigators were envied by their peers. Most ships had two of them. K-122 only had one. Navigators stood no duties other than their navigation watch, and they were excused from Party-political duties, which only increased the envy.

Tverdokhleb pushed his black-rim glasses off the tip of his nose and bent over the chart. He lifted a mechanical compass, placed it on the chart, and walked it out from what he calculated was the location of the K-122 to the nearest bit of shore jutting into the ocean. Only a few seconds passed before

Tverdokhleb tossed the compass onto the chart and shouted, "Captain, we are thirty kilometers from shore. But we are less than ten kilometers from where the seabed starts to rise."

Yakovitch—and most everyone else in the control room—glared at Tverdokhleb; they were under quieten ship orders and here the navigator was shouting.

"Very well," Bocharkov replied.

Folks in the control room exchanged a few glances before returning to their work. If the captain was unconcerned, then they had no worries.

"How far out do you think the American is?" Bocharkov asked.

Kalugin shrugged. "I have no opinion, sir. I still believe we are picking up convergence noise."

"But we have never lost the sound," Ignatova said.

"I know, but the sound seems to have a rise-and-fall quality to it."

"Let's return to our base course. I want to be off the harbor entrance before dusk. Give us some time to do a little reconnoiter before we enter."

Ignatova nodded sharply. "Aye, sir."

"Oh, and, XO, keep us off the shoals and shallow waters as long as possible. I want the option of sprinting back into deep waters if we have to."

"Aye, sir." Ignatova turned and left the vicinity of the periscope, where the captain preferred to stand. Moments later the XO was talking with Yakovitch near the helmsman and planesman.

A few minutes later when Bocharkov looked forward, Uri Tverdokhleb had left his position—a cigarette dangling from his lip—and was talking with the XO and the OOD.

A moment of possession passed over Bocharkov. He wondered if American captains felt an ownership of their ships and submarines as he did right now—*right this very moment*—of the K-122.

Ignatova broke his thought. Standing beside his XO was Lieutenant Kalugin.

"Captain, we need to come to course zero-four-zero. For the most part, the remainder of the navigation leg will keep us within Philippine national waters. If we remain at five knots we will not arrive until after dark."

"How far from Subic Bay are we?"

"We are around eighty kilometers. At five knots, it will take us nearly ten hours to reach the bay. The sun will have set by then, sir."

Bocharkov grunted. "Speed?"

"We need to be at least twelve knots to reach the harbor in about four hours. It will be around eighteen thirty hours, but we will have about three to four hours of daylight left for observation."

Bocharkov looked at Kalugin. "If we kick our speed up to twelve knots, will the American detect us?"

Kalugin licked his lips, then replied. "Sir, if we are going that speed when the American slows down, then most likely he will detect us."

"Maybe he can't hear us and we can only hear him," Ignatova offered.

Kalugin shook his head. "I am very sorry to say, sir, that if we can hear him, then he has the same water conditions as us, and if his sonar team is as good as ours, then he will be able to hear us."

Bocharkov nodded. "Here's what we will do, XO. The American is slowing down now. Most likely to listen to whatever it is we have on board or on our hull that tells him where we are. When he speeds up again, I want to put fifteen knots of noise in the water. Zoom ahead of him on course zero-four-zero." He looked at Kalugin. "Will you be able to track him if we are doing fifteen knots?" Bocharkov asked, already knowing the answer.

The officer ran the back of his hand across his forehead. "No, sir. Once we exceed twelve knots, my passive sonar capability is severely limited."

Bocharkov grunted again. "How often is the American slowing down?"

"He has not changed his routine, Captain. About every thirty minutes he slows down. Sometimes he slows to such a speed that he is undetectable."

"Okay," Bocharkov said, gaining both officers' attention.

"Here is what we are going to do, XO. When Lieutenant Kalugin tells you the American is increasing his speed, you will wait until the high speed revolutions of the American warship are sufficient to mask our own underwater noise. Then increase speed to fourteen knots for twenty minutes, then reduce speed to eight knots." He turned and slapped Kalugin on the top of the man's chest. "Lieutenant, you are most important for this. When we reduce speed, you have to regain contact with the American. When you regain it, I want to know his bearing. I want to know if he has changed his course, or if he is continuing to turn toward us." He let out a deep breath.

No one said anything.

"Life does not get more exciting than this, does it?" Bocharkov asked with a broad grin.

Ignatova nodded. "I am not sure I need this excitement."

Kalugin produced a weak grin, his eyes shifting between the XO and Bocharkov.

Bocharkov laughed. "Lieutenant, pay no attention to the XO's sarcasm. Ukrainians are not known for their humor." He took a deep breath. "This is why we are submariners. Not for the thrill of riding beneath the waves, but the thrill of playing hide-and-seek with the enemy." He patted his stomach. "Gets the adrenaline flowing."

"BRIDGE, this is Combat. Bring her down to eight knots," the voice from the 12MC echoed on the bridge.

"That's my warrant officer," the boatswain mate of the watch said aloud to the helmsman.

"Yes, Boats," the young seaman on the helm replied as if he had heard the statement numerous times during the morning watch.

"All ahead, one third. Make turns for eight knots!" Lieutenant Goldstein snapped from the center of the bridge.

A second young sailor standing near the helmsman grabbed the handles of the annunciator and pulled them back.

In the aft depths of the *Dale* the engineers saw the speed rung up from the bridge. Sailors clad in soaked T-shirts and dungarees started a sweltering choreography of movements—shouting out what they were doing as they turned knobs, flipped switches, and rerouted steam to slow the revolutions of the shafts. Flashes of whistling steam shot out from valves, raising the already hundred-plus temperature another few degrees.

Off the stern of the ship, the cavitation of the props churning the huge twenty-knot wake began to dissipate as the ship slowed to its quiet underway speed of eight knots.

CHIEF Stalzer flipped another page of the paperback book he was reading. Whoever this "Anonymous" was that wrote these crotch novels, he really knew his stuff. The vibration through the hull of the ship as it slowed shook the shelf in front of the sonar console, causing the papers, scissors, and other loose items on it to move, advancing toward the edge.

"Jesus Christ, we're never going to get to Olongapo with all this stopping-and-starting shit," Stalzer said to himself. He reached up and pushed the stuff back away from the edge of the shelf as the vibration eased.

Stalzer spun the chair around, parted the curtains, and looked toward the rear hatch. "Damn you, Oliver. You picked a hell of time to take a crap." He looked forward and saw the XO talking to Warrant Officer "Tiny" Smith. "Yeah, a hell of a time," he whispered.

Bad enough with the XO running around with his anal personality, but having the first division officer—a former boatswain mate master chief—up here acting like some god-fucking officer was enough to ruin his day.

He dropped the curtains and turned back to the sonar display. Oliver probably talked Burkeet into this sprint-and-walk travelogue. He folded the ear of the page he was on and tucked the book in his back pocket. His pack of cigarettes was in the right sock nestled alongside his ankle.

"Come on, Oliver, before the officers work their way here to see if we have any contacts."

Stalzer lifted the headset and put it on. The cavitation of the ship, the vibration of slowing down, and waiting for the speed to settle out would take a few minutes. Then the passive sonar would calibrate itself and start processing the surrounding underwater sounds. Five minutes, Stalzer calculated, before any noise in the water would be displayed or before he would hear anything.

The curtain snapped back. Both the XO and Smith stood there. The XO seemed shocked. "Chief, didn't know you were standing watches."

"Oliver has the runs, sir. Something he ate."

"Anything on sonar?"

Stalzer shook his head. "It'll take a few minutes for the waters to settle out, and then we should see."

"Let me know if you get anything," Warrant Officer Smith said, his Andy Devine voice grating on Stalzer's ears.

How did a no-load like Smith ever make warrant officer? "Yes, sir, Warrant."

The curtain fell back in place. Stalzer turned back to the sonar console. He smiled.

Tonight he would be in the Moroccan Ratoosie Bar, and Maria would be waiting for him. Tiny, thin, dark-haired Maria. Lots of bar girls named Maria in Olongapo, but Stalzer only cared for this Maria.

"I love you no bullshit, sailor, buy me Honda," he said softly, smiling at his attempt to imitate her Filipino accent. Thirty minutes upstairs with her and then he would have the rest of the night to get knee-walking, commode-hugging drunk.

Tomorrow might not be fun recovering, but by God he was a sailor, and sailors had a reputation to live up to—and he intended to live up to it tonight. Oliver could stay aboard as part of the watch. He was the intellectual asshole who'd convinced Burkeet—the little shit—to keep searching for commie-pinko submarines when they could almost smell Olongapo. A century ago the crew would have mutinied and keel-hauled Oliver.

"SIR, recommend course zero-seven-zero," Lieutenant Goldstein said to MacDonald.

MacDonald set his cup down in the holder on his chair. "Very well."

"Left ten-degree rudder, steady up on course zero-seven-zero!" Goldstein ordered.

"Left ten-degree rudder," the helmsman replied, swinging

the helm one full turn before grabbing it sharply as it passed one full circle. "Coming to course zero-seven-zero!"

The young novice seaman manning the annunciator stepped over to watch the third-class at the helm.

MacDonald grinned. It was moments such as these he felt the magnetism of command, of knowing the fate of the *Dale* rested in his hands.

Someday that young seaman would be driving the ship. He imagined the anticipation of the young man was tremendous wanting to take over the helm from the qualified sailor on it.

Unless you have held the wood grain of the helm in your hands and watched the needle show the angle of the rudder, you can never know the boost of knowing that when the ship heeled to port or starboard it was because of you. There were lots of "hearts" to a ship. The engine room was a heart. Combat was a heart. The crew's mess was a heart, and even their berthing compartments could be considered a heart. But the brains of the ship, that determined where every heart on board went, was the bridge, and within the bridge that heartbeat was the helm.

Motion at the navigational plotting table caught his eye. The duty quartermaster was wetting the tip of the pencil with his tongue. MacDonald watched admiringly as the second-class leaned over the logbook and wrote down the exact orders given by the officer of the deck along with the time of the order. Navy logbooks were the bible of a warship, capturing every presence of the captain on the bridge and every order given that changed what a warship was doing as it cut through the waves of the oceans.

"Passing zero-niner-zero!" the helmsman announced.

—

A beep through the headset caught Stalzer's attention and he glanced up at the console. He shut his eyes and took a deep breath, his stomach growling. Not now. Not this close. Mechanically, he spun the round ball mounted in the shelf, shifting the sensitivity from one set of hydrophone banks in the hull-mounted sonar to another. The signal grew slightly stronger, but not much. He looked at the data on the spoke. Fifty hertz reflected on the readout. Fifty hertz meant it was not an American submarine. It had to be one of the Soviet Echo submarines, but what was it doing this close to the Philippines? He could not tell yet if it was a convergence or a direct sound spoke.

Wonder what the commie-pinko's doing this close to Subic Bay? Probably watching. He pushed the headset tighter against his ears, closing his eyes. Watching Subic Bay was not near as much fun as being in Olongapo. If the Soviets knew what fun waited in Olongapo, they'd surrender now. The signal began to fade.

"What the fuck?" Stalzer cursed. He shifted the sensitivity around the hydrophones, trying to regain contact. "Where in the hell did you go, my asshole commie buddies?"

THE helmsman shouted, "Passing zero-eight-zero!"

MacDonald nodded in acknowledgment, turning in his chair to watch the helmsman. Sailors were professionals, and regardless of how many times he walked by the ones on board, they truly amazed him with their knowledge and professional tenacity. The helmsman was no different.

The third-class boatswain mate carefully spun the helm a quarter turn to the right. The sailor's tongue protruded slightly as he bit on it, while his eyes concentrated on the compass mounted above the wooden helm. Below the ocean surface, two huge rudders responded to the directions of the helm and began to straighten.

The boatswain mate of the watch leaned over to watch. The helmsman and the trainee were his responsibility. It was a badge of professionalism for a boatswain mate to meet course changes dead-on—slide into them gently. One degree past the ordered heading was easily masked, but two were a dead giveaway, and three degrees earned you a slap upside the side of the head by the BMOW.

The compass mounted above the wooden helm slowed as the *Dale* crept the last few degrees to zero-seven-zero. Zero-seven-eight, zero-seven-seven . . .

The helmsman slowly brought the helm back a quarter

turn, allowing for the slight delay the change in rudders would impose on their course. The compass seemed to stop at zero-seven-four. The helmsman grimaced, his tongue withdrawing into his mouth as his teeth clenched. It was not lost on him that he had the BMOW and a newbie watching over his shoulder. Zero-seven-three—then, almost as if by magic the ship steadied on zero-seven-zero.

"Steady on zero-seven-zero!" the helmsman shouted, letting out a deep breath and grinning from ear to ear.

"Very well!" Goldstein replied.

The quartermaster of the watch notated the new course in the log.

"About fucking time," the boatswain mate of the watch whispered to the helmsman.

"It was perfect," the third-class replied with a smile. "Like always."

With a grin, the BMOW winked. "Don't let it go to your head, Stewart."

THE signal disappeared as the curtain parted and Oliver stepped inside the cramped space. "Sorry, Chief. Must be something I ate. I hurried back as soon as I could."

Stalzer tossed the headset onto the narrow shelf. "About time, Oliver. Next time, call one of your friends out of their rack and make him relieve you."

Stalzer stood and shifted to one side as Oliver took the headset and sat down. Stalzer looked up and saw that the hydrophones were still pointed in the direction of the lost signal. *Oh, well,* he thought. *Either Oliver will find it or he won't.*

"You get anything, Chief?"

Stalzer guffawed. "If I had gotten anything, you think I would have jumped up as soon as you walked in?"

Oliver shook his head. "I'll start a search pattern. Any orders?"

"Yeah, keep Warrant Officer Smith up-to-date even if you don't have anything—otherwise he'll be pestering you throughout the watch."

"Aye, Chief."

"I'm going down to the goat locker. Gotta get ready for the sea-and-anchor detail."

"Chief, do you have the liberty watch schedule yet?"

"Yeah, I do," Stalzer replied, tapping his head. "It's right up here and you got the first duty night in port."

"Chief, I had it last time, in Guam."

"Duty aboard ship in Guam is a boon. Ain't nothing to do ashore on that island except avoid the snakes."

"Can I exchange duty with someone?"

Stalzer nearly said no, but then said, "If you can find another sonarman who'll take your place, then I guess it's okay."

Oliver smiled. "Thanks, Chief."

"Don't thank me. You still got to run a chit through me and the lieutenant. And I'll want to see both of your signatures on it. Yours and whoever is going to stay on board to do the 3M maintenance checks."

Oliver's smile faded. "Chief, I'm the only one who knows how to do the preventive maintenance checks. Can't I do them tomorrow?"

Stalzer shook his head and laughed. "What if we have to get under way tomorrow, Oliver? You want to be the one to tell the skipper why we're behind in our PMS?"

Oliver slipped the headset down over his ears. "No, Chief, I wouldn't want to be the one."

Neither would I. Stalzer scratched his chin. "On second thought, Oliver, you can have liberty tonight once we are tied up and they release the liberty parties, but tomorrow night, I want you on board doing the preventive maintenance."

Oliver smiled. "Gee, thanks, Chief."

"Don't thank me. We're getting in late. Won't be much time for Olongapo anyway. You know where I'll be." Stalzer stepped through the curtains, the circulating air ruffling them slightly as they settled back into place.

"Yeah, you'll be in your rack reading your crotch novel," Oliver whispered to himself.

He looked at the sonar console in front of him and began to systematically rotate the hydrophones at a very slow rate, listening for anything that might be the Soviet Echo he had tracked for nearly twenty-four hours. If he could find it, then

Stalzer would stay out to sea another day. He leaned forward, one hand moving the hydrophones and the other pressing the headset against his ear. Just a spike, he told himself. Just a spike and he could be tracking the pinko-commie again.

"THEY have slowed down, sir," Starshina Zilkin said, glancing up at Bocharkov. His hand held the headphone tight against his left ear.

"Did they detect us?" Kalugin asked.

Zilkin looked at the weapons officer. "I do not know, Lieutenant. They were slow when we picked them up. That is why I called you, Captain," Zilkin said.

"Any indications the Americans have changed course?"

"No, sir, but the American destroyer is not too far from us," Zilkin offered. "It has a right-bearing drift. The noise from its shafts, I believe, is decreasing, which means it may be heading slowly away from us. We may be in its baffles."

"Do we have a course on it?" Bocharkov asked.

Zilkin shook his head. "I am doing a passive plot on the bearings. Estimated speed is around eight to ten knots, Captain."

Ignatova walked up behind Bocharkov. Bocharkov turned. "What do you think, XO?"

"I think it is heading to the U.S. naval base at Subic."

Bocharkov grunted. "I think you are right."

The three officers stood silently as Zilkin continued to track the American destroyer. The sonar operator continued to pencil in lines of bearing from the K-122.

"It is on a base course," Zilkin said.

"And that is?" Ignatova asked.

"I think the course is between zero-six-zero true and zero-seven-five true. I make its speed between seven and ten knots."

Bocharkov grunted again. "This may be our chance, XO."

"It may be, Captain."

Bocharkov nodded, but after several seconds of his failing to elaborate, Ignatova asked, "And what is our chance with this, Comrade Captain?"

"Maybe we can ride into Olongapo in its baffles? It will mask our noise."

Ignatova nodded. "Wanted to be sure it wasn't something dangerous."

Bocharkov smiled. "It is definitely not something dangerous I want to do. But it will make our Spetsnaz happy." He glanced at the clock on the bulkhead. It showed five in the afternoon. The Pacific sun would be bright above the waves.

"XO, let's get back to the control room. I want you to take the conn and ease the boat into the baffles of the warship."

A few seconds later the two officers stood in the center of the control room.

Bocharkov touched the XO on the shoulder. "Have Tverdokhleb give us a course to deep waters in the event we have to run for it. If the Americans detect us, then we will need a quick escape route."

Ignatova nodded and stepped away to confer with the officer of the deck, Lieutenant Yakovitch.

The forward hatch opened. Lieutenant Vyshinsky spotted Bocharkov and walked to him. The communicator had a message board tucked under his arm.

"Ah, Lieutenant, you have decided to come out of your dark spaces," Bocharkov said, reaching for the afternoon message board.

Vyshinsky blushed. "Yes, sir." He cleared his throat. "I am to relieve Lieutenant Yakovitch as the officer of the deck."

Bocharkov nodded as he flipped through the messages quickly. Twice a day the K-122 came to periscope depth and deployed a long communications antenna that stretched for a hundred meters behind the submarine. The antenna would float quickly to within a couple of meters of the surface, where the continuous submarine broadcast could be recorded. Then, twice a day, the communications officer would search down Bocharkov and Ignatova so one of them could read the mostly routine messages. Much like the American and British navies, the Soviet submarine force was the silent service. It seldom broadcast or acknowledged any messages unless required to do so. The lessons of World War II with the German and Japanese navy codes had not been lost on the generations of submarine sailors who followed.

Bocharkov stopped flipping. Usually he glanced at the messages, ignoring the supply messages and casually ignoring the "love-the-Party" sermon messages. But some did require his attention or were of oblique importance, such as the one he read now. He let out a deep sigh and folded the attached message on the board. "Make sure the XO reads this one, Lieutenant."

He watched as Vyshinsky walked toward Ignatova. If what the message said happened, the Americans would be even angrier to know why a Soviet submarine was in their harbor. They would believe it had to do with the event Moscow believed was going to happen sometime in the next few days. The K-122 had to be inside the harbor, do the mission, and get out within the next forty-eight hours.

SEVEN

"GENTLEMEN, take your seats. The admiral has arrived and will be here shortly."

MacDonald leaned back in his chair until it rested against the wall of the conference room. On the blackboard at the front of the room someone had printed the words "Beacon Torch" in the center. He looked at his watch. The meeting was supposed to start at ten hundred. He looked at the large hand clock above the chalkboard. It was already ten fifteen. Not like Green to be late.

The senior captains—the four-stripers who really ran the navy—sat around the shined mahogany table. "Four-stripers" referred to the four quarter-inch stripes that encircled the end of the sleeves on the navy dress blue uniforms. The tropics were too hot for dress blues. Everyone wore khakis, except the senior officers at official functions.

The skipper of the *Kitty Hawk* sat in the first seat to the left of the head of the table. While MacDonald was not completely sure, he was fairly confident that the Marine Corps brigadier general seated across from the *Kitty Hawk* skipper was the commander of the landing forces embarked on the amphibious carrier. Beside the general was the four-striper who was the skipper of the amphibious carrier, the USS *Tripoli*.

Everyone had a job. And everyone had a specific place to sit based on rank. MacDonald sat along the outside wall of the conference room. Two more years and he would be at that table.

One of the captains turned in his chair to lean toward MacDonald.

"Skipper, Joe Smith," he said extending his hand.

MacDonald came forward, the front legs of the chair hitting the wood floor with a short bang. "Captain."

"You're Danny MacDonald, aren't you?"

"Yes, sir," he answered, wondering who Joe Smith was.

"I'm on the admiral's staff. Reporting from the navy staff at the Pentagon. Heard a lot of about you and your tin can. Wonderful job on those submarines. I know the admiral was happy."

MacDonald smiled. "When Admiral Green is happy means he's less grumpy."

Smith laughed. "Let's just say he was tense but overall very satisfied. I thought it was a wonderful ASW effort on your part, and you did it without the help of our fine navy aviators. Well done." Smith turned back to the table.

MacDonald nodded to himself. If the admiral was satisfied, then that was something he could pass along to the crew who gave up a couple of days of fine navy liberty in the Pacific port that offered anything a sailor of the sixties could want.

A heavy-set four-striper from one of the auxiliary ships burst through the doorway of the conference room. Sweat stains inched down both sides of the khaki shirt. The captain mopped his face with his handkerchief and in a heavy Southern accent mumbled something about humidity and heat and why he never returned to the great state of Georgia during the summer months. Accompanied by slight laughter, the late arrival looked toward the front of the room. "Whew," he mumbled loudly before hurriedly taking his chair at the table.

Another late arrival rushed through the door, worked his way along the narrow lane between the knees of those against the wall and the backs of those at the table. He was a thin man—seemed nervous to MacDonald, but if you were late to one of Green's meetings, you had reason to be nervous—and the man's red hair could use a trim.

The daylight twinkled off the silver oak leaves on his khaki collar. *Awful young to be a commander,* MacDonald thought. The collar devices looked almost new. Different year group—not a competitor for the captain selection board next fall.

MacDonald would be looked at early for selection. Everyone received an early look, and sometimes the magic wand of the kingdom would reach down and touch the head of a perceived hot runner. Seldom happened, and he had great doubts, with only this tour as a commanding officer, of it happening to him. But his record was good. He knew it. His bosses definitely knew it. And many of his peers whom he considered competitors had either screwed up or shipped out. So maybe he had a chance.

The redheaded commander tripped over the feet of one of the men, who reached out and steadied him before he could fall on anyone.

"Thanks."

A bit clumsy, MacDonald thought. He watched the officer as the man continued his progress—accompanied with "excuse me's"—toward one of the few empty chairs in the room; the one beside him.

"Anyone sitting here?" the commander asked.

MacDonald shook his head. "Nope. It's free."

The man dropped his notebook on the chair and smiled, revealing a bright set of straight teeth—he must have spent a lot of time in a dental chair.

Before sitting down, the man stretched his hand out to MacDonald. "Hi, I'm Ron Kennedy, skipper of the *Coghlan.*"

A fellow destroyer skipper. Might not be a bad sort after all. MacDonald smiled and introduced himself as they shook hands. "Skipper of the *Dale.*"

Kennedy sat down. "Looks as if we've got two of the destroyers with the group."

MacDonald pointed out the two other destroyer skippers with the group.

"Four of us." Kennedy's eyes widened as he leaned too close to MacDonald. "That's a lot of destroyers for a battle group, don't you think?"

MacDonald shook his head. "No. It's probably not enough."

"You could be right." He chuckled. "I heard one of our destroyers lost track of an Echo II submarine yesterday. I forget which one. I wonder if the admiral is pissed over them losing it?"

MacDonald's lips tightened. How could the admiral be angry with the *Dale*? He caught Smith turning slightly in his chair to look at Kennedy. Finally he replied, "I doubt the admiral is upset."

The Dale *had* done things no other destroyer had done with the Soviets. And, as Captain Smith pointed out, there were no airborne ASW assets out there helping him.

"I mean, if you have contact, it has to be something monumental to cause you to lose them."

"I suppose you have to have been there to appreciate it."

Kennedy nodded. "The *Coghlan* has the best damn ASW team in the fleet." He jabbed his thumb into his chest. "My crew won the battle excellence award for ASW before we left San Diego."

"Gentlemen, the admiral," a lieutenant commander positioned near the front door announced.

MacDonald recognized him as Wayne Powers, the admiral's executive aide.

Everyone stood to attention. The sound of chairs scraping on the tile floor and the rustle of pant legs rubbing against each other replaced the low ebb of conversation that had filled the room.

"At ease," Admiral Green announced as he entered the room.

No one moved, waiting for him to sit.

"I said at ease, you bunch of seadogs. I'm going to be standing, so sit down so everyone can see what a real sailor looks like."

Light laughter filled the room, along with the noise of sliding chairs. An unfamiliar captain stood near the lieutenant commander at the door. He must have arrived with Admiral

Green. As MacDonald watched, the captain, who remained
standing in the open doorway, began to fill a pipe with tobacco. Around the table, most of the captains lit up cigarettes.

Green held a pointer in his slim hands as his eyes roamed
the room. When he spotted MacDonald, he stopped. "Gentlemen, I want to introduce you to Commander MacDonald for
those who don't know him. Stand up, Danny."

His face was still glowing red from Kennedy's stinging
remark.

"Danny, are you blushing? Now, don't be modest. Gentlemen, Commander MacDonald and the crew of the *Dale* have
spent the last forty-eight hours chasing two Soviet Echo submarines that had been trailing the *Kitty Hawk* battle group.
One, if not both, of those submarines was caught flat-footed
by VQ-1's reconnaissance aircraft as it was surfaced simulating the launch of cruise missiles against us."

The captain at the door nearly dropped his pipe.

Green continued. "The intelligence gained from disrupting the Soviets when they are doing these exercises gives us
insight into what we can expect to see when the bubble goes
up and we have to bomb those commie bastards back into
the Stone Age."

Green paused and took a sip of water from the glass on the
lectern. "Commander MacDonald and his crew arrived in the
vicinity of the submarine and covertly chased the son of a
bitch, eventually catching him on the surface with a member
of his wolf pack. Then they chased one of the two submarines
for nearly another whole day before losing him."

He set the glass back on the lectern.

"Let me tell you. If we had wanted to sink those two submarines, we could have done it and it would have been done
because of the professionalism of the crew of the *Dale*. Well
done, Commander," Green finished and clapped his hands.

Applause came from around the room. Captain Smith
turned and shook MacDonald's hand again, his eyes on Kennedy. "As I told you, the admiral is very pleased with the
Dale."

When Smith turned around, the commander sitting on
MacDonald's right shook his hand also, offering congratulatory comments.

When MacDonald turned around, Kennedy reached out and shook his hand and whispered, "Can a young commander eat crow now, or would you prefer it served hot later?"

"Okay, Danny, sit down. You've had your moment of glory so now you have to return to the navy leadership mantra of 'What have you done today for the fleet?'"

Several laughed as MacDonald sat down.

Kennedy leaned over and whispered, "Did I ever tell you about my ability to stick my foot in my mouth? My apologies, Skipper."

MacDonald nodded. *Apologies? You can go to hell, my fellow skipper who has no idea what a live ASW operation is really like.*

Admiral Green cleared his throat. "Gentlemen, I asked you here this morning to discuss Beacon Torch. I know you are aware of some aspects of it, but every one of you, your ship, and your crew are going to be living it, breathing it, and eating it for the next three months. What happens after those three months will be up to the enemy."

Green nodded at the lieutenant commander, who quickly stepped to the front and pulled down the map behind the admiral, a topographical map of the Vietnams.

"We are heading to Yankee Station." Green slapped his pointer against the Gulf of Tonkin.

Yankee Station was the notional spot in the Gulf of Tonkin where American aircraft carriers launched and recovered their aircraft. Yankee Station was far enough out to sea to discourage even the most foolhardy of the North Vietnamese ships or fighters from trying to attack.

"When I say 'we,' I mean the *Kitty Hawk* battle group. The *Tripoli* Amphibious Task Force will head toward Vietnam." Green moved the pointer away from the map, and while tapping the free end of it on his left palm, he continued, "That's the simple operational plan, but we all know simple is something applied to what landlubbers do. Nothing is simple about operating a battle group so every element arrives together, steams together, and fights together."

Green paused with another sip of water, before continuing. "By June 18—two weeks from today—we are going to be providing air support to an operation led by the Marines in the *Tripoli* Amphibious Task Force to hasten the end of this godforsaken war. We may even drive the communists back across the DMZ and stop the domino-effect commie-bastard leaders in Peking and Moscow want." He took a deep breath.

"Maybe it means we are going to invade the North?" Kennedy whispered.

MacDonald ignored the comment, keeping his eyes on Green. Kennedy obviously didn't know the admiral's reputation.

"No, Commander, it does not mean we are going to invade the North," Green answered.

MacDonald smiled. Green's keen sense of hearing was legend in the fleet.

"Yes, sir," Kennedy answered.

"But then again I have to tell all of you that the administration is under a lot of pressure. Every day in America demonstrators are tearing up our cities, destroying property, and, worst of all, spitting on returning servicemen. The decaying lack of will within America for this war is spreading. You spend four years winning a world war and it takes six to win a regional conflict? You got to ask yourself whose hand is in this pie."

Green lifted the pointer again and touched the area of the demilitarized zone separating the two Vietnams. "The exact landing area is top secret—as is this briefing, if you get my drift."

The captain at the door stepped inside and gently pulled the door shut behind him.

"The *Tripoli* will close the coast under air protection of the *Kitty Hawk* battle group." Green pointed toward MacDonald. "We will detach a surface action group, led by Commander MacDonald, to provide naval gunfire support and antisubmarine protection."

MacDonald's head lifted slightly. This was a first-heard for him. Not only was Green known for his keen sense of hearing, slight paranoia, and love of the sea, but he was also known for enjoying the thrill of springing surprises on subordinates. And for being on his third wife.

The news of commanding a SAG was a surprise MacDonald appreciated. So the *Dale* would have another chance in a different venue to prove as effective in it as it had in ASW.

"Congratulations," Kennedy whispered.

"Commander, you sure talk a lot," Green said with a tilt of the head. Every head in the room turned toward where the admiral was looking.

MacDonald was surprised to see everyone looking at him. He was going to throttle this Kennedy before the briefing was finished.

"Aye, sir," Kennedy replied.

The stares shifted slightly, much to MacDonald's relief.

"Earlier the same talkative officer offered Commander MacDonald . . ."

Yes, he was going to throttle this Kennedy.

". . . the opinion that maybe we were going to invade the North." Green shook his head. "To the best of my current information, which is in the top secret portion of your Beacon Torch operations message, is that we are not, but we want them to think we are. That means we mention nothing of our destination."

The door to the conference room opened and two sailors entered pushing a small cart filled with pastries. Another two entered through the rear door with a large unplugged coffee urn.

Green smiled. "Even an admiral has to stop for morning coffee." He looked at his watch. "Let's take a ten-minute break and then we'll continue. Gentlemen, I do not see this being a short briefing, if you get my drift."

MacDonald glanced at his watch as the noise of moving chairs and standing bodies blocked his hearing and view of the admiral. Another pet peeve of the mercurial flag officer was "clock watchers." Green's time was their time, so don't piss him off by being caught looking at a clock or your watch. He had been known to order all watches tossed into the center of a table if he caught more than two men glancing at their wrists.

"My apologies for being such an asshole earlier," Kennedy said in a soft voice. "It's the Irish in me. Can't keep dumb thoughts to myself."

MacDonald smiled. "That's all right," he said as calmly as possible.

"But you should know, with an Irish name like MacDonald."

"It's Scottish," he said sharply. *Lord, don't put the* Coghlan *in my SAG. I might sink it instead of hitting the targets ashore.*

MacDonald stood. "Excuse me, Commander. I need to call my ship."

Kennedy stood also. "Guess if we want any sticky buns and hot coffee we should push our way to the front."

"I think I'll pass," MacDonald said, as it seemed Kennedy was not going to move until he did.

Kennedy nodded. "I would like to talk with you after this meeting to get a feel for how you want to do the surface action group . . ."

"Sorry. It's much too soon to discuss how we'll split up the duties, and definitely too early to determine how the operations will be divided."

"I just thought—"

MacDonald nodded sharply. "You have to understand Admiral Green. He enjoys surprising folks with their assignment; more so when there is an audience to enjoy the surprise with him."

"I understand. By the way, the name is Ron."

"Plus, I have to sit down with my operations team and work up a plan. The good thing is the *Coghlan* and the *Dale* have the five-inch guns we'll need to support the troops when they go ashore."

"Just want to make sure you recognize that the *Coghlan* is smaller—less trim—than the *Dale*. Means we have more flexibility to do some innovative things such as dashing up the river for close-in naval gunfire support."

MacDonald cocked his head to the side. "River?"

"Mekong or one of the other large ones in Vietnam."

MacDonald smiled. "I think we both need to review the charts once we are sure where the Marines are going to land. But I will remember that, Commander."

Kennedy nodded and then started weaving his way to the coffee.

Motion caught MacDonald's eye from the front of the room. It was Admiral Green gesturing for him. A minute later of congratulatory handshakes and pats of the back, MacDonald stood near the admiral.

Green pointed at his mouth as he chewed. "One moment," he mumbled. A second later he swallowed. "Sorry about that. Carrier food is good and it is always plentiful, but nothing beats an Olongapo cinnamon bun." The admiral wiped his hands on the paper napkin, wadded it up, and tossed it into the nearby waste can.

"Danny, me boy, that was not bullshit about you and your crew with those two Echo submarines. You did more in two days than the rest of the navy has done against the Soviet submarine threat all year." Green laughed. "Would not surprise me to see the KGB take the captains of those two boats and shoot them both. Wouldn't surprise me in the least. At least all our navy does is write you a letter of reprimand. Any submarine captain worth his salt would never get caught on the surface."

Captain Smith walked up.

Admiral Green turned. "Joe, have you met Danny Mac-Donald?"

They shook hands again. "Yes, we have, Admiral."

"Danny, Captain Smith was recently selected for admiral. He's going to fleet up in a month to be vice commander Cruiser-Destroyer Group One."

"Congratulations, sir," MacDonald said.

Smith waved it off. "And don't pay attention to what Kennedy said. He's a lot more like you than his comments showed. Just a little younger."

"Yeah," Green said. "Deep selected for lieutenant commander and now commander. He's about two years ahead of his year group." Year groups identified the officers by their year of commissioning.

"Must be doing something right," MacDonald said.

"I wonder if the navy knows he's from a different Kennedy family," Smith offered.

"Don't know, don't care," Green snapped. "If he can handle the *Coghlan* as well as Danny commands the *Dale*, then we'll have a hell of an ASW team." He faced MacDonald. "We got a problem, Danny," Green said softly.

MacDonald's attention was piqued.

"The Soviets are convinced we are going to invade North Vietnam." He motioned forward the captain in the doorway. "This is Captain Norton. Alexander Norton is an intelligence officer being detached to my staff. Alex, give Commander MacDonald a quick dump on what you told me this morning."

Norton groaned. "Sir, we should do this in a special compartmented intelligence facility—a SCIF."

"Captain, I'm the admiral and this is my intelligence compartment." Green waved his hand around himself drawing the outline of an umbrella over their heads. Tell him."

"Yes, sir." Norton faced MacDonald. "The two submarines following the *Kitty Hawk*—"

"Are we sure there were only two?" Green interrupted.

"Yes, sir, we are pretty sure. We keep track of all the Soviet warships, so the process of elimination and knowing where the others are operating tell us not only how many could have been out there, but which ones also."

"Anything else we need to know, Alex?" Green asked.

Norton shook his head; wavy black hair, about an inch too long by navy standards, fell out of place. "The only other crisis continues to be the Middle East one."

"Shouldn't bother us; we're half a world away."

"Shouldn't, Admiral, but, the Soviet Navy views the Middle East as one of their growing spheres of influence. Anything we do there, they will react here."

"Let's hope they keep their guns in their holsters or the *Kitty Hawk* will blast them back into the nineteenth century."

"Yes, sir. That we could definitely do," Norton replied calmly, and then he cleared his throat. "With Egypt ordering the United Nations to withdraw its peacekeepers and then closing the Gulf of Aqaba to Israeli shipping earlier last week, things are going downhill rapidly."

"What's the latest?" Captain Smith asked.

"We received a report this morning from the Office of Naval Intelligence saying the Jordanian Army is massing along Jordan's border with Israel. That brings to three the number of Arab armies—Egypt, Syria, and Jordan— surrounding Israel."

Smith's eyes narrowed. "Do we think they are going to attack Israel?"

Norton took a draw on his pipe as he nodded. "Why would you spend the money, rhetoric, and ego on sword rattling unless you intended to do just that? Nasser is leading the rhetoric. Egypt has always been the strength, power, and key to controlling the Middle East. When Egypt snaps its fingers, the other Arab nations jump in line."

"If they are going to attack, when do we think they will?" Green asked.

"Good question, Admiral. I would expect something this week, but not later than a week from today. Not on a Friday—that's their Sabbath, and Saturday is the Jewish Sabbath. If I were the Arabs, I would do it next Saturday, if Israel waits that long."

"You think they'll do something?" MacDonald asked.

"Who?" Green questioned.

"The Israelis," MacDonald replied.

Norton shrugged. "The Israelis are surrounded. We are the only ally they truly have. They will weigh what they do with what we will support."

"Do we know what President Johnson will do?" MacDonald asked.

"He won't support them," Green said adamantly. "The president has his hands full with Vietnam, the riots, and the demonstrations. I don't think the American people would support a new war."

"We can't stand by and watch the Arabs destroy Israel," Smith said.

Green let out a deep breath. "We have our own war here in the Pacific. We'll have to hope the French mission to Egypt is able to defuse the situation."

"French mission?" Smith asked.

"The French have sent a delegation to meet with Nasser. To try to defuse the situation and get the Egyptians to pull back from the border with Israel," Norton answered.

"And if they fail?" Green asked.

"If our mercurial French ally fails, then we'll have to wait and see if the Israelis can pull another surprise victory."

"The Syrian and Egyptian armies are Soviet-trained," MacDonald said.

"If I were the Israelis, I'd be more concerned about the Jordanian Army," Norton added.

"Why's that?" Smith asked.

"They are British-trained. Until a few years ago, the Jordanians always hired a retiring British general to be their chief of the army. The Jordanians are well trained, well educated—in comparison to the Egyptian and Syrian soldiers—with high morale, extreme professionalism, and confidence. The key for Israel will be keeping the Jordanians contained. The good news for the Israelis is the Jordanian Army is the smallest of the Arab armies."

"Seems everywhere you look in this modern age of 1967, there's something propelling us toward a nuclear war with the Soviets," Green said. "Regardless of what President Johnson may or may not do—and, regardless of what I think—I cannot see America standing by and letting Israel lose."

The three officers nodded in agreement.

"Do you think there is a chance they may divert the *Kitty Hawk* and *Tripoli* to the Middle East?" MacDonald asked.

"There is always a chance," Green replied. He looked at Captain Smith. "Joe, we should check our supplies to see what we have if such an order came down."

"Aye, sir, will do that after the briefing."

"Meanwhile, we need to get back to our own piece of the geopolitical show called Beacon Torch," Green said. "We will have to let the Sixth Fleet worry about Israel." He turned to Smith. "Joe, when we get back to the carrier, take a look at our emission control status. Let's see how we can curtail our radars and communications to reduce detection by those commie bastards."

BOCHARKOV stepped into the control room. The sound of the pumps operating quietly on the deck below kept a soft vibration constantly permeating the K-122. He made a mental note to have this vibration quieted when the K-122 went back into the shipyard.

"Captain in control room," Chief Diemchuk, the chief of

the watch, announced. Near the hatch where Bocharkov entered, a young starshina made a notation in a green logbook.

"Status?" Bocharkov asked, looking at Ignatova standing near the periscope.

Near Ignatova stood Lieutenants Golovastov and Dolinski.

Just what he needed to take a tense operation inside the U.S. Navy bastion of Subic Bay and make it better. Both the GRU Special Forces gung-ho "kill and take no prisoners" Spetsnaz and the Party-political "working together for a Socialist tomorrow" *zampolit*.

God, how he hated to have to see the *zampolit* before lunch. There ought to be a Soviet Navy directive forbidding *zampolits* to talk to their skippers until after lunch—No! Make it dinner.

"We remain at one hundred meters depth, speed zero."

"And our location?" Bocharkov asked, intentionally ignoring both junior officers.

"A slight right-bearing drift, Captain, when the tide ebbed out an hour ago, but other than that we are five hundred meters southwest of the supply depot of the Subic Naval Base. We are also about the same from the edge of Olongapo Bay."

"How much depth do we have under us?"

Ignatova shrugged. "We do not know, Captain. At one hundred meters we know the American aircraft carriers can come into the port, but unless we use our depth ranger, we won't know."

Bocharkov looked at Tverdokhleb sitting at the navigation table. "Uri, what is the bottom like inside Olongapo Bay?" Bocharkov turned to Ignatova. "Did he tell you?"

Ignatova smiled.

"Muddy, Comrade Captain. Mud with shifting shallows. I do not recommend entering it. Our draft is much too deep to go too far into it."

"Yes, sir, Captain. He did tell me. As soon as I entered the control room, Lieutenant Tverdokhleb was telling me, telling them, and probably calling around the boat to make sure everyone knew to stay out of Olongapo Bay. I take it he told you?"

Bocharkov grunted. "He called me to tell me."

"Do you want to take a depth ranger?"

Bocharkov shook his head. "Not yet." He looked at the clock on the wall. Ten fifteen. The K-122 would have to wait another twelve hours before they could commence the Spetsnaz operation.

"Lieutenant Dolinski, what are you doing in the control room?" Bocharkov asked.

"Just observing, sir."

"Then go observe somewhere else. We don't have much room here."

"I asked him to come with me, Comrade Captain," Golovastov said. "Sir, Lieutenant Dolinski is a *zampolit* like me. He has been providing me some very good ideas since his arrival."

Ignatova turned. "Are you a *zampolit* now, Lieutenant?"

A tight smile crossed Dolinski's face as his head rose. "Of course, Captain Ignatova. Once a *zampolit*, always a *zampolit*. Lieutenant Golovastov is fairly new. When I saw the challenges here on the K-122, I thought I could give him the benefit of my experience."

"Well, I hate to stop the two of you from your professional sharing, but do you think it could be done better somewhere else?" Bocharkov asked, forcing his voice to remain calm. What challenges? What was it about young zealots that gave them the omnipotence to believe they had the answers to every damn thing in the world? "The crew here in the control room has their hands full keeping the boat level, steady, and quiet. The fewer hands here the better."

"What I was showing Lieutenant Golovastov, sir, was how his Party-political work could be integrated into the operations of a boat. How it could be used to increase solidarity regardless of rank," Dolinski replied, ignoring Bocharkov's order. Instead, Dolinski clenched his fist and continued. "Five fingers are useless in a fight unless curled into a fist. It is something Yasha can create on the K-122." Dolinski paused. "Of course, that help would be alongside you and the XO." His tight smile broadened, but the Spetsnaz's eyes locked with Bocharkov's.

"I think you have a bright idea, Lieutenant Dolinski," Ignatova said. "Now, I must insist, as the captain asked, that the two of you take your discussion elsewhere. We have a boat to get ready for tonight's mission. You, Lieutenant Dolinski, are the mission for tonight."

Bocharkov grunted. "Lieutenant Dolinski, are you ready for tonight?"

The man snapped to attention. "Sir, the Spetsnaz are always ready."

Ignatova looked at Dolinski. "Maybe, Lieutenant, you should take Lieutenant Golovastov with you? It would be the right thing to do." The XO turned his attention to the *zampolit* of the K-122. "Lieutenant Golovastov, what do you think? I think Lieutenant Dolinski is right about how the right Party-political approach to working together can enhance teamwork. Maybe if you went with the lieutenant tonight, you would gain even further insight into the principles Comrade Dolinski is sharing with you." He looked back at Dolinski. "I believe what you said would apply across the Soviet Navy, would you not agree?"

Dolinski's smile disappeared. "I think not, sir. The role of the *zampolit* is to indoctrinate and guide, to observe outside the chain of command, and to offer suggestions to improve solidarity and Party correctness—not to do the operations."

"But you are doing operations," Ignatova said, his voice sharp.

"It was my choice to move into this field, comrade."

"Good," Bocharkov said with a heavy sigh. "Now, if you two would excuse us, we have work to do for tonight when you take your principles and your operational skills into action on American soil."

"You mean Filipino soil," Golovastov said. "The imperialists have enslaved this Asian country—"

"Lieutenant, you are correct," Ignatova said, his voice rising. "We are in dangerous waters with a dangerous operation to do. I know where you are going with this idea and I think it is a great idea."

Golovastov looked surprised.

"You are going to use it as topic one for a Party-political meeting later. Tell me quickly: Am I right?"

"Yes, sir. You are right. I will use it as a topic for tonight's Party-political discussion."

Dolinski glared at Ignatova, then with a curt sideways nod

added, "You are right, Captain Ignatova. This is a great topic for a Party-political discussion."

Ignatova looked at Bocharkov. "We are blessed with two *zampolits* on board the K-122."

Dolinski and Golovastov saluted and marched out the aft control room hatch.

"Blessed is not the word I would have used, XO."

"Golovastov is going to be hard to live with once this Dolinski fills his head with how *zampolits* can improve operations," Ignatova said softly.

"And he is easy to live with now?"

Lieutenant Alex Vyshinsky, the communications officer, stepped through the forward hatch, stopping as his eyes adjusted to the lower light of the compartment. Bocharkov saw the officer and waited. Communicators seldom left their little empire unless necessary.

Vyshinsky saw Bocharkov and Ignatova. He walked quickly toward them.

"More directions from Moscow most likely," Ignatova said softly.

Steps before he reached them, Vyshinsky, stuttering slightly with the first word, said, "Captain, I have a top secret message from Moscow."

Ignatova raised two fingers and dipped them. "Two points."

Vyshinsky held the metal message board out with his left hand while saluting awkwardly with his right. "Here it is, Comrade Captain."

"Comrade," Ignatova said, shaking his head. He looked at Vyshinsky as Bocharkov took the message board. "Captain is sufficient, Alex, or comrade, but both together is a waste of air aboard a submarine."

Bocharkov motioned downward. Last thing needed was an interview with the *zampolit* while this Lieutenant Dolinski was filling the political officer's narrow mind with bullshit and ideology.

Ignatova nodded. Vyshinsky stood silently, his glances bouncing from Bocharkov to Ignatova while Bocharkov read the message. Halfway through the message, Bocharkov said, "Damn," and kept reading. Wordlessly, he finished and passed it to Ignatova.

Ignatova quickly scanned the message before looking up at Bocharkov. "Damn!" His eyes went back down and this time he read each word. Ignatova pulled the metal top of the message board down, holding the board away from the communicator when Vyshinsky reached for it. "One moment, Lieutenant."

Ignatova looked at Bocharkov. "We have to finish this mission tonight and get the hell out of Subic Bay."

Bocharkov nodded. "You are right." The clock showed ten twenty five. "By this time tomorrow I want to be at least a hundred kilometers away from Subic Bay. Make sure the department heads are aware of this."

"Sir," Vyshinsky stuttered. "It is a top secret message."

Bocharkov grunted. "Won't matter if the Americans catch us here and know the same thing Moscow does, now will it?"

"No, sir," the communicator answered, his Adam's apple rising and falling.

"XO, I want the K-122 in deep water by this time tomorrow."

"They do pick their times, don't they?" Ignatova said sharply. He handed the message board to Vyshinsky, who quickly left the control room.

"Too bad we don't have allies with any sense of patience," Ignatova said. "Maybe we can send Dolinski and Golovastov to them."

EIGHT

DOLINSKI slammed the hatch behind him as he stomped into the forward torpedo room. Starshina Cheslav Zosimoff, squatting near the hatch, stood. Shaking his head, he spun the wheel securing the watertight hatch behind Dolinski.

Squatting on the deck around the opened containers were Lieutenant Motka Gromeko, Chief Ship Starshina Burian Fedulova, and Dimitry Malenkov, the only petty officer who spoke accent-free American. The boat's Spetsnaz team had been hard at work preparing for tonight's mission.

Gromeko stood, brushing his hands together. "We've been waiting for you."

Dolinski crossed his arms. "Looks as if you did not wait long. Have you found what you were looking for?"

Gromeko shook his head. "Not sure what we are supposed to be looking for, Uri." He started around the small compartment, pointing at each box as he turned. "Here we have the electronics, which are unfamiliar to all of us, but I know this coil of wire will turn into the antenna. That is why—"

"Why I am here, comrade? You don't know what you are looking for because I am the technician." Dolinksi looked around the crowded room. "Without me, there is no mission, and if you start screwing around with this stuff and break anything, lose something, or cause it to malfunction, then, the mission is kaput."

"This box has uniforms in it," Gromeko continued, ignoring the outburst. "I presume they are American Navy uniforms, but we are not sure how to wear them or when. . . ."

"That is my job to show you."

"And this box has weapons. We have weapons on board the K-122, but these weapons . . ."

". . . are designed to work underwater, if we need them," Dolinski finished. He uncrossed his arms. "If you had waited until I returned, we could have done this more orderly."

"Since we did not know where you had gone or what you were doing, I decided—as the senior lieutenant on the team—to start preparations."

Dolinski's eyes widened. "So we do not have any problems ashore, comrade, while on board the K-122 you are the senior officer. Seniority among lieutenants is like virtue in a whorehouse. It matters little." He pointed to the escape trunk above them. "Once we enter the escape trunk, I become the senior officer for this mission. I was not sent here as an advisor."

The silence in the torpedo room seemed to last forever before Gromeko cleared his throat. "You are the technician. I will value your advice, comrade. Seniority may be like virtue in a whorehouse, but in this whorehouse I am the madam," he said as he stood. Then he added, "But we will discuss the operation with the captain before we depart, to get his advice. He is ultimately responsible."

Dolinski opened his mouth to argue, but seemed to think better of it and shut it.

"Shall we go over your plan?" Gromeko asked, squatting again. He was nervous about this. Surely Dolinski and the GRU had some sort of plan for what they were going to do once ashore. They had not rehearsed the operation, not even to go over it in detail. Just words about sailing into the harbor, sitting on the bottom—which the captain quickly dismissed—and then frogmanning it ashore. What then?

"You worry too much, Motka," Dolinski said as he unbuttoned his shirt pocket. From the pocket he pulled a black pouch and tossed it on the makeshift table created by the tops of the crates. "Here is the chart of the American base."

Gromeko picked up the black pouch and unzipped it. Unfolding thin sheets of paper, he laid them on the crate tops and smoothed out the creases. The map was barely readable, but was sufficient to guide them to the target, if it was accurate. Small boxes represented buildings and block Cyrillic lettering identified what each building was.

Dolinski squatted down beside them. He shifted the papers slightly so the diagram faced him. "Right here," he said, tapping a small building on it. "Right here is where we are going to go. It is their telephone point of presence—a PoP as the Americans call it. Right here, every telephone on the base and every temporary telephone hooked up to every ship in the harbor transect each other. It is the heart and soul of the telephones supporting the American's Subic Naval Base. Right here is their vulnerability and our opportunity."

Starshina Zosimoff now stood looking over Dolinski's shoulder at the map.

Gromeko and the blond-haired Chief Ship Starshina Fedulova exchanged questionable glances. Dolinski chuckled. "It's not complicated, comrades." His finger walked the path between lines of warehouses, from the telephone switching building back to the harbor. "We will come out somewhere along here—the south side of the harbor." His finger moved to the right. "See this mark here?"

"Yes," they said in unison.

"That is a huge drainage pipe. It is here we will leave our tanks and suits, and put on the American dungaree uniform."

"Dungarees? Like blue jeans?" Zosimoff asked. "Can we keep them afterward?"

Dolinski looked up, and then back at the paper. "Not the same thing. They call their working uniforms 'dungarees.' "

"Are we sure they will fit us?" Fedulova asked, lifting up one of the shirts. There are exactly five here and there are five of us."

Dolinski shrugged. "Mine fits. We have your uniform measurements at headquarters, Chief Ship Starshina Fedulova. Unless you have put on great weight, yours should fit you well."

Fedulova rubbed his fingers on the fabric. "Which is which?"

Dolinski flinched.

"We will try them on later, Chief, and mark them accordingly," Gromeko said.

Fedulova dropped the shirt back onto the pile and nodded. "They are not much to look at it."

"We need to try them on now, Comrade Lieutenant," Starshina Malenkov said quietly.

"Why?" Dolinski demanded.

Malenkov stood to attention. "Because, Comrade Lieutenant Dolinski and Comrade Lieutenant Gromeko, if we have to make alterations to them, we will have time. The Americans are very attentive to things in uniform. They will recognize something out of place, and if it is one of their starshina chief petty officers who see us, he will surely stop and comment on what he sees."

"It will be dark," Fedulova offered.

Malenkov shrugged. "It is only my opinion. I may be wrong."

"He could be wrong," Gromeko said, raising his hand. "And if he is wrong, so be it, but it will not hurt us to try on the uniforms and make sure they fit, make sure they are accurate." He looked at Malenkov. "Do you know how an American uniform should look on the person wearing it?"

Malenkov paused, then shook his head. "I only saw the American military in what they called their dress uniform . . ."

Dolinski reached down and pulled up a light blue dungaree shirt. He tossed it to Malenkov before glancing around at the others. "Let's do it. The starshina is right."

Thirty minutes later, with Malenkov and Zosimoff having to trade dungaree trousers because of the length, Gromeko was satisfied the uniforms were sufficient for their mission. Even Dolinski agreed.

Then their attention focused on the map in front of them. Gromeko nodded at Dolinski.

Dolinski put his finger on the map, and as the others listened, he started to talk. As he explained the operation for tonight, he made it seem so simple that Gromeko unknowingly relaxed slightly. Knowing what was expected and seeing some prior planning improved his confidence that they would be able to do this. He knew that once American sailors hit Olongapo, the lures of the city captured their capitalistic fever. As Dolinski wound down, the GRU officer asked if anyone had questions. When none were forthcoming, he stood.

"These," he said, pointing at the electronics, "are the most important thing for the success of our mission. I will need thirty minutes inside the telephone switching building once we get there. Your job is to see that I am not disturbed."

"If we kill anyone, they will know—"

"Know nothing, Lieutenant Gromeko," Dolinski finished. "People die all the time in Olongapo. What is one more death to a nation dealing death to our allies on a daily basis?"

Gromeko looked up, but said nothing.

"Nothing is the answer." Dolinski paused. "The Americans will launch an investigation, find some guilty sailor, and send the pleading man off to prison for something he did not commit." He shrugged, and then looked around at each of them. "But you are right in that if we kill someone or do something that draws attention to our presence, eventually someone may figure out what has happened."

"How about your electronics?" Starshina Dimitry Malenkov asked. "Even the Americans check their systems on a schedule. They will eventually detect the additional gear you are installing."

Dolinski sighed. "You may be right, Malenkov, but by the time they discover the equipment and dismantle it, we will have the information we want."

"What information is that?" Fedulova asked.

Dolinski glared at the chief for a moment, and then sighed, "Not everything we will do tonight will be known to you. Some things are best unknown."

"What does that mean?" Gromeko asked, curious.

"It means the chief—and the rest of you—do not have the need to know. Your job is to get me to the telephone switches and provide guard while I am in there." He squatted beside the box with the electronic gear, rooting through the loose wires. "We are going to have to rewrap these wires." He lifted a small box in his hand. "See this?" he asked, holding it up.

They nodded. Gromeko said, "Yes." He was growing weary of this lieutenant. The sooner Dolinski was off the boat the better.

"When I finish, the lights here along the front must shine green. That will tell us the system is operational and able to transmit. So when I finish the installation, we will have to conduct the test when we return to our wet suits."

"Why don't you test it immediately after you install the system, comrade?" Chief Fedulova asked.

"We cannot test at the building. It has to be done from a distance. The lights will glow green near the installation, but we have to ensure a signal is transmitting when we leave. The antenna will have been wound around the wires leading from the building to the telephone pole outside. One hundred meters from the system should be sufficient to know it works." He set the black electronic system down and wiped his hands on his dungaree pants.

"Enough," Gromeko said. "Lieutenant Dolinski is here for his technical and engineering know-how. Our job is to get him to the building, protect him long enough for him to do his job, and then get all of us back safely to the K-122."

It was at that moment that it dawned on Gromeko that Dolinski had never done a mission. This was the GRU lieutenant's first. Dolinski was one of these desk-jockey intelligence analysts who for some reason get chosen to do something like this. A slight chill went up Gromeko's back. They were going into enemy territory, where nothing would give the Americans more pleasure than to capture or kill them.

"Let's get out of these American uniforms and get them stored in the watertight bags we are going to be carrying," Dolinski said.

Gromeko looked around the torpedo room at the other Spetsnaz. He and his team had done a few special missions—in Vietnam. Of his team he was confident, but here they were escorting a GRU specialist onto foreign soil. Someone who was vastly overconfident and underexperienced.

Gromeko looked at Dolinski and for a moment their eyes locked. It was if the GRU officer recognized that Gromeko knew his limitations. Dolinski looked away first, grabbing one of the loose cords and wrapping it between his thumb and small finger to form a figure eight. "Wish you had not undone everything," Dolinski muttered as he wrapped.

Gromeko looked at his watch. It was one o'clock. Lunch would still be being served for another hour. Ten hours until they would do this.

"Lieutenant Dolinski, would you go over your expectations again? Chief Fedulova and Starshina Zosimoff, we will need to add times onto the mission: How long will it take us to reach shore? How long will it take us to change out of our suits, tanks?" He nodded at Dolinski. "Your map is faint. Do you know how far from the beach the telephone building is?" He put his finger on the map. "What is the length of each of the buildings between which we are going to traverse?

Dolinski squinted his eyes for a moment. Then he shook his head. "I figure they are about one hundred meters in length. They are nothing but warehouses. All warehouses are built the same—rectangular." Dolinski spun the map around to face Gromeko. "These two buildings near the beach are warehouses. We have to walk between the warehouses. Then there is an open space until we reach the next two buildings. At the end of those two buildings is the telephone switching building."

"Does anyone know how long these warehouses are?"

Fedulova, Zosimoff, and Malenkov shook their heads.

"Let's figure each warehouse is one hundred meters long by fifty meters wide." Gromeko was guessing, but a guess was better than a complete surprise.

"These are big warehouses from the photographs I saw," Dolinski said.

Gromeko nodded. "That may be, but we are trying to build a timetable now. Something that should have been done where there was more intelligence on which to build." It was a remark aimed at Dolinski. Gromeko waited a second for the man to explode, and was surprised when the GRU officer instead started working on his second loose cord.

"We will have to know how long you will need to do your work, Lieutenant," Gromeko added.

"I will need no more than thirty minutes."

"Wow!" Fedulova said. "That is a long time."

"It is. Lieutenant Dolinski, can you do it in a shorter period?"

"Lieutenant Gromeko, I will hurry, but not at the expense of the mission. It will do us no good for me to hurry through the installation only to discover when we reach the beach that it was flawed. For then we will have to return to the building."

There was a moment of silence before Gromeko said, "That is reasonable. Chief, figure thirty minutes into the timetable."

Dolinski finished the second cord, then set them both alongside the box. He put the small electronic boxes he would need later into the box first, and then laid the cords on top. Then his eyes started searching around the compartment. "Did you see a tool box—a leather carrying case with small screwdrivers, pliers, and wire strippers?"

Everyone started looking. "I do not recall seeing it," Gromeko said.

"It was in the box," Dolinski protested. "It has to be here. Those are the tools needed for the installation." He lifted two waterproof bags from the bottom of the box. "We will use these to carry the equipment with us."

OLIVER pulled aside the curtains to the sonar compartment. The vacant space with the silent console lay in front of him. His head still pounded from the night ashore. He had returned with several *Dale* shipmates and a few new ones they had picked up downtown, singing pornographic ditties dedicated to the tittie bars of Olongapo. He was not sure how he'd climbed into his rack. How could so much fun hurt so much the day after?

"About time someone from Sonar showed up."

Oliver turned. It was Lieutenant Burnham. He let out a deep sigh. "Sorry, Lieutenant, I was unaware we were to have anyone down here on watch."

Burnham guffawed. "You don't. I'm the command duty officer and doing my rounds. Are you going to be in Combat?"

"Yes, sir. I have my PMS to do."

"Preventive maintenance service—PMS. Leave it to the navy to find some way to associate unpleasant things for the ship with unpleasant things for women."

"Sir?" Oliver asked, confused. "Don't you mean preventive maintenance schedule?" He should have taken an aspirin.

"Petty Officer Oliver, never correct an officer. Sometimes we are right."

Petty Officer Banks walked up. Burnham's attention diverted, Oliver stepped inside.

"Want to have a cigarette on the fantail?" Banks asked Burnham.

"Sure, why not? After the horrid mass-produced food we had for dinner, anything is better. Including a coffin nail."

Oliver listened to the footsteps moving away. His stomach growled. He should have gone to dinner, but Sunday meant sleeping in, doing just about anything he wanted. He reached below the small ledge that ran along the front of the sonar console and flipped the power switch. Then he leaned back in the seat, aware of an incredible thirst. While he waited for the equipment to warm, Oliver stepped out into the silent combat information center and walked to the scuttlebutt.

"Scuttlebutt" was an old nautical term identifying the water kegs on sailing ships. Since a lot of gossip and chatter occurred around the water fountain, the term "scuttlebutt" over the years had come to mean water fountain, gossip, and useless chatter.

The hatch leading to the bridge was open. Oliver stuck his head into the bridge area. It was vacant also and the lights were out. The gray haze of dusk was settling over the harbor. He stepped completely onto the bridge and out onto to the port bridge wing, taking in the complement of ships anchored and moored around the gigantic harbor. A welling of pride filled his hungover body. Where else could someone from a small cotton mill village like Whitesburg, Georgia, find himself in the Philippines looking at what had to be the mightiest navy the world had ever seen? And he was part of it.

He was never going to leave the navy. He was going to

enjoy the world. Enjoy the liberty ports. Even if it was a lie that sailors had a girl in every port. He could barely afford a girl in Olongapo, much less every port.

Oliver turned, heading back to Sonar. On the back shelf, near where the boatswain mate of the watch stood alongside the microphone to the 1MC, was a stack of paper cups. He took several of them and went back to Sonar. Along the way, he filled one of the cups with water. At Sonar, he stashed the other cups in one of the file cabinet drawers.

The hum of the equipment filled the small space now. He flipped on the screen and waited the few minutes it took for the green display to warm. Then he hit the diagnostic switch, letting the cursor roll along the screen, checking out the display. He downed the water, stood, and returned to the scuttlebutt. When he came back and sat, the cursor blinked near the top left-hand side of the screen.

He shut his eyes.

"OLIVER! You asleep!"

His eyes opened wide and he jumped. "No, Chief!" he shouted back.

A hand slapped him upside the back of his head. "Don't lie to me, shithead," Chief Stalzer said with a laugh. "I heard about you last night, coming back shit-faced." He laughed more. "Did you hear about the sailors on the *Coghlan*?"

Oliver shook his head.

"They tried to sneak a bar girl on board the tin can. Guess a couple of sailors distracted the quarterdeck watch while a couple more handed the girl over the lower aft portion of the destroyer. Had her nearly to their berthing area when the duty master-at-arms caught them." He laughed. "Talk about bad luck."

"What did they do to them?"

Stalzer shrugged and tittered into the door facing. "Whoa there, Stalzer," he said to himself. He looked back at Oliver. "What did you ask?"

"I asked, what did they do to them?"

Stalzer shrugged. "Who knows? I would have given them

a medal if they had succeeded. They would have made a fortune out to sea. What are you doing?"

Oliver reached over to the file cabinet and opened the bottom drawer. "I am doing what you told me to do, Chief. I'm doing the PMS."

"Damn fine thing you are, too," Stalzer said, leaning forward.

The smell of stale cigarette smoke on the chief's civilian shirt whiffed across Oliver's hangover-sensitive nostrils. His stomach growled.

"You have to eat when you have a hangover," Stalzer said. "Eating and drinking water and chucking down aspirins are the prescriptions for surviving a great time on the town."

Oliver grunted as he pulled out the white PMS cards covered with small lines of instruction, numbered sequentially.

Stalzer reached up and pulled the clock from the wall, holding it behind his back. "Without looking at your watch, what time is it?"

The smell of beer joined the odor of stale cigarettes. He was going to be sick. "I don't know, Chief."

Stalzer brought the large navy clock around front of him. "Let's see. For the Marine Corps, Mickey's little hand is on eleven and his big hand is on eight. For the air force, it is nap time, so they have never seen this time of night. For the navy, it's twenty-three forty. Twenty minutes to midnight and you expect me to believe you only got here to do the PMS?"

Oliver let out a deep sigh. "Damn, Chief. You just get back from downtown and decide to come up here and give me shit?" he said softly.

"Petty Officer Oliver—beloved of the captain and the division officer—I came up here to just see for myself if you would be here." He turned and after several tries hung the clock back up. "Did not come up here to give you a hard time. Fact is, you are one good sonar technician and you are going to make one hell of a great master chief petty officer."

Oliver looked up at the chief. "You're drunk, Chief."

"Duh! We are in Olongapo, aren't we?" Stalzer replied.

Oliver nodded.

"Then of course I'm drunk. And you're ugly. Tomorrow

morning, I'm going to be sober, but you're still going to be ugly."

Oliver gave a slight smile. "Churchill."

"Churchill?"

"Yes, Chief. Churchill said that to some lady who told him the same thing."

"Did he really?" Stalzer asked, curiously.

"That's what I heard."

"Damn. All this time, I thought I said it." Stalzer turned and stepped into the combat information center. "Tomorrow is a Monday, Oliver. Don't stay up so long that you miss quarters tomorrow morning. Zero seven thirty sharp."

"You sleep well, yourself, Chief," Oliver said. For a moment he thought well of his division chief. Maybe the alcohol loosened the mind to where you did speak the truth, or your basic emotions of love, honor, and obey—Wait a minute! That was what his girlfriend wanted when he left Whitesburg.

"I'm going to bed." Stalzer started away, and then stopped. "By the way," he said from around the corner, his footsteps coming back. "Here's a couple of letters for you that came earlier today." Stalzer tossed them over Oliver's back, one landing on the small shelf and the other one faceup on the deck. "Sorry," Stalzer mumbled before he turned, nearly falling before righting himself and disappearing aft toward the chief's quarters.

Oliver reached down to pick up the letter on the deck, recognizing the writing as his brother's. His brother was in Vietnam supporting the navy on a riverine craft, plying the dangerous waters of the rivers. He'd wanted to join the army so they could be stationed together, but the army recruiter said no way, with both of them being the only sons of the family. Some worry-wart reason about a family losing both of them in combat at the same time.

He laid this letter on top of the letter on the shelf. When he did, he realized he had three letters, not two. One of the remaining letters was from his mom. She wrote him nearly daily. The other was from the "girl he left behind." After three years in the navy, Oliver had come to believe that every sailor had a "girl he left behind." He lifted her letter and smelled the Woolworth's perfume she wore and imagined her running her finger along the edges of the letter. This was one letter he was looking forward to reading, and he fought the urge to do so, but he had to finish the PMS. He looked at the clock. It was ten minutes to midnight. By the time he finished, it was going to be one in the morning. Good thing he had dozed off. He felt much better. Then his stomach growled. "Ummm." Mid-rats were being served in the mess.

He laid the PMS papers on the shelf. Then he looked again at the clock. The chow hall was only two decks away and half the destroyer's length. He could go grab a sandwich and be back here in twenty minutes. He pulled together the curtains as he stepped into the darkened combat information center.

Behind him, the slight rise of an underwater noise spoke detected by the starboard-side hydrophones went unnoticed. When the clock showed midnight, Oliver was nearly at the chow hall.

"RISE slowly," Bocharkov said quietly.

The command went from his lips to the officer of the deck, who relayed it quietly to the chief of the boat, Uvarova, who stood over the planesman and near the helmsman.

"Ten-degree angle, heading three-three-zero," Uvarova reported to the command.

This was the critical moment. If the Americans were going to detect the K-122, this would be it. Changing the ballast load created noise in the water. Through his feet Bocharkov could feel the pumps belowdecks. Someday maybe a Soviet scientist would come up with some way to muffle all underwater sound. At least for the Soviet Navy. Would not want the American submarines to be any quieter.

He nodded when Ignatova stuck his head into the control room. "I am heading to the forward torpedo room, Comrade Captain."

Bocharkov nodded again as the head disappeared. Ignatova would call him once he arrived.

"Passing fifty meters."

He was bringing a Soviet nuclear submarine to periscope depth in the middle of an American fleet anchored and moored in an American-controlled harbor in Philippine territory. For a fleeting moment, he imagined how easily he could sink many of them with his torpedoes. A spread of eight, three for each of the carriers—the *Kitty Hawk* and the *Tripoli*—then one each for two of the smaller ships. His rear spread of six would also be useful. Then he would sprint to the opening of the harbor while his crew loaded another round. By then, fire and damnation would be erupting over Olongapo Harbor. With fire and explosions comes confusion. He could probably launch another spread from his rear tubes . . .

"Captain, we are passing thirty meters."

He nodded. It would rival Pearl Harbor, when the Japanese sunk the American Fleet. It would also cause America to overreact, as they were prone to do. Within the K-122 he would be one famous Soviet captain until they surfaced near Kamchatka. By then, hundreds of missiles from both sides would have passed one another in the dark of space to explode across half of the globe, destroying the motherland of both nations. He swallowed. *It is good we keep these fantasies in our minds.*

A vision came to him of his wife, his two sons, and the newest member of the family, his daughter. Without doubt, the same fantasies crossed through the minds of the Americans, along with realizing the fate of their families if they ever lived them out.

"Passing twenty-five meters."

"Make your depth fifteen meters, Lieutenant Commander Orlov," Bocharkov said. For tonight he had ordered his most senior officers to the important positions. His operations officer, Orlov, was the officer of the deck. The XO was to be with the Spetsnaz mission team until they had departed the boat. Then the forward torpedo tube team would man their position. He had given strict orders there was to be no preventive maintenance or anything that required opening the outer doors of the torpedo tubes. While he might imagine and bask in the fantasy of sinking the American fleet, he would only use the torpedoes to cover his escape. He glanced at the clock. It was five minutes to midnight. Sinking one or two American warships would not cause World War III.

The internal intercom buzzed. Starshina Chief Trush

grabbed the handset. A second passed. "Captain, the XO is in the forward torpedo room awaiting instructions."

"Very well," Bocharkov replied. No one was going anywhere until he was assured everything topside was clear. Meanwhile, everyone was in place awaiting his orders. "Up periscope."

Bocharkov swept the lens around the harbor. Every ship was lighted from bow to stern. On the farther side of the harbor, the American aircraft carrier *Kitty Hawk* was moored pierside behind the smaller amphibious carrier *Tripoli*. There were few ports with the depth of Olongapo Harbor, in which either of those two ships could tie up alongside the pier.

As he turned the periscope, movement caught his eye and he quickly turned the scope back to the left. A small landing craft was passing about one hundred meters dead astern. He focused the lens, then pressed the button. "Distance?"

Orlov replied, "Ninety meters."

"Ninety meters," Bocharkov repeated.

"Target?"

"Small boat," Bocharkov replied, then leaned away from the lens. "What we call a landing craft. I believe they call them liberty launches—carrying the sailors and marines from the ships anchored in the harbor to the shore and back." He continued his sweep. Less than three hundred meters in the direction of the stern and nearer than the carriers were several "small boys." He counted at least one cruiser and three destroyers. The auxiliary ships—oilers, ammunition ships, repair ship—were anchored off to his starboard side. It must be from those huge ships that the liberty launches were plying their trade.

The intercom beeped again. Orlov grabbed the handset. "Control room." Several seconds passed. "Captain, XO reports the team is ready when you are."

Bocharkov nodded. He had a bad feeling about this, but emotions were something navy officers ignored when orders were involved. He mentally crossed his fingers. "Tell them about the liberty launches. I presume there will be more." He turned the periscope aft so it pointed east to the area where the Spetsnaz team would land. At least the site for the mission was not near the main base. This was far enough way from the piers so the team could have some shadows. Rocks and concrete tridents filled the uphill beachhead between the slight waves of the near-calm harbor and the narrow road above it. He focused the periscope. There was the dark circular opening that must be the main flood drain Gromeko had described. The team would use it to store their flippers, tanks, and gear until their return. He turned the scope upward, glad to see stars. Maybe it would not rain, but then this was the Philippine tropics.

NINE

FINALLY, Bocharkov stepped away from the periscope. "Down periscope. Lieutenant Commander Orlov, ensure Sonar is alert to any passive noise in the area. I want those small boats tracked as well as any new sources." He looked at the clock. It was fifteen minutes after midnight—Monday morning. The sun would rise around zero five thirty.

"We are doing that, Comrade Captain."

"Why do the Americans call them liberty launches?"

" 'Liberty' is the time the Americans are ashore corrupting the natives. The small boats take them back and forth in teams to continue the imperialist indoctrination of the natives with the American dollar."

"Lieutenant Commander Orlov, you are filled with lots of information trivia."

"I think I should say thank you, Captain."

Bocharkov grunted and then turned to the navigator, who sat hunched over his charts at the forward end of the compartment. "Lieutenant Tverdokhleb, when is sunrise or false dawn? When is my periscope going to be easily seen from the decks of the nearby Americans?"

The officer leaned back, an unlit cigarette dangling from

his lips. Tverdokhleb reached up and pushed his black-rimmed glasses back off his nose and against his eyes.

If the man ever looked at the sun, he would burn his eyes out, thought Bocharkov.

"Sir?"

"I asked, when is sunrise?"

Several seconds had passed with Bocharkov glancing at the clock when Tverdokhleb announced, "Zero four seventeen hours, Comrade Captain."

Bocharkov nodded. That meant false dawn would be about thirty minutes before that, but the mountain range behind Olongapo should block that out. From his review of the charts earlier in the day, he knew that false dawn was just that in Subic Bay: false. Dawn broke suddenly when the edge of the sun came over the top of the mountains. By four seventeen, he needed to be in deep water or near it. After sunrise, any speed he might put on to make their escape ran the risk of creating a wake on the surface. A wake that would be invisible to the K-122, but easily discernible to an American lookout.

He cleared his throat. "Tell Captain Second Rank Ignatova that he may release the team to their mission."

"Aye, sir," Orlov replied.

Was that a smile he saw on the operations officer's face? Could it be that this "thing" they were doing was having a positive effect on the crew? The officers, chiefs, and sailors standing the watch seemed quieter, seemed more alert—but then they should be, in the heart of the American fleet. He smiled. Damn. It did feel good doing something to the Americans instead of diving, running, and evading them. Maybe what the K-122 was doing was a turning point for the Soviet Navy.

"And after the team has departed the boat, Operations Officer, start making preparations for us to leave. I want out of this enemy harbor before zero six hundred."

Ignatova put the handset back in the cradle. "The captain says it is time. There are landing craft shuttling American sailors back and forth between their ships and the shore. You will have to be careful of them."

"Aye, Comrade Captain," Dolinksi answered.

Gromeko hoisted his tank onto his shoulder. "The escape

hatch is too narrow for the tanks," he said to the team. "You will have to carry them like so." He held his single tank to his chest. "Once outside the escape trunk, put your tank on. I will be waiting."

"I will go last," Dolinski said.

"How about the gear you will need?" Ignatova said, looking at the two waterproof bags sitting between the two officers.

"I will take one with me," Malenkov replied. He reached down and slid the bag between his feet. "Like this, sir, inside the escape trunk."

"Then he and Chief Fedulova will carry it between them to shore," Gromeko added.

"I and this starshina"—Dolinski pointed at Zosimoff—"will carry the other bag the same way. Ashore, we will only have one of them to carry."

Ignatova nodded, then stepped forward and shook hands with each of them. "Go with speed and safety." He glanced at his watch as he moved near the hatch to be out of the way of the departing team. "You have two hours twenty minutes. Time?"

"Gromeko looked at his deep-sea wristwatch, then at the clock on the bulkhead of the forward torpedo room. "Time is zero zero twenty-two."

"We will work the two hours twenty minutes from zero zero thirty," Ignatova said, looking at the analog clock with its small hand on twelve and the large hand on twenty-two. He doubled-checked his wristwatch against the bulkhead clock.

"Let's go," Gromeko said, moving under the hatch. He pulled down the narrow ladder and climbed. A spin of the hatch wheel and in a few seconds he was inside. Fedulova climbed halfway up the ladder and handed Gromeko his tank before securing the watertight door.

Gromeko's shoulders touched the sides of the escape trunk. He clasped the single tank against his chest, pressing his back against the curvature of the trunk. In the darkness of the trunk, he could not tell how the tank was resting against the other side. The mouthpiece fit securely in his mouth, his teeth clenched on the rubber tubing, making sure the rush of water did not dislodge it. His right hand was above his right shoulder so he could reach the wheel once the hatch filled. The sound of hydraulics announced the flow of water.

Water began to fill the darkened escape tube designed for abandoning the boat rather than what they were doing. Gromeko's breathing was shallow in the tight confines. It seemed minutes until the seawater filled the trunk. Then, effortlessly, Gromeko spun the wheel above him and pushed upward against it using his feet for leverage. The hatch opened, and he was halfway out of the trunk when he was able to take his first deep breath of tank air. He was relieved to be out of the man-made tomb.

He let himself settle on the forward deck of the K-122 before reaching forward to push the hatch down. He spun the small wheel, securing the hatch for the next man. Then he slipped his tank onto his back. Down below in the forward torpedo room, the lights would have told those waiting when he had opened the outer hatch and when he had closed it. They would pump the water out and the next Spetsnaz would soon follow him.

By the time Malenkov emerged, Gromeko was fully outfitted, with his tank on his back and his flippers off his belt and on his feet. Malenkov handed his tank to Gromeko, did an about-flip in the water, and dove headfirst back into the escape trunk. A second later he emerged tugging the bag with him. Gromeko secured the hatch for the third member.

OLIVER pulled the curtains back, careful not to spill the paper cup of "bug juice." They frowned on having the sugary fruit-flavored drink everyone called "bug juice" drunk anywhere except topside and in the chow hall. But he was alone and he still had an hour of work—if he didn't find anything wrong—to finish.

He looked at the clock on the bulkhead. Midnight plus twenty-five. He was going to be one tired puppy in the morning, whether he caught any shut-eye or not. Why did the chief have to be such a prick? Maybe being a prick was part of the personnel qualification standards for getting to wear the khaki uniform with the anchor on the collar?

He set the cup on the narrow shelf, watching it closely as he leaned down to pick up the preventive maintenance schedule from the plastic sleeves taped to the side of the small file cabinet. He opened the two-page card and scanned it.

He took a sip of his drink and laid the PMS card in front of him. All you had to do with PMS was go down the card, step by step, doing each item as it asked. Thankfully, this card did not require any tubes. He just had to check each hydrophone individually for attenuation and sensitivity. What the hell did they think he had been doing for the past two days with that Soviet submarine? Sipping tea and telling shitty sea stories? For a moment, Oliver thought about gundecking the checks—mark them as being done and slip the card back in its plastic cover—but just because others might have gundecked their preventive maintenance did not mean he would.

Oliver flipped off the sonar connection to all the hydrophones and waited a few seconds for the electronics to wind down. Then he flipped on the starboard-side hydrophones.

He lifted the cup and took a deep swig of the drink, his cheeks wrinkling at the sugar surge going across his tongue. What was the difference between a sea tale and a fairy tale? A sea tale starts with "This ain't no bullshit" instead of "Once upon a time." He choked at his own joke, spraying slight droplets of bug juice on the scope.

"Damn." He grabbed a nearby rag and started wiping away the stuff before it dried to a crusty spot, which the chief would spot in a minute and keep him away from Olongapo for two nights instead of one.

As he wiped, he noticed a slight noise spoke on the number four hydrophone. He pressed the headset tighter against his ear because the noise was in the same frequency range as the Echo submarine he had tracked for two days. Oliver wondered what noise from one of the navy's ships in port could be almost—no, absolutely—identical to a Soviet submarine electrical generator. Could he also just barely detect a sound behind this fifty-hertz noise?

He shut his eyes. His stomach growled. Fifty hertz! Soviet and Warsaw Pact nations' electrical sources put out fifty hertz to American sixty hertz.

Why would he be hearing "his" submarine inside the

harbor—No! He lifted the headset off his ears. Must be some sort of convergence zone peculiarity causing the submarine noise to bounce into the harbor. Oliver looked around. He licked his lips, aware of the dryness, and took a deep breath. What he should do is get the chief up here, but the chief would never get out of his rack. Lieutenant Burnham was the command duty officer, but by now he was in his stateroom.

He slid out of the seat and stood. The spike coming from the hydrophone showed the noise originating off the starboard side of the *Dale*. What was anchored behind them? He dashed out of the sonar space, through the dark confines of Combat, toward the hatch that separated the war-fighting heart of the ship from the bridge. Quickly he undogged the hatch and stepped onto the bridge for a brief moment before running out onto the starboard bridge wing, where he leaned against the railing.

Nothing! As far as he could see there was nothing between the *Dale* and the starlit natural barrier that curved back toward the entrance. He checked to see that the logistic ships anchored off the stern were nowhere near the noise spike, even though he knew it was a Soviet submarine he was hearing. To the left, the huge lighted silhouettes of the *Kitty Hawk* and *Tripoli* blocked his view of the guarded pier.

Oliver shut his eyes, swallowed. He looked at the waters, his eyes scanning back and forth along the line of bearing where the noise spoke originated. A minute later his eyes crossed the natural barrier. Somehow, if that noise was coming through the entrance, it had to be bouncing off something in the harbor to change its direction.

"What you doing, Matt?"

Oliver turned and looked up. It was Seaman Cleary. Oliver looked back at the water, then up again.

"You ain't about to jump, are ya?" Cleary laughed. " 'Cause if you do, I ain't jumping in to save you. Not with ole hammerhead patrolling the harbor."

Oliver shook his head. "Naw. I'm not about to jump, Tim. What are you doing on board?" he asked casually, turning his attention back to the dark waters of Subic. His mind roared over the possibilities of how he could be detecting a Soviet submarine while tied up pierside.

"Damn good thing you're not jumping, because I got the watch."

He should tell someone. Doctrine called for any contact that an operator was unsure of to be reported. But Oliver would be a laughing stock because no way he should be picking up a Soviet submarine.

He looked up. "Where's your sound-powered phone?"

Cleary lifted an arm from the railing and jerked his thumb over his shoulder. "Can't wear those things in this heat. Makes your ears sweat and I break out in a prickly heat. Besides, you can't hear the command duty officer when he's trying to sneak up on you. Ruins a good nap on watch," Cleary joked.

The noise of a liberty launch drew their attention. Laughter from sailors returning from a night on the wild side of Olongapo City reached their ears. A group were shouting, "Shit Man Fuck!" at the top of their lungs like rowdy cheerleaders celebrating an unexpected win. Raunchy laughter from the chorus followed each rendition.

"Lucky bastards," Cleary said. "If I had not had a physical discussion with some fucking chief off the . . ." He stopped, then added, "Damn. I forget, but it was one of the ships in the harbor. But I showed him. I took my face and beat the shit out of his fist."

Oliver looked up again. "Don't move! I'll be right back." He dashed through the hatchway.

Behind him, Cleary's voice carried. "Why? Why can't I move?"

Oliver dashed through the bridge, ducked as he ran through the hatch, and used his hands as he dodged around the equipment in Combat to get to Sonar. Breathing heavily, he pulled the curtains apart and stared at the display. The noise spike was still there.

He was back on the bridge wing in seconds, looking up at the signal bridge. Cleary was gone. He started up the ladder.

"Hey, man! Why can't I move?"

Oliver stepped off the rung back onto the deck of the bridge wing. He cupped his hands and looked up at Cleary. "Tim! I need you to call Mr. Burkeet and tell him to come to Sonar."

"Why?"

"Because I need him, Tim. I don't have time to explain."

Cleary snorted. "Shit, man, we're in Olongapo and stuck on board while every sailor in the fleet is out there enjoying the beer, flesh, and tossing quarters into Shit River."

"Tim, if you don't—"

Cleary raised his hand. "I can't call the lieutenant. I only have comms with the quarterdeck and Mr. Marshall is the in-port officer of the deck. You know what a dickhead he can be. You come up and call him."

"Who is the junior officer of the deck?"

Cleary's lips pursed as he concentrated. "I'm not sure," he said after a few seconds. "I think it is Boats Lowe."

"Tell Manny to come to Sonar."

Cleary smiled and threw a thumbs-up at Oliver. "That I can do."

Oliver disappeared off the bridge wing.

Moments later he was back in Sonar, his headset on his ears, when a sound like a quick flood of water rode across his ears then stopped. He concentrated. Only thing that could make an underwater noise such as this was an outer door opening, like the outer tube on a torpedo. He shivered. This was getting weird. His instructors had told him the oceans played havoc with noise sometimes, sending it hundreds of miles before someone heard it. Other times, you could be on top of a submarine with it making all kinds of noise—their sailors could be banging steel wrenches against the hull—and you wouldn't hear a peep.

GROMEKO waited outside the escape trunk, slowly moving his flippers to remain stationary. The hatch opened and the last member of the team, Lieutenant Dolinski, emerged, turned, and dove back into the escape trunk to pull the remaining bag free.

When he pulled it out, Gromeko leaned forward and secured the hatch. He made the thumbs-up sign to the other four, received same, and then looked at his fluorescent compass. He pointed in the direction they needed to go.

Chief Fedulova and Starshina Malenkov grabbed a handle each on their bag and started in the direction Gromeko pointed. Gromeko hovered. He looked in Dolinski's direction as the officer and Zosimoff grabbed the handles of the other bag. Then he turned and swam quickly to get ahead of Fedulova and Malenkov.

Behind him the submarine waited at periscope depth. Ahead, less than a hundred meters, was the shore and the thrill of doing a mission. Gromeko had no doubt they would do this without ever being detected. After all, who would believe a Soviet Spetsnaz team was skipping and jumping around the U.S. Naval Base at Subic Bay?

A long, dark shadow swam past between them and the submarine, its Jurassic-age body rippling smoothly through the nighttime waters.

"UP periscope," Bocharkov said. He squatted and flipped the handles down as the hydraulics lifted the scope. He pressed his head against the rubber fitting as he rode the scope to the surface. The shipboard lights seemed so close as he studied the ships. On one of the destroyers he could make out a sailor standing watch on top of the bridge.

OLIVER heard the hydraulic noise and wondered what was making it. It wasn't ballast pumps because they were different. This sound was smooth and it disappeared after only a few seconds.

The telephone on the bulkhead rang.

He slipped off his headset. "Sonar," he said in greeting.

"Oliver, this is Lowe. What the fuck are you doing?"

"Boats, I need Mr. Burkeet up in Sonar."

"It's after one in the morning, Oliver. You want me to wake the young lieutenant and tell him you want his ass up in Sonar?"

"Yes. It's important, Boats."

"So is sleep and passing a watch without a lot of officers running around loose," Manny Lowe replied. Then he whispered, "I got Marshall up here. Ain't that enough for a sailor to have to put up with?"

"Look, Manny, I wouldn't ask this if it wasn't important."

"Then why don't *you* go wake him up?"

"Because I have my equipment up and operating. I can't leave it on."

"Then turn it off."

"That's the problem."

"What's the problem?"

"I can't turn it off."

"If you can't turn it off, then it's the chief you want, not Lieutenant Burkeet. Burkeet can barely turn on and off his stateroom light, much less—"

"Look! Are you going to wake the lieutenant or what?"

Oliver heard Marshall ask Lowe who he was talking to. For a good minute, Oliver had to wait while Lowe told the lieutenant junior grade engineering officer about their conversation.

Finally Lowe said, "You got a pencil?"

Oliver scrambled around a moment and came up with one of the Skilcraft black ballpoint pens the navy had in abundance. "I got a pen."

"Here's his extension; you call him. Mr. Marshall said if you call bothering the quarterdeck again he's going to have you up to see the XO."

Oliver wrote down the number, hung up without saying good-bye, and dialed the extension. It rang for a long time without anyone answering. He should have known the lieutenant would be ashore or at the officers club with everyone else. Finally he hung up the telephone, turned back to the sonar console, and put the headset on. Probably best thing to do was not tell anyone. They'd laugh over his concern about hearing Soviet submarine noises while tied up pierside. After a few minutes he lifted the PMS card and started doing the preventive maintenance schedule even as periodically a new noise would pass over his headset. Each time, Oliver glanced at the console. It took about ten minutes for him to realize that whatever noise he was hearing, was always on the same bearing—two seven two. The clock showed ten minutes after one.

GROMEKO'S fingertips brushed the bottom before he saw it. He blinked a red light behind him twice, then glanced upward. Lights from the poles along the road bled into the waters. He swam upward a few meters until his head broke the surface. Behind him he heard the others surface. They were less than twenty meters from the rocky barrier that made up this portion of Olongapo Harbor.

A hand touched his shoulder. It was Dolinski. Zosimoff treaded water to the other side of the man. "There," the GRU officer said, pointing to his left.

The dark circular shadow outlining the huge drainage pipe was about fifty meters in that direction. Gromeko nodded, looked around, and pointed in that direction for Fedulova and Malenkov, who were behind the other three. He dove, knowing the others would follow. Along the shallow waters near the shore the five Spetsnaz members moved quietly, their flippers barely stirring the surface as they inched their way to the opening ahead of them.

Less than ten minutes later, the five men were inside the pipe. A trickle of water ran through the center of the ten-foot-wide drain. Without talking, they quickly removed their tanks, flippers, and gear. Malenkov reached into the bag and pulled out the chief's uniform. He was slipping on the black leather shoes by the time Gromeko was buttoning up his dungaree shirt.

Gromeko stepped to the edge of the pipe and flashed three dots three times with his red flashlight. Then he put it away. His watch showed ten minutes after one. He snapped his fingers, drawing everyone's attention, and pointed at his watch. Everyone looked at his own and understood. They were five minutes behind schedule.

Zosimoff was the last to finish. He tucked the 9mm pistol inside the top of his pants and pulled the dungaree shirt over it. The others did the same. "Do not pull the pistols unless we have no choice. Does everyone understand?"

They nodded and said, *"Da,"* in unison. The voices echoed inside the drain, causing everyone to go silent. Gromeko wondered for a moment if the team was up to this challenge.

Dolinski walked alongside each of them, checking their uniforms, making sure the line of the shirt, the belt buckle, and the zipper of the dungaree trousers were aligned. He slipped his fingers inside the top of Gromeko's trousers. "Nice tight fit, comrade," he whispered.

Malenkov went first, slipping around the side of the pipe and working his way slowly up the steep, dangerous side of the rocky barrier. Gromeko realized that any of them could slip and break an ankle right here. Better here than up there, he thought.

Gromeko followed. At the top, Malenkov reached over the railing of the wooden fence paralleling the road and helped him over. Dolinski followed with his bag, then Fedulova and Zosimoff were right behind him.

"We are ashore," Dolinski said.

"Sir, no Russian, please," Malenkov said in near accent-free English.

Gromeko nodded in agreement, putting his finger to his mouth.

"That way," Dolinski said in Russian.

They crossed the street. A line of warehouses stretched along the road. Closed gray doors large enough for trucks to drive through graced the ends of each warehouse.

"They all look the same," Zosimoff whispered.

"The building we want is behind the second row of warehouses," Dolinski replied.

Malenkov stepped ahead of the other four, shaking his head.

Gromeko knew what the young starshina was thinking, but none of them spoke English like he did. They had little choice but to use Russian. "Try to keep quiet," Gromeko said in heavily accented English.

"I don't speak English," Dolinski said aloud, "Besides," he shrugged, "do you see any Americans here?" He motioned up and down the street. "They are either all asleep or in one of their drunken orgies in town."

"Orgies?" Fedulova asked. "I've always wanted to see one of those."

"I would like to do more than see one," Zosimoff added quietly.

Malenkov stopped and turned. "Your voices carry."

Gromeko agreed. "No more talking. Comrade Dolinski,

you lead the way. You have a better knowledge of the location."

For the next five minutes no one spoke as they walked along the side of the road, straggling out with Malenkov in front. Dolinski and his satchel swinging alongside his right leg followed close behind the Spetsnaz sailor. Gromeko and Zosimoff were a meter apart. Chief Starshina Fedulova sauntered along in the rear, casually looking in every direction, as if expecting any moment for the Americans to jump out of the shadows from between the warehouses or come roaring down the road with their guns blazing.

Around the corner ahead of them the headlights of a car lit up the road.

"Get into the shadows," Fedulova said, stepping off the road.

"No!" Gromeko growled. "It is too late. They'll see us." He grabbed Zosimoff and draped his arm over the sailor's shoulders. "Hold me up as if I just finished a gallon of vodka."

The car appeared and slowed as it neared the five sailors, then stopped abreast of Malenkov.

A head appeared in the open window along with a flashlight. "What's going on here, Chief?" the man asked as his flashlight passed over the face of each of the men.

Malenkov jerked his thumb back at Gromeko. "Got a drunken sailor I'm taking back to the ship." He turned back to the team. "Keep walking. I didn't tell you to stop." He motioned.

"Shouldn't be out here, Chief," the man inside said as he withdrew his light. The left arm appeared, showing the stripes of a first-class petty officer.

"I know, and they're going to know in the morning when the boss sees them."

The petty officer laughed. "Well, this is a restricted area. Shouldn't be out here, but I'll let you go this time. I don't want a drunk vomiting in my car. What's your name, Chief?" the first-class asked, holding up a clipboard. "Gotta tell my chief when we get back to Security."

"Malenkov," Malenkov said. "Chief Malenkov."

"What ship are you on, Chief?"

"USS *Kitty Hawk.*"

"Oh, wow," the sailor said, shaking his head. "I have never had a hankering for duty on board a carrier. Too big and you never get to know everyone, and with the exception of Olongapo, most times you have to anchor out and take liberty launches for a beer."

Malenkov smiled. "I have to get back to my ship," he said, pointing down the road.

"No problem, Chief. And don't worry. Our chief never turns in other chiefs."

Malenkov nodded. "Thanks, sir. That is good." And he kept walking. Dolinski nodded as he walked by the open window.

"Did you hear that?" the first-class asked the unseen person on the shotgun side. "He called me sir. Chiefs can be sarcastic bastards, can't they?"

"Tell him your parents are married," the unseen person replied.

As Fedulova reached the window, the driver put the car in gear and drove off down the road.

The car disappeared around the bend behind them.

"It will be back," Dolinski said.

"How do you know?" Gromeko asked.

"It's a dead end. They will travel about another five or six kilometers before turning around and coming back along this road. We have to get off the road."

They were near the end of the row, with only two warehouses remaining. After a moment's hesitation, Dolinski pointed down the dark alleyway that separated the nearest two warehouses. He stepped off the road and onto the gravel.

Malenkov followed, then Gromeko and the others. Chief Fedulova waited a moment to give the other four more space, and then he disappeared into the shadows beside the building.

The telephone switching building should be at the end of these warehouses, according to the outline Dolinski had shown them. Gromeko hoped he was right. His left eye stung as a bead of sweat rolled into the corner of it. Instinctively he reached for a handkerchief that was not there, before using the long sleeve of the dungaree shirt to wipe his eye. In front of him Malenkov did the same a few minutes later.

"THEY should be ashore," Orlov said.

"I have not seen their flashlight signal, Officer of the Deck."

"Aye, sir. Orders?"

"We assume they made it and either they forgot to signal or I missed the flashes." Bocharkov sighed. He grabbed the handles of the periscope and spun it slowly in a three-hundred-sixty-degree arc. "No new contacts."

Since the departure of the Spetsnaz team, the control room of the K-122 had been collecting the name and disposition of every warship anchored and tied up pierside at Subic Naval Base. Bocharkov had also been collecting the location of the cranes and trying to identify the various buildings ashore. Never before had a Soviet submarine had the opportunity to see the inside of this harbor except through fuzzy satellite photographs. If he only had a camera. Something GRU should have thought about when they were deciding this mission.

"WELL, there you are again," Oliver said aloud. He looked at the clock. "Little past one thirty." He tossed the preventive maintenance sheet onto the deck. He tapped the scope with his index finger. "You're out there somewhere, aren't you? Out there, outside the harbor, waiting for us to come back out and play chase." An exasperated sigh escaped. "Couldn't do it if we wanted right now. Crew is out partying and I'm too pooped to pop."

Oliver took off the headset. That was the third . . . or was it the fourth . . . time he had heard the hydraulic sounds coming through the headsets. "Periscope," he said aloud. "You son of a bitch! You're bringing up your periscope every few minutes."

He pulled a pad of legal-size paper over, glanced at the clock, and wrote down the time. Then he looked at the other times. This was the third. A quick subtraction showed that each time was ten minutes apart. How often previously had the Echo raised its periscope?

"You got to be at the harbor entrance," Oliver said aloud, the grayness of fatigue disappearing. "I got you, you son of a bitch. You're outside the harbor watching us. Waiting for us to appear." He drummed the pencil on the small shelf. "Why?"

"What's the problem, Oliver?"

He turned. Lieutenant Burkeet stood in the opening. It was 1:45 A.M.

"THIS is the building," Dolinski said quietly.

Across an open space, a small two-story building, painted the same dark gray as the warehouses, stood alone. Multiple lines ran from nearby telephone poles into a central box hidden on the left side of the building. No lights were showing through the bars protecting each of the small windows lining the building front. And a metal bar with a large lock sealed the main door.

"We got to get in there," Dolinski said.

"Do you have the tools to do this?" Gromeko asked. "Or do we blow it?"

Dolinski's forehead wrinkled. "Blow it?" he asked sarcastically. "Why would we blow it? Let the Americans know someone has been here?" He opened the satchel and pulled a small box out.

"We have to get these lights out," Gromeko said, ignoring Dolinski's tone. "No one is going anywhere unless we do." He pointed at Fedulova. "Take Zosimoff and work your way to the right. Look for the main electric box."

"Yes, sir," Fedulova answered, stepping quickly to the right, tapping Zosimoff on the shoulder. "Come, comrade."

"Malenkov, come with me." Gromeko looked at Dolinski. "Wait until the lights are out."

"Takes too long," Dolinski said. "Wait here in the shadows, provide backup." Without waiting for the others, he stepped into the opened lighted area and crossed toward the building.

Gromeko looked to where Fedulova and Zosimoff had disappeared. Arguing with Dolinski was bad for the team.

Everyone needed to know who the central authority was so they knew whom to obey. Dolinski was usurping the chain of command.

When the Spetsnaz lieutenant was halfway across the opening, Gromeko said, "Let's go. Spread out."

He stepped out into the light and started to follow. He and Malenkov separated right and left. To the right Fedulova and Zosimoff had disappeared around the ring of light, probably hidden on the other side, near the next row of silent warehouses.

Dolinski walked up to the entrance door to the small telephone exchange. A light overhead lit up the white Dixie-cup sailor hat that had tilted downward to stop at his eyebrows.

Gromeko licked his lips. A whistle broke the silence for a moment, causing him to flinch. It came from the left, far away, and then went quiet. He assumed it was some American sailor trying to get the attention of another. Suddenly the lights went out.

"Govno!" Dolinski said aloud.

Gromeko looked around, his eyes still adjusting to the sudden darkness. Dolinski turned on his flashlight, the light shining on the locked door. Gromeko rushed forward to join the other lieutenant.

"How are you doing?" he asked quietly.

"I am doing not so well, comrade. My eyes are blind."

"Mine, too. But we'll adjust quickly." And they did. First the background light began to be discernible, followed quickly by the starlight. Gromeko squinted when he looked at the door where Dolinski had his flashlight pointed. A red lens covered the flashlight, producing a red light to work by.

"Here," Dolinski said. "Hold the light."

Gromeko took the flashlight and focused the beam on the locked door.

Dolinski unzipped the small pouch he had and pulled out two small tools. "Locksmith tools," he mumbled.

He slipped a small, flat metal tool out and flipped it open. A tiny round wire-like protrusion clicked into place. The end of the wire bent around at a slight angle. Dolinski pulled another tool out.

This one was straight with a slight flat blade on it—reminded Gromeko of a tiny screwdriver.

Dolinski worked both tools into where the key would go, slid them around, and a slight click could be heard as the door unlocked. "We can go in now, comrade," Dolinski said, pushing the metal bar up and out of the way. "But once I open this door, most likely an alarm will sound somewhere on this base, telling someone that the door is ajar. We can expect company soon afterward."

"How long?"

Dolinski shrugged. "How do I know? I don't even know what I will find when I do open the door. If the banks of switches are secured behind another door, then most likely we will be pressed to finish before we have company."

"I will deploy the men."

Dolinski shook his head. "As much as I would like to show the Americans how Russians are prepared to die for their country, I don't think we would accomplish anything by doing it here."

"I will still deploy the men," Gromeko insisted.

"They are deployed. Tell them if the Americans show up, it is better that one or two of us are captured than everyone. They are to warn us, then slip away to warn the submarine."

Gromeko agreed. He disappeared into the shadows. Dolinski waited. Within two minutes he was back. "Fedulova and Zosimoff found the main fuse box and pulled the lever. Chief Fedulova understands."

"Then you should go join them."

Gromeko shook his head. "No, you will need someone to hold the light and to help."

Dolinski nodded. "Okay, here we go." With that he turned the knob and pushed the door open. Row upon row of switchboards with cables running from one female plug to another were revealed as the light moved along the bay of equipment. Dolinski stepped inside, the light continuing to move back and forth across the switchboards. "I am looking . . . ," he mumbled.

Gromeko turned at the door and pulled his pistol. "You have twenty minutes."

Dolinski chuckled. "Not hardly. Don't forget that some-where on this base someone is looking at the alarm and wondering why it went off. Eventually they will send someone. Fifteen minutes if we are lucky."

"Then, hurry."

"There it is," he said, the light focused on several pieces of equipment with no plugs in them. He laughed. "Five minutes is all I am going to need here. It will take longer to string the antenna. Give me five minutes. Looks to me, Motka, that we may be out of here in fifteen minutes."

Gromeko nodded, unseen by the other lieutenant.

"HEY, Chief!" Turnipseed, the petty officer at the security consoles, shouted. "I got an alarm on the telephone center."

Chief Bellis tossed the latest issue of *Sports Illustrated* onto the table, pulled his legs off it, and stood up. "It ain't raining," he said, walking to the front door and opening it. The humid heat of the Philippine night hit him in the face.

He shut the door, letting the air-conditioning wash over him. "Though it's humid enough to be raining over there. Anything else lighting up?"

"No, Chief," Turnipseed answered. "Nothing else. If it's a rain short, then it's raining only near the warehouses."

The front door opened and Petty Officers Forster and Meeks stepped inside.

"Wow!" Forster said. "That feels good."

"Didn't you two just come from the warehouse side?" Bellis asked.

Forster nodded. "Sure did."

"Was it raining?"

"Naw," Meeks answered, as he opened the nearby refrigerator and pulled a bottle of Coca-Cola out. He grabbed a nearby church key and pried the top off. "Only thing we saw was a chief and a couple of sailors taking one of his drunks back to the *Kitty Hawk*." He turned the drink up and chugged.

"Don't forget to put your quarter in the tin," Turnipseed said.

"You'll get your money."

"*Kitty Hawk*?" Bellis asked.

"That's what the chief said," Forster answered.

"What were they doing over there?"

"Like Meeks said, Chief, they were taking a drunken sailor back to the ship."

"That doesn't sound right," Bellis answered, stepping away from the front of the air conditioner. "The *Kitty Hawk* is way over on the other side, nowhere near the warehouses, so how in the hell did the chief find his drunk over there?"

"Had to be lost," Turnipseed offered.

"Or taking a night walk for the solitude," Meeks put in with a laugh. "There were five of them."

"Five? What are five sailors doing in the oh-dark-thirty hours of the morning over there? Better yet, answer me how in the hell did they get over there?" Chief Bellis finished. He pointed at Forster. "You two get back in the patrol car and get your butts over to the telephone switching building and check on it. Wouldn't surprise me if your sailors decided to take a leak and are trying to find a head. If they are, you bring them back to Security so that chief and I can have a friendly chat."

"Ah, come on, Chief. It's nearly two in the morning," Forster whined.

"It ain't. It's fifteen minutes until two and in the time you've spent here whining to me about doing what I've told you, you could be halfway there."

"Ah, Chief, we just finished an hour in that car. There's no air-conditioning," Forster objected.

"Well, next time, you'll learn to get all the information."

"Can we have guns this time?" Meeks asked. "Guns always make me feel safe."

"No, you can't have a gu—a piece. It's called a goddamn piece, Meeks, and I wouldn't trust you with a gun. Goddamn Arkansas razorback! You'd shoot someone just to see if it's true that guns kill."

"Oh, they kill all right, Chief. I just don't want someone else finding out on me."

"Come on, Meeks," Forster said. "Let's go." He grabbed his Dixie-cup hat and jammed it on his head.

Meeks opened the refrigerator again and grabbed a second soda. "You want one?"

"Yeah, but I want a Sprite soda."

"That's seventy-five cents!"

"You'll get your money, Turnipseed. Christ," Meeks said, looking at Forster. "You'd think Mama Turnipseed owned the damn thing."

"He does," Forster said as they shut the door behind them.

"Chief, Meeks owes me seventy-five cents."

"That's your problem."

Bellis walked to the desk, picked up the telephone, and dialed the Subic Operations Center. A moment later he was talking to the command duty officer, a Lieutenant Wagner with a deep Bostonian accent. Bellis quickly brought the lieutenant up-to-date on the security light emanating from the telephone switching building near the warehouses. Wagner said he was going to send a couple of marines out that way. The chief asked that they not shoot Forster and Meeks, as much pleasure as it would bring.

"What'd he say?" Turnipseed asked, reaching up and tapping the light again, as if the act would cause it to go away.

"He said he didn't trust a bunch of us enlisted to resolve a security light so he's sending the marines out to check on it."

Turnipseed shook his head. "That's Lieutenant Wagner for you. He don't trust nobody. Sending marines to check on a faulty security light is like sending . . . like sending . . . well, you know."

"Yeah, I know," Bellis said quietly, glancing at the door. He had a bad feeling about this. Marines and sailors were known to have misunderstandings. Olongapo was a great place for having them.

TEN

THE knocking woke him. MacDonald raised himself onto his elbows and turned on the table lamp. The bulkhead clock showed five minutes to two. "Come in!" he shouted.

Joe Tucker and Lieutenant Burnham entered, stopping just inside the stateroom door.

"What's wrong, XO?" MacDonald spun around in the bed, planting his bare feet on the small throw rug Brenda had given him after seeing the sparse compartment he would call home for three years.

"Just got this in from Naval Intelligence, sir. Top secret," Joe Tucker said, as if that explained everything.

MacDonald reached for the message board. Burnham stayed near the door, as if positioning himself for a quick exit. Draftees such as him should not be allowed to avoid it by joining the navy.

"About our Echo submarines?" If it was, it was something that could have waited until morning.

Joe Tucker shook his head. "Best you read it."

"Mr. Burnham, turn on the overhead light, please."

Burnham flipped the switch. The overhead white light filled the small stateroom.

The two khaki-clad officers waited while MacDonald sat on the edge of his rack in his T-shirt and Skivvies reading the page-and-a-half message. He glanced at Joe Tucker once while reading. The world gone crazy. A minute later, he closed the metal covering over the message.

"What do you think?"

Joe Tucker cleared his throat. "It might explain why we had a tattletale and two cruise missile submarines doing an anticarrier exercise against us last Thursday."

MacDonald looked at Burnham. "Your thoughts, Woodrow?"

"Sir, I agree with the XO."

"Not much we can do about this," MacDonald said, tapping the message board. "It's half a world away."

"There is an operations plan being prepared for the chief of naval operations to release. It would divert the *Kitty Hawk* battle group to the Middle East."

"Says here that Naval Intelligence expect the Israelis to launch a preemptive strike sometime in the next few hours. Once that happens, we have only two ways to the conflict. One is to overfly Saudi Arabia, which isn't a belligerent at this time; the other is to enter the Red Sea, which the navy won't allow an aircraft carrier to do. It bottles us up. Kind of like sending one into the Persian Gulf."

"Means we go around the tip of South America."

"By the time we got there, the fighting would be over." MacDonald bit his lip. He handed the message board to Joe Tucker. "The Israelis aren't going to wait for us. What's the status of our steam plant? We still have steam?"

"I authorized them to secure engine room number one earlier today, Skipper. There were some steam pipe repairs that needed to be done."

"We can't get under way?"

Joe Tucker shook his head. "We are scheduled to be here another two days. Stillman and I discussed the idea of securing one today; they'd do the repair work and scheduled maintenance through the night. Then tomorrow we'd do the other steam room. So if we had to get under way, we could, on the other engine room, and bring the other up within a day."

MacDonald nodded. Stillman was the mustang chief engineer of the *Dale*. Mustangs were a rough lot. They were enlisted men who had somehow managed to receive a commission based on their technical knowledge. "Keep engine room number two up and ready for emergent departure, in the event this Naval Intelligence notice is accurate."

"If it's not, then it will be the Arabs who will attack," Burnham said, drawing the attention of both senior officers.

"Why do you say that?" MacDonald asked.

Burnham crossed his arms and leaned against the bulkhead. "They've been moving—"

"They?"

"Skipper, the 'they' is Egypt and Syria," Burnham answered, then continued as if he were in a classroom. "Jordan has increased its presence along its border, but has been silent on the war drums that Egypt and Syria are beating." He shook his head. "No, sir—they're going to war, so either Israel will do the preemptive thing or Egypt and Syria will blitzkrieg across the border and do what they have been promising."

"What promise?" Joe Tucker asked.

"Push them into the sea, eradicate Israel, kill every Jew—man, woman, and child—in the country."

MacDonald nodded. "Thanks, Lieutenant, but I cannot see the world standing by and watching something like that happen."

Burnham uncrossed his arms. "The world has stood aside in our lifetime, and if not at this time or in this place, we will see it do it again."

"Out of our area of operations right now," MacDonald said. "Anything else?" he asked, looking at Joe Tucker.

The sound of footsteps came from the passageway outside. Lieutenant Burkeet stuck his head inside the stateroom.

"Looks as if I'm hosting a wardroom party up here," MacDonald said, drawing the navy-issued gray blanket over his knees and Skivvies.

"Skipper, XO, OPSO," Burkeet said. "I hate to bother you, but Oliver insists he has the Echo submarine on passive sonar."

"Can't be," Joe Tucker said.

Burnham made a downward motion with his hand. "Man

must have just come back from liberty." He looked at Mac-Donald. "Still living in his glory of tracking the thing for two days."

"I listened to the noise he was listening to," Burkeet protested.

Joe Tucker shrugged. "Most likely a noise from one of the other ships in port."

"Has Chief Stalzer listened to it?" MacDonald asked.

Burkeet shook his head, recalling stumbling into the chief when Stalzer was returning from downtown. "I'm not sure he's on board."

Burnham laughed. "Oh, he's on board all right; just not sure we'll be able to wake him." Everyone looked at Burnham. "He came back aboard before midnight. I'd say he had a few before returning."

"If he was able to walk aboard, then he's able to get up and go double-check whatever it is that Oliver has," MacDonald snapped. Several seconds of silence passed. "Look, Don, you go wake your chief and get back to Sonar. The rest of you get out of here so I can dress."

DOLINSKI stood up. He wiped his hands on the fake U.S. Navy dungarees. "That should do it."

"We can go?" Gromeko asked from the doorway.

"Not yet," Dolinski said as he walked briskly toward Gromeko. "I've got to string the antenna." He squatted by the knapsack, shined his red-lens flashlight into it, and pulled a coil of wire from it.

"Antenna?"

"It's easy. I am going to connect it here to the monitoring system. Then I will run it to one of the poles outside: a line antenna. It will also turn the lines into antennas to help transmit the conversations our system picks up."

"All that fresh wire will be noticed."

Dolinski shook his head. "I won't be using all of this. Just enough to— Why am I explaining this to you, comrade? You know nothing about electromagnetic waves and propagation."

I know about arrogance, Gromeko thought, turning his attention toward the outside once again. He watched as Dolinski wound the wire through and under the overhead wires and then with a long blade made a hole to slip the coil of wire through.

Nearly a minute passed before Dolinski stood. "It is done. Now we go outside." Dolinski walked quickly toward Gromeko, bent and without stopping grabbed his knapsack and walked briskly by him.

Gromeko followed, holding the pistol in his hand. He had pulled it a few minutes ago as his anxiety grew over what he considered inordinate time being taken by the whistling Dolinski. "Have you tested it?"

"We are too close to test it. We will test it once we are in the drainpipe."

Dolinski picked up the coil of wire from the ground outside. He tossed it up so it went over the top of the lines running from the building to the nearby telephone pole. He did is several times. "There! That should do it."

Unwinding the wire, the Spetsnaz officer walked backward to the pole, then holding the coil with one hand, he started to climb the steel rungs protruding from the pole. Stopping at the top, he pulled the wire tight, then wound it around the lines there several times before cutting it.

"Here!" Dolinski said to Gromeko, dropping the coil down to him.

Gromeko caught the wire and put it into Dolinski's knapsack. A moment later the two officers stood side by side. Dolinski's eyes traveled along the lines running from the building to the top of the pole.

"Too dark to tell if it sticks out."

"It doesn't stick out, Motka," Dolinski said. "I just wanted to make sure it was not sagging."

From a distance the sound of a siren caused both officers to pause. "Think they are coming here?" Gromeko asked.

"If they had any type of security here on the base, they would have been here minutes ago." Dolinski grunted. "Maybe we will be lucky and it will be their marines."

A second siren joined the first.

"We should hurry." *Or we may be unlucky and it will be their marines.*

"On second thought, maybe tangling with their marines

would ruin our covert mission." Dolinski laughed. "Though I would enjoy a chance to see if they are as tough as they say." With that, he broke into a run. Gromeko followed.

When they reached the alley where they had entered, the other three Spetsnaz waited.

"Let's get out of here," Gromeko whispered, twirling his finger in the air.

The five men took off at a run, Fedulova slowed to bring up the rear. Zosimoff sprinted forward taking the point. Malenkov was slightly behind him, knowing his English would be the only thing that might buy them time to reach the waters.

They passed the first set of warehouses and were between the last rows when car lights lit up the end of the warehouse on the left. Zosimoff stopped, squatted, and whistled. Malenkov caught up and squatted beside him. Both had their pistols out. A siren accompanied the car light.

Gromeko dashed to the right and Dolinski to the left, both men flattening themselves against the warehouses. Behind them, Chief Fedulova went to one knee on the gravel-filled terrain.

Across from Gromeko, Dolinski had the strap from the knapsack across his left shoulder. His pistol was in his right hand.

Gromeko licked his lips. Fighting their way off this base would endanger their mission, and it would not take long for the Americans to discover the K-122.

The lights disappeared even as the sound of the engine and siren grew. The car was going down the alley on the other side of the warehouse where Dolinski had taken cover. Gromeko stepped into the center of the alley. "Go! Go! Go!" he shouted, figuring the siren would cover his shouts.

The five men were up, back in the center of the alley, sprinting toward the road. If they could get in the water, nothing would stop them.

As Zosimoff reached the road, a fresh set of lights blazed around the corner. He was caught in their light. Malenkov dove to the right side for the shadows.

"Halt! Stay right where you are!" an American voice commanded.

Gromeko motioned Dolinski to the right. Both men

sprinted along the edge of the shadow. Behind them the siren was fading as the car drove between the next row of warehouses. Gromeko glanced back, but Fedulova was nowhere to be seen. But he was back there, Gromeko knew that. No Spetsnaz left another. What was the French saying, "One for all and all for one"? It could have been the motto for the Special Forces of many nations.

Zosimoff opened his left hand and let the pistol fall onto the ground.

"Sarge, he's got a gun!"

Familiar clicks like a quick cacophony of crickets told Gromeko and the others that there were more than two or three hidden behind the bright lights. Though Gromeko could not see them, he knew weapons were aimed at Zosimoff. He touched Dolinski and the two officers hurried forward.

"Raise your hands!"

Zosimoff stood, his head turned toward the unseen men hidden by the end of the right warehouse.

Malenkov reached the end of the warehouse, his back pressed against it. "Raise your hands!" he said in Russian.

Zosimoff raised his hands.

"Put them on top of your head!"

The sound of running boots on the graveled road drew their attention. Gromeko and Dolinski reached the area near Malenkov.

"Get him, men! Knock his ass on the ground! Hemmings, you get that piece!" Three marines in full utility uniforms, carrying M-14 carbines, came into sight. Running full-tilt at Zosimoff. The first one drew his weapon back as if intending to smack Zosimoff in the face. The other two kept the barrels aimed at what they thought was a wayward sailor available for some Marine Corps attention.

Zosimoff moved fast as the first marine reached him, shoving his right palm into the man's nose and grabbing the carbine as the man yelled in pain on his way down to his knees. Before Gromeko could shout "No," Zosimoff had fired an automatic burst, taking out the other two men. Gunfire erupted as bullets ripped into Zosimoff.

Malenkov leaned around the end of the building, took aim, and fired four quick shots in unison.

Behind them, the sound of another siren grew. Gromeko glanced back. Headlights were coming down the alley behind them.

The gunfire tapered off. Gromeko dashed forward, grabbed Zosimoff, and pulled him into the shadows. He glanced to the right, counted two other marines. One of them was pulling the other to the other side of the warehouse.

"Now!" Gromeko shouted. He lifted Zosimoff over his shoulder. "Into the water!"

The car behind them rocketed up on its rear wheels as it left the alleyway of the rear set of warehouses. It slammed down on the gravel before plummeting into the alley where the Spetsnaz team was stalled. Two bullet shots rang out. The tires on the left side of the car exploded, causing the driver to lose control. The car drove into the warehouse with a loud crash as it hit. Cursing from inside told Gromeko whoever was in there was still alive.

"I'm going to kill them!" someone shouted from the open window of the car.

Malenkov dashed across the road and took position on the other side. A pepper of gunfire hit the gravel, sending bits over his head. He fired a couple of shots at the marines.

Gromeko walked as fast as he could across the road, the weight of Zosimoff holding him down. Dolinski walked alongside, firing his pistol calmly, without aiming, at the end of the warehouse where the last two marines were. "That will keep their heads down."

"That was Russian, Sarge!" one of the marines shouted.

Gromeko was unable to make out the reply. His English was not as good as Malenkov's. He reached the other side. Malenkov stood to help ease Zosimoff down. A bullet caught Malenkov in the chest, knocking him backward into the water. Malenkov turned and pulled himself toward the rocks, holding onto it.

"How badly are you hurt?"

"I am fine," Malenkov said, running his hand over his chest.

"Just a little blood is all." He held up his left hand covered in blood. "And I seem to have lost my pistol."

Gromeko and Dolinski lay down on the rough rocks leading to the water. "Where is the chief?" Dolinski asked. He leaned up and fired another shot at the marines.

"Stay there, Starshina Malenkov," Gromeko said. "We're coming."

One of the marines dashed to the truck, reached in the driver's side door and pulled his walkie-talkie out. The sound of urgent words could be heard by the Soviets. There was little doubt that this place was going to be flooded with reinforcements at any time.

Fedulova ran from his position at the warehouse toward the truck. The marine on the walkie-talkie didn't see him until too late. Fedulova pistol-whipped him across the face, and then put the barrel against the man's face. He looked at the other marine at the end of the warehouse and in Russian told him to drop it.

Gromeko doubted the American understood the words, but the intent was obvious. Instead of dropping his weapon, the marine fell back into the shadows.

"Leave him, Chief!" Gromeko shouted. He looked at Dolinski. "Help me," he said, nodding down at Zosimoff.

Fedulova whipped the pistol against the captive's head, knocking him out, then stood and sprinted toward the officers.

By the time the two men were at the edge of the water, the chief had come over to the side of the road. "Sir, let me help."

"Get Malenkov," Gromeko said. "We got Zosimoff."

Within a minute, the five men were in the water, treading it softly as they eased out into the harbor away from the lights. Then they turned left, working their way toward the drainpipe. Behind them, the sound of voices and shouts filled the night for the first few minutes, before sirens joined the group. Gromeko wondered for a moment how American prisons were.

"OKAY, Oliver," Chief Stalzer snapped, running his handkerchief over his face, wiping away the water from his quick splashes at the sink when they woke him. "What in the hell do you have?" he asked, the words trailing off when he caught sight of Burkeet sitting on the other chair.

"Oliver thinks he has the Soviet Echo on sonar, Chief."

"Inside Subic? Could be, but they'd be so far out; it would be an anomaly, sir. I doubt we are picking up a Soviet submarine tied up pierside here, sir. We got too much self-generated noise from this many ships parked about the place."

"The skipper is on his way down, Chief. I would like you to see what Oliver has. I would like to be able to tell the captain exactly what we have."

Oliver wanted to shout. He wanted to stand up and tell them both to go to hell. He wanted to cry, too. This was the Echo. He knew it. And he had doubts the chief would agree with him, because the chief was just like that. Deriding him all the time and even more so since he had been the main man tracking the submarine.

"Give me the headset," Stalzer said, snapping his fingers as he held his hand out.

Oliver handed it to him.

Then both he and Burkeet watched as Stalzer listened to the noise. "I don't hear anything."

"UP periscope," Bocharkov said, his eyes riding the eyepiece on the way up. Belowdecks, the sump pump kicked in.

"I thought I told everyone to secure everything!" he said sharply, leaning away from the eyepiece. "Secure those pumps! Now!"

Orlov grabbed the microphone and relayed the order to Engineering.

OLIVER put the headset on. Almost immediately the sound of hydraulics filled his ears. "I hear something."

"Lieutenant, I'm telling you there is nothing there."

Oliver took the headset off. "Here, Chief. Maybe there wasn't anything when you had them on, but there is something now." As Stalzer took the headset, Oliver reached up and turned on the speaker.

The sound of hydraulics was drowned out by the rise and fall of another piece of equipment.

Stalzer pressed the headset against his ears. He reached

forward and tuned the passive sonar, watching the frequency readout of the noise. He paused at fifty hertz, and then rapidly moved it to sixty hertz, paused, then back to fifty. A deep breath filled the chief's chest. He lifted the headset. "Damn!"

On the speaker, the rising and falling sound of the equipment stopped.

Stalzer looked at the readout. "Shit, man, fuck, Oliver." Then the chief looked at Burkeet. "He does have a Soviet submarine, sir."

"Heard that hydraulics?" Oliver asked, smiling. "Damn, I knew it."

"That was a periscope coming up, and the louder noise was one of those well-made Soviet pumps. Stupid skipper to keep those pumps working if he is just outside Subic Bay."

"So Oliver is right? We have a Soviet submarine inside Subic Bay?"

"Sir, Subic Bay is a big-ass bay. He could be a hundred miles from here, his noise riding the underwater currents."

Oliver squirmed with pleasure in his seat. "Damn, I knew it."

Stalzer slapped him lightly upside the back of the head. "Don't be so happy about it."

"It's too loud to be a hundred miles out, Chief."

Burkeet looked at Stalzer. "You think?"

Stalzer ran his hand across his face. "Sir, I may have exaggerated with saying a hundred miles. The sump-pump noise is something that would ride for miles, but the hydraulic noise of the periscope is not that loud. Most times you have to be in direct path to hear it." He sighed. "I know there is going to be no living with Oliver, but the only way Oliver could be getting this," he said, shaking his head, "is if that submarine is within ten to fifteen miles of the *Dale*."

"Could be closer."

Stalzer slapped him lightly upside the head again. "Yes, Oliver, it could be closer. It could a few hundred feet away, but it ain't. What submarine would be stupid enough to come this close. . . ." His voice trailed off.

No one spoke for a few seconds, before Burkeet chuckled. "Right, Chief. You're joking, aren't you?"

Stalzer shook his head. "I can't think of any other way a

noise spike that cuts right into the harbor barriers west of us could be picked up by a destroyer tied up pierside, sir. I know water plays a lot of tricks on us with sound, but I've never seen anything like this."

The sound of footsteps drew their attention. The captain stuck his head inside the small sonar cavity just as the sound of hydraulics filled the space. The clock read ten minutes after two.

"HE'S dead," Dolinski said as they dragged Zosimoff out of the water and onto the rocks below the drainpipe.

Gromeko nodded.

Fedulova and Malenkov swam up. Gromeko and Dolinski helped pull Malenkov out of the water and into the pipe.

Fedulova followed, turning over on his back, breathing heavily. "Damn, you weigh a lot, Malenkov."

"I don't think it is me," Malenkov gasped.

"How do you feel?" Gromeko asked.

"My chest is on fire."

"Help me," Gromeko said to Dolinski. The two officers pulled Malenkov farther into the drainpipe.

Dolinski sat down on the curved side of the pipe while Gromeko and Fedulova laid the wounded Spetsnaz warrior along the bottom of the pipe. A narrow stream of water rose up along the man's shoulders until it flowed around Malenkov's arms, continuing its gravity-fed journey to the exit.

Dolinski's hands rooted in the knapsack until he found the small receiver. He lifted it, unstrung two loose earpieces, and put them on. He turned on his flashlight, the red light illuminating the controls on the receiver as he duckwalked to the edge of the pipe.

Gromeko opened the wounded sailor's dungaree shirt. The bullet had penetrated the upper left part of Malenkov's chest, near the underarm. Bubbles of blood came out every time he took a breath.

"Looks as if it has hit your lung, Malenkov," Gromeko said. Turning to Fedulova, he ordered, "Give me the first aid kit."

Fedulova grabbed one from one of the divers' belts lying along the sides of the curved pipe.

"Lieutenant Dolinski and Chief Fedulova, go ahead and get out of those clothes and into your gear."

"In a moment," Dolinski said. "One more minute," he mumbled softly, pressing the right earpiece against his head. He smiled. "The mission is a success. I can hear the telephone calls of the Americans."

"Then get changed," Gromeko snapped.

"I am already doing that," Dolinski replied, wrapping the earpieces around the receiver and jamming it into the knapsack. "I am already doing that," he repeated.

Fedulova and Dolinski worked as quietly as possible, pulling off the American dungarees and slipping into their underwater gear.

Gromeko worked on Malenkov. It took a couple of minutes to get gauze over the wound, run tape across it, under Malenkov's arm, and around the neck on the other side.

"Feels better already," Malenkov said softly. He put his hands down and attempted to push himself up. He moaned as he collapsed back onto the bottom of the pipe.

"Don't move," Gromeko said. He grabbed a nearby diver's belt and worked it around Malenkov's waist. "This will keep you from bobbing to the surface."

Malenkov chuckled. "To die on enemy soil is to die for our nation. I just never expected to do it this soon."

"You're not going to die," Gromeko said. "All you have is a bleeding chest wound."

"Just a bleeding chest wound?" Malenkov asked with a hint of sarcasm and a smile barely visible in the shadows. "Lieutenant, you can't take me with you."

"Here, let me talk with Malenkov while you change, Lieutenant," Fedulova said.

"We can't leave his equipment with him," Dolinski said.

"We aren't going to leave him."

"We can't take him with us. He is right. He is dying. Leave him here, if you want him to live." Dolinski shrugged. "If he does live, then the Americans will take care of him. They take care of everything."

Gromeko put his face a few inches from Dolinski. "We do not leave our shipmates behind," he said, accenting each word separately.

"He will endanger all of us."

"Then we will be endangered together."

"The lieutenant is right, sir," Malenkov said. "Leave me, but leave me a weapon. That way you will not have to worry about the Americans capturing me."

"Quiet, everyone." No one spoke as Gromeko quickly changed.

Chief Fedulova and Lieutenant Dolinski waited at the mouth of the drainpipe, watching for signs of the Americans. Above them, the noise of vehicles passing back and forth told them the warehouse area was flooded with U.S. marines.

Small beams of light searched the waters where they had fled earlier. With each sweep the lights moved along the road.

Dolinski jerked his thumb at Malenkov. "It will not be long before someone thinks of looking in this pipe. Starshina Malenkov is right. Leave him. Give him a weapon. He will die like a true Spetsnaz."

"Looks as if the boats we were told about are coming this way, Lieutenant," Fedulova said.

"Where?" both Lieutenants asked in unison.

"There," Fedulova answered, pointing past Dolinksi toward the piers where the destroyers were tied up.

"Could be the liberty launches we were told about."

Fedulova shook his head. "Most likely they are, but most likely they have been requisitioned to search for us."

Motion to the far left caught their eyes as new running lights appeared around the end of one of the huge logistic ships anchored a hundred meters or so from the piers.

"Those are moving fast," Fedulova observed.

Gromeko stumbled away toward his gear. The curved pipe was not made for walking. He sat down on the rippled curved body of the pipe and put on his flippers. "I am ready." He looked at Malenkov. "This is going to be painful, but you can do it, Starshina Malenkov."

"It is about time we go," Dolinski said. "If the K-122 hears the commotion, the captain may have to choose between the four of us and the one hundred thirty officers and men on board."

Fedulova nodded, his lower lip pressing his upper lip upward. "I could see where the captain would have a very hard decision to make."

"Let's go," Dolinski said.

"First, we clean up our mess. Open your knapsack." Gromeko looked at Fedulova. "Get me some rocks, heavy ones."

"What for?" Dolinski asked.

"If we have to drop these knapsacks, then we want them on the bottom of the harbor, not floating on the surface."

Fedulova eased over the side of the drain into the water, his head disappearing beneath the waves.

Dolinski opened his knapsack. "What for?" he asked.

Gromeko crammed their American uniforms into it. "We can leave these uniforms behind."

Dolinski held up his knapsack. "We cannot leave this behind."

"I know, but the uniforms we can."

Fedulova surfaced, placing several rocks on the edge of the pipe. "Is that enough?" He picked up a couple more rocks near the edge of the pipe. "These are bigger"

"Let me put some rocks in your knapsack, Uri," Gromeko said to Dolinski.

"My knapsack is not going to be dropped," Dolinski said.

"We may not have a choice. If the Americans capture . . . or kill us, then we do not want the knapsacks bobbing to the surface with our bodies."

Dolinski looked as if he were going to argue, but instead he opened his knapsack.

Gromeko nodded. He tossed a belt to Fedulova. "Put this on Zosimoff. Then he grabbed the knapsack and started cramming Malenkov's and Zosimoff's wet suits into it. He reached over and pulled the American uniforms from Dolinski's knapsack. "Put these together in the event we have to ditch them."

"I thought the rocks were for that."

Gromeko nodded. He picked up several of the rocks and tossed them into both knapsacks. "That should take them to the bottom, if we have to let them go." He leaned over to Malenkov. "You still with us?"

"I have not gone anywhere, sir."

"Lieutenant Dolinski, help me put his flippers on."

With the flippers on, Gromeko leaned over the man. "I have to lift you to put your tank on."

Malenkov nodded, but neither expected the cry of pain that escaped. For several seconds they waited for the Americans to appear over the edge of the pipe. When nothing happened, Dolinski and Gromeko helped Malenkov through his painful slide to the edge of the pipe. Fedulova, already treading the water at the end of the pipe, reached up and helped Malenkov into the water.

Fedulova took the face mask off, dipped it in the water, and then slid it over Malenkov's face. Malenkov raised his right hand in a weak sign of "okay."

"Chief, you stay with him. Lieutenant Dolinski, you carry the knapsacks. I will tow Zosimoff's body with me."

"One question, Lieutenant?" Fedulova asked.

Gromeko nodded.

"How do we get his body into the K-122 once we're there? The tube is only big enough for one person at a time."

"It'll work. The person in the tube has nothing to do but shut the top hatch. We can do that from the outside."

A minute later the heads of the four Spetsnaz warriors dipped beneath the waters and disappeared from sight. Blood trailed from the bandaged wound on Malenkov and the dead body of Zosimoff. Gromeko glanced at his diver's watch. The fluorescent hands showed fifteen minutes after two.

In the drainpipe behind them, starlight revealed a coil of wire that had fallen out of Dolinski's knapsack.

ELEVEN

"WHAT are your recommendations?"

"We could go active on sonar," Chief Stalzer said.

Joe Tucker shook his head. "Against regulations to do that in port. You don't know what damage you're going to do."

"Don't know if someone is in the water," Burnham added. "Fry their ass."

"Not really," Burkeet said. "Could destroy their eardrums if they're near the sonar."

"XO, we can always request permission from Subic Operations Center. They can authorize it," Burnham said.

MacDonald raised his hand. "I have to tell Admiral Green. Meanwhile," he pointed at the XO, "Joe Tucker, the *Coghlan* is parked farthest from us. Out near the end of the pier. I need to talk with their skipper and get them involved in this."

Joe Tucker's eyebrows furrowed. "*Coghlan*?"

MacDonald nodded. "The admiral would have to get us permission to use sonar. It would take some time for that to happen, but if we can get another ship to activate its sonar, maybe we can get a passive noise triangulation on this possible submarine."

"Why don't we take the motor whaleboat and take off along the line of bearing?" Oliver asked.

"How's that?" Burkeet asked.

"If we drag a line or wire behind it, it only has to be periscope depth, about fifty feet. If the submarine is in the harbor, we'll snag it."

"Sounds simple," MacDonald added.

"Too simple," Joe Tucker said.

"Better than sitting here," Stalzer said. When everyone looked at him, he added, "Sorry. I was thinking out loud."

"Chiefs have been known to do that," Joe Tucker said with a smile. "Chief's right, Captain. Let's do both. Let's send the motor whaleboat out along the line of bearing to see what they can see, and I'll wake up the sonar team on another ship."

"Sounds like a plan, but let's do the triangulation before we start putting boats in the water. Meanwhile, I will contact Admiral Green," MacDonald said. He reached over and patted Oliver on the shoulder. "Good job, sailor. I guess the other question I have is, what are you doing here in the middle of the night?"

"The chief wanted me to do the PMS today," Oliver replied. "I didn't finish it yesterday and it needed to be finished by quarters tomorrow morning."

MacDonald looked at the chief. "Well done, Chief Stalzer."

"Thank you, sir. I try to keep our team to a schedule."

Stalzer failed to see Burnham roll his eyes.

Boatswain Mate Manny Lowe appeared back of the group standing in the doorway to Sonar. "Captain, XO!" he said.

Everyone turned.

"What is it, Boats?" MacDonald asked.

"There's been an incident ashore, sir. Subic Base Operations is warning everyone to be alert. They've had some sort of shooting near the warehouses."

"What kind of shooting?" Burnham asked.

"Don't know, sir. They just said for all ships to increase their security until they have apprehended whoever was shooting at the marines."

"Anyone hurt?" Joe Tucker asked.

"Don't know, sir. They just said to increase our security."

* * *

GROMEKO tugged the dead weight of Zosimoff with him. The weights in the diver's belt made it harder. He looked up through the clear water and could make out the shadowy outlines of the other three, above and ahead of him. They would reach the K-122 minutes before him.

The weight of the dead man was forcing him to swim deeper than the others. He wondered for a moment if he was going to be able to make it. Then he shook his head. Spetsnaz warriors never had thoughts such as this!

Fedulova and Malenkov were traveling in tandem. Gromeko glanced upward. He could make out Malenkov's weak kicking. Good! The man was still alive. Dolinski would reach the submarine first. He hoped the GRU Spetsnaz officer would let Malenkov go first.

His eyes dropped as he kicked a little harder. Zosimoff's head bounced off Gromeko's stomach as he swam, and when he kicked his flippers for forward motion, his calves and feet hit the body. It was the only way he could move, dragging Zosimoff slightly behind him.

A dark shadow blocked the starlight for a moment. Gromeko looked up, thinking a boat had passed over them, but there was nothing there. Must have been a cloud or a piece of harbor flotsam. He would have heard the engine of a small boat. But boats were heading this way.

The shadow passed again, but Gromeko ignored it. He concentrated on keeping Zosimoff's body alongside him. The K-122 could not be too far ahead of them.

"UP periscope," Bocharkov ordered, flipping the handles out, and riding the lens up through the water. He turned the periscope, starting his three-hundred-sixty-degree reconnaissance visual. As he hurried around the compass heading, he passed a series of running lights, causing him to bring the periscope back, focusing on the scene to his right.

"I have multiple small boats leaving the north side of the harbor," he said.

"Sir, I have lots of noise spikes of small motors coming from the same direction," Chief Diemchuk announced.

Bocharkov focused the lens with his fingers, concentrating on the boat in the middle. "Looks like a landing craft," he said slowly, as he shifted the lens onto another boat to the right of the first one. "Second contact bearing zero-two-four appears to be a patrol boat. The hull is too dark to identify, but the fluorescents riding its bow wake show greater speed than the other one." He leaned back from the periscope and looked at the clock on the bulkhead. It was twenty minutes after two.

"Do you think they have detected us?" Orlov asked.

Bocharkov bit his lip. He nodded. "That is always a possibility, but the destroyers are still tied up ashore and have yet to move."

"THERE it is again, sir!" Oliver shouted.

"We heard it on the speaker," Stalzer said, patting the petty officer on the shoulder.

Both sonar technicians looked at the captain.

"What do you think?" he asked Burkeet.

Every head turned to the ASW officer.

"I agree with the chief and Petty Officer Oliver, sir. It sounds like a periscope."

"Could be outside," Burnham said.

Stalzer shook his head. "It would be the first time I've heard a periscope rise from this distance. It would be near impossible for us to hear a periscope rise if it was even at the edge of Subic Bay."

"The bearing goes through Subic Bay and out to sea," Burnham argued.

"This one isn't out in Subic Bay. It's in the harbor."

Everyone looked at Stalzer.

"I know, I know," Stalzer said. "I don't believe I said it either. It's impossible. A Soviet submarine is inside an American-controlled harbor? It is as dumb as an American submarine . . ."

Everyone stopped.

MacDonald stepped outside Sonar and hurried to the nearest telephone.

"Where's he going?" Burnham asked.

"Probably to call the admiral," Joe Tucker said as he pushed past Burnham to follow MacDonald. At the curtain, he turned. "Lieutenant Burkeet, keep recording the noises. We'll need them later."

"Aye, sir."

MacDonald was at his chair in Combat. Nearby, hanging on makeshift hooks along the edge of an electronics bay, were several metal-covered logbooks. He grabbed one labeled "Olongapo," flipped over the metal cover, and started rifling through the messages.

"What you looking for, sir?" Joe Tucker asked as he stepped up.

"The telephone number of the *Coghlan*."

"The *Coghlan*?"

"I would estimate he's nearly a half mile from us." His finger traced the numbers downward until he found what he wanted. "Ah! Here it is." He quickly dialed the number. "If we have a Soviet submarine inside the harbor area, then a half-mile separation will be sufficient for us to get a location on it."

As the phone rang, he turned to Joe Tucker. "If this Ron Kennedy can get his sonar team up and tracking this noise, then we'll know real fast if it is an anomaly or if we have an intruder in the harbor."

A sleepy voice answered the other end. It was not sleepy when MacDonald explained to his fellow skipper what he wanted. When he hung up, he turned to Joe Tucker. "Now I'll call the admiral." He sighed.

"You know Green will be over here in minutes," Joe Tucker warned.

MacDonald nodded, his finger misdialing the second number. He hit the disconnect and redialed. He knew he was doing the right thing, but even doing the right thing could make you the butt of jokes for decades to come.

* * *

GROMEKO knew he was falling farther behind the three men ahead. He no longer could make them out, so now as he pulled the weight of Zosimoff along, he glanced at the wrist compass every few seconds to stay on course. The submarine should be at periscope depth and as low as he was swimming; he would run right into it—unless it had left.

Something bumped him on the left side, knocking him to the right and causing him to lose his grip on Zosimoff. Without thinking, he quickly reached back, luckily grabbed the sleeve of the dungaree shirt, and pulled the body back to him. What in the hell was that?

He looked right and left, treading water for a few moments, then attributed it to more flotsam in the heavily polluted waters of the harbor. He started swimming again, kicking harder, trying to make up for time he was losing. If he arrived at the K-122 after—

He was hit again. This time his hand trailed along the side of the thing that hit him. It took several seconds for it to pass. Shark! He had been a diver long enough to know. The blood from Malenkov and from Zosimoff had led it, or them, to him. He kept swimming.

Sharks circled their prey before dashing forward. They glided up, rubbing their skins, which were one continuous work of taste sensors, against their prey to determine if it was edible. Then they attacked, ripping and tearing their prey to threads with teeth honed by evolution since the age of dinosaurs. Gromeko had just been rubbed.

He stopped. The water was murky and he would hardly see the shark if it attacked. He pulled the knife from his ankle scabbard. And he waited. He allowed Zosimoff to drift downward slightly to give him room for the attack. The sound of his speeding heart filled his ears. To die as shark bait this far from home doing a mission in enemy waters—where was the irony of that?

Suddenly Zosimoff was jerked from his grip. The last he saw of the body was the waving hair as it disappeared downward. Without waiting, he turned and continued swimming toward the submarine. He picked up speed without carrying the body, but somewhere behind him was a big shark, and he did not know if Zosimoff would sate its appetite.

* * *

"SOMETHING is happening," Bocharkov said.

Ignatova stepped into the control room. "It's nearly two thirty," he said. "Thirty minutes before they are due back."

Bocharkov nodded. "Prepare for an emergency exit, Lieutenant Commander Orlov." He turned to Ignatova. "Return to the forward torpedo room, XO. As soon as they are on board we are going to head out. Too much activity topside for me."

"Do you think they know we are here?"

Bocharkov bit his lower lip. "Don't know. All I can do is watch the destroyers now. With only small boats surfing across the harbor, the worst they can do is accidentally run into the periscope."

"Maybe the Spetsnaz team has been discovered," Tverdokhleb said, seated at the navigation table, one leg over the arm of the chair and his left hand drumming a cigarette on the table.

Bocharkov and Ignatova looked at the taciturn navigator.

Tverdokhleb shrugged. "If they have run into resistance and managed to escape, maybe the Americans saw them jump into the harbor. Maybe that is why we are seeing hundreds of boats scattering across the water." He shrugged again. "Just thinking out loud."

"Hundreds of boats?" Orlov asked.

Bocharkov shook his head. "Tens of boats is more accurate, but our esteemed navigator may have a point." He turned back to the periscope. "Run up the radio antenna and get the communications officer up here immediately."

THE telephone rang. MacDonald picked it up. While they waited for the *Coghlan*'s sonar team to man their position, he had moved the telephone outside of the *Dale* sonar compartment.

"*Dale* speaking," he answered. He acknowledged the voice on the other end and then hung up. "Admiral Green is on his way over."

"I hate it when I'm right," Joe Tucker mumbled.

The telephone rang again. This time it was the lead sonar

technician on the *Coghlan*. MacDonald handed the telephone to Stalzer. What would happen now would be that the *Coghlan* and *Dale* operators would focus on the same noise, each take a line of bearing on the signal, and then draw the lines outward until they crossed. Where they crossed would reveal the location of this mysterious signal that everyone seemed hell-bent on identifying as a Soviet Echo class submarine.

The officers stepped out of the sonar compartment to give Stalzer and Oliver room to work.

"I can't believe the Soviets would be this dumb," Burnham said, his voice trailing off as everyone looked toward him.

"I think he is outside the harbor. Inside, he is too close for his cruise missiles," Joe Tucker said.

"Probably related to the expected attacks later today," MacDonald offered.

"What attacks?" Burnham asked sharply. "In Vietnam?"

MacDonald shook his head. "Not now, Ops. Later." Only one thing made sense to MacDonald. If this submarine was inside the harbor, it was spying. It was reconnoitering the Americans, gaining intelligence for when the two largest fleets in the world would fight for dominance of the seas. From some of his own intelligence-gathering missions just outside the twelve-mile national water limits, he knew exactly what this submarine was doing if they were "dumb" enough to be inside the harbor. Neither navy doubted that someday they would have that showdown. What if this was it?

"Most likely a sound propagation anomaly," Joe Tucker said, his eyebrows furrowed.

Stalzer leaned into Combat, straddling the doorway. He held his hand over the mouthpiece of the telephone. "*Coghlan* is turning up its gear, sir," he said to Burkeet. "It'll be another five minutes before they're ready."

MacDonald looked at the clock on the aft bulkhead of Combat. It was two thirty in the morning. It was going to be a long day for him. He tried to recall when he'd last had eight hours' sleep in a row.

"Why would they be out there, Captain?" Burkeet asked MacDonald.

MacDonald pinched his nose. It had been a long time,

probably before they departed Pearl Harbor on the first leg of their deployment from San Diego.

"They've been trailing the *Kitty Hawk* battle group since we left Japanese waters," Joe Tucker answered. "They're waiting for us to come out. I hate to think what it would mean if we have one sitting a few thousand yards from us."

"Could be," MacDonald added. "You never know with Mad Ivan what he is up to, but I doubt seriously he'd attack us inside the harbor."

"Why, sir?"

"Well, Lieutenant Burkeet, remember Pearl Harbor?"

The ASW officer nodded.

"We are still looking at photographs and movies of the event. Even today we recoil from what happened on December 7. Have you ever read about the Battle of the Aleutians or the Battle of the Solomons?"

"I studied them at the Academy," Burkeet answered.

"Those two battles were at sea. Sea battles are more palatable to the world than those that rage ashore like Pearl Harbor. At sea, when the battle is over, the ocean covers the battlefield, and peace reigns from horizon to horizon." He paused. "That's why I don't think this is a hostile act in terms of blood, guts, and gunpowder."

MacDonald glanced up as Boatswain Mate Second Class Manny Lowe stepped through the opened watertight hatch.

"Sir, the officer of the deck sends his respects and sent me to find you."

"You found me, Petty Officer Lowe. What is it?"

"Sir, Subic Operations Center has issued a report of intruders near the warehouses. Apparently there has been gunfire and some marines are either dead or wounded or both. They think the intruders escaped into the harbor . . ."

A shiver went up MacDonald's spine. He didn't need the *Coghlan*'s line of bearing, for he knew in his gut the Echo was sitting in the harbor out there. What in the hell were the Soviets trying to prove? A surge of anger welled up inside of him.

". . . and they are asking all ships to be alert for swimmers."

No one spoke for a moment, then Joe Tucker asked, "Any more information than that?"

Lowe shook his head. "No, sir. But I remember when I was here last year, the Filipinos had been slipping inside the fence and breaking into things, stealing stuff. Could be they're just getting more brazen, sir. Maybe this time they brought guns with them."

"Dumb if they did," Burnham said. "The Filipino police will have them dead and buried by morning if they catch them."

"Ops," MacDonald said. "Bring the ship to general quarters."

"GQ?" Joe Tucker asked.

General quarters was the naval term for bringing a ship from peacetime sailing to battle status, ready to fight and defend itself. It was not something done in port—except too late in Pearl Harbor on December 7, 1941.

GROMEKO swam, fighting the fear in his mind. Sharks were the scourge of sailors and others whose profession took them into the ocean. In the dark waters of Subic Bay, imagination fed fear, and fear was more a killer of men than sharks. This he knew.

Most times sharks and sailors kept a watchful and respectful eye on each other, but not this time. He could barely see his hands in front of him because of the murkiness of Subic Bay. Fear could eat up the oxygen in a diver's tank in seconds instead of minutes. He counted his breathing rhythm, forcing his mind to concentrate elsewhere. Gromeko told himself there was little he could do if the shark returned. But he kept the knife in his hand as he swam.

With Zosimoff gone, the trail of blood was gone also. Maybe the shark was full now. Maybe the shark had lost him, but he knew if it wanted him it would return. The eyesight of a shark isn't what takes it to its prey. It is the smell riding the currents, or the out-of-synch vibration created by a human in the water, or a combination of both.

He stretched his left arm out as his right came back alongside, the knife held blade-outward so he wouldn't cut himself.

He did not want to stop to put it back in the scabbard, and then, if the shark returned, he wouldn't have time to reach it again.

His right leg came up as his left leg went down, the flippers propelling him forward. One thing the encounter had done was cause Gromeko to lose track of time. What if he had swum over the K-122 and was now working his way into the center of Subic Bay?

The blow came suddenly along the same side as before, knocking Gromeko end over end. Instinctively he tightened his hold on the knife. The rough skin of the shark rubbed along the suit, doing the "taste test." Gromeko's arms and legs spread out, helping him regain his balance. He treaded water a second or two, until he recalled that the shark had come from below to take Zosimoff. He turned upside down, holding the knife tightly, waiting for the attack.

It came as suddenly as the taste test, emerging a few feet from him, the faint light from above casting a pale gray shadow across the creature's opened mouth.

"Hammerhead" flashed through Gromeko's mind even as he rolled to the left.

His knife cut a narrow slash through the part of the shark where its right eye lay. The shark twisted back and forth as it moved to the left, away from Gromeko. The tail caught him again, knocking out his mouthpiece.

Water flooded his mouth before Gromeko could stop his inward breath. He coughed as he fought to get his mouthpiece reseated. The knife hit his temple in the effort. Blood in the water would only help the hammerhead find him again, but he had no time to think about whether he had accidentally cut himself or not.

He treaded water, upside down, waiting for the next attack. After about a minute when nothing happened, Gromeko forced himself to look at his compass and continue in the direction in which he hoped the K-122 waited. The drumming of his heartbeat filled his ears. He had fought a giant shark. Whether he had won or not would be determined by whether he was standing inside the submarine.

* * *

"RAISE the communications antenna," Bocharkov ordered, leaning back from the periscope.

"The communications antenna?" Orlov questioned.

Bocharkov's eyebrows furrowed. "Was my voice unclear?"

"No, sir—I mean, sir . . ."

"Just raise the antenna." Bocharkov turned to Lieutenant Tverdokhleb. "Uri, you speak good English, don't you?"

Tverdokhleb dropped his unlit cigarette on the chart and looked up from his seat. "I have studied it at the university. I understand it better than I speak it."

"Get over to the harbor common radio and tell me what the Americans are saying."

Internationally, channel sixteen was the harbor common frequency used by ships whenever they encountered another ship at sea, entered or departed port, or needed to communicate with a ship that did not have a known frequency.

"Communications antenna raised," Orlov reported.

"Turn on the radio."

A moment later English filled the control room.

Tverdokhleb stood and meandered over to the radio. He stared at the speaker for a bit, then turned. "It seems, Captain, that they are searching for someone or something in water."

"Do they say what?"

"No, but they are launching boats to search the waters of Subic Bay along the shore. Apparently they have had a confrontation ashore."

"Could it be our men?"

Tverdokhleb shrugged and then turned back to the speaker.

Bocharkov put his eyes to the lens of the periscope and swept the area around him. To his north lay the piers and the main part of the American naval base. South was Cubi Point Naval Air Station. Escape lay west. Behind the K-122, east, were the warehouses and the telephone switchboards where his Spetsnaz team was . . .

Bocharkov leaned back and looked at the clock. It showed twenty minutes to three. "Ten minutes until they return. They would be in the waters now," he mumbled under his breath. Then he looked over at Lieutenant Commander Orlov. "Officer of the Deck, tell Engineering we move in fifteen minutes."

"Fifteen minutes, aye," Orlov repeated, jerking the microphone off its cradle to relay the information to the chief engineer.

THE *clong-clong-clong* of general quarters shook the sleeping awake and startled those already awake. Sailors scrambled from their bunks, jumping on one leg as they jammed the other through their dungarees, bumping into one another as they rushed to dress. Most had open shirts or no shirts as they raced up and down ladders toward their assigned battle stations. Most figured the *Dale* had a major fire for GQ to be sounded. No one but the few around Sonar knew the truth.

Through the rear hatch to Combat rushed an influx of sailors and officers racing to their consoles and flipping switches, the hum of electronics filling the room along with several voices shouting instructions. As he stepped into Combat, Lieutenant Kelly saw the captain, hurried over, and saluted. "What's going on, sir? Fire?" He continued buttoning his khaki shirt as MacDonald turned.

"We may have a Soviet submarine inside Subic Bay," MacDonald replied, sounding calmer than he felt.

"Bullshit! Oops, sorry, sir? A Soviet submarine inside Subic Bay?" Kelly glanced into the sonar compartment and saw Oliver there. His shoulders visibly fell. "Did Oliver pick him up?"

"Seems so."

"Sir, do you want Combat brought all the way up to fighting status?"

"Would not have sounded general quarters if I hadn't, Lieutenant." He knew Kelly was thinking the same thing he had when he came to Combat: Maybe Oliver wanted more than his moment of glory tracking the Echo. MacDonald grunted. If so, the crew would be punishment enough for the young sonar technician.

Stalzer lowered the telephone. "*Coghlan* has their sonar up, sir. I've passed them the frequency on which we have our contact."

And, MacDonald thought, *I will be the laughing stock of the pier.*

Admiral Green stepped through the rear hatch. "What's going on, Danny?"

"Attention on deck!" Burnham shouted, snapping to attention.

"Carry on," Green replied, returning MacDonald's salute. "Bring me up-to-date."

"My apologies, Admiral, I didn't hear them bong you aboard."

"You didn't because I told them not to do it. You had GQ going at the time."

Kelly hurried off toward the center of Combat, his voice shouting, "Report," as he tucked in his shirt. Around Combat, voices began to report the status of their consoles as they warmed up.

For the next several minutes MacDonald told Green of Oliver's detection, of how the sailor was performing PMS at midnight and detected the signal, and how Chief Stalzer had confirmed the noise as a Soviet submarine. Green seemed unconvinced, preferring to believe the signal was just an ocean phenomenon of sound. No Soviet submarine would dare penetrate an American-controlled harbor.

Stalzer's face turned red as he realized the humiliation he was going to feel and receive from the other chiefs if this was just a sound anomaly. He could hear the jokes in the goat locker. His throat felt dry. Then a voice on the other end of the telephone drew him away from the admiral and the skipper.

"Let's say you're right, Danny," Green said. "What are your intentions if he is out there in Subic Bay? It's really Philippine waters, not ours."

"I would cast off and engage it, sir."

Green nodded, his lips pursed. "Be kind of hard to drop depth charges inside Subic Bay. Right now Security has about twenty or thirty small boats out there looking for some sailors who shot up the marines." Green's voice trailed off. "*If* they were sailors," he mumbled, his hand rubbing his chin.

At that moment, MacDonald knew the admiral had switched from a nonbeliever to considering that the idea of a Soviet submarine might be true.

"Sir, the *Coghlan* reports a bearing of one-six-zero."

Burnham leaned over a chart of the bay, drawing a line from the pier where *Coghlan* was tied up. "Our bearing?"

"I hold the contact bearing one-seven-two, sir!" Oliver replied.

Burnham realigned the wooden ruler and ran a line from where the *Dale* was parked along the bearing. Then he grabbed up a metal compass, spread the legs, and measured from *Dale* to where the two lines intersected. Both MacDonald and Green looked over Burnham's shoulder.

Burnham leaned away from the table. "Four hundred yards, sir."

"Impossible."

MacDonald stuck his finger on the warehouses at the far eastern end of the naval base. "Within swimming distance, sir."

"How long until you can cast off?" Green demanded.

"We have one engine room on line. Enough power to shift colors, sir."

Green stuck his hand out. "Chief, give me that telephone."

Stalzer let go of the telephone as if it were on fire.

"*Coghlan*, this is Admiral Green. Put your skipper on the telephone."

For a minute Green asked Ron Kennedy the same question. *Coghlan* had both engine rooms stoked and ready to cast off. The admiral ordered the other destroyer to report to the *Dale*, and he wanted both ships under way ASAP! Then Green called the Subic Operations Center and ordered them to have every ship in port go to general quarters and remain there until otherwise ordered. He tossed the telephone back to Stalzer.

Stalzer caught it and quickly dialed the *Coghlan* sonar room. Within moments, the sonar technician from the *Coghlan* was on the other end. They were going to lose this landline when the two destroyers cast off.

GROMEKO saw the outline of the K-122 below him. It was only then he realized that in the last minute of swimming he had slowly risen in depth. He glanced behind him and below expecting to see the open mouth of the hammerhead bearing down.

Motion drew his attention. The outline of Dolinski. His knapsack flowing alongside him, heading downward toward the bow of the K-122. The wounded Malenkov and Chief Starshina Fedulova followed, dragging the second knapsack between them. Gromeko kicked harder. He estimated they were fifty to seventy meters in front of him. The clarity of the water had improved greatly since they'd left the muddy area nearer the shore.

"SIR!" Orlov shouted.

"Quiet!" Bocharkov whispered, motioning downward.

Even in the blue light of the control room, Bocharkov saw Orlov's face darken.

"Sir, XO reports noise overhead forward torpedo room."

Bocharkov looked at the clock. It was five minutes to three.

"Sir, Chief Engineer Matulik reports ready to engage."

"Tell him to be prepared for my orders."

"Captain, it seems the Americans have alerted their ships. At least two of them are preparing to get under way," Tverdokhleb said.

When Bocharkov looked at him, Tverdokhleb pointed to the radio. "I think they have told tugboats to go help two ships get under way. And I think one of the ships told them they did not have time to wait for tugs."

"Which of the ships? What class of ships? Destroyers?"

Tverdokhleb shrugged. "I don't know, sir. I don't know the English for their class of ships. I think one of the names is *David* or *Dale* or *Davida*."

"Chief Ship Starshina Uvarova," Bocharkov said. "Look up the American order of battle and see what class of ship the *David* is."

MACDONALD and Green stood on the port bridge wing of the *Dale*, watching the sailors ashore single up the eight lines holding the destroyer to the pier. Then MacDonald started the orders to free the destroyer from land. Once they were free, the colors of the United States flying from the stern of the warship would be shifted to the mainmast. Such was the tradition of shifting colors once free of the shore, for every warship in the world, a tradition passed along from the British Navy when it ruled the seas in the nineteenth century.

When every line was aboard, with the exception of the number one line running through the bullnose of the bow, MacDonald put a left full rudder on and ordered rotations on the shafts for one knot. The stern of the destroyer eased away from the pier. As if backing out of a parallel parking slot, MacDonald waited until the stern was clear of the cruiser parked behind him before he ordered the number one line cast off.

"Shift colors, under way!" the boatswain mate of the watch whistled through the 1MC speaker system.

"Rudder's amidships! All back one third!"

The *Dale* sped backward, clearing the cruiser. MacDonald raised his binoculars in the darkness and scanned the waters behind the destroyer. "All watches report!"

Inside the bridge he heard the contacts coming in from the topside watches.

"Tell them to search my stern, make sure we don't have anyone out there."

The admiral stepped inside the bridge and walked over to the boatswain mate of the watch. "Okay, Boats, where do you hide the coffee here?"

"SIR, I believe one of the ships is under way," Tverdokhleb said.

"Which one?"

"Captain, I'm not even sure I heard it correctly."

"It is not the *David*. It is the USS *Dale*," Uvarova said from where he stood between the planesman and the helmsman. "It is the destroyer."

"It is the same one that tracked us last week," Orlov added. "Sonar has it on passive sonar."

"Officer of the Deck, what is the status in the forward torpedo room?"

Orlov lifted the handset from its cradle and relayed the question to the XO. Ignatova's reply was easily heard by Bocharkov. "We are draining the escape hatch for the first one."

GROMEKO touched the deck of the submarine. The hatch was open. Dolinski and Fedulova were helping Malcnkov into the narrow confines. Fedulova held the tank while Dolinski guided the wounded man into the hatch. No one looked toward Gromeko. When Malenkov's head disappeared, Dolinski pushed the tank inside with him and closed the hatch. Fedulova spun the wheel to secure it.

"HATCH is sealed, XO!" Chief Starshina Diemchuk said.

"Commence draining."

A full minute passed before the light changed from red to green. Diemchuk reached up and spun the wheel. The hatch opened and residual water spilled into the submarine. Malenkov fell the six feet to the deck, groaning as he rolled over.

Diemchuk bent over the sailor. "He's wounded, sir." Diemchuk held up a hand covered in blood.

"Get the others inside!"

Diemchuk shoved the watertight hatch shut and spun the wheel. He pulled the hydraulic lever. The light quickly turned red as water began to fill the escape tunnel. Topside, the Spetsnaz had no signal to tell when they could open the hatch. They used their watches to estimate when it was time, then they would spin the wheel. If the escape tube was not full, the topside watertight hatch would not open.

Ignatova grabbed the nearby handset. "Doctor to forward torpedo room on the double," he broadcast through the boat. He had no sooner hung up than the intercom connecting the control room to the forward torpedo room buzzed. He wasted no time in telling Bocharkov that Malenkov was wounded.

Three minutes later, Dolinski dropped to the deck. Malenkov was being helped onto a stretcher.

"What happened out there?" Ignatova asked.

Dolinski ignored the XO's question as he watched the corpsman and another medical person lift the stretcher and carry Malenkov out of the forward torpedo room. He looked at Diemchuk. "Is he still alive?"

"He is."

"I asked, what happened out there?"

"Captain Second Rank Ignatova, may we get the others inside before we start our debriefing? We do not have much time."

The next through the hatch was Chief Starshina Fedulova. Gromeko was the last to drop to the deck. As he did, Diemchuk closed the hatch.

"Where is Zosimoff?" Fedulova asked Gromeko.

Gromeko pulled his face mask off. "A shark got him."

There was silence for a moment. Then Dolinski said, "I told you we should have left him back there."

"We never leave our wounded or dead behind," Fedulova said, staring hard at Gromeko.

"It's better than deciding halfway here to let him go," Dolinski said.

Still breathing hard, Gromeko sprang toward the GRU Spetsnaz. "I did not let him go. A shark grabbed him away from me."

Dolinski sneered. "It is a story that I may have used also, if I thought others would think less of me."

The punch caught Dolinski on the left side of the chin, sending the officer forward into the torpedo tubes. The GRU Spetsnaz officer spun away and came up with his knife.

"Stop it! Stop it, immediately," Ignatova commanded, stepping between the two officers. He pointed at Dolinski. "You! Get out of here and report to Medical." He looked at Fedulova. "Go with the lieutenant and have him checked out by the doctor. Call me with a status report on Malenkov."

The intercom buzzed. Diemchuk grabbed the handset, his eyes wide as they spun between the two lieutenants. "Forward torpedo room," he answered.

Dolinski put his knife back in the scabbard. "We will meet again, Lieutenant." Then he walked toward the hatch, his shoulder nudging Gromeko as he passed. At the hatch, he turned. "If I had said I was going to bring one of the men's bodies back, I would have. I would not have lost my nerve and—"

"I said, that's enough!" Ignatova commanded, stretching his palm out. "Go." He looked at Fedulova. "You are to stay with Lieutenant Dolinksi."

"I don't need a babysitter, Captain Second Rank Ignatova."

"And I don't need someone running around my boat seeking revenge. We'll discuss this later when tempers are cooler."

"Sir," Diemchuk interrupted. "The captain wants to know—"

"Tell him everyone is on board. Tell him I am on my way to the control room."

WHEN the bridge wing of the *Dale* neared level with the bridge of the cruiser, MacDonald leaned in. "Right five-degree rudder, steady on course one-seven-zero." He glanced at the navigator. "Lieutenant Van Ness, what's my depth on this course?"

"Sir, you have a hundred fifty fathoms as long as you stay on this course. To your left are the mud flats. Depth drops rapidly to ten fathoms." One fathom was the equivalent of six feet or 1.83 meters.

"Coming to course one-seven-zero, speed one knot," the helmsman replied as he spun the wheel. The compass in front of him spun slowly as the *Dale* crept away from the pier.

Unseen from the bridge, the sound-powered talker on the stern of the *Dale* walked across to the port side and watched the distance close slightly between the destroyer and the cruiser as the *Dale* moved forward. He had pushed the talk button and opened his mouth to warn the bridge, when through narrowed eyes he realized inches were growing between the *Dale* and the starboard side of the cruiser.

The sailor released the "push to talk" button. An explosive release of air escaped as he hurried over to where the port side of the *Dale* curved into the aft end.

The two ships were less than eight feet from each other as the sailor watched the separation increase. Looking up, he saw the cruiser's topside watch looking down at him. They both waved, and then the sailor on the cruiser disappeared.

Looking around and seeing no one watching, the *Dale* sailor nervously shook a cigarette out and lit it.

He had let out his first puff when three blasts of the horn came from farther down the line of ships moored pierside. Another destroyer was backing away from the dock. He reported the observation to the bridge.

"Sir, aft watch reports *Coghlan* under way."

"Very well," MacDonald answered, stepping briskly to the 12MC and pushing the button to Combat. "Combat, this is the captain. *Coghlan* is under way. Have her take station three hundred yards on my starboard side and steady up on course one-seven-zero, speed two knots."

"Two knots?" Lieutenant Goldstein asked.

MacDonald nodded. "Bring revolutions up to make speed two knots, Officer of the Deck." He looked at the clock. It was five minutes past three.

"Aye, sir."

Green walked over to MacDonald, a fresh cup of coffee in his hand. "Seems to me you ought to light off your active sonar, Danny."

"Sir, we have to get permission from Base Operations—"

"Then it seems to me you're wasting time. Give them a call. It'll take them a few minutes to alert the ships so we don't blow up anyone shifting munitions or lose the ears of a few sonar technicians who might be doing their own preventive maintenance at oh-dark-thirty in the morning."

TWELVE

Monday, June 5, 1967

BOCHARKOV spun the periscope aft, quickly focusing the lens. He could see the running lights of the destroyer. It was definitely under way—disconnected from the pier and backing away, five hundred meters away. He leaned back from the lens, his hands never leaving the handles. "Bring the boat to course two-seven-zero degrees, speed four knots."

"Sir, another warship is under way. I hear bridge-to-bridge communications between tugboats and a ship called the . . . I think, the *Coughing*," Tverdokhleb said.

"That would be the USS *Coghlan*," Orlov corrected. "It has a Kennedy as the skipper."

Bocharkov nodded as he listened to his earlier orders filter to the helmsman.

"He's the one we were briefed on before we departed Kamchatka," Orlov added.

Bocharkov acknowledged the comment, but he also knew this Kennedy was not a Massachusetts Kennedy. Once intelligence discovered no relationship, the *Coghlan* had become just one more American warship to track—and to sink—when ordered.

"Steady on course two-seven-zero, speed four knots, sir," Orlov reported in a calm, low voice.

"Sir, I should return to my post," Tverdokhleb said. "There are shoal waters we must avoid."

Bocharkov agreed. He wanted to vacate Subic Bay as soon as possible. A hundred meters of depth was enough for a submarine to evade an ASW effort in the open ocean, but it was not much when you were enclosed on three sides in a bay.

Tverdokhleb hurried across the control room and slid into the chair at his plotting table. He picked up a ruler, laid it out on the chart, and ran a pencil along it. Bocharkov knew the navigator was laying out a dead reckoning line along course two-seven-zero. Dead reckoning was where the position of a vessel was determined by the time of travel along the course being taken. It was good for short distances and navigating in channels and harbors, but out to sea, over long distances, the ocean currents skewed the position.

"Make a log entry," Orlov said to the starshina responsible for the log, "for zero three zero five hours, showing K-122 at sixteen meters on course two-seven-zero, speed four knots."

Bocharkov lifted his forearms off the handles of the periscope for a moment, feeling the tingle as the blood flow increased.

"Officer of the Deck, Navigator! You have two hundred seventy meters beneath the hull," Tverdokhleb reported.

Bocharkov grunted. He could not go down now. The charts Tverdokhleb was using were out of date, and harbors were notorious for undocumented wrecks.

He lowered his forearms onto the handle again, leaning forward, his eyes on the lens. Right now it was more important to see what the Americans were doing as he maneuvered the K-122 to the open ocean. Once there, no destroyer could catch him.

The two destroyers filled his scope, but their running lights had a right-bearing drift, meaning they were still on their original course, to where the K-122 had been.

He needed no one to confirm the Americans were onto his presence in the harbor. Why hadn't they turned on their active sonar? he asked himself, but he knew the answer even as he asked it.

It was the same for the Soviet Navy. Active sonar was a powerful instrument. To use it in closed waters such as Subic Bay and Olongapo Harbor could cause ammunition to explode. It could seriously damage or destroy sensitive instruments, kill divers, and even burst the eardrums of sailors manning sonar.

He leaned away from the periscope. "Lieutenant Commander Orlov, prepare for the Americans to use active sonar."

"Inside the harbor?"

Bocharkov let out a deep sigh. "I am sure they will not ask for permission."

"Aye, sir."

"Tell me, Lieutenant Commander Orlov, what can we expect the Americans to use if they do fire on us?"

"Sir, you have reported lots of small craft in the harbor. Sonar confirms at least a dozen small boats topside. The only weapon the two American destroyers have at this short distance is their over-the-side torpedoes. And if they fire them, then they run the risk of hitting one of their own small boats."

Bocharkov mumbled his acknowledgment. "We would not see them preparing to launch unless we saw them manning the topside surface vessel torpedo tubes."

"And it is still dark topside." Tverdokhleb snorted with a short laugh. "But in little over an hour, the skies will begin to lighten. Then we can see them clearly if they try."

Bocharkov started to correct the navigator, but Tverdokhleb was right. He could watch the destroyers now, but he needed more light to see what they were doing topside. And more light meant more opportunity for them to see his periscope.

"Make your speed five knots."

"Recommend course two-nine-zero in ten minutes. Depth will remain the same, but it will parallel the shoal waters near the United States navy airfield. You may want to stay near the shoal waters, if the Americans intend to use active sonar."

Bocharkov was surprised. Tverdokhleb did not strike him as an officer who understood underwater tactics. Keeping close to shoal waters—without running aground—might confuse an active-duty sonar ping. The ping would get the submarine, but it would get the rocks and debris behind the submarine also.

"Cubi Point," Bocharkov said aloud.

"Sir?" Orlov asked.

"Cubi Point is the American airfield off our port bow. It also has shoal waters running alongside it." Bocharkov looked at the bulkhead clock. "Change course to two-zero-zero at time zero three seventeen."

Orlov looked at the log keeper and saw the young starshina notating the entry.

"SIR, the contact is moving," Oliver reported.

"Course, speed, direction?" Burkeet asked, his words running together.

"I have a right-bearing drift, sir. I have cavitations in the water. Slow speed, but he's moving, sir."

Burkeet grabbed the sound-powered handset from its cradle and relayed the information to both Combat and the bridge.

ON the bridge, MacDonald reseated the handset. "Lieutenant Goldstein, are you ready to assume the deck?"

Goldstein saluted. "Yes, sir, I am. We are on course one-seven-zero, speed two knots, and are at general quarters. Admiral Green is embarked—"

"Thanks, Lieutenant," MacDonald interrupted. He lifted his head slightly. "This is the Captain. Lieutenant Goldstein has the deck."

"This is Lieutenant Goldstein! I have the deck!"

At the navigation table, the quartermaster of the watch wrote into the logbook the time at which the captain transferred the bridge to Goldstein.

"Any directions, sir?" Goldstein asked.

"I'm going to Combat. Be prepared for course and speed changes, but you are not to exceed six knots without my direct orders." MacDonald looked at Green. "Admiral, would you care to join me?"

"*Would I care to join you?* Why, Captain MacDonald, thank you for asking."

Crossing the bridge toward the hatch leading to Combat, Admiral Green handed his empty cup back to the boatswain mate of the watch. "Good coffee, Boats."

"Captain off the bridge!" Boatswain Mate Manny Lowe shouted as MacDonald followed the admiral through the watertight hatch. At the plotting table the duty quartermaster glanced at the clock on the bulkhead and notated the time when the captain left the bridge as 3:21. He also notated Admiral Green's departure.

"WHAT you got?" MacDonald asked Burkeet. Joe Tucker stood to the right of the officer, the XO's head more inside Sonar than in Combat, where the others stood.

"Oliver has the submarine on a left-to-right drift, sir. Not a lot of speed, but looks to me as if he's trying to head to open water."

"Have we reestablished comms with *Coghlan*?"

"No, sir, not yet, but Radio says they are working with *Coghlan*'s radio shack. They expect to have it soon."

"Tell Radio to work faster."

"Aye, sir." Burkeet nodded at Stalzer, who relayed the useless order. The issue was seeding the cryptographic cards into the readers. Those cards were the key to secure communications and required two-person control at all times. The communications officer, Lieutenant Junior Grade Alton Taylor, and Radioman Chief Petty Officer Bob Caldwell had just opened the safe that held the cryptographic material. They would have to audit the open package, select the material for today, and then sign for its use. On the other end a curt Chief Caldwell told Stalzer to "eat shit and die," that they were working as fast as they could.

Stalzer put the handset back in its cradle. "Chief Caldwell said only a few more minutes."

MacDonald looked at Joe Tucker. "XO, see what you can do."

Joe Tucker stepped through the nearby aft hatch, heading toward Radio.

MacDonald turned to Green. "Sir, recommendations?"

"Well, Danny, what do you recommend? Do we want to

stop him from reaching open waters, or do we want to startle him to the surface here?" The admiral pointed toward the bow of the ship, hidden by the bulkhead that separated Combat from the bridge.

MacDonald's eyebrows furrowed into a deep "V." He took a deep breath. "I would say chase him, get near him, and let him know we know he is here."

Joe Tucker was back through the hatch. "A few more minutes and they will have comms with *Coghlan*."

Both MacDonald and Green nodded. Green turned back to MacDonald. "No weapons. If he surfaces, then it will be a coup for us in the world's press. The Philippine government will be furious; other Asian countries will be rushing out to check their harbors." Green nodded again, biting his lower lip for a moment, before a big smile spread across his face. "But we don't attack him." Then, after a slight pause, he added, "Damn it."

Burnham walked up to the officers. "Sir, just double-checked with Subic Operations Center. They're saying they're working to give the all clear for us to commence pinging."

"Would the Russians consider pinging them an act of war?" Green asked.

MacDonald nodded. "They could. If they know what we know is going to happen in the next few hours."

Green guffawed. "Oh, Danny, you are funny sometimes. No one knows what we know."

MacDonald felt his face turning red. *You don't know what you don't know* was something a previous skipper of his used to say whenever someone was emphatic about something. *You don't know what you don't know.*

"But if they do know, Admiral, then they may be concerned we are going to sortie right by Vietnamese water and continue—"

"You may be right, Danny," Green interrupted, biting his lower lip. "If the only reason the Soviets have been this brazen is because of what the Israelis may be planning, then . . ." Green's voice trailed off. A second or two passed before he continued, his voice serious, "Jesus Christ, Danny. Guess even us admirals get a little arrogant about our own wars, don't we? So wrapped up here I missed the global picture—forgot about how the Soviets view everything."

"Yes, sir," MacDonald said, wondering what the admiral was talking about. "But we haven't heard anything definite. Maybe the intelligence is off. Maybe the Israelis are not going to attack."

"Don't agree when I'm berating myself, Captain. Admirals are always right, even when they are wrong."

"Should we relay this information to Subic Operations Center, sir?"

Green did not answer the question. He glanced around at fully manned Combat, then back at MacDonald. "They were spying on us for a lot more than our war. Maybe they are here to pull a Pearl Harbor on us, fire an array of torpedoes."

"Sir, I would think they wouldn't have enough torpedoes. . . ." One moment Green had discounted the Soviet submarine attacking and the next moment his pendulum of thought had spun to the other end.

"Didn't you report two submarines on the surface?"

MacDonald acknowledged the report. Joe Tucker had stepped away from Sonar and was listening to the admiral.

"There is another scenario we have to consider, Danny."

MacDonald felt a shiver up his spine as intrinsically he reached the same conclusion. "The other submarine could be outside the port—preparing to launch cruise missiles simultaneously with this submarine's torpedoes."

Green clapped his hands. "Right!" With a sigh, he added, "Don't you hate it when great minds think alike?"

"We don't know that for sure," Burnham said sharply. "We don't know they are about to attack us, sir." He looked at MacDonald. "Skipper, I hope we aren't planning on attacking—"

"I believe, what Lieutenant Burnham is saying—" Joe Tucker interjected.

Green motioned downward, shaking his head. "It's a worst case scenario, gentlemen. We never want to think America is ever going to suffer another Pearl Harbor. Subic Bay is not another Pearl Harbor, unless the Soviets have submarines off Pearl Harbor, San Diego, and Norfolk, Virginia. But if we prepare for the worst, then we won't be disappointed or surprised." He looked at Burnham. "Well, Lieutenant, do you think we should call 'Big Apple'?"

Big Apple was the code word for everyone to prepare for

an imminent attack—a surprise attack, a missiles-in-the-air, inbound type of attack. Everyone tied up ashore, who had steam available, would immediately get under way. The open ocean was the destination, for warships are meant to fight on the seas, not tied up pierside.

Burnham shook his head. "Admiral, we'd have a mess on our hands trying to pursue this fellow and maneuver around a bunch of ships trying to reach the ocean."

"By the time the ships got under way, we would have settled with the submarine," MacDonald said.

"I agree." Green looked at Burnham. "Tell Subic Operations Center we need ASW aircraft outside Subic Bay. Tell them there might be a second Soviet submarine out there on the surface." He looked at MacDonald. "That should get the airdales' rocks off."

Burnham hurried away from the admiral and MacDonald.

Green looked at MacDonald. "Put the *Coghlan* ahead of the submarine—between it and the open ocean, but keep the other destroyer to your west also. Meanwhile, Danny, let's make sure we keep the *Dale* within firing distance for your over-the-side torpedoes." He looked at Burkeet and Joe Tucker. "Tell your Sonar if they hear something they even think is the opening of the outer doors of that submarine's torpedo tubes, I want to know."

"Aye, sir. I would like to be able to use active sonar if they open their torpedo tubes."

"Permission granted." Green looked at the man. "In war, we don't wait for permission from those ashore."

"We have secure comms with the *Coghlan*," Burkeet said from the entrance to Sonar.

IGNATOVA stepped into the control room as the sonar operator turned to Orlov.

"Sir, I have the contact to our starboard speeding up. He now has a left-bearing drift. That will put him ahead and to the west of us if he continues."

"The other contact?"

"It appears to be in a slight turn. I think he has contact on us and is shifting his course to come closer."

Ignatova continued to the periscope, watching Bocharkov twist it from starboard to aft and back again. He looked at the clock. It was three fifteen. It seemed so much later.

Bocharkov leaned away and looked at the clock also. Two minutes until they turned. He nodded at Ignatova as he turned to Tverdokhleb. "Navigator, take us as close as you can to the shoals."

"Captain, the team is back aboard," Ignatova said as he reached Bocharkov.

"Status?"

"Malenkov is seriously wounded, and according to Gromeko a shark attacked them. Zosimoff is gone."

"Gone?"

"Apparently killed in a firefight with the Americans ashore. Gromeko was bringing his body back to the boat, but he said a shark attacked them and jerked Zosimoff's body away from him."

"A shark?" Bocharkov asked with disbelief in his voice.

"A shark. Dolinski called him a coward. I had to break up—"

"Two minutes until turn!" Orlov announced.

"We'll talk later, XO. Right now, make sure the boat is rigged for combat. I know we set it when we came into the bay, but check it again."

Ignatova turned to carry out the orders.

"Captain Second Rank Ignatova," Bocharkov called. "Make sure we have torpedoes in each tube."

"The aft torpedo tubes have two tubes with decoys. The forward torpedo room has only two sailors because—"

"The mission is complete. Re-man it immediately." Then, Bocharkov returned to the periscope. He intended to reach the open ocean. Then he thought, what would he do if he was unable to make it to the open ocean? Would he fire on the Americans? Take as many of the enemy as he could?

Without removing his eyes from the lens, Bocharkov added, "And tell them they are not to open the outer torpedo doors without my direct order."

"Aye, sir."

"Very well," Bocharkov replied. Then his thoughts turned for a moment to Gromeko.

Shark? More likely Gromeko let the body drift away rather than slow down his return to the K-122. It was what he would have done, but then he was not Spetsnaz, he was a destroyer sailor. Gromeko would be explaining himself to the investigation committee upon return to Kamchatka.

STALZER put his hand over the handset, tapped Burkeet on the arm, and said, "*Coghlan* reports bearing two-six-zero, sir."

Burkeet nodded. "I'm going forward to the antisubmarine warfare team and see how they are doing. See if they are copying the same thing you are."

"Roger, sir. They are copying the same thing I am," Stalzer said, obviously feeling rebuffed. "They hear the same thing I do."

"Understand, Chief. Didn't mean it like it sounded. I want to see their plot."

Stalzer stuck his head back inside the sonar compartment. "Sometimes I think Burkeet doesn't trust us."

Oliver bit his tongue. Anything told to Stalzer was soon known around the ship. Good news traveled fast when Stalzer knew it. Bad news traveled faster.

"Chief, I hold the contact bearing two-seven-zero true."

The destroyer started a slow turn. Oliver looked at the compass above the passive display console. The ship was coming right. "What do you think, Chief?"

"I think we are coming onto course two-seven-zero."

Oliver nodded. He knew that, he told himself.

DOLINSKI walked into the control room trailing his knapsack after him.

"What are you doing here, Lieutenant?" Ignatova asked.

Bocharkov leaned away from the periscope, now pointed toward the aft quadrant of the boat. He caught a glimpse of Dolinski near the XO, but his attention was on watching the two destroyers, so he quickly returned to his surveillance.

The running lights of the destroyer off his starboard beam showed a starboard bow aspect. Would he be able to avoid a confrontation?

He pressed his eyes tighter against the eyepiece. There, he had thought it: confrontation. Seldom did they ever run into the Americans without some sort of confrontation. The high seas made it convenient. Several seconds passed before he leaned away. "Officer of the Deck, the destroyer behind us is in a left-hand turn."

"Captain, Sonar reports the warship off our right aft quarter in a slow left-hand turn," Orlov reported.

"Very well."

"Two minutes to course change," Orlov announced.

"Two minutes twenty seconds," Tverdokhleb corrected.

Bocharkov nodded. Ignatova and Dolinski were approaching him. Now was not the time to discuss either the mission or the confrontation in the forward torpedo room.

"Captain, Lieutenant Dolinski wants to connect his receiver to the communications antenna."

"Why?"

"He says—"

"Sir, if I can connect this," Dolinski interrupted, holding up a small receiver with earphones and trailing a red and black clip, "to the antenna, then we can listen to the American telephones. Hear what they are saying."

"Do you speak English, Lieutenant?"

"No, Captain, but Malenkov does." Dolinski pointed at Tverdokhleb. "The navigator does. I am sure there are others who do on board."

Bocharkov grunted. "Right now, I know what the Americans are thinking and what they are doing. They are trying to either bottle me up so I have to surface, or cause me to screw up and run aground before we reach the open ocean."

"Aye, sir," Ignatova answered.

"But, sir, I am offering you insight into the Americans that only this can provide." He held up the receiver set.

"All the intelligence in the world isn't going to help me in the next half hour."

"Time to turn: two minutes!" Tverdokhleb announced.

"Two minutes," Orlov echoed.

"Sir, intelligence can shave minutes off a tactical problem and days, weeks, months off a strategic one."

Bocharkov opened his mouth to order the young lieutenant away, and then thought better of it. "Thank you, Lieutenant Dolinski, for your insight, but right now my eyes are my intelligence and they are watching two American destroyers trying to cut us off."

"Second contact is on right-bearing drift, bearing zero-two-zero!" Orlov announced.

Bocharkov pointed toward Sonar, at Tverdokhleb and toward Uvarova. "Everything I need to survive is right here in this room with the exception of the engineers. Once we get out of Subic Bay, Lieutenant, you can hook up your contraption and play it as long as we are periscope depth. Now, if you will excuse me," Bocharkov finished, glancing at Ignatova.

"But, if it doesn't work—"

"Lieutenant Dolinski, if it doesn't work! What would you have me do? Surface the K-122, put a rubber raft over the side, and send you back to fix it?"

"Come on, Lieutenant Dolinski," Ignatova said, touching the GRU Spetsnaz officer on the arm. "I'll show you where you can test your system."

The aft hatch opened and Lieutenant Vyshinsky, the communications officer, entered, looking straight at Bocharkov. Bocharkov caught the stare. Vyshinsky held up a message board. "Take it to the XO," Bocharkov said aloud. Didn't these officers realize the precarious situation they were in? Didn't they realize how narrow a chance the K-122 had of making it to the open ocean?

"Time to turn: one minute thirty seconds," Tverdokhleb announced from his seat.

"One minute thirty seconds," Orlov echoed, "until time to turn!"

"Recommended course two-zero-two," Tverdokhleb said.

"New recommended course two-zero-two!" Orlov repeated.

Shoal waters and the rocks leading to shore were protection. Bocharkov looked at the clock. The rocks and shoal waters would not mask the noise the K-122 was putting in the water, but if the Americans decided to go active sonar, it would disrupt the pings and help hide him.

"Come to course two-zero-two," Bocharkov acknowledged. The Americans were going to go active. He would. Then he realized how he could use it to his advantage and quickly called Lieutenant Commander Orlov to him. It would be dangerous, but he knew it would work. It had better.

Ignatova, with the communications officer in tow, approached Bocharkov. "Skipper, you had better read this," he said, handing a message to him.

THE speaker for the Navy Red secure communications squeaked like fingernails down a chalkboard, drawing chill bumps racing across everyone's arms. MacDonald's hands were halfway to his ears when it stopped and the familiar synchronizing bagpipes of the cryptographic keys replaced the nerve-wracking initial sounds.

"Lieutenant Burnham!" Joe Tucker shouted across Combat. "Turn the speaker down. Now!"

The volume decreased almost immediately.

"*Dale*, this is Subic Operations Center. How do you read me?"

"I read you five by five," Burnham replied.

The aft hatch opened. Two sailors from the mess decks came into Combat. One was carrying a large rectangular tray filled with hot pastries. The other carried a coffee container and paper cups.

"Finally," Green said in a soft voice. "A ship that recognizes the needs of an aging admiral."

"Dale, the USS *Wrangell* is wrapping up ammo transfer and will be done within the next five minutes. Once we have the all clear from her, you will be cleared for active sonar operations. Be advised we have multiple small boats searching the harbor for intruders. We will have to ensure they have no one in the water. Do you copy? Over."

"Subic, this is *Dale*. We copy. Out," echoed the voice of Lieutenant Burnham.

Burnham looked at Joe Tucker. "XO, if they are searching for people in the water, doesn't that mean that those people might be in the water when we turn on active sonar?"

"They're intruders," Green snapped. "If they're in the water when *Dale* goes active, then they'll get out of the water quick enough." Green turned to MacDonald. "Well, Danny me boy, what are your intentions?"

"No change is my recommendation, Admiral."

"Think he knows we're onto him?"

"Yes, sir. Without doubt he's been watching everything on periscope. Plus, if he is smart, he will be monitoring our harbor common channel 16 frequency. He'll know we have two ships under way."

"Most likely the gunfire ashore had nothing to do with a rowdy party, you know?"

MacDonald nodded. "It has crossed my mind that we don't issue pieces to our sailors," MacDonald said, using the nautical term "pieces" instead of "guns."

"What could they have been doing?"

"I heard the altercation was near the warehouses."

Green nodded. "Security had an alarm from the small building holding the telephone switching units." He laughed. "If they were trying to tap our telephones, they're going to be wasting a lot of time monitoring them, unless they enjoy small talk, phone sex, and pleas for money from momma-san."

MacDonald had not known about the alarm's location. If they were tapping the telephones, they would know a lot more than the admiral figured. Logistics was the primary topic of discussion over unclassified lines. Had to be so. Most supplies originated with commercial firms, which did not have cryptographic systems capable of protecting sensitive but unclassified information.

"I suggested to the base commander they get that cryptologist Norton . . . I forget his first name . . . out of his BOQ room and get him over to the telephone switching building. They're supposed to be the technical eyes of the navy. Maybe he can detect if they've done anything to our telephones."

"Yes, sir."

"Of course, maybe we'll be lucky and they did something to reduce the telephone bill."

"Sir." Stalzer motioned from Sonar. "The contact is in a turn again. Looks like a slow turn to port."

Green and MacDonald stepped over to the sonar compartment. Stalzer squeezed inside to the left of Oliver, while Burkeet pressed against the bulkhead along the right.

Joe Tucker stepped away from the opening and headed forward. "Skipper, I'll be at the plotting table with the ASW team."

MacDonald nodded. It would be the plotting table that would show the navigational track of the contact as well as the topography of Subic Bay. They might hear the immediate changes here at Sonar, but if they were going to fight the intruder, it would be from the charts of the ASW team.

Everyone remained silent as Oliver repeated the compass headings as the contact changed course. When he called, "Contact steady on course two-zero-five," a collective sigh filled the compartment. The one worry with trailing a submarine was missing a maneuver where the contact was positioning for a firing solution.

A minute later, Joe Tucker rejoined them. "Captain, appears the submarine has aligned itself along the shoals of Cubi Point."

"Means less water beneath his hull to take evasive action," Green offered.

"Yes, sir, but it might also mean this skipper expects us to use active sonar. Active sonar doesn't work well in shallow water. It bounces and reverberates all over the place," MacDonald said.

"How long until he reaches those shoal waters?"

"Admiral, he is already in them, sir," Joe Tucker replied.

The familiar bagpipe sound filled Combat, almost immediately followed with the call sign of the Subic Operations Center calling the *Dale*.

"*Dale* here. Go ahead," Lieutenant Burnham replied.

"You are cleared for active sonar. I say again, you are cleared for active sonar."

Topside the sailor manning the aft sound-powered telephone watch reported the red stern lights of the small boys heading back toward the piers of the Subic Naval Base. He also reported the activity on five of the warships as they prepared to get under way. The sound of horns cascaded over the military installations surrounding Subic Bay and Cubi Point

Naval Air Station, waking everyone as the American base ramped up to a possible attack. Many of the sailors who would normally be on board would find themselves left behind if the warships received orders to cast off lines, but every ship in the United States Navy kept the minimum number of officers, chiefs, and sailors on board to get under way at a moment's notice. This event would be critiqued for lessons learned, which would be noted, and soon forgotten as time eroded memory of the event.

"Think we should give active a try?" Green asked.

MacDonald nodded. "If we can get one ping off him . . ."

Green shook his head violently. "That's not why I want us to go active, Captain. I want that son of a bitch to know we know he is there." He guffawed. "After all, isn't as if he can go anywhere." He nodded. "Where is the *Coghlan*? I want her to zip ahead of the contact. Get the *Coghlan* between it and the open ocean. Tell him to stay silent and he is not to use active sonar without my permission. Let's box this son of a bitch in."

MacDonald acknowledged the order and looked at Joe Tucker, who saluted and moved toward the main part of Combat, where Lieutenant Burnham stood.

"Once we go active, Danny me boy, what do you think this contact is going to do? What would you do?"

MacDonald bit his lip as he thought about the question.

"Why do you think he edged himself closer to shoal waters?" Green continued. "And if he has the same charts we do of Subic Bay, he's going to know that those shoal waters are mostly man-made, filled with huge rocks and debris. Had to do it so the runway would stretch far enough out for the air traffic it was handling."

"He could open his torpedo tube doors while masked by the active sonar," MacDonald offered.

Green nodded. He chuckled. "Worst case for us. He opens his torpedo tube doors. We miss it. Then we take short-range torpedoes down our nose."

"Yes, sir."

"He may do that, but he won't fire. Let's assume for 'worst case' planning he does do that."

"I already have ordered our decoys ready for launch at my orders."

"They'd be good in open ocean. They may not work as good inside the shallower waters we are in. Shallow water—air-launched decoys?" Green shook his head. "Most likely the torpedoes would hit us before the decoys hit the water." Green looked around Combat. "What do we do?"

"We close the contact, sir."

"Do what?"

"Close the contact. If we are nearly on top of him when we activate our sonar, we'll be too close for his torpedoes to activate. Even if he fires them, he'll miss us."

"You're right, Danny. But when they miss us, they're going to seek out the nearest target that is viable. We have an entire battle group behind us, and one or more of them will become an inferno."

"We can launch decoys now."

Green shook his head. "We have to weigh what we do with what we think is going on in the mind of that Soviet skipper. He is as scared as we are nervous. Scared and nervous make for volatile bedmates."

"STEADY on course two-zero-two," Orlov announced.

"Sir?" Ignatova asked.

"I heard," Bocharkov told Ignatova, then announced loudly, "Very well. Distance to shoal waters?"

"Fifty meters," Tverdokhleb replied. "We are fifty meters maximum from shoal waters." The navigator looked up, pushing his bifocals off the end of his nose and against his eyes. "But these charts are old. I recommend going no closer."

"How old?" Ignatova demanded.

Old? A hell of a time to decide to tell us that, Bocharkov thought.

"Three years."

Bocharkov relaxed. A three-year-old chart was nothing. He had sailed from Kamchatka with charts five, six, and one time with a chart ten years old.

"We should be worried?" Ignatova asked.

"Only for the bow," Tverdokhleb said calmly. "The bow will announce shoal waters when it hits them."

"XO," Bocharkov said, drawing Ignatova's attention. "When

the Americans go active, I want to open the aft torpedo tube doors. All of them."

Ignatova nodded. "The Americans will hear us opening the doors."

Bocharkov nodded. "It is a risk we have to take."

"Aft torpedo tubes five and six are decoys. One through four are ready to fire."

Bocharkov grunted. "You don't expect me to fire torpedoes at the Americans, do you?"

Ignatova shook his head. "If they fire at us?"

Bocharkov gave a quick chuckle. "Then we will fight our way to the open ocean."

"Sir!" Orlov shouted from near the sonar console. "Contact Two to our north is in a left-bearing drift. It is increasing revolutions on its shafts."

"It is increasing speed to get ahead of us. It is moving into attack position," Ignatova said softly.

"No," Bocharkov countered. "The Americans are no fools. They are moving the ship to block our sprint to the Pacific. They know we have to try to escape eventually, so they are preparing for it." But the message from Moscow changed things. What if the Americans knew what Moscow had sent?

"Maybe we should take a chance with the decoys now."

Bocharkov pursed his lips as he shook his head. "No, XO. Not yet. Sometimes a slow escape is better than none. We will continue along this slow pace, letting the shallow water disrupt their sonar."

"If it doesn't, Comrade Captain, then . . ."

"Then we'll have less water overhead when we swim to the surface" Bocharkov whispered. Then he shook his head. "Sorry. Bad joke. Vladmiri, the main thing right now is patience. Patience is the key to defeating the Americans. Patience and good Soviet engineering."

"Then we're screwed."

"Another bad joke, XO."

THIRTEEN

Monday, June 5, 1967

"SIR, we are steady on course two-zero-zero," Lieutenant Burnham reported. "Time zero three two zero."

MacDonald glanced at the bulkhead clock where the hands showed three twenty in the morning. "False dawn?"

"I'll check, sir." Burnham turned and walked to the hatch separating the bridge and Combat. Within seconds he returned. "Eastern sky is lightening. Navigator says dawn is zero four thirteen, sir. Also, Skipper, Lieutenant Goldstein recommends no turns to port without a navigation check. He says the new course will bring us within a thousand yards of shallow water."

MacDonald looked at the bulkhead clock. Nearly forty-five minutes until dawn. "Tell the forward watches to keep alert for a periscope."

Burnham acknowledged the order as he hurried to the main section of Combat.

"You think he will have his periscope up, Danny?" Admiral Green asked.

"I would if it was still dark. We're too close for our surface radar to reflect it and at this fast-paced speed of three, four knots, the contact won't be making much of a wake."

"True," Green said, nodding. One of the mess cooks handed the admiral a fresh cup of coffee. "But it will still be making a wake." He sipped. "What's the fluorescence like inside Subic Bay?"

"Not much. Too much pollution—oil, sewage."

"Doesn't smell like Shit River."

Burkeet stood astraddle of the entrance to the sonar compartment. His head spun back and forth between the admiral and captain, pretending not to eavesdrop as they talked and strategized the next course of action. Simultaneously, the young officer listened to Chief Stalzer and Oliver talk about the sounds coming across the sonar. He had learned another valuable lesson, too. Junior officers should be seen and not heard.

Burnham returned, breathless. "Sirs, Subic Operations Center says don't light off sonar! They have had a snafu with the *Wrangell*. They're estimating thirty minutes now."

Green and MacDonald exchanged glances.

"Said when the ships went to GQ, the pierside working parties sent the Filipino laborers home. *Wrangell* is standing up a working party and expect to have the remaining ammunition off the pier and inside the skin of the ship in thirty minutes."

"Thirty minutes is a long time in antisubmarine warfare," Green offered.

"Thanks, Lieutenant," MacDonald said. "Relay my thanks to the Operations Center and tell them . . ."

". . . And tell them from Admiral Green that we are going to turn on the sonar in twenty minutes with or without their permission."

Burnham saluted, did an about-face, and hurried off to relay Green's comments.

"Dangerous if the *Wrangell* has exposed munitions, sir," MacDonald said.

Green shrugged. "Naw. Won't be dangerous. I was over there earlier today. Everything, including munitions, is just as your lieutenant said: They are on the piers. I don't think sonar in the water is going to leap above the waves and cause them to explode unless it rips up the stanchions and the munitions fall into the water. If that happens, we'll have more problems than worrying about sonar causing an explosion." He snorted and then glanced at the ASW team working the passive bearings between the *Dale* and the *Coghlan*. "*Plus*, I want to make this bugger sweat. Coming into an American port—*even if it is technically owned by the Philippines*—and thinking he can get away with it."

The aft hatch opened and the communications officer, Lieutenant Junior Grade Alton Taylor, stepped into Combat, a metal message board tucked neatly beneath his left arm. The khakis looked laundry-pressed, with two creases cutting neatly through the front pockets. MacDonald and Joe Tucker still wondered how long until the Naval Academy graduate lost his military bearing to the heat of Southeast Asia.

"Admiral, Captain, my respects, sirs," Taylor said. "Captain, I have this urgent message from Commander in Chief U.S. Pacific Fleet."

Green snorted. "I wonder what Big Al wants now."

"Admiral Johnson?" MacDonald asked.

Green shook his head. "No, I'm thinking of Al *Snotgrass*, one of the one-stars on his staff. Al is always wanting something and not averse to using the admiral's name. 'Snotgrass' was the nickname given to Admiral Albert Samuel Griffin when he was a midshipman along with the rest of us." Green smiled. "It was for an incident involving lots of beer and long grass in front of the Annapolis bar we were in." He tapped the message board. "Message?"

MacDonald flipped over the metal top and quickly read the message before handing the board to Admiral Green. "In this case, sir, it appears 'Big Roy' sent the message."

"Don't get cocky, Danny," Green said, taking the message board.

"Then again, reporting an unfriendly submarine contact in Subic Harbor probably had the old man out of his rack and into his shoes fairly quickly." Green took the clipboard and read the message. As the admiral read, MacDonald watched the flag officer's eyes rise for a moment, just before Green pulled the metal top down. He flipped the top closed and handed the message back to the communications officer.

"Looks as if they believe the contact we are pursuing might be part of a preemptive strike."

"Why would they believe that?"

"Because the Israeli Air Force attacked the Egyptian and Syrian airfields at zero seven fifteen Israeli time. That's two hours, fifteen minutes ago, gentlemen." Silence greeted the announcement. "Commander Seventh Fleet has ordered all ships in the fleet to prepare to get under way. He does not want to be caught with his pants down."

"Six hours difference between Israeli time and ours here; means it's around nine thirty. What do you think, Admiral?" MacDonald was surprised. His voice seemed steady, but there was this feeling that he was standing at the precipice of World War III and that *Dale* might be on the forward edge of starting it.

Around them, Burnham had moved closer, Burkeet had stepped out of Sonar.

Green shook his head. "I think our intelligence analysts are wrong. If our Soviet foe was going to do something as stupid as that, Crazy Ivan would have already done it." Green pointed to the port side of the ship, in the west direction. "It would already be raining cruise missiles from that other submarine out there and this son of a bitch would have spread torpedoes all over Subic Bay."

"Maybe they don't know about the Israeli attack yet, sir."

"You could be right, Skipper. We just found out, and the news is over two hours old. But when you cut through the holy war crap, the Middle East has been embroiled in since 1947, we and the Soviets have had a lot of opportunities to trade a few missiles." Green chuckled. "It hasn't happened yet, and I don't think either they or us are prepared to fight over another Middle East war yet."

"They're doing a little spying," Burnham offered.

"I think you are right, Lieutenant. But, then," Green added with a sigh, "I have been wrong before. But if I am wrong, then let the Soviets start it."

No one said anything.

"Okay, everyone," MacDonald said. "You heard the news. Now, get back to your positions."

Green looked at MacDonald. "This is a very long way from the safety of the Soviet coastline. It's a spying mission that has gone awry—very awry—for them." Green paused and looked at the message board. "And very sensitive for us."

"You think they were involved in the shooting ashore."

Green shrugged, then nodded. "Most likely. But then who knows for sure? We haven't had any serious gunfire inside the navy base since that chief decided Vietcong were landing near Cubic Point. Fortunately, he didn't kill anyone."

"I don't think they know the Israelis have already attacked."

Green stroked his chin. "I don't know, but I hope they do."

"Sir?" MacDonald exclaimed. "Why would we want them to know?"

"If the captain of that Echo class knows what we know, then he's as aware as we are of how a shooting confrontation might escalate our eyeball-to-eyeball wariness to a higher plane."

MacDonald thought of MADD—the Mutual Assured Destruction Doctrine. The doctrine said that in an exchange of nuclear warheads, there were no winners—only losers. So for lovers of life, MADD had become the overarching umbrella for a shaky peaceful coexistence. MADD would never work if either party worshipped death over life. Religious fanatics would laugh at MADD as they rushed into the arms of Allah.

"Admiral, Petty Officer Oliver picked up the submarine about the time the Israelis attacked."

BOCHARKOV leaned away from the periscope, put thumb and forefinger on each side of his nose, and rubbed his eyes.

"Steady on course two-zero-two."

"Time to next turn?"

When Tverdokhleb did not quickly answer, Bocharkov shouted out the question in his direction. "Time to next turn, Lieutenant? Didn't you hear me?"

Tverdokhleb put both hands on the table. "Sir, we can turn anytime, but we will have to turn within thirty minutes because we will be leaving the shoal waters."

"Okay, Navigator, which direction?"

"West?"

"West what? Quit making me ask the questions."

Tverdokhleb quickly took a ruler and ran a pencil line with it. "Next turn is in twenty minutes, sir. Base course is two-seven-zero. I would recommend ten to twelve knots."

"Won't that make us easily detected by the Americans?" Orlov asked.

"I think they have already detected us, Lieutenant Commander Orlov," Ignatova answered. He was nearing the navigation table.

"Make it so," Bocharkov said with a grunt. Once he increased speed above ten knots, then he would lose his own passive picture of the Americans. He would not know if they were sprinting ahead of him or if more had joined the pursuit. At least in this modern age of 1967, he did not have to worry about depth charges. *No, now they drop torpedoes onto you from the sky.*

Over at the navigator's plotting table, Ignatova was in deep, animated discussion with Tverdokhleb, both peering closely at the chart, their fingers tracing patterns on it.

Bocharkov went back to the periscope. He focused it aft. The bow light of the warship was easily discernible. It did not appear to him that the ship was trying to close or pull over the top of them. If that happened, both ships would collide because he had no depth in which to disappear. He pulled the scope to the left, peering off his starboard side. The running lights of the warship in that direction were pulling left. That warship was racing to get ahead of them but not at such speed its sonar would be affected.

"The running lights of the contact to starboard show it is an American destroyer."

"Aye, sir," Orlov acknowledged.

"Sir," Ignatova said from beside him.

Bocharkov leaned away from the periscope. "What is it, XO?"

"I have gone over the plan with our navigator. Eventually we are going to have to run for it."

"I prefer to say we are going to 'evade' to 'we are going to have to run.'"

"Yes, sir. I do, too. The way to the open ocean is due west. Ten minutes on any westward course shows at least one hundred meters of water beneath us."

"So we have to avoid the Americans for about ten minutes before we can head for the dark Pacific beneath us?"

Ignatova nodded. "The question is, when do we do it?"

Bocharkov looked at the clock. "It is three thirty five now." He looked over at Orlov. "Officer of the Deck, come here, please."

When Orlov arrived, Bocharkov started speaking. "The Americans are going to want to use their active sonar. No one attacks only on passive sonar—too much room for error."

"You think they are going to attack us?" Orlov asked.

Bocharkov shook his head. "No, they know as we do that neither of us can afford a confrontation except on the high seas. But they will want to embarrass us, force us to the surface, or hold us down. To do that, they are going to have to use their active sonar."

Ignatova nodded. "Active sonar will turn this submarine into a brass drum."

"Precisely," Bocharkov agreed. "With us inside it. So we have to get out of here before they can make that happen."

"Maybe they are unable to go active sonar right now. Maybe they don't want the Philippine government to know that a Soviet Navy submarine penetrated within striking distance to their fleet," Ignatova suggested.

"Make no mistake about it, Vladmiri," Bocharkov said. "They are going to go active on their sonar."

"Why haven't they yet?"

Bocharkov grunted. "Who knows how the Americans think. One moment they are as sane as us, the next moment they are off on a wild tangent to save the world in their image." He shrugged. "Regardless of what the American government may want to do, I know the captains of the destroyers trailing us want to go active sonar. Right now, they are pleading with someone for permission . . ."

". . . or they are waiting until they have their forces properly deployed," Ignatova finished.

Bocharkov nodded. "When the destroyer to our starboard reaches a position between us and the Pacific, I expect the destroyer behind us to become more aggressive. It will be the one to go active."

"Then what, Captain?"

"When they go active with their sonar, the shoals and rocks to our port side should disrupt the return signals. That should cloud their displays, creating an inaccurate picture. It will take less than a minute for them to shift back to passive."

"Afterward, they will stay on passive," Orlov said.

Bocharkov nodded. "For a while. But during those few seconds we have an opportunity."

"What if they are not going active because they know what will happen with us this close to a rocky shore and in shallow water?" Ignatova added.

Bocharkov sighed—a deep sigh—before taking a deep breath. "Then it will be rough inside the K-122 while they are active." He turned to Orlov and in a near whisper said, "When they go active, Officer of the Deck, I want to come to course two-two-zero."

He pointed at Ignatova. "XO, you go check the recommended course and see if our navigator's comment about the ocean depth *anywhere* to our west applies to that course."

Bocharkov lightly poked Orlov in the chest, leaned forward, and in a soft voice said, "I will give the order. You will execute it and you will bring the speed up to sixteen knots during the turn, reducing it to ten knots when we steady up."

"A knuckle," Ignatova said with a smile.

"Knuckle" was the nautical term for when a ship made a quick turn at high speed, churning the water behind it and creating an artificial barrier that reflected active, and confused passive, sonar. Bocharkov knew it would present an opportunity for a less competent sonar operator to mistake the knuckle for the submarine.

"Once on course two-two-zero, we will have ten minutes. Ten critical minutes in which we cannot head deep; we will be cavitating—putting noise in the water." He paused, looking at each of them before continuing. "And we will be vulnerable. If the Americans are going to attack, this would be most advantageous for them."

· "XO, go check on Tverdokhleb. I want you on top of Tverdokhleb while we are doing this, checking his navigation and making sure when I order us deep, we have water beneath the keel to answer the call."

"CAPTAIN MacDonald," Admiral Green said, cradling the cup of coffee in his hands. "Give Subic Operations Center another call and tell them it is zero three three zero. We are going active."

MacDonald nodded, and motioned Burnham to his side. A few seconds later the combat information center officer was moving back to the center part of Combat. Both MacDonald and Green watched as Burnham lifted the red handset.

"Should shake them up, shouldn't it?" Green asked.

Before MacDonald could reply, Burnham shouted from where he stood. "Subic says all clear for active, sir!"

"Amazing what a little flag power can do for overcoming operational inertia."

"TIME, zero three three zero," Orlov announced.

Bocharkov looked at Tverdokhleb. "Position?"

"One hundred meters port side, depth fifty meters. Recommend steer course two-two-zero."

Bucharkov looked at Orlov. "Make it so, Officer of the Deck. Come to course two-two-zero, maintain four knots."

Bocharkov rubbed his eyes before leaning forward and looking through the periscope. The warship was still there, less than one hundred meters to his rear. One hundred meters to his left were rocks that would tear the bottom out of the K-122, and one hundred meters behind him was a ship that would sink him. He wondered briefly what the captain of the destroyer was like. Like him, he knew the man would be trying to guess what the K-122 would do next. Just as he was trying to figure out what actions he could do without causing the Americans to think they had been fired upon. Any misunderstanding between them right now would reverberate all the way to Moscow and Washington—if it had not already.

The communications officer, Lieutenant Vyshinsky, came

through the aft watertight hatch. Accompanying him was the *zampolit*. Just what he needed right now—a bunch of Soviet-indoctrinated bullshit. What he needed was a couple hundred meters of water beneath his keel. Then he could handle anything.

"IT'S that time, Danny," Green said, glancing at the clock on the bulkhead, then his watch.

MacDonald looked. The clock showed fifteen minutes to four.

"The contact is in a turn!" Stalzer reported in a loud voice, his head quickly disappearing back into the sonar compartment for a moment before reappearing. "Right-hand turn. It's a slow turn, Captain, Admiral, but she's turning."

Green grunted. "Could not ask for better-trained contact," he said with a smile. "In a couple of seconds our target is going to be broadside to us with his torpedoes unable to fire against us. He is going to have to maneuver if he intends to attack." He clasped his hands behind his back. "Now is the time to ping them like sardines in a can. Not a damn thing he can do about it without it being mistaken for a hostile act."

"Lieutenant Burkeet, when I give the word, I want one ping," MacDonald said, holding up his right index finger. "Just one pulse."

"Tell Subic what we are about to do, Lieutenant!" Admiral Green shouted.

"Admiral, I need to be on the bridge now," MacDonald said.

Green nodded. He leaned toward MacDonald. "Give it five minutes before you order active sonar. I should follow you up in a few minutes, and I'll take care of Subic if they try to delay our actions."

MacDonald nodded once, then turned and hurried forward, heading toward the bridge. If the Soviet Echo—everyone thought it was an Echo submarine because that is what they had chased around the Pacific for a couple of days. It was definitely a nuke and it was definitely not theirs and it was definitely not a coastal-hugging Chicom diesel. He opened the hatch to the bridge and stepped through to the announcement by the navigator of "Captain on the bridge."

Goldstein hurried over to MacDonald. MacDonald walked by the officer of the deck, nodding at Ensign Hatfield, who was standing near the center of the row of windows that lined the bridge from the edge of the port bridge wing to the edge of the starboard bridge wing.

Goldstein did a quick turn and trailed MacDonald, his hand holding the binoculars to his chest so they wouldn't bounce against his body.

MacDonald stopped in front of the 12MC internal communications device. He turned to Goldstein. "We're going to activate sonar. When, I'm not sure, but I do know what the Soviet—I mean the contact—will do once it hears the ping. The skipper of the submarine is going to be at least antsy. He is going to want to position his boat to defend against an attack by us. If, or when, he starts maneuvering to align his forward or aft tubes toward us, we are going to have to do some quick maneuvering."

"Aye, sir," Goldstein acknowledged. "Ensign Hatfield, I want you behind the helmsman. When I give course-speed changes, you double-check the helmsman. Make sure we don't pass them."

MacDonald's eyebrows rose. He had never imagined Goldstein as a take-charge sort of guy. He turned back to the 12MC and pressed the button for Combat. "Combat, this is the captain."

"Captain, Combat here, sir," Lieutenant Burnham replied.

"Tell the torpedomen to stand by the SVTTs." SVTT stood for surface vessel torpedo tubes.

"Aye, sir."

MacDonald hurried to the port bridge wing and leaned over the railing, looking aft toward the port-side surface vessel torpedo tube mount. He heard the shouts of the watch and knew the sound-powered telephone talker was relaying Burnham's orders, but he couldn't make out the words. The shadows of the men, moving in the last shades of night before the dawn, told him they were uncovering the three-tubed torpedo launch system. He would have to turn the *Dale* to fire either of them at the contact dead ahead of the destroyer. He took a deep breath and stepped away from the railing. He was prepared to launch torpedoes if he had to. They only had a three-nautical-mile range, but the contact was less than a half mile ahead of them.

"Sir," Goldstein said from the doorway. "Combat reports over-the-sides are ready."

"Mr. Goldstein, to fire our torpedoes, we will have to maneuver the ship. I think a ten-degree rudder and a ten-degree course change will be sufficient right now, but keep abreast of where the contact is relative to *Dale* and be prepared to uncover whichever SVTT is best for launching the torpedoes."

"Aye, sir," Goldstein acknowledged and quickly stepped back into the bridge, stopping immediately at the navigation plotting table.

MacDonald watched for a moment as the officer of the deck's finger ran across the chart. He knew Goldstein was checking the surrounding waters. A ten-degree rudder that ran them aground would ruin the day. He heard noise aft and turned in time to see the sailors swing the over-the-sides so the tubes pointed out. "Over-the-sides" was nautical slang for the torpedoes fired from the SVTT.

MacDonald stepped back into the bridge and walked briskly to the 12MC. He pressed the button for Combat, then also the ones for Sonar and Engineering. He had three of the ship's general quarters positions on the line.

"Combat, Engineering, and Sonar, here's what we are going to do," he started, and then quickly went through his plan for a single ping. When everyone had acknowledged, he paused and took a breath. "Sonar, contact status?"

"Contact is steady on course two-two-zero, speed estimated between three and four knots."

MacDonald glanced out the window in front of him. About a thousand yards off his bow was a Soviet submarine with its starboard side facing him. It would be easy to sink the enemy arrogant enough to penetrate the waters of America's foreign navy base. A bit of a thrill raced through him at the thought of seeing the bow of a submarine break the surface before it sunk to the bottom. He both wanted to do it and hoped the decision to do so never came.

"I want a single ping. Only one," he finally said, glancing

at the clock mounted on the bulkhead behind the helmsman. It showed ten minutes to four.

"Roger, sir," Burkeet answered. "One ping."

In the background he heard Admiral Green add, "Make it low-power, Lieutenant. Too much power will have the sonar ricocheting off the rocks and bottom."

Why didn't I think of that? MacDonald asked himself.

"Officer of the Deck, come to course two-three-zero, speed four knots." This would clear the port torpedo tubes for launching the Mark-32 torpedoes.

He heard the ping of the sonar as it reverberated through the destroyer, knowing that belowdecks the noise would startle those not prepared.

"HOLD it, hold it!" Bocharkov said as the loud echo of the sonar ping faded. "They used low power on their sonar," he added. The captain of the destroyer was a smart opponent, he decided. He looked at Vyshinsky and handed the message board back to him. "You and Golovastov, return to your station."

"But, Captain," Golovastov objected. "This is a message from Moscow. It is an order—"

"I said, leave my control room. Now!"

Out of the corner of his eye, Bocharkov saw Ignatova smile for a moment before turning back to look over the shoulder of Tverdokhleb.

Vyshinsky turned and hurried away immediately. The *zampolit* stood in front of Bocharkov for a couple of seconds before angrily turning and following the communications officer.

"Turn?" Orlov shouted.

Bocharkov's attention returned to the boat. He shook his head. "Not yet." He looked at Ignatova. "Did you get the time?" He had no doubt that Golovastov would go directly to the political officer's private stateroom and start writing his superiors about how Bocharkov disobeyed orders from Moscow. His argument would be that he wasn't disobeying them. He was executing them. A deep sigh escaped.

"Fifteen seconds, sir."

"Fifteen seconds?"

"Yes, sir, from ping to fade."

Fifteen seconds from the time the ping hit the K-122 until the echo faded. Fifteen seconds he had in which to create a knuckle and start his sprint to the open ocean. He might have a whole minute of confusion once he started maneuvering, before the Americans reestablished contact. If they lost contact as he hoped.

"Bearing to the American warship?"

"Which one, sir?"

"Both!" he snapped.

"Contact One bears zero-two-zero true, estimated range one kilometer. Contact Two bears two-seven-zero true, estimated range five to seven kilometers. Contact One is constant bearing; noise shows it seems to be maintaining constant range. Contact Two has a distinct left-bearing drift, high rotation on its shaft. It seems to be opening distance from us."

Bocharkov grunted. He looked at Ignatova. "Your thoughts, XO?"

"They are attempting to box us in as you have noted, Captain. This seems to remain the most likely scenario. The course change of Contact One can only mean one of two things. Either he is repositioning to help box us in, or he is clearing his torpedo weapon systems so he can launch. I think I would prefer the first alternative, but . . ."

"But we both know he is positioning to launch torpedoes. The question for us is whether this means he intends to launch or is more likely a defensive maneuver."

"They could also be positioning themselves so the one nearest us can launch torpedoes at short range while Contact Two is preparing to launch its rocket-propelled torpedoes."

"You think they are going to attack?" Bocharkov asked with disbelief. "I don't."

Ignatova shook his head. "Neither do I, sir. But it is an option the Americans are giving themselves."

Bocharkov grunted. "We are playing the usual cat-and-mouse game; only we are playing it in shallow waters." He slapped the handles of the periscope. "We have got to get to deep water."

"Aye, Captain," Ignatova said.

"Officer of the Deck, get ready. When I give the order, I want a right full rudder, all ahead full. My next order will be for a left full rudder, maintaining all ahead full. The orders will come almost back-to-back." Bocharkov looked at the anxious faces in the control room. "Periscope down."

Bocharkov stepped back as the hydraulics lowered the periscope.

"BRIDGE, Combat! We got him, sir. Dead ahead six hundred fifty yards."

"Any course or speed change?"

"Negative, sir. Contact remains on course two-two-zero, heading toward the open ocean."

The clock read five minutes until four.

"Give him one minute, Lieutenant Burnham, then one more ping. A single ping and no more."

"Aye, sir. Captain, port and starboard over-the-sides are ready. Six tubes loaded. Port SVTT is choice of weapon, sir. With your permission, am having them set for short range. That way they'll go active as soon as they hit the water."

MacDonald's eyebrows lifted. "Belay that order, Lieutenant. Set them for two hundred yards run before they go active." Good initiative, but wrong decision. A launched torpedo became its own boss, subject to finding a target—any target. It had no way of telling if what it locked onto was a friendly or hostile.

"Yes, sir. Will do."

"And make sure it is destroyed if it goes farther than a mile. Don't want to accidentally sink the *Coghlan*." He paused. "Also, make sure that *Coghlan* knows our intention and that they are to wait for our order before they fire."

"Aye, sir."

A few seconds passed before Burnham added, "Sir, time to next ping is zero four hundred."

He nearly asked why the wait, but knew it was either because of Green or Subic Operations Center. Either way, three more minutes meant three more minutes for the contact to wonder what was going to happen next. "Very well, make it so."

BOCHARKOV looked at the clock. "It's been nearly three minutes since the last pulse."

Ignatova walked up. "The navigation picture looks as accurate as the charts permit, Captain."

"Three minutes since last pulse."

"I know. I wonder what it means. Continuous pulses would keep the boat roiling in reverberations."

"I think it means they just wanted us to know they know we are here."

"I think they already knew that we knew."

"Probably, but with a single pulse, I think they are also telling us they don't intend to attack. They are playing the cat-and-mouse game as we are." Bocharkov smiled.

"Or they have the information they need for a two-prong attack."

Bocharkov grunted. "They have had that information for over half an hour." He shook his head. "No, they may want us to surface, if they can make us. The delay in sending out another pulse tells me they no more want a hot event than we do."

"You may be right."

"XO, when we start the turn, I want you over at the firing panel. I want the torpedo doors opened. Do it while the ping is still echoing." Then he added in a loud voice, getting everyone's attention, "Maybe the Americans will miss the opening of the torpedo doors in their euphoria."

"Euphoria?"

"They are probably as happy as we are. We have detected the entire U.S. Asian Fleet in port and they have managed to find themselves an unknown submarine inside their harbor. Now, which side has the best tactical advantage?"

"We do?" Ignatova asked.

"Of course! Whichever way we fire, we have a target. They only have one direction in which to fire."

The men in the control room laughed. These times of confrontation with the Americans were filled with tense minutes of anxiety punctuated with seconds of ass-tightening fear. He needed his men to have confidence. He needed to show it.

Right now, all he felt was a strong desire to pee. "Combat syndrome" they called it at Grechko Naval Academy. In moments of fear a strong desire to void the wastes from the body took over. He grunted, drawing the attention of those nearby. A holdover from mankind's caveman roots.

Bocharkov looked up at Orlov. "Time since last ping?" he asked aloud.

"Two minutes, sir," Orlov answered.

"Anytime now, comrades. Be prepared." He looked at the clock. "Prepare for a sonar pulse," he said.

A slight rustle accompanied his orders as everyone leaned forward at his position, or tightened his hands on the various handles, the helm and ballast controls. Even the XO seemed to move closer to the torpedo firing mechanism.

Movement forward caught his attention as Uvarova squeezed the shoulders of the two men manning the planes. "This is what you are trained for," the chief of the boat whispered. Though softly spoken, Uvarova's deep voice rode across the silence of the control room like a comfortable mantra. A couple of sailors nodded in agreement.

Ignatova picked up the handset and pressed the *Boyevaya Chast'* 3 button. "Forward and aft torpedo rooms, this is the control room. Prepare to open doors on aft torpedo tubes." Satisfied of the answer, Ignatova lowered the handset and nodded at Bocharkov.

"Remind them not to fire torpedoes without my order," Bocharkov cautioned. "We are going to fire decoys, but also at my order."

Ignatova nodded, keyed the handset, and relayed the order.

All they could do now was wait. The execution time was in the hands of the Americans. For a brief moment, Bocharkov wondered what he would do if the Americans failed to ping again. He grunted. No way. Once you were committed to the final phase of an antisubmarine warfare event, you followed it through. American doctrine called for three pulses to finalize a firing solution. A slight chill traveled up his spine. What if they went to the third pulse?

"**CONTACT** status?" MacDonald asked from the bridge, his mouth about a foot from the 12MC speaker. The clock read zero three fifty-nine. A deep sigh escaped as he straightened.

"No change, sir. Contact remains on course two-two-zero, estimated speed four knots."

Time for the second ping, he thought.

"Lieutenant Burnham, it's that time. Where is my pulse?" His finger rested on the toggle that switched the voice box from listen to speak. Looking out the port side of the bridge, he could detect the approaching dawn against the silhouette of the hills to the east.

He turned to Goldstein. "Remind the topside watches to keep alert for signs of a periscope." What would he do if they spotted it? Photograph it? Speed up and run over it?

"Aye, sir," the officer of the deck replied before relaying the order to the sound-powered phone talker positioned near the boatswain mate of the watch to the left of the helm.

"Sir, Admiral Green said permission granted."

His finger pushed the toggle downward. "Very well, Lieutenant Burnham, tell Sonar they can transmit a single pulse at this time."

On the bulkhead behind the helmsman the black second hand touched the twelve on the clock.

"Aye, sir."

BOCHARKOV looked at the clock. Anytime now.

He still jumped when the second pulse hit the K-122, but he was ready. "Right full rudder! All ahead full!"

The nuclear-powered engines kicked in almost immediately. The K-122 leaped, tilting left as the submarine surged forward like a wild stallion released from its stall. From barely making way, to foam roiling the water less than twenty meters above them. Everyone grabbed hold of something to steady themselves. Bocharkov grabbed a nearby railing that separated his periscope position from the main control room.

"Passing two-three-zero!" Orlov announced, then continued to rattle off the turn degree by degree.

Ignatova was on the intercom. He would be ordering the outer torpedo doors opened. Bocharkov neither felt the vibration of the doors opening nor heard the grind of the hydraulics that should have accompanied the act.

"Passing two-five-two! Passing sixteen knots."

Bocharkov waited. The deck and bulkheads vibrated with the strain of the tight turn as K-122 continued to increase speed. The helmsman leaned into the helm, keeping the K-122 fighting the urge of the boat to steady up on a course—any course.

"SHE'S coming around!" Oliver shouted. "The contact is increasing speed and bringing her bow around."

Green stuck his head into the sonar room. "What!"

Chief Stalzer grabbed the extra headset and pressed them against his ears. "The contact is turning. It's in a fast turn. Its bow is turning toward us!"

Green's head disappeared.

"BRIDGE! This is Combat!"

MacDonald pressed the toggle switch. "Captain here."

"Danny, this is the admiral. The submarine is moving into attack position; it's in a right-hand turn at high speed, bringing its bow around!"

MacDonald's throat tightened. This is what he was trained to do. He shook his head slightly at the thought. He turned toward Goldstein. "All ahead flank! Steady as she goes!"

This should offset the turn of the contact, causing *Dale* and the contact to be starboard to starboard as if passing each other. If the submarine did do something stupid and launch a torpedo, the wire guiding it would break before it could be guided to the *Dale*. Additionally, closing the contact meant getting the destroyer inside the range of the Soviet torpedoes, where they would be unable to lock on them. He thought of the "ring around the rosy" song girls in grammar school sang.

He pushed the toggle switch. "Combat, prepare to fire torpedoes at my command; starboard-side over-the-sides."

"Roger!" came Burnham's reply.

For a moment he wondered if Green would step in. He hoped not. This was his ship and his battle, but Green was the admiral in charge and as the commander Task Force Seventy, he could do anything he fucking well pleased. "Just not now," MacDonald mumbled to himself.

"RELEASE decoy!" Bocharkov shouted. "Left full rudder, maintain speed."

It took several seconds for the submarine to respond to the new orders.

"I have lost the contacts," the sonar operator reported.

Orlov did not bother repeating the announcement. Bocharkov had heard it and ignored it. They were passing eighteen knots in shallow water. All his passive detection capability was gone.

He thought he felt the slight vibration of the decoy as it was launched, but the K-122 was shaking so bad he wondered for a moment if it was just his imagination.

STALZER lifted his headset. "That son of a bitch has his torpedo tube doors opened."

"You hear them?" Green asked.

Stalzer bit his lip and nodded. "I heard something. It was definitely a torpedo tube door opening or closing."

Green pulled his head back from the doorway to Sonar, looked around, and grabbed a nearby sound-powered phone talker. "You got comms with the bridge?"

"Yes, sir," the young sailor stuttered, his eyes glancing down at the admiral's hand holding his arm.

"Good. You stand here at Sonar and start passing everything they say up to the bridge." Then Green released him and hurried forward toward Burnham.

"It's turning! The submarine is in a hard left turn . . ."

Both Stalzer and Oliver pressed their headsets against their ears. "It's gone! I got noise in the water, but it's gone."

Green turned. "What do you mean it's gone?"

Stalzer and Oliver relaxed the pressure.

"It's back. We got it." Oliver reached up and moved the pointer on the display slightly. "Wow! It's bearing dead ahead again; no bearing drift."

Stalzer's eyes squinted for a moment and then opened wide. "We have a decoy in the water! That's no submarine; that noise I heard was it launching a decoy."

"STEADY on course two-four-zero, reduce speed to eight knots." Bocharkov then turned to Tverdokhleb. "Time to deep water?"

Tverdokhleb flipped his ruler along the chart, running a pencil line down it. His tongue protruded slightly from between clinched lips.

"I said, how long until deep water?" Bocharkov repeated.

The vibration of the earlier maneuver and speed was slacking off as the K-122 slowed and steadied up on a new course.

The navigator looked up. "Maybe seven minutes on this course at speed eight knots."

"REDUCE speed to six knots!" MacDonald shouted.

The *Dale* vibrated as the speed rapidly decreased. It would take a minute or so for the destroyer to come down to six knots.

Motion to his right caught MacDonald's attention. It was the running lights on the *Coghlan* and they were on a constant bearing. He pressed the toggle. "Combat, Skipper. What is the *Coghlan* doing?"

A second passed before Burnham's voice came back. "Last report showed two-seven-zero at ten knots, sir. That was ten minutes ago."

"I hold him constant bearing."

More valuable time passed before Burnham replied. "Sir,

we are calling him. The radar repeater shows he has changed course and is closing us."

MacDonald grabbed the bridge-to-bridge radio handset. The bridge-to-bridge was the opened radio that every ship in the world carried that allowed them to communicate not only with one another when their paths crossed, but with Harbor Control when they approached a port, and the tugs that many times helped guide them into and out of ports.

"*Coghlan*, this is *Dale*. I hold you on constant bearing. Request you change course-speed."

"*Dale*, this is *Coghlan*. We have had to change to course two-zero-zero to maneuver through a mess of fishing boats. Will be maneuvering back to base course two-seven-zero in a few minutes."

"*Coghlan*, we are engaged in serious maneuvering and you are constricting my—"

"Sir," the quartermaster called from the navigator's table. Lieutenant Goldstein was walking toward the table. The quartermaster of the watch bent over the chart, dragging a pencil down the line of a ruler. "*Coghlan* is less than three miles and is CBDR. Unless she changes course in the next fifty seconds, we are going to be in extremis."

FOURTEEN

"**STEADY** on course two-two-zero! Speed eight knots," Orlov announced.

The aft hatch opened. The *zampolit* Lieutenant Golovastov and the GRU Spetsnaz Dolinski entered together. Bocharkov saw the neatly folded message in Golovastov's hand. Now was not the time for this.

"Depth?" Bocharkov asked.

"Sixteen meters."

That was good. They had just done some high-speed turns and the planesman expertise—under the chief of the boat's close supervision—had kept the K-122 at the same depth. He was happy they had not breached the boat or hit the bottom.

Ignatova motioned to Golovastov, who glared back, but continued toward Bocharkov. Dolinski ambled quietly behind the *zampolit*, ignoring the XO's motions. The time for politics was before the battle, not in the middle of it.

The two men marched right up to where Bocharkov stood.

"Lieutenant Tverdokhleb! What is my depth? Where am I?" Bocharkov shouted, his eyes burning into Golovastov, who now stood in front of him, Dolinski slightly behind the *zampolit.*

"Sir, we are two kilometers off Cubi Point. Charts show fifty meters of water beneath the keel."

Bocharkov nodded, his eyes never leaving the *zampolit.* Fifty meters was twenty more than he'd had minutes ago. "Time to deep water?" he asked aloud.

"Five minutes," Tverdokhleb answered.

"Five minutes," Orlov repeated.

"Is it light above me yet?"

"Fourteen minutes until dawn," Tverdokhleb said.

Bocharkov glanced at the clock.

Ignatova put the weapons console handset in its cradle and started toward Bocharkov. He saw the movement. "XO, tell Engineering my intentions are to stay on course and speed for the time being. Once the Americans have regained contact, we will conduct a similar maneuver again along with decoys. We'll need power to do it."

It was a meaningless order. Ignatova stopped and glanced for a second at the two junior officers standing in front of Bocharkov, before returning to his position.

Bocharkov was surprised to see Orlov move closer to his position, away from the center of the control room where the office of the deck normally stood when the boat was at general quarters.

Finally, Golovastov cleared his throat.

Bocharkov ignored it. "Raise periscope," he said. He'd take a quick look around and then lower it before some alert topside watch on the destroyers saw the wake that eight knots would create around the tube.

"Excuse me, Captain," Golovastov said.

The noise of the hydraulics raising the periscope masked Golovastov, so Bocharkov ignored him as he bent to unfold the handles on the scope. He pressed his eyes against the eyepiece and rode the scope up. Let the two junior officers stand there. Let them wait on display for everyone to see. He was trying to save the ship, not read some Party-political message from Moscow. If it were important, it would be from the commander Pacific Fleet.

"Sir, Contact Two has changed course," Lieutenant Yakovitch, the assistant weapons officer, said, sticking his head inside the control room from the sonar space. "It is CBDR—constant bearing, decreasing range."

"Bearing?" Bocharkov asked as he spun the periscope toward his starboard side.

"Bearing three-zero-zero true, sir."

"Speed?" Bocharkov asked as he aligned the scope with the compass bearing.

A slight pause occurred before Yakovitch replied, "Contact is at twelve knots."

"Twelve knots?"

Yakovitch acknowledged the speed of the contact.

Bocharkov grunted, but his eyes never left the periscope as he focused on the running lights. Twelve knots was too fast for most destroyers to have passive contact. The American sonar pulses were coming from Contact One, the combatant behind them. The lights blurred into focus. It took him only a couple of seconds to tell he was looking at the port bow of the destroyer. Bocharkov glanced at the compass. Same bearing.

"Our contact behind us?"

"On course two-zero-zero, sir, slight left-bearing drift."

If the two destroyers continued on their courses, he would have a narrow window in which to escape. He grunted again. How could he—

"Captain, I must insist you acknowledge Moscow's message."

Bocharkov stepped back quickly. "Lower periscope."

As the hydraulics kicked in, he jerked the message from Golovastov and quickly scanned it. Then he handed it back. "Are you satisfied?"

"Sir, Moscow is ordering you to abandon this mission."

"What the hell do you think I am doing, Lieutenant? And you," he said, pointing at Dolinski. "Didn't I tell you to get the hell out of my control room?"

Dolinski's head jumped slightly as Bocharkov caught the Spetsnaz lieutenant off guard. Bocharkov knew what Dolinski wanted to see. He wanted to witness the *zampolit* taking him down a notch so he could go back and make his own report through his channels.

Dolinski snapped to attention. "Comrade Captain, I need to fully test the installation. To see if it works."

"And you want me to run up the periscope? Stick an antenna in the air?"

"It would not take many minutes, sir."

Bocharkov grunted. "It either works or it doesn't. It is too late to be concerned about it, don't you think?"

"But, it is part—"

"Look, we will test it later."

"I need to test it now, sir."

Bocharkov held up his hand. He looked at the two men. "Now, listen to me, you two. I am trying to save the boat. That message is useless to me right now. Your intelligence apparatus—whatever it was—is something we have no control over now. It is too late. And you are endangering our lives. Now, both of you get the hell out of my control room, and I don't want to see you again until I call for you!" Bocharkov punctuated his words with his index finger jabbing at the men. He was unaware he was also stepping toward them.

Golovastov bumped into Dolinski as he stumbled backward, catching the Spetsnaz off balance. Dolinski pushed the *zampolit* forward, causing Golovastov to nearly bump into Bocharkov.

Without warning, Golovastov dashed toward the forward hatch. Dolinski nodded at Bocharkov with no expression across his face. Then the Spetsnaz lieutenant turned and casually followed the fleeing *zampolit* out the forward hatch.

Chief Ship Starshina Kostas Uvarova stepped over to the hatch and checked the watertight seal before nodding at Bocharkov. "It is sealed," he said.

Bocharkov took a deep breath. This wasn't over. The two *zampolits* would make trouble for him through their separate pipelines. But he had to survive this before he could worry about his future.

"Give me status on the contacts," he ordered. While he listened to the same status from a minute earlier, he envisioned how events might unfold with the two American destroyers. What could he do and when could he do it to give the K-122 more breathing room toward the deep water?

"Four minutes to one hundred meters," Tverdokhleb announced.

One hundred meters was better than fifty, but it still wasn't enough to lose the Americans. He needed three hundred, then a thousand, then unlimited depth to escape and evade the clumsy destroyers. What would he do if he were the captain of one of the destroyers? Helicopters? The Americans had been experimenting with these unmanned DASH helicopters that seemed to take off and disappear over the horizon to never be seen again.

No, if he were the Americans, he would keep his forces in position for an attack and, once ready, sprint forward to try to drive the K-122 to the surface. He needed time, and he needed a sound layer of water between him and the surface to mask the noises being generated by the K-122. Two sound layers would be manna from heaven.

The isothermal layers of water would bounce his passive noise downward and send the American sonar pulses upward. Give him those conditions and he would lose the Americans in minutes.

"Water beneath my keel?"

Tverdokhleb shrugged. It was never good when a navigator shrugged.

"Do you know?"

"Sir, these charts are old. They indicate less than seventy-five meters. If we could do a depth—"

"It would tell the Americans where we are," Bocharkov snapped. He should have thought of that while the Americans were pinging, when he might have been able to mask a single ping downward to find the bottom.

DOLINSKI grabbed Golovastov outside the control room. "We have a problem, comrade."

Sweat poured from the brow of the K-122's *zampolit*. The man nodded, taking in a deep breath, his chest shaking with the effort.

Dolinski pulled his handkerchief from his pocket. "Here, wipe the sweat from your face."

"I think the captain is dangerous," Golovastov muttered.

Dolinski gave a slow nod in agreement. "We need to tell Moscow."

"We can't," Golovastov objected.

Dolinski smiled. "We are the representatives of the Party. We can do anything we want when we feel our nation is endangered."

"What can we do?"

Dolinski quickly explained his plan. A minute later the two men were walking toward Communications. Golovastov had a worried look on his face. He also knew the incident in the control room had injured his prestige in front of the crew. By the time the two of them reached the communications compartment, he had regained some of composure. Here the communicators would not know of the confrontation in the control room.

"*DALE,* this is *Coghlan.* We are turning back to base course two-seven-zero. Be advised there are numerous Filipino fishing boats north and northwest of us heading out to their favorite fishing grounds."

Goldstein lifted the bridge-to-bridge microphone.

"Tell them to use Navy Red for their communications," MacDonald said, referring to the secure comms.

Goldstein nodded. "Roger, copy all. Please shift to Navy Red."

The voice from the *Coghlan* acknowledged the transmission.

They were lucky he didn't bead window them. "Bead window" was the cover term transmitted in the open to tell the user he was transmitting classified or sensitive information.

MacDonald pushed the toggle switch of the 12MC and relayed the information about the fishing boats to Combat. Then he added, "Have we reestablished contact with the submarine?"

"That is a negative, sir," Mr. Burnham replied. "Too much clutter in the water. Do you want us to pulse them again?"

It takes a minimum of three pulses for a good targeting solution. If he turned on the sonar for the third pulse, would the Soviet captain react, thinking the next thing he would hear would be American torpedoes headed his way? If he did, would he fire first?

"How close are we to the contact?" MacDonald asked.

"Last status was five minutes ago, Captain. At that time we had him six hundred yards, sir. We were closing at the time. The enemy submarine was on a course of two-two-zero at four knots. When we hit him with the second pulse, he went balls-to-the-wall on speed, turned left, put a knuckle in the water . . ."

"How do we know it was a knuckle?"

"It faded within a couple of minutes. The submarine also released a decoy, but it failed to fool our sonar team."

"If the submarine increased speed, then we ought to be hearing the cavitation."

"We think it went silent, hiding behind the noise of the cavitation and the noisemaker it released."

"Very well." He put the handset back in the cradle and looked over at Goldstein. "Slow to four knots."

He listened as the order cascaded from the officer of the deck to the helmsman, each one in the line of command repeating the order given him. At the navigation plotting table, the quartermaster grabbed the logbook and wrote the time of the order along with the order given. Somewhere in Washington, D.C., every logbook of every warship that ever sailed under the American colors was stored.

MacDonald wanted to be in Combat. Navy tradition had the captain on the bridge, but warships were fought from the combat information center in this modern era. He walked the length of the bridge, peering forward. Off his bow, somewhere beneath those dark waters and within a mile of him, was a Soviet submarine. Angst built as he waited for his sonar team to regain contact. To lose a submarine within a mile of you inside American-controlled shallow water was not good. He stopped and wondered for a moment if maybe the *Dale* could have passed over the submarine.

MacDonald pushed the toggle switch the next time his pacing took him by the 12MC. "Combat, Captain. Have we regained contact?"

"We are working on it, sir," replied one of the officers.

"Very well, Lieutenant. Ask *Coghlan* if they have contact."

"We have, sir. *Coghlan* does not have contact with Alpha One either."

"Alpha One?

"We have designated the submarine contact as Alpha One, sir. Never know, we might have another one . . ."

". . . as a probable submarine, sir."

"With your permission, Captain, I believe we can upgrade that to definite submarine. It's the Echo we tracked earlier, is my understanding. That is what the sonar technicians, Chief Stalzer and Oliver, are saying, sir."

"Have we put out a situation report—a SITREP on this?"

"Initial SITREP went out within a minute of us detecting the probable submarine, sir."

MacDonald stayed bowed over the voice box a few seconds longer before pushing the toggle switch again. "Well done, Lieutenant, and it is definitely a submarine. That we have already decided. Let's not waste time calling it a probable submarine."

"Thank you, sir. Well-trained crew."

MacDonald straightened. He turned to Goldstein. "Officer of the Deck, I'm going to Combat. You have the bridge and the conn."

"Aye, sir."

They watched as the skipper walked past the helm, around the radar repeater, and passed by the plotting table to reach the aft hatch port-side.

The boatswain mate of the watch announced, "Captain off the bridge," as MacDonald undogged the hatch and stepped off the bridge and into Combat. At the plotting table the quartermaster of the watch made a quick notation as simultaneously he was taking bearings from the topside watches to shore and drawing the lines on the chart.

"Stayed longer than I thought," Ensign Hatfield said.

Goldstein smiled before replying, "Keep your attention on the job at hand, Ensign."

There seemed to be a spring in Goldstein's steps as he walked the bridge, double-checking course and speed and acknowledging the quartermaster's periodic repeats of where the ship was located, nearest point of land to their left, and distance to shoal waters. The captain must have a lot of respect

and confidence in his ability as OOD to leave the bridge at a
time such as this.

"CAPTAIN in Combat," the chief of the watch announced as
MacDonald entered. Seated near the captain's chair above the
radar consoles, an operations specialist third class petty officer made a notation in his logbook. A captain's presence on a
warship was never without notice.

"Carry on!" MacDonald said as he maneuvered past the
tight confines of the Forrest Sherman class combat information center.

No space was wasted, and when the ship manned battle
stations such as now, there was little space left to walk. Sailors pressed against their consoles or squeezed into a narrow
space, or put their backs against the bulkhead to allow Mac-
Donald room to pass them. A chorus of "excuse me, sir" graced
his passage.

At the entrance to Sonar, Admiral Green stood talking
with Joe Tucker.

"Joe Tucker, would you take the bridge, please."

Joe Tucker saluted and started his own journey through the
mass of equipment and sailors toward the bridge.

"I wondered how long you could stay up there before realizing this is where we fight ships today."

"Longer than I thought, sir." MacDonald stuck his head
inside the sonar compartment. "You got anything?"

Both Stalzer and Oliver had their hands on the earpieces
of their headsets, pressing them down against their ears. They
both shook their heads and replied in unison, "No, sir."

"We've lost the little son of a bitch," Green said from over
MacDonald's shoulder. "Gonna be one hell of a ribbing if we
don't regain him."

Ribbing? This submarine may be planning to shoot, Mac-
Donald thought.

Green smiled. "I know what you're thinking, Danny. If the
Soviet asshole had wanted to fire on us, he would have already done so."

"How about the other submarine outside the harbor?"

"We don't know there is another submarine outside there.

We 'supposed' there was one when we initially detected this one. But you may have been missing the transmissions ongoing between Subic Operations Center, the marines ashore, and the small flotilla of search craft that is convoluting this effort of ours."

"I may have, sir," MacDonald replied, knowing the admiral was right.

Green let out a burst of air. "Methinks our earlier suspicions about the bastard below us being here on a spying mission have been proven right. And I think our spooks are better than their spooks."

"They may have him again, sir," Burkeet said, his head jutting out from around the open curtains of Sonar.

MacDonald and Green stepped closer.

"What you got?" MacDonald asked softly.

Oliver lowered one earpiece. "I think I had the coolant reactor pump again, sir. Hard to tell. But it's gone now."

"Were you able to get a bearing on it?"

"No, sir, Captain. I got a quick noise and then it faded."

Stalzer looked at the two officers, glanced at Burkeet, and then said, "Admiral, Captain. We should go active, sir."

"It would be the third pulse," MacDonald said.

"I mean go active and stay active, sir," Stalzer said, his words running together.

"He might think we are fixing to fire on him," Green said.

"And he might not," Lieutenant Burkeet offered. "At this depth, neither his torpedoes nor ours are going to be very effective. Too much bottom clutter, too much Subic-generated noise in the water, and if we fired a torpedo, we'd run as much risk as he would of it hitting one of our ships."

"We know that, Mr. Burkeet, but right now that submarine captain has got to be one nervous asshole," Green said. "Nervous assholes tend to do things with emotion rather than logic."

"Sir, if we don't find him and he reaches deep water . . ."

MacDonald stepped away quickly, saw the nearest sound-powered telephone talker, and grabbed him. "Ask the bridge where the nearest deep water is."

A moment passed. "How deep they want to know, sir?"

"Five hundred feet or more?"

"What are you doing?" Green asked from behind him.

"Sir," the young seaman replied. "Nearest water that depth is directly off our starboard beam about four nautical miles."

MacDonald moved toward the center of Combat, where Lieutenant Burnham stood. "Lieutenant, bring the *Dale* onto course two-seven-zero, speed ten knots." He turned to the ASW plotting table, where the Gold Team had their clappers, rulers, and pencils scattered on the chart. The chart outlined the depth contours of Subic Bay. He looked at where the submarine was last located and the time notated beside the pencil mark. A quick glance at the clock on the bulkhead showed him there had been nearly ten minutes of no contact.

"Won't that take you across his bow, Danny?" Admiral Green asked.

"I don't think he is on a course that would take him toward the northern shoreline of Subic Bay."

"So, your thoughts?"

"He's heading to deep water. He's always been heading toward the open ocean and deep water. All he wants to do is escape and get into water where he can maneuver."

Green nodded. "Right now we have him, Danny. Once he hits the open ocean, he's a nuke. He can get below the layers and be miles away before we know it." Green scratched his chin. "In that case, Danny, maybe you ought to send the *Coghlan* farther out. Put him six to ten miles outside the bay so when the submarine detects the *Dale*, the nervous Soviet skipper will make a maneuver *Coghlan* can detect and pursue."

MacDonald gave the orders to reposition the *Coghlan*. The *Dale* tilted slightly to port as it came about on the new course to starboard. The submarine had to be within a mile.

"What was the contact's last course?"

"Two-two-zero, sir. Then it disappeared."

"It's gone back to two-zero-zero," MacDonald said.

"How do you know, sir?" Burnham asked.

"Do you think you know what he is doing now?" Green asked with a fresh cup of coffee in his hand.

"I think I know what he is going to do."

"What?"

"He doesn't know he's given us the slip, so he is watching

and tracking us. He hasn't changed his destination. He is still heading toward deep water and he wants to make it before we regain contact." MacDonald looked down at the chart once again. He put his finger on one of the depth contours. "See here, sir."

Green leaned forward.

"He was heading toward this part of the ocean when we hit him with the second pulse. This is the nearest entry to deep water. He knew we were going to go active for a second pulse, and when we did he was ready. Our friend bought time with the knuckle and the noisemaker, and he's making the most of that time to reach deep water. He's not doing four knots anymore. He's doing about ten knots, and in about another five minutes he is going to reach a depth that will give him some maneuvering capability—not much, but enough."

"So I was right."

"Sir?"

"I said he was on a spying mission, not an attack mission. If he is trying to escape, he's not here to take out the American fleet."

DOLINSKI stormed into the communications room. Vyshinsky was nowhere to be seen. The GRU Spetsnaz did not know that the communicator was heading toward Engineering to use this time for his mandatory training on the reactors. Junior officers must qualify in every watch station on a Soviet submarine to be considered for submarine insignia.

The two young starshinas in the communications room jumped to attention when the *zampolit* and Dolinski entered.

"As you were, comrades," Golovastov said, motioning them down. His stomach rumbled, but the deference the two men gave helped restore some of the confidence disturbed by Bocharkov. After all, he was the representative of the Party— *bullshit*! He was the Party on board the K-122.

Dolinski walked to the far rack of equipment and ran his finger down the protruding switches and toggles. He shoved aside several cables connecting the receivers and the antennas. Finally, he turned to the nearest sailor. "Where is the control for the floating wire?"

The starshina quickly took Dolinski to the control.

"If I hit this switch, the antenna will deploy?"

"Yes, sir, but we are at battle stations, sir. The captain—"

"Do you know who he is?" Dolinski interrupted, pointing at the *zampolit*.

The sailor nodded. "He is Lieutenant Golovastov."

"Right. And now we are doing the work of the Party."

The other starshina stepped forward. "Sir, if you are going to deploy the antenna, our orders are to notify conn so they are aware the wire is out."

"The *zampolit* is taking over the communications room for now," Golovastov stated, straightening visibly. After all, he was the *zampolit*, and had the *zampolit*'s duties, which included protecting the interests of Moscow—the Communist Party. Under his orders, he could commandeer the boat if he thought it prudent in the interest of the Party and the Soviet Union.

Dolinski hit the switch. A red light came on, accompanied by the slight hum of the small hydraulic motor that controlled the antenna. The wire was one hundred meters long and was used for both receiving and sending long-range messages when submerged. Most of the Soviet Fleet broadcast could be received by the small antenna that was part of the periscope system.

The senior starshina hit the *Boyevaya Chast'* channel 5 switch and quickly asked for Lieutenant Vyshinsky to return to Communications.

"GOT a new sound in the water," Oliver said, his eyes going from Lieutenant Burkeet to Chief Stalzer.

"They're trailing wire, sir. They're reeling out their antenna!" Stalzer added, his fingers white from pressing the earpieces against his head. "Damn."

Burkeet glanced at MacDonald and Green, whose heads filled the open doorway.

"Why would they do that?" MacDonald asked.

Stalzer was leaning over Oliver, tweaking the directional beam.

"Bearing two-zero-zero," Oliver reported.

"That will affect his maneuvering ability," Green added.

MacDonald nodded. "Might be true what they say about the Soviets."

"You mean they can't take a shit without Moscow's permission."

MacDonald gave a slight nod to the admiral. "I was thinking something along the lines of getting off a situation report to Moscow. They could do the same thing through their conning tower antennas. Why would they trail a wire that is probably a hundred meters long . . . Damn!"

MacDonald's head disappeared.

"What?" Admiral Green asked, following the skipper.

MacDonald grabbed the sound-powered telephone talker standing near Sonar. "Tell the bridge to come to course two-seven-zero, ten knots for two minutes!"

"What's going on, Danny?" Green asked, his bushy eyebrows furrowed into a deep "V."

"They are trailing a wire that is going to come directly back to us. If it goes near the shafts, it's going to wrap around our propellers, sir. I need to move the *Dale* west of the contact."

The destroyer leaned to starboard as the steam plants kicked in and the *Dale* began to pick up speed.

The sound-powered talker acknowledged an unheard voice and looked at MacDonald.

"Coming to course two-seven-zero, speed ten knots!" Burnham shouted from the front of Combat.

"Sir!" the sailor shouted.

MacDonald and Green looked at him.

The sailor looked toward Burnham and then back at MacDonald and Green. "I meant that sir, sir" the sailor said, pointing at the combat information center watch officer. "Mr. Goldstein sends his respects and reports ship turning to two-seven-zero, speed ten knots."

MacDonald looked at the clock on the bulkhead.

"Smarter captain than we give our adversary credit for," Green said.

"Yes, sir," MacDonald mumbled, his eyes on the clock, his mind calculating how much space the ship would open to the west of the contact. He looked at the sailor. "Tell the bridge I want to come to course two-two-zero at zero four fifteen and at that time reduce speed to four knots."

Green nodded when MacDonald turned to him. "Glad I came along for the ride, Danny." He sighed. "I think I'm going to go to the bridge for a while and view the sunrise. You shout if you need me."

MacDonald was surprised at the relief he felt when he watched the back of the admiral amble toward the hatch separating the bridge from Combat. He wondered for a moment if he would have been able to exhibit the self-discipline needed to clear the way so his subordinates could do their job.

"Sir, we hold passive contact on the submarine," Burkeet said.

"Range and bearing?"

"Bearing is one-seven-zero, sir. No range, but the bearing appears to be constant. He has to be close."

"Then he has either returned to his original course of two-two-zero and we are paralleling him, or worst case is we could be on a collision course with him. That is his true bearing, right?"

Burkeet nodded. "Yes, sir."

"WHAT is going on?" Bocharkov shouted.

"We have the wire going out, sir!" Ignatova shouted from the Christmas tree panel near the firing control.

"Orlov! What the hell—"

"I have given no order, Captain!"

"XO, Chief Ship Starshina Uvarova! Lay forward and tell the communicator to reel in that wire. If I have to make quick turns to avoid the Americans, we are going to wrap that wire around our shaft and blades!"

Ignatova was right behind Uvarova at the hatch as the two men raced toward the communications compartment.

"What is he thinking?" Bocharkov muttered, referring to Vyshinsky, his young—and now dumb—communicator. "Commander Orlov! Keep us steady on this course and speed."

"Sir," Tverdokhleb said. "We are approaching the seventy-five-meter depth."

"You sure?" Orlov asked.

"How can I be sure?" Tverdokhleb snapped. "We have been shifting and speeding up and speeding down." Then with a sigh, he continued, "Captain, I think we are over the seventy-five-meter depth, but I would give it another couple of minutes at four knots to be sure."

"Lieutenant Commander Orlov, make your depth fifty meters." He didn't have time to wait. "Take her down easy and keep us on this course."

"Make my depth fifty meters, aye. Take her down easy. Planes ten degrees!"

The planesman pulled the hydraulics control handles back. The sound of water filling the surrounding ballasts barely registered through the thick double hull of the Echo submarine. Bocharkov knew the Americans would hear the noise, but if they missed the sounds of trailing the communications wire, then they sure as hell wouldn't hear the ballast tanks. He had to get water over them. He had to escape.

"WHAT are you doing out here?" Ignatova demanded when he saw Lieutenant Vyshinsky standing in the passageway outside of Communications. And why in the hell were the two communications starshinas out here with him?

"Sir, the *zampolits* ordered us out." Vyshinsky and the two sailors were standing at attention, their backs pressed against the far bulkhead across from the communications compartment.

"*Zampolits*? You mean Mr. Golovastov?"

"Yes, sir. He was with the other *zampolit*, Lieutenant Dolinski. They said they had Party business and we were to leave while they answered Moscow."

Ignatova wanted to slap the officer. He turned toward the hatch. "Are they the ones reeling out the wire or did you—"

"No, sir! I told them not to," the senior starshina answered sharply. "I was ordered not to inform the conn."

Ignatova spun the handle, opening the hatch to the communications compartment. He stepped inside, Uvarova immediately behind him. Vyshinsky followed. The two sailors stayed in the passageway, peering inside.

"What are you doing?" Ignatova shouted.

Dolinski calmly turned. Golovastov stepped to the left of the GRU Spetsnaz, his eyes switching between Ignatova and Dolinski.

"Captain Second Rank Ignatova," Dolinski said. "We have a message from Moscow that must be replied to—"

"And it will be, Lieutenant!" Ignatova looked at the two men. "Why did you order the communicator away from his battle station? And who decided to reel out the wire without orders from the captain?" Without waiting for a reply, he stepped between the two officers and switched off the system. The whine of the hydraulics tapered off.

"Don't do that, comrade," Dolinski said, his voice threatening.

"Don't tell me what to do," Ignatova said, not deigning to look at the junior officer. "You two have endangered the boat when we are engaged in hostile actions. When we return to Kamchatka, you will be charged—"

"We will be charged with upholding the power of the Party by recognizing you and Bocharkov as counterrevolutionists!" Dolinski interrupted.

Ignatova flipped the switch the other way. The small engine whined into life. The gauge above the switch showed that the wire was rewinding. "When we get there, we will let the navy determine who has done the most damage."

Dolinski guffawed. "You and your comrade captain have done the damage. And it will not be the navy who will determine it. Now, step away from the antenna, comrade, or I will be forced to hurt you."

Ignatova turned. Dolinski was less that a foot from him, causing the XO to step back, his back coming up against the panel behind him. "Do not threaten me, Lieutenant. That is mutiny." The fact that he was facing a Spetsnaz-trained killer was not lost on Ignatova.

"No, Comrade Captain Second Rank. This is not mutiny. It is reclaiming the boat for the Soviet Union."

"Who gave you the idea that you could determine what is good for the Party and what is good for the Soviet Union?"

Dolinski looked at Golovastov. "We did. We two *zampolits* have decided that what is happening on board the K-122 is anticommunism. That is our job. To do the Party-political training and guide fellow comrades toward the values of communism and the importance of the Party."

"And this is going to allow the K-122 to escape from the Americans? You are—"

Dolinski reached forward and grabbed Ignatova.

Dolinski never saw the blow coming. The fire extinguisher hit him on the back of the head. The GRU Spetsnaz collapsed in a heap on the deck. Uvarova stood over the lieutenant.

Ignatova and Uvarova looked at each other. Golovastov fell back several steps until the bulkhead stopped him.

"My apologies, XO," Uvarova said. "I did not mean to hit the good officer. In the Party-political training provided this voyage by Lieutenant Golovastov, he cautioned us that we should always be alert for those who espoused the Party's ideals for their own ambition." He looked at Golovastov. "Thank you, comrade, for your tutelage."

The equivalent to a United States Navy master chief, Uvarova hefted the fire extinguisher and chuckled. "Must have slipped."

"Get the master of arms down here, Chief Ship Starshina Uvarova." Ignatova turned back to the panel. "Lieutenant Vyshinsky, get your ass back in here and re-man your battle stations."

Then, as an afterthought, Ignatova added, "And contact the doctor to hasten to Communications if he is not busy."

"Lieutenant Golovastov, you are confined to your stateroom until further notice. Do you understand?"

Golovastov nodded quickly. "Yes, Comrade XO." He looked down at Dolinski. "And the lieutenant?"

"From the looks of the chief of the boat's following of your orders, Dolinski will be in the hospital for a while. I will point out that he acted under your orders."

"But, sir . . ."

"Get your ass out of here, Lieutenant!"

On the gray deck of Communications, a small of pool of blood was growing beneath the GRU Spetsnaz's head. The man's chest moved, so he was not dead, which was good.

FIFTEEN

Monday, June 5, 1967

"HE was making a lot of noise," Stalzer said from beneath his earphones.

Oliver looked up at the chief. "I think they shut down the wire for a moment. The noise dropped off, but it's back now."

Stalzer shrugged. "Could just be environmentals, Oliver." The chief looked at Burkeet. "They could be still reeling it out, or have decided that when we shifted our position beam to them instead of dead astern it meant they couldn't attack us with their radio antenna, so they are reeling it back in." He smiled.

"Bearing?" MacDonald asked.

"Bearing one-six-zero from us, sir," Stalzer answered.

MacDonald drew back. "Course and speed?" he asked the sound-powered phone talker.

A couple of seconds passed as the sailor quizzed the bridge. "We are steady on two-two-zero, speed four knots."

"Give the admiral my respects and inform him that unless otherwise directed, I intend to pulse the target again."

The sailor nodded, pressed the "push to talk" button, and relayed the information to the bridge. A second or two passed before he relayed the admiral's acknowledgment.

Maybe Green had stepped out of the decision-making process for a while and the prosecution of the target was truly his. Then again, he knew the admiral too well.

"Sir," Burkeet said. "The chief and Petty Officer Oliver believe the contact has increased its speed. It is hitting at least ten knots and drawing away from us."

MacDonald looked at the sailor. "Tell the bridge to increase speed to ten knots." He saw Burnham watching from twenty feet away, in the center of Combat. MacDonald looked at the Combat watch officer. "Tell *Coghlan* we are going to pulse the contact again."

Burnham nodded in acknowledgment and grabbed the handset from the cradle of Navy Red.

MacDonald turned back to Sonar. "Pulse him once." He held up one finger. "Only one ping and at low power."

A couple of seconds passed before he heard the single sonar pulse. MacDonald envisioned the three-hundred-sixty-degree circle as the pulse traveled outward. It not only hit the K-122 and started its trip back to the *Dale*, but the pulse hit the hull of the *Coghlan* and the small boats still searching the harbor in response to the earlier firefight ashore. The return pulse brought information on every contact it hit, but it was the one bearing one-eight-zero Oliver placed the tip of his pencil on.

"Contact now bears one-eight-zero, right-bearing drift, range two thousand yards."

"He's pulling away from us," Stalzer added.

MacDonald nodded. The contact was increasing separation. That might not be a bad thing. Increased distance increased MacDonald's weapon choices. Plus, the last thing he wanted was to run over the conning tower of the Soviet submarine—not much danger of that with a one-nautical-mile separation. It would not only create a major embarrassment for both nations, but he would find himself sitting at some desk ashore while the "green board" figured out how in the hell he screwed up.

"Relay the information to the *Coghlan*," he told Lieutenant Burnham, who had moved closer but remained within reach of the handsets aligned overhead near the center of Combat.

* * *

"RELEASE a noisemaker," Bocharkov ordered as the echo of the American sonar ebbed through the K-122. "Lieutenant Orlov, tell Sonar to tell me where the other contacts are above us."

"Bch-3, this is Bch-1. Use the American pulse to identify the topside traffic. Where are the two destroyers?" Orlov ordered through the intercom.

Orlov looked toward Bocharkov. "Sir, do you want to change course or speed?"

"No." A rapid change of course and speed might convince the Americans he was maneuvering into attack position. He had the aft outer doors open, with four of them loaded with armed torpedoes. He figured the Americans knew that or why else would they change their position from aft to beam. No, they were in position to attack, if they wanted. So far, they had only chased, keeping a reasonable distance from him.

He grunted. They want us to get away. They no more want us here than we want to be here right now. *Too much paperwork,* he had heard a senior admiral once say when they thought they had an American submarine in Soviet waters. *Too much paperwork.* So the Soviet battle group had collected information on the American submarine until it disappeared beneath the layers in the open ocean. *Too much paperwork.* He laughed, drawing the attention of those in the control room. He wondered if the Americans had a similar expression.

Now it was time for the K-122 to reduce everyone's paperwork.

The forward hatch opened and Ignatova entered—alone.

"Control room, I say again: This is Sonar. We have Contact One bearing zero-zero-zero, range one thousand eight hundred meters, right-bearing drift. Contact Two bears two-seven-zero, range three thousand meters, with a left-bearing drift. We have multiple small boys in the water."

Bocharkov heard the report. It told him the unknown destroyer that had been on his tail was on his beam now, drifting backward to his former position if he and Contact One maintained current course and speed. It was also going slower than the K-122. Was this the plan of the destroyer's skipper? He would know soon, because the American sonar team would have the speed of the K-122 calculated soon. He glanced at the clock. Within three to five minutes they would have the speed calculated. If the destroyer changed its course and speed, then he would have better knowledge of the adversary's plan.

"Make your speed five knots." *Let's not make it easy for the Americans.*

"Make my speed five knots, aye," Orlov responded.

That should confuse their sonar team for a little. He looked at the clock. This was a first for him, he realized. A slow-speed antisubmarine operation with both him and the adversary creeping through near-shoal waters. The other warship was still increasing distance from him and putting itself between the K-122 and the open ocean. Once he reached the deep Pacific, he would care little where the Americans were deployed, for he knew the K-122 would easily evade them.

But there was one threat Contact Two represented. The increased range gave the destroyer more weapon options. As long as Bocharkov remained within a thousand meters of Contact One, all that warship could do was fire over-the-side torpedoes, *which was bad enough.* The other contact could fire its antisubmarine rockets, or ASROCs, meaning he would not even know they were coming until the rocket-fired torpedoes splashed into the water above him—too late for evasion in this shallow water.

This would be something for the tactical journals, if he lived through this and the assaults on his loyalty he would face from the *zampolits* once they returned to Kamchatka.

Ignatova reached his side and whispered a quick synopsis of the events in the communications compartment.

"He is with the doctor?" Bocharkov asked.

"I left him with the chief of the boat."

"Let's hope the doctor is soon there, before Uvarova decides to administer his own version of medical care," Bocharkov replied.

"I think he already did."

The slowing forward momentum of the K-122 eased the vibration in the control room as the boat reduced speed to four knots. A slight smell of oil whiffed through the control room. Both Bocharkov and Ignatova looked at each other, but the smell quickly dissipated.

"Course, speed, status?" Bocharkov asked.

"Two-two-zero, passing six knots heading to five. Contact One continues with right-bearing drift—now off our aft starboard quarter bearing zero-two-two."

"Navigator, how long to deep water?"

Tverdokhleb leaned back, bracing both hands on the plotting table, his glasses balanced precariously on the end of his nose. "If we are where I think we are, Captain, and you continue on course two-two-zero, then five minutes to deep water."

"Comrade Navigator, it was five minutes to deep water twenty minutes ago!"

"But we have been maneuvering, sir. We have changed course; we have changed speed . . ."

"Officer of the Deck, make your course two-seven-zero and your speed ten knots." Enough of this guessing. If the Americans wanted to attack, they would have already. He needed to get to deep water. He didn't know if the Americans had their instructions from higher headquarters or were waiting for them. Either way, time was of the essence.

"Make my course two-seven-zero, speed ten knots, aye."

The K-122 leaned to the right as the huge Echo class nuclear submarine commenced a fifty-degree turn to starboard.

"Depth?"

"Fifty meters, sir."

"Make your depth one hundred meters." Before Orlov could echo the command, Bocharkov cautioned, "Slowly. We want to go down slowly."

"Make my depth one hundred meters, five-degree plane, aye."

The boat continued its right tilt as the bow edged downward. The chief of the watch had taken Uvarova's position and had his hand on the hydraulic levers, pulling back, letting more water into the ballast tanks.

Bocharkov tightened his hands on the nearby railing. If the bow hit the bottom at this speed, the chase would be over.

* * *

"WE are losing him," Oliver said.

Stalzer shook his head. "He is turning and diving," he said, tapping the rainfall display on the sonar console. "I heard the ballast tanks taking on water."

"Not much depth here," Burkeet said.

MacDonald stuck his head out of Sonar, looked at the sound-powered phone talker. "Ask the navigator what the depth is here."

"Right-hand turn," Stalzer said, his finger tracing the pattern on the sonar scope. "That third pulse must have convinced him we're about to fire on him."

MacDonald ignored the comment.

The aft hatch opened and Chief Caldwell entered, carrying the familiar message board in his right hand. The radioman chief secured the hatch before turning to MacDonald. "Sir, message from COMSEVENTHFLEET." He handed the metal board to MacDonald.

"Sir, the navigator says there is about three hundred fifty feet beneath our keel."

"He's trying to get as much water between him and us as he can."

MacDonald nodded. "But he's also maneuvering and changing speed."

"Maybe he does believe we are maneuvering into attack position," Burkeet added. "Maybe he's maneuvering for a better attack position."

MacDonald thought a moment about that. The Soviet captain knew as well as MacDonald that a grenade over the side was the warning to surface. He had not played that hand yet. He sighed. "I don't think so. I think he knows as we do that if either of us was going to attack, we would have by now."

"Maybe he's waiting for directions from Moscow," Admiral Green added from behind MacDonald.

"Welcome back, sir."

Lieutenant Burkeet stepped back into Sonar.

"What you got?"

MacDonald brought CTF-Seventy up to speed on the maneuvering, the latest contact position, and then finished with "He's going to cross our bow in a few minutes with this drift and our speed."

"Looks as if the contact is steadying up, sir," Burkeet added.

"Course?"

A second passed as the ASW officer conferred with Chief Stalzer. "Around two-seven-zero."

"Still descending?"

"We have steady passive contact at this time, sir. He may have leveled off."

MacDonald lifted the message board and quickly read the message. His stomach tightened as he reached the end of the short directive.

"What's wrong, Danny?"

MacDonald handed the board to Green, who quickly read it, before handing it back to MacDonald. "So it's sink him or make him surface."

"We need to drop a grenade over him, sir," MacDonald said. "Warn him to surface."

"You have underwater comms. You have any of the San Miguel spooks on board? Any of those Ruskie-speaking fools we can get to tell him to surface or face attack?"

MacDonald shook his head.

"Ask the *Coghlan* if they have any communications technicians on board."

"PASSING eighty meters, speed four knots."

Bocharkov looked back at Tverdokhleb. "Any advice, Navigator?"

Tverdokhleb's hands came away from their grip on the edge of the plotting table as he turned in his chair and quickly read the course, speed from the gauges above the helmsman. Bocharkov turned away as the navigator started marking the chart in front of him.

"Make your depth ninety meters."

"Making my depth ninety meters, aye." The planesman eased off the angle, bringing the submarine level. "Am at ninety meters, speed five knots, course two-seven-zero."

"Captain!" Tverdokhleb said in a loud voice. "If we come to course two-nine-zero, we will quickly hit five hundred meters."

"Are you sure?" A cigarette dangled unlit from the corner of the navigator's mouth. Bocharkov's eyes locked with his. He saw the uncertainty in them.

"Sir, the new course will make it look as if we are turning back toward the American contacts. It will point our bow at Contact Two, Captain," Ignatova cautioned.

Bocharkov nodded. "Make your course two-nine-zero, speed ten knots."

"NO, sir. He has their van on board. They've installed it in the old DASH hangar, but the communications technicians have not embarked. They are scheduled for embarkation on Thursday."

"Well, so much for a good Monday," Green added. He put a hand on MacDonald's shoulder. "Time for the grenade."

"The contact is maneuvering again, sir," Burkeet said from the doorway of Sonar. "He is dead ahead with his bow dead on *Coghlan*. We are only ten degrees off his aft tubes."

"His outer doors could be opened," MacDonald offered.

"Why would you say that?"

"He released a noisemaker in his last maneuver, Admiral. I believe the Echo class submarines have to fire their decoys from their torpedo tubes."

"If the man is any kind of competent skipper, his outer doors—fore and aft—have been opened since we started chasing him. Though it is hard to call it a chase dashing ahead at ten knots and lollygagging at four while we dodge fishing boats and search craft inside Subic Bay."

Chief Stalzer's head appeared again. "He is steadying up on course two-nine-zero and we are starting to see intermittent gaps in the passive signature, sir!" His head disappeared back inside.

"Looks as if he is going deeper."

"How deep can you go in three hundred feet of water?" MacDonald turned to the sound-powered phone talker. "Ask the navigator the depth ranges coming up."

"Sir?" the young sailor asked, confused over the question.

"Sir," Lieutenant Burnham answered from the center of Combat. "We have the charts here, sir. If the contact continues on new course, he is going to be over depths of fifteen hundred feet heading downward to two miles."

"We'll lose him," Green said softly.

"Tell Weps to break out the grenades and lay to the bow on the double." MacDonald did not wait for Burnham to answer. He hurried forward, heading toward the bridge. The navy clock on the forward bulkhead of Combat struck one bell. MacDonald glanced up: zero four thirty hours. It seemed much longer.

"CAPTAIN on the bridge," Ensign Hatfield announced as MacDonald stepped onto the bridge.

"Bring the *Dale* right to course two-nine-zero, increase speed to eight knots." He wanted more speed, but he needed Sonar to maintain contact on the Echo.

The rings of the annunciator near the helmsman accompanied the order for increased speed. Down in the engineering spaces, the chief engineer saw the request and started shouting out the orders to make it happen.

MacDonald plucked the Navy Red handset from its cradle. "*Coghlan*, this is *Dale*—Charlie Oscar speaking. Is your skipper there?"

Down below in Combat, everyone heard the call over Navy Red. Several heads turned to listen. Green, with coffee cup in hand, moved closer to the speaker.

A second passed before Kennedy answered. "Captain, Charlie Oscar *Coghlan* standing by."

"Ron, Danny here. Have received a 'flash' message from Commander Seventh Fleet ordering us to either bring the submarine to the surface or sink it." As he said it, he felt a slight chill go up his spine. He reached behind him and pulled the sweat-matted shirt away from his body.

"Roger, sir."

"I would like for you to ready your ASROC in the event we need it. My intentions are to pass overhead his position and drop the first of three grenades. I would prefer to have him surface than for us to have to sink him."

"I agree, sir. A little humility and embarrassment is a lot better than feeding the sharks."

MacDonald thought he detected something approaching joy in the man's voice. Happiness was not what he was feeling right now. He licked his dry lips. He had never fired a torpedo in anger. Even with the occasional navigational near misses with the Soviets in their navies' never-ending dog-and-cat chase games, never had he imagined he would be in a position where he had to fire on them. The U.S. Navy trained for the day when it would happen, but that day was always over the chronological horizon.

The old World War II films of massive surface and subsurface war were reminiscences of the past. Today's war at sea was fought by aircraft and missiles. Down below in that floating coffin, which men called a submarine, were husbands, fathers, sons—just as in the ships above it.

"Captain, did you copy my last?" Kennedy asked.

"Copy all, Ron. Once I have sailed over him and dropped the grenades, I will immediately bring the *Dale* to flank speed and head out of the area. That is going to put the contact in my baffles. I will be blind until I can come out of the turn and clear them. I will switch ASW control to you."

"We have him tracked also, Captain. I have shifted my course to give me a left-bearing drift on the target. This gives me some added space away from his bows. But it also brings the contact between us."

"In two miles, Ron, the contact is going to have fifteen hundred feet of depth to play with. We need to stop him before he reaches it."

"Aye, sir. *Coghlan* is ready to execute any orders given—immediately. I have a constant firing solution being worked on the target."

For a moment, MacDonald questioned if that was a good thing to know. "I don't want you to fire unless he does something hostile."

"He may fire on you, sir."

"I don't think he will, Ron. I think he may speed up and go deeper."

Several seconds passed before Kennedy replied. "Copy all."

Motion outside the windows on the bridge caught MacDonald's attention. It was the weapons officer Lieutenant

Kelly. Trying to keep up with the young weps's brisk walk was the gunner's mate chief Benson. The chief's belly bounced over the belt line of pants about two inches too small.

"Roger, sir. If he goes deep, we can always go to constant pulse on the sonar."

MacDonald's eyebrows furrowed. "Let's don't do that, Ron, unless we are prepared to fire, and I suspect we would have to do it ASAP, because if I was him, I'd fire first." What was this Kennedy thinking?

"Aye, sir."

"Roger, out." MacDonald jammed the handset back into its cradle. "He might blow us out of the water along with the submarine," he mumbled.

"Sir?" Goldstein asked.

"Nothing," MacDonald answered as he walked by the officer of the deck and headed toward the port bridge wing. He grabbed the megaphone from its storage locker near the hatch. Goldstein stopped at the hatchway when MacDonald stepped onto the bridge wing.

He raised the megaphone, pulled the trigger to speak, and the chill-rending screech of electronics filled the outside air for a second before he could. At the bow, Weps and the gunner's mate chief looked toward the noise. MacDonald slapped the megaphone once and the screech disappeared.

MacDonald explained the sequence of events. As he talked, he noticed Chief Benson reach over and take the grenades from Kelly. In another time he would have smiled.

"KEEP taking her down," Bocharkov said.

"Aye, sir. Passing one hundred meters."

Bocharkov looked over at Tverdokhleb. "What is the depth beneath me, Navigator?"

"At least one hundred meter—"

"We just passed one hundred meters! So it has to be more."

Tverdokhleb put the unlit cigarette in his mouth and bent over his chart. The man looked up and smiled. "We have to be over the three-hundred-meter line, sir."

"Are you sure?"

Tverdokhleb slapped his palm on the table. "I know where

we are, sir. I am positive. I am one hundred percent positive."
Then, in a soft mumble, Bocharkov heard the man say, "Otherwise we would have already hit the bottom."

Bocharkov looked at Orlov. "Officer of the Deck, take us down to two hundred meters, increase plane angle."

"Making my depth two hundred meters, increase angle to twenty degrees."

The K-122 tilted sharply as the extra ten degrees were applied to the angle. Bocharkov glanced at the Fathometer as Orlov announced, "Passing one hundred twenty-five meters." They would be in deeper water in seconds. The clock on the bulkhead showed twenty-five minutes until five. Dawn had broken above the water.

"Sir," Ignatova said from near the firing console.

Bocharkov looked. His XO was pointing at the temperature gauge that measured the outside water temperature.

"Ten degrees of change in last fifty meters."

Bocharkov grunted. They were passing through a layer. Finally some good news. The layer would help shield their passive noise. A grinding sound squealed through the control room.

"What the hell?" Orlov said aloud.

Chief Ship Starshina Uvarova stepped through the forward hatch. "It's the sump pump clearing the water out of the bilges!" Uvarova said in a loud voice, stepping quickly to the intercom.

"Shut it off! What is it doing on in the first place?" Bocharkov snapped.

"Engineering, Control Room," Uvarova called, his finger pressed so hard on the Bch-5 button it was white. "Secure the main sump pump, immediately."

Almost immediately, the squeal stopped, to be replaced by a soft winding down of the motor.

"Ease planes to five degrees," Orlov ordered.

Bocharkov glanced at the depth reading—they were approaching two hundred meters. He looked back at the navigator, who was leaning with his left shoulder against the forward bulkhead, his body crouched forward slightly as he right hand tapped his pencil on the chart.

"Lieutenant Tverdokhleb, what is our depth?"

The man straightened in his chair. "We should be over the three-hundred-meter curve of the bottom, heading toward a deeper depth of fifteen hundred." Tverdokhleb laid his wooden ruler on the chart, took a metal compass, and walked the distance with it. "Ten minutes until unlimited water."

"Bring her up to ten knots!"

OLIVER eased his headphones back on his ears. "I bet that screwed up their hearing."

Stalzer did the same. "If there was any doubt we still had them passively, they have erased it." He smiled.

"What was it?" Burkeet asked.

"Don't know," Stalzer said, shaking his head. "It was one of their pumps, I think."

"The chief is right, sir. That was a pump." Oliver pointed at the console. "I can hear it winding down."

"Must have had a bearing jump or something."

Burkeet stepped out of Sonar, nearly bumping into Admiral Green. He quickly told the admiral about the noise, and then hurried toward Lieutenant Burnham so the captain could be notified.

ON the bridge, MacDonald listened to the report. Maybe the submarine was beginning to feel its mechanical limitations. Naval Intelligence said the Soviet submarines were basically pure pieces of shit. Maybe they were right.

"Thanks, Lieutenant Burnham. It's time for the grenades. I will take control of the maneuvering up here. You plot the submarine at your end and let me know if it changes course or speed."

"Aye, sir. We now have sound-powered comms with Weps on the bow," Goldstein announced.

MacDonald looked out the windows. One of the forward topside watches stood beside Chief Benson, who cradled two of the grenades in his left hand with the other held in his right.

"Okay, Combat, give me some course changes to take us over the submarine." MacDonald released the toggle switch.

Burnham started to talk, and as he proposed course changes turning the *Dale* to the left, MacDonald nodded at Goldstein, who translated the recommendations into conning commands. At the helm, Ensign Hatfield continued his watch over the shoulder of the helmsman. The duty quartermaster penciled in the orders being given in the green logbook. With every entry, the second-class petty officer looked at the clock on the bulkhead behind the helmsman. MacDonald glanced at it, also. It was twenty minutes until five.

"Captain," Burnham called. "Radio has asked permission to switch from the night frequencies to day. I have told them not to, sir. I'm concerned about the time it will take them to change the cryptographic keying material plus synch up on new frequencies."

"Very well," MacDonald answered. He looked out the opened port hatch. The sun was creeping up from behind the mountains to the east. Radio frequencies that were good for the night were barely useful during the day because of the sun. He looked at the clock. They should be all right on the night frequencies for a little bit.

He picked up his binoculars, slung them around his neck, and moved to the port bridge wing as the ship came smartly left, centering on a course that if the submarine surfaced would cause the two warships to collide due to emergent maneuvering. Over the mountains to the east, the sun's rays were breaking, and morning began to descend down the slopes heading toward Olongapo City, the harbor, and Subic Bay.

"Two minutes to over contact," Goldstein announced, looking at MacDonald.

MacDonald nodded in acknowledgment.

"Sir! Combat reports the submarine has increased speed!" Goldstein shouted.

"Increase speed slightly," MacDonald said in a calm voice.

Burnham recommended a slight course change to starboard.

The *Dale* picked up speed, and the bow came to the right a few degrees as the destroyer edged closer to crossing over the center of the contact. He wondered if the submarine knew what they were doing. He wondered if their sonar team was as good as his.

"CONTACT One has increased speed and his course has changed to a constant bearing," the sonar technician announced.

"Looks as if they are closing?" Ignatova asked.

"They could be," Orlov added softly.

Bocharkov grunted, drawing everyone's attention. "They are about to either cross over us to show they know we are here or . . ." He let his sentence hang. He was going to say, "or they are preparing to attack." But he didn't, and he did not say those words because, like him, if the captain of the American warship had wanted to attack them, he would have done so long ago. But then orders do change.

"It was the pump," Orlov said. "It gave away our position and now the American warship is closing."

There was silence for a moment, before one of the starshinas in a shaking voice asked, "Why?"

"They must be losing us," Bocharkov said, not believing his words. "We are going deeper. Everyone is to concentrate on his job. Do your job well and we will be having our congratulatory drinks before lunch."

A couple of the sailors laughed and a few smiled, but the tension was growing in the blind confines of the Soviet K-122 Echo class submarine.

Bocharkov glanced at the depth, but could not see past Orlov, who had stepped between him and the XO near the firing console. "What is our depth?"

"We are passing two hundred twenty meters."

"Level off," Bocharkov snapped. "Make your depth two hundred thirty meters." His last order was two hundred meters.

Orlov gave the orders leveling the planes, and the Soviet submarine easily came to final trim at two hundred thirty meters.

"I make my depth two hundred thirty meters, Captain," Orlov reported.

"Very well. Make your speed ten knots." Bocharkov

looked at the navigator. "Lieutenant Tverdokhleb, what do I have to my right?"

"Right?" Tverdokhleb asked softly, then straightened sharply in his chair—almost at attention. "We have Subic Bay, sir. On this course we will have open ocean. Unlimited depth. To the left . . ."

"Right now—what do I have?"

Tverdokhleb shook his head. "I would recommend two-six-five degrees, Captain. We will reach fifteen-hundred-meter water in the same time, but we will have broader initial width of that depth until outside territorial waters." There was a slight pause. "That is my best recommendation on where I think we are."

"Officer of the Deck, make your course two-six-five, speed ten knots. No cavitation in the turn."

"Making my course two-six-five, speed ten knots, aye."

Bocharkov reached up and grabbed an overhead pipe as the K-122 slowly turned to starboard. Hopefully the temperature gradient above them would shield their turn.

"**BRIDGE,** Combat. We've lost contact with the target."

"Last position?"

"Five hundred yards dead ahead, sir. Target on course two-two-zero . . ."

MacDonald heard voices in the background, then the 12MC went quiet for a second before Burnham continued, ". . . and appeared to be in a turn."

MacDonald looked at the clock, his eyes fixing on the red second hand. "Prepare to drop the first grenade at my command."

He listened as the sound-powered phone talker relayed the command to the weapons officer and gunner's mate chief standing near the bow.

"Drop the first one." He pushed the toggle switch on the 12MC and warned Combat that the first grenade was on its way.

Less than ten seconds passed before he saw Chief Benson pull the pin and throw the grenade overhand much like a good right fielder trying to head off a runner at home plate. Mac-Donald did not see the grenade hit the water.

A few seconds later, the 12MC blared with Burnham's voice. "We have the explosion. Sir, the submarine was still a good five hundred yards ahead of us."

"I dropped it, Lieutenant, so he knows we are approaching and what we expect."

"Aye, Captain," Burnham acknowledged. "Am not sure he heard it since we were not directly overhead and we were more or less in his baffles."

"*Dale*, this is *Coghlan*," blared the Navy Red from the speaker overhead.

Ensign Hatfield hurried from his position and jerked the handset from the cradle. "*Dale* here. Go ahead."

"This is Captain Kennedy. Is your Charlie Oscar there?"

MacDonald reached over and took the handset. "Ron, this is Danny MacDonald."

"Captain, we show a small explosion. Was that your grenade, and if so, do you have the contact beneath you?"

MacDonald explained the grenade and the distance from the submarine. He went on to tell him that they had lost passive contact. After a few seconds MacDonald agreed to Kennedy's proposal for the *Coghlan* to transmit a single sonar pulse to relocate the contact.

"CAPTAIN, we have a small explosion off our starboard side aft, sir," Orlov reported.

"Probably a grenade," Ignatova added. "Means they want us to surface."

"Passing one hundred seventy-five meters, speed ten knots. Steady on course two-six-zero."

Bocharkov grunted and smiled. "Means they have lost us. Means the layer worked. Officer of the Deck, make your speed twelve knots."

"Make my speed twelve knots, aye."

He looked at Tverdokhleb, who was smiling. The navigator held up a spread-fingered hand. "Five minutes, sir. Five minutes and you can go as deep—"

The pulse echoed through the control room, bringing conversation to a halt. Bocharkov looked at the Fathometer; it showed them coming upward to two hundred meters depth.

"Make your depth three hundred meters," he commanded.

"But, sir . . . ," Tverdokhleb said, his words trailing off.

"What?" Bocharkov barked.

"We are only over the three-hundred-meter curve."

"Let's hope it is tapering downward."

"Making my depth three hundred meters, aye."

"Increase planes angle . . ."

"Leave them at five degrees," Bocharkov interrupted. If they hit the bottom, better to do a glancing blow than slam into it.

"**BRIDGE,** Combat. We had a faint couple of seconds of contact with the target, distance one thousand yards. It must be beneath an isothermal layer. Contact is on a course of two-six-five, but we do not have a speed."

"Very well. Give me a course and speed to get over the top of the contact."

"Sir, already have it. Recommend course two-six-eight, increase speed fifteen knots for three minutes, sir. That should put us in close proximity to the contact. Then I recommend another single sonar pulse to refine location."

MacDonald stood at the 12MC for a few seconds before turning to Goldstein. "Officer of the Deck, bring us onto course two-six-eight and increase speed to fifteen knots." The speed would render the passive sonar capability of the *Dale* useless, but since they had already lost the noise signatures of the submarine, it was a moot issue.

Overhead, he listened to Burnham in Combat passing information to the *Coghlan*, whose sonar pulse had located the contact.

"Steady on course two-six-eight, speed fifteen knots," the helmsman announced.

MacDonald turned to the sound-powered phone talker. "Tell the bow to ready the second grenade."

"**THAT** was the third pulse," Ignatova said.

"I think it was because they lost us, XO." They were both

thinking of the American ASW tactic of three pulses and then fire. Bocharkov's hand tightened on the overhead pipe.

"I have increased blade rates on Contact One," the sonar technician reported.

Orlov looked up at Bocharkov, who nodded at the officer.

"Make your course two-eight-zero, and reduce speed to four knots."

"Aye, sir," Orlov replied.

The K-122 tilted to starboard as the submarine changed course. The bow was still tilted down as the submarine approached the three-hundred-meter mark.

The blow came suddenly, knocking the boat off course to the left, shaking everyone in the control room and knocking Ignatova into the firing console. Bocharkov found himself on the deck near the periscope. He jumped up.

"Make your depth two hundred meters. All stop!"

"Making my depth two hundred meters, angle twenty degrees!" Orlov shouted.

Bocharkov did not respond. The groan of metal filled the submarine as it continued downward. Bocharkov glanced at the gauges across the compartment. "Status!"

"Passing two hundred fifty meters. Continuing down."

"All astern!"

The boat shook as the shafts changed their direction.

"Passing three hundred meters."

The cigarette fell out of Tverdokhleb's mouth and he made the sign of the cross on his chest.

The boat shook. The vibration rattled as the propellers fought the downward angle of the K-122.

"SEND out a single pulse the minute after the sound of the second grenade fades," MacDonald said, agreeing with Kennedy's request.

He nodded to the sound-powered phone talker. "Tell Weps to drop the next grenade."

The sailor acknowledged and quickly passed on the information. MacDonald watched the word being relayed on the bow to Lieutenant Kelly, who turned to Chief Benson. The gunner's mate chief's arm went back in a large windup and then came forward. This time MacDonald saw the grenade hit the water. Several seconds passed before Combat reported a successful explosion.

Grenades were practically harmless against a submarine. Even if they bounced off the hull before exploding, the damage would not be great enough to sink the contact. At least that was what MacDonald had been taught, but then he doubted that anyone had really tested the theory.

BOCHARKOV took a deep breath when he felt the nose of the boat begin to tilt upward. A couple of starshinas were helping Ignatova to his feet. Blood coated the XO's forehead, dripping onto the man's white shirt.

"Depth three hundred seventy-five meters, speed eight knots, course . . . course two-five-eight."

Maximum depth for an Echo class submarine was three hundred meters. Two things this had proved. One, the K-122 could survive below three hundred meters, and, two, there had been more than three hundred meters of water beneath him.

"What was that?"

"I think it was an outcropping or something," Orlov offered.

"It was most likely an old derelict," Tverdokhleb said in a shaky voice. "Just an old relic."

Whatever it was, K-122 had hit it dead-on, the boat would have come to the surface—a few bits at a time.

"Damage report and get the medical officer to the control room."

Chief Trush helped Ignatova to a clear spot near the bulkhead and sat him down. Ignatova raised his hand and nodded at Bocharkov, which sent blood splattering down the XO's shirt.

"Any more injuries?"

Uvarova was holding his arm, but still at his position near the planesman. The chief of the boat did not turn at the question. "Chief Ship Starshina Uvarova, do you have anyone injured?"

A deep sigh escaped Uvarova before the man responded. "No, sir. My men are okay."

"How about you?"

Uvarova turned. "Captain, I am okay." He raised his arm slightly. "I hit my arm on the hydraulic levers, sir."

"Is it broken? Am I going to have to pull your teeth to get you to tell me?"

"I think it may be broken, sir, but I still have the other arm."

Bocharkov turned back to looking at the gauges. "Have the doctor look at it when he arrives. Navigator, recommended course."

"Recommend return to course two-six-zero, remain at present depth of two hundred meters. You are still five minutes to unlimited depth."

"We are always five minutes until unlimited depth, Lieutenant Tverdokhleb."

Unlimited depth for an Echo II submarine meant anything over one thousand meters. The only limit to how deep the submarine could go was the ability of its hull to withstand the water pressure. Bucharkov recalled one report showing an Echo II reaching nearly four hundred meters before it sprang a leak. K-122 had gone to three hundred seventy-five.

"We have another explosion, sir, off our stern . . . in the baffles."

Second grenade. "Distance?"

"Faint."

A minute later the sound of a sonar pulse from one of the warships reached the control room. This time Bucharkov felt no hit. He heard the pulse as everyone else did, but there was no strength to it. He looked at Orlov just as the aft hatch opened and the doctor stepped into the compartment.

"I think the pulse missed us," Orlov said.

"Ask Sonar."

He watched as the doctor squatted beside Ignatova. "When you finish with the XO, Doctor, look at the chief of the boat's arm."

Dr. Nosova nodded.

The epiphany hit Bucharkov as he walked back toward his position near the periscope platform. He knew why the sonar missed them and the grenade explosion was barely audible. He changed direction and hurried toward the navigator. Tverdokhleb half-rose as the captain approached. "Quick. Show me where we hit the obstacle."

Tverdokhleb sat down, picked up his pencil, and drew a circle around a spot on the chart. "About here, Captain."

"Show me where we are now."

The navigator put the tip of the pencil on a short line. "Right here. We are about two to three hundred meters from where we hit, Comrade Captain. We are still drifting forward on course two-six-five."

"How much depth do we have beneath us?"

"We are still at the three-hundred-meter curve, Captain. But we must have more depth available than the charts show . . ."

"If we are still at the three-hundred-meter curve, Navigator, then why did we hit this . . . this thing when we were passing two hundred fifty?" he snapped.

"Because, sir, it is not on the chart."

Bocharkov turned to Orlov. "Come here, Burian."

Almost immediately the officer of the deck stood beside the captain.

"What depth were we when we hit the sunken derelict? Two hundred fifty?"

"No, sir. We were passing two hundred seventy-five meters."

Bucharkov looked at the two junior officers, then turned to Tverdokhleb's chart, twisting it slightly on the plotting table. "Listen. We have two American warships—let's call them destroyers—placed here and here based on the bearings Sonar has been passing us, right?"

Orlov agreed.

"Here is where we hit the obstacle. From the sound of the hit, it sounded as if we hit something metallic. It was definitely an uncharted sunken vessel."

"Or an outcropping. It could also have been the bottom," Tverdokhleb said.

"It couldn't have been the bottom because when we glanced off, we continued downward. Besides, Lieutenant, you said it was a derelict. Make up your mind on what it was and stick with it."

"My apologies, sir."

Bocharkov grunted. "Regardless, we have hit something and that something is higher than the bottom. I think your first instinct, Navigator, was right about it being an old sunken vessel. Which means it is not on the chart. Then, maybe you are right, but instead of it being man-made, maybe it's a mountain or an outcropping. Whatever it is, it is between us and the Americans." He looked at Orlov. "You said their pulse did not hit us, right?"

"Sonar confirms no indications it detected us."

"Why?" Bocharkov asked, then continued before Orlov could reply. "Because of what we hit. It is shielding us from their sonar, but once they pass over it, they are going to regain contact with us, if we are not over open ocean."

A broad smile passed over Orlov's face. "Means we have an opportunity to evade them, sir."

Bocharkov grunted. "Well said, Lieutenant." He looked down at Tverdokhleb. "What I want from you, Uri," Bocharkov continued, tapping the navigator on the shoulder, "is to listen to the contact information Sonar is passing and plot the American destroyers. Lieutenant Orlov, you are to stand here and provide recommendations to me on course changes to keep that underwater whatever between us and the Americans. Lieutenant Tverdokhleb, you are the key to getting us out of this." He looked at both officers. "Do you know what that second grenade meant?"

They shook their heads.

"It means they are going to drop one more, and if we don't surface, then they will attack us."

The officers exchanged glances.

"Your orders, sir?" Orlov asked.

Bocharkov looked at Tverdokhleb. "Officer of the Deck, make your depth two hundred fifty meters, make your course two-eight-zero, and make your speed ten knots."

Orlov turned and started back to his position near the helmsman. As he walked, he repeated in a loud voice, "Making my depth two hundred fifty meters, maintaining course two-six-five, and coming to speed ten knots, aye!"

An echo of his commands came from the helmsman, as the starshina shifted the wheels slightly. At the annunciator, the chief of the watch, Trush, passed along the speed command and reported when the engine room acknowledged the new order.

Uvarova watched, holding his broken arm, as the planesman eased the angle of the planes mounted on the conning tower of the Echo. "Easy, easy," the chief of the boat said softly.

The K-122 started to pick up speed from the slow drift. Bocharkov looked down at the chart. Tverdokhleb shifted the chart back so it faced it him. With the fine tip of the pencil the navigator drew a slight line from where they were and put a time on it.

Orlov must have told Sonar what Bucharkov wanted, because almost immediately the passive bearings to the two destroyers began to roll aloud through Combat. Tverdokhleb whipped his compass along each bearing and drew a faint line. On the chart the navigator had drawn a circle to identify where the something—possibly an underwater knoll—was they had hit.

"Make your course two-seven-zero," Bocharkov said.

"Make my course two-seven-zero, aye," Orlov replied.

The helmsman acknowledged the officer of the deck's order and eased the helm to starboard, bringing the K-122 ten degrees to starboard. The K-122 was heading out of Subic Bay. The open Pacific Ocean beckoned only miles away.

"How will this affect our masking by the underwater object?" Bocharkov asked Tverdokhleb.

The navigator bent over his chart for a few seconds, then straightened. "We have about five minutes of cover before Contact Two will have a straight line to us."

Bocharkov nodded and then started back toward his position near the periscope. He did not know if this was going to work or not. He had no idea of how wide or high whatever they'd hit was. For all he knew they could find themselves unmasked at any moment, like a virgin at an orgy.

The only way he was going to know was if it worked—or didn't.

The muffled sound of another explosion was heard through the skin of the submarine. It was faint, but sufficient to reach inside the K-122.

"That's the third one," Ignatova said from his sitting position, a bandage now covering the top of his head. The XO was being helped to his feet. Ignatova shrugged off the hands and stood before the weapons console. "I am ready, Captain."

"Make aft tubes one and two ready in all respects," Bocharkov said. He did not want to fire on the Americans, but if he had no other choice to save the K-122, he would.

"Tubes one and two ready, sir," Ignatova replied.

Bocharkov looked at the clock. It showed zero four fifty.

"Steady on two-seven-zero at two hundred fifty meters, speed ten knots, sir."

"Very well," Bocharkov said, with more confidence than he felt.

SIXTEEN

CAPTAIN Norton faced the banks of telecommunications equipment before him. One hand held the briar pipe he puffed, while the other traced invisible lines in the air as his eyes traveled along the massive maze of wires that ran from the fronts of the telephone switching system to disappear around the back of each piece.

Growing daylight broke through the small windows of the building. He pulled a handkerchief and wiped the first beads of sweat from his forehead. He folded the khaki hat in his hand and jammed it under his belt. The temperature inside this building would hit over a hundred today, he surmised. He removed the pipe long enough to yawn and scratch the stubble of the morning shadow across his chin.

"Chief, tell San Miguel to send a couple of huge fans in the logistics van. Tell them we will need them this morning."

Chief Welcher nodded. "Aye, sir. I'm going to check on the main van and see if it has left yet. Plus I want to do another check of the outside. We got some daylight now." He stepped outside the building.

Norton had forbade any communications over the telephone lines with San Miguel until he figured out what this contraption was and how it came to be installed inside the Subic Bay telephone switching system. He now knew where it came from and was sure he knew how it came to be installed here.

The Marine Corps captain stepped into the small building, drawing Norton's attention.

"Captain, we have secured the perimeter, sir."

"How far down the road have you put forces, Captain Lewis?"

"As you requested, sir. No one will be able to reach this end of Subic today without wading through my marines."

Norton nodded. "Well done, Captain."

"Captain," Norton said, causing the young officer to stop and turn. "My condolences on the marines' losses last night. I know everyone killed and wounded was a comrade of you and your men. They were also our comrades."

"We're going to get them, sir."

Norton started to say something, but better the man believed his words than know the truth Norton had reached in the hour he had been here.

"You are right, Captain," he finally replied. "We're going to get them," he said, his words trailing off as his eyes returned to the strange contraption he had found. He stuck the pipe back between his lips. Blue smoke curled from the bowl as his teeth lightly trapped the stem.

"Yes, sir, we will. Did you hear about the action in the Middle East?"

"I did. Seems the Israelis have wiped out the Arab air forces, doesn't it?"

"Yes, sir. Kind of dumb of the Arabs to start telling everyone what they were going to do weeks ago and start preparing to do it and not expect the Israelis to do something."

"It is a strange and dangerous world in which we live, Captain. Back to the security," Norton said, stirring the conversation away from the newest Middle East war.

For the next five minutes the two officers discussed Norton's orders for the security and where to mount the ingress and egress to the area. The fewer people who knew what he knew the better.

Chief Welcher stepped into the narrow space between the

marine officer and the bank of equipment. "Captain," he said, looking at Norton. "I found where it's connected."

Welcher glanced at Norton and then Lewis. When it became apparent the marine officer was curious over the chief's words, Norton said, "Captain, that will be all. Thanks again for securing the area and relay my regrets to your men."

Lewis opened his mouth to say something. Norton knew the man was going to ask why they had secured the area, and he was prepared to lie and tell him it was because it was a crime scene. But the marine officer apparently changed his mind, and he stepped out of the doorway into the rising humid heat of the Philippines, which filtered into the fan-cooled area of the switching room.

"Tell me about it."

"Fairly simple, sir. A thin wire antenna trails from the telephone line here in the switching room to the top of the telephone pole. They just wrapped it around the heavier telephone cable."

Norton walked to the rear of the racks of equipment, where the bulk of connecting wires ran from the top of the telephone switching bank to the wall, disappearing through it to the outside. He turned on his flashlight and searched the wiring. "I don't see where it connects here."

Welcher had followed the navy cryptologic officer. He reached up and traced his hand along the wires, searching for something. "I don't see or feel anything either, sir. Maybe once we have more light we can tell better."

Norton went back to the contraption. "Looks as if whoever did this did not expect it to stay long before it was discovered."

"Piss-poor installation."

Norton grunted. "Works though," he said, a puff of blue white Carter Hall smoke whiffing from his lips and the bowl of the pipe. "On the second hand, Chief, maybe they wanted us to find it. Think we're right to leave it attached? Maybe safer for us to pull it out and destroy their mission. At least, someone would have a lot of explaining to do if it failed to work. What do you think? Leave it or pull it out?"

"Sir, I'm a chief. I'll do what you tell me to. We already have it. We can rip it out anytime, box it up, and ship it to the

Foreign Technology Exploitation office at Office of Naval Intelligence, or we can take it back to San Miguel."

"We could do all of those. I think we'll leave it in. Kind of a gesture of goodwill between us spooks," he joked. "Let them think for a few days they were surreptitious enough to fool us." Norton looked the out-of-place equipment over closely without touching it. "Is there some way we can connect this to only one line or two? Right now, I'm not sure how it is determining which telephone lines to monitor."

Welcher leaned over, the two heads nearly touching. The beer aroma of Olongapo coming from Welcher and the sweet tobacco smoke of Norton's pipe mixed around the two men.

"Captain, I think we can do it, but we run the risk of destroying the instrument once we start messing with it."

"The van from San Miguel will be here in two hours, followed by the logistics van." He fanned his face. "Let's hope they remember to send the fans."

"Which teams are coming with the group?"

"I asked for the operational deception team." He looked at Welcher. "Did you find out if it had left yet or not?"

"I wrote the message for transmission and one of the runners has left with it for Subic Operations Center. Not being able to talk with them directly makes this a hard way to exchange information."

"No choice, Chief, until we know what we are up against. Until then, every conversation made by telephone by anyone on the base, whether it is the Cubi Point airdales or the Subic Bay ship drivers, their conversations are being transmitting into the ether."

"I don't think it can monitor every conversation, sir."

Norton shook his head. "I think you are right, Chief. I would offer most likely it sets itself to active lines and stays there."

"Only one transmission line outside and it's a wire antenna. Can't transmit a lot. Probably one conversation at a time."

Several more puffs of smoke rose from the bowl as Norton nodded. "You're probably right, Chief. Would do them little good to listen to sex talk between the sailors coming into port and their wives back in the continental United States." Norton shook his head. "No, they're going to want to monitor the talk between Subic Operations and the ships tied up here."

"The problem, sir, is I don't know how to find out how or what this thing is monitoring without taking it off. This contraption makes me think it is a receiver. And I don't know any receiver that also transmits." Welcher shook his head. "Know what I think, Captain?"

"Tell me, Chief."

"I think it roams the circuits looking for something that is active. Kind of what you were saying. When it finds someone in a conversation, it quits roaming, starts monitoring, and starts transmitting, until there is a click as they hang up, or a certain number of seconds pass with no conversation or something like that. Then it starts searching the telephone lines again for activity."

"Well, we won't take it apart yet, Chief. We'll try some external exploitation. See if we can find the frequency this thing is transmitting its data on, and from there, we'll extrapolate how it works."

"Should be able to limit the lines it is monitoring, if it is more than one."

"That's why our deception team is on the way, Chief."

The muffled sound of an explosion reached their ears.

"Another grenade," Norton said.

"That's the third one. Ten minutes until five," Welcher said, tapping his watch.

"Might not need our team if our ships are preparing to fire on the Soviet intruder."

"You think we have a Soviet submarine inside Subic Bay, sir."

Norton motioned the chief over. "Look here," he said pointing to the underside of the monitoring system they had found.

Welcher leaned down. "CCCP" was embossed in bright white Cyrillic letters on the equipment. "Union of Soviet Socialist Republics," Welcher mumbled. "Not very smart spies, are they?"

"Smart enough to get in here and put the system in place. If they had not encountered our security forces, it might have been days, weeks, or even months until we found it. No telling how much damage could have been done from them puzzling out the operational intelligence they would have gleaned from what they heard."

"They're in for a surprise when our folks arrive," Welcher chuckled. The chief leaned closer, ran his finger along the rough bottom of the foreign equipment.

Norton smiled. "That they are, Chief, that they are."

Welcher laughed. "Well, I'll be damned, sir. There's something here." He leaned down to look at the bottom of the foreign system. Welcher ran his fingers over it again. "Someone has scratched something into the bottom."

"What is it?"

Welcher pulled his flashlight and squatted. Looking up at the scratching, he started spelling the Cyrillic letters out.

"I studied Chinese and Vietnamese, Chief. I don't know Russian."

Welcher flicked off the flashlight and stood. He chuckled. "Can't say this is the Russian equivalent to 'Kilroy was here,' but someone has scratched 'Greetings from Dolinski.' "

"Is that a city or someone's name or what?"

Welcher shrugged. "It just says, 'Greetings from Dolinski' and beneath it is yesterday's date: 'June 4, 1967.' And it's scratched into the metallic casing, sir." Welcher laughed. "The son of a bitch wanted us to know who did this."

Norton grunted. "Or where the system came from. Strange. I couldn't see one of our spooks doing that."

They both laughed.

"WHO threw the third grenade?" MacDonald demanded, rushing to the port-side bridge wing. He lifted the megaphone, pulled the talk trigger, and barely let the electronic squeal fade before he was shouting, "What the hell are you doing, Weps? I didn't order the grenade."

Lieutenant Kelly and Chief Benson raised their arms and shook their heads. Kelly cupped his mouth and shouted something, but the wind swept the words away from MacDonald.

MacDonald touched his ears and shook his head. Kelly

ran in the direction of the bridge wing. He cupped his lips again and shouted, "Sir, we haven't thrown the third one."

MacDonald's eyebrows arched. Then who did? He had turned to go back into the bridge when Goldstein filled the hatch. "Sir, *Coghlan* called. They accidentally dropped a grenade over the side."

MacDonald rushed to the Navy Red and grabbed the handset. Before he could call the *Coghlan*, the bagpipe sound of the crypto gear synchronizing filled his ears.

"Dale, this is *Coghlan*. Is your Charlie Oscar there?"

"Ron, this is Danny," MacDonald answered. "What is going on?"

"We had a little mishap over here, Captain. I had my men standing by to drop grenades in the event you needed us to help in the warning phase. Unfortunately, one of the pins fell out—"

"Fell out? How in the hell does a pin fall out?"

"Well, this one did, Captain, so we had no choice. The chief tossed it overboard."

MacDonald was furious. He wanted to scream obscenities at the redheaded captain of the *Coghlan,* but what would it accomplish? The damage had already been done and the *Dale* was approaching the datum where the contact was last reflected.

"CAPTAIN," Orlov said from his position near the helm. "Sonar reports Contact One off our aft starboard quarter is continuing to close."

Bocharkov grunted with a nod. Everyone in the control room knew the third grenade would be the last warning the Americans would give. The contact closing on them would be the one to attack. The torpedoes would splash into the water above the K-122 and begin a circling search until their homing devices detected the submarine. Then they would straighten and head directly toward the K-122, small sonar pulses locking on the submarine as the torpedoes drove toward the Echo's propeller area. If they disabled the Echo propellers, the best case would be that the K-122 would survive the attack. If the ballasts still operated Bucharkov could surface and surrender, but if the ballasts were damaged also, then the K-122 would settle to the bottom.

He thought the water was still too shallow to implode them, so in time the Americans would rescue them, hold them up for the world to see, and then return them to Mother Russia, where all of them would disappear for allowing themselves to be caught. And the Americans would have an entire K-122 submarine to exploit.

"Captain?" Ignatova asked.

Bocharkov blinked a couple of times. "XO?"

"Sir, I asked if you want to open the forward torpedo doors."

Bocharkov took a deep breath. Most likely whatever they'd hit still protected them from being detected. If the Americans knew where they were, they would not have dropped the grenade so far away. Most likely he could open the forward tubes without them hearing the telltale sound.

"Open all outer doors, fore and aft tubes," he commanded.

If they were going detect him opening one or two torpedo tube doors, they might as well hear him opening all of them. After all, they were the ones who dropped the third grenade. All he wanted to do was leave the area.

"Opening outer doors fore and aft, aye!" Ignatova acknowledged. "Outer doors aft open with exception of five and six. Opening forward torpedo doors."

Bocharkov listened as the commands were passed to the two torpedo rooms and acknowledgments returned from them as the doors were opened. He now had twelve torpedoes at his command. Even if he failed to sink either American ship, he could give the crews of both of them moments of sheer, exhilarating panic when his torpedoes filled the top feet of Subic Bay.

"Aft tubes five and six replenished with decoys. Outer doors opened aft tubes five and six."

He had two of the four aft tubes ready to fire. The six tubes in the forward torpedo room were also ready now.

"Sir, Sonar says the third grenade came from Contact Two, not One. Contact One dropped the first two."

The farthest American warship had dropped the third grenade. Why did they change for the third grenade?

"Sir, Contact One is picking up speed and remains heading toward us."

So they had not lost the K-122 as he'd thought. If that was right, then they knew he had opened his torpedo doors. They knew he was able to fire first or retaliate if they fired. He hoped that was a good thing.

"Sonar has reduction in revolutions on Contact One."

Why is Contact One slowing? Bocharkov asked himself.

"SLOW our speed to five knots," MacDonald said. What was the Soviet captain thinking? What would he think if he were in his Soviet counterpart's position? Everyone in every navy in the world that had a submarine force knew what the three grenades meant. The submarine had to have detected the third grenade. What would he do if he heard the third grenade? Would he fire first? Would he wait? Could the Soviet captain afford to wait? MacDonald wasn't sure he could. .

"Coming to five knots, sir," Goldstein said.

"Very well . . . ," MacDonald answered, his words trailing off. The clock on the bulkhead showed zero five hundred hours. A slight breeze flowed through the opened port-bridge-wing hatch, through the bridge, and out the opened starboard-bridge-wing hatch. The humidity of the Philippine day remained behind as the breeze tapered and ceased. MacDonald lifted his arms, feeling the sweat beginning to stick his T-shirt to his underarms. It was just another glorious day in the Orient.

He pushed the toggle switch on the 12MC. "Combat, Bridge. Have we regained contact?"

"Not yet, sir. Recommend active sonar."

MacDonald bit his lower lip. "Not yet, Lieutenant." If he sent a single pulse now, the submarine might think it was the final firing solution, and if the Soviet captain intended to fire, he would fire when that pulse reached the submarine.

The rear hatch opened and Admiral Green stepped onto the bridge.

"CTF-Seventy on the bridge!" the boatswain mate of the watch announced from his position near the 1MC system.

"Morning, Admiral," MacDonald said as the World War II veteran walked up alongside him. Bright sunlight shined through the port windows of the bridge.

"Seems to me, Danny, you got a handful right now."

"Yes, sir. If we ping him, sir, I am concerned he might think we are fixing to launch torpedoes and fire first. If we don't, we might lose him."

Green pursed his lips as he nodded. "It's a damned if you do, damned if you don't situation."

"Any suggestions as CTF-Seventy, sir? After all, you are the officer in tactical command."

Green smiled. "Yep. I am the OTC, but you are the skipper. You have your orders. I notice you slowed down, so I wanted to ask why."

MacDonald shared his reasoning with the admiral.

After a few seconds of listening, Green interrupted. "Danny, you have your orders. Eventually we were going to drop that third grenade anyway. Eventually, the Soviet Echo is going to surface, or continue running for the open ocean, or fight us. But our orders are not to let it reach the open ocean. It either surfaces or we sink it."

"Sir, did you always follow orders in World War II?"

"Unfair question, Danny. In World War II we did not have the communications and over-the-shoulder rear echeloners watching our every move and offering their candid observations and giving their great orders without knowing the tactical situation at the time. We had something called commander's intent."

"Not very clear, Admiral," MacDonald said.

"We still have commander's intent. It's Commander in Chief Pacific Fleet's intent the Soviet submarine does not escape. It is your job to execute whatever measures you can to make it happen. In today's navy, unlike in World War II, we got such reliable communications everyone can watch and critique what you do."

"Sir?"

"You have your orders, Danny. Now, if you will excuse

me, I have to go to the head and get rid of some of this coffee. I'm going to be gone for about five minutes."

With that, the venerable gentleman disappeared through the rear hatch, leaving MacDonald to decide how to successfully execute the Commander in Chief U.S. Pacific Fleet's orders. If he followed the orders, he endangered his ship and the men on it. If he didn't follow the orders, the Echo was going to escape.

"Bring her back up to ten knots, Officer of the Deck. Maintain course two-six-five."

"Captain, Combat," came the mechanical voice through the 12MC. "Sonar reports they may have detected the opening of the contact's outer doors. And they got a bearing on the submarine; it's two-seven-zero."

"Very well," MacDonald responded. So the *Coghlan*'s third grenade must have done the trick. Not Kennedy's fault; just MacDonald's responsibility.

He pushed the toggle switch. "Combat, Captain. Do we have steady contact with the submarine?"

"Not completely, sir. Sonar had a couple of seconds of passive noise coming through the hydrophones when the submarine opened its torpedo tubes. Just enough to identify what the noise was and get a bearing. Bearing was two-seven-zero."

MacDonald acknowledged the information and turned to Goldstein. "Sam, ease the *Dale* to course two-seven-zero, maintain ten knots."

"Aye, sir," Goldstein acknowledged, then in a loud voice he continued, "Helmsman, five degree starboard rudder, steady on course two-seven-zero, maintain five knots."

MacDonald listened for several seconds as his course change passed from the officer of the deck to the helmsman; then the helmsman echoed the order as he turned the helm with minimum rudder to bring the *Dale* ten degrees starboard. Ensign Hatfield stood with his hands folded behind him, looking over the shoulder of the helmsman.

Nearly a minute passed before MacDonald sighed and pushed the toggle switch on the 12MC. "Combat, this is the Captain. Make the over-the-sides ready to fire at my command."

"Request permission to secure the running lights, sir," Goldstein said.

"Permission granted."

The port red running light on the left side and the starboard green running light on the right side were turned off along with the mainmast and the stern white lights. Lights at night told other ships not only the direction the contact they were watching was traveling, but also the size of the ship. Combinations of lights on the mainmast sometimes also revealed the class of ship they were observing. And at other times, they told the observer what the ship was doing, such as towing a barge.

MacDonald pressed the 12MC. "Combat, this is the Captain. Make sure the *Coghlan* is aware of the combat situation—"

"Sir, I passed the information personally to their combat information center watch officer," Burnham interrupted.

MacDonald flinched. He did not like to be interrupted. "Very well," he said in a sharp tone. "Now tell them to be prepared to launch their ASROC on our command."

"Yes, sir. I will pass along the orders. Captain, I have informed them over Navy Red that we are preparing to launch our over-the-sides."

"Make sure they understand that we are doing this as a precautionary step. At this time, I have no intention of firing."

"Aye, sir, will do."

The *Coghlan* had already dropped the grenade accidentally. Last thing he and they needed was for the redheaded stepchild to "accidentally" launch a couple of ASROC torpedoes onto the target. There was no recall of a torpedo launched. They were going to circle until they found a target or ran out of fuel. Meanwhile, the contact would definitely launch theirs. Of that, MacDonald had no doubt. No skipper would stand by and accept an attack from an adversary.

The Navy Red secure communications net gave off its familiar bagpipe squeal as the cryptographic keys between the two ships synchronized. Then Burnham began passing the tactical information. A couple of times the lieutenant and his

Coghlan counterpart had to repeat the information, but as it rose over the mountain the sun was playing havoc with the nighttime frequencies.

MacDonald listened to the passing of information with excruciating angst.

"XO," Bocharkov said. "Make aft tubes one and two ready in all respects."

"Aye, sir," Ignatova replied.

Bocharkov's mouth felt dry. He had never fired a torpedo in anger or in combat. He grunted. Anger? Combat? Were they different? Surprising to him, a calmness he had not felt earlier seemed to have settled on him as he reached this critical moment of making a decision. He knew once the decision was made, he could follow the rote to conclusion.

Should he fire first? If he did, the Americans would launch their torpedoes almost instantaneously. The one advantage he might have would be if they had lost constant contact with him because of his depth and the underwater obstruction he hit minutes ago. Sonar seemed positive that the last pulse by the Americans had failed to detect the K-122. But what if they were wrong?

"Contact One has changed course," Orlov reported, his voice louder than normal. "A small change, but one that lines—"

"New course?" Bocharkov asked.

"A few degrees to the right—"

"What is the course?" Bocharkov barked.

"Two-seven-zero, sir."

After a couple of seconds, Orlov added, "Sonar says the turn may be in response to them detecting us opening our torpedo doors."

"Very well." The decision was being taken from him by the Americans. Was this going to be another instance where a Soviet warship—in this case his—would back down rather than act?

"Contact One has steadied on course two-seven-zero. Sonar reports increased revolutions. Contact One is picking up speed."

Bocharkov grunted. He had been wrong. The Americans

still had contact on the K-122. Maybe opening the forward outer doors had done it; then again, maybe the Americans never lost contact. He never lost contact with them.

"Sir, Sonar says the course change indicates the Americans still have contact on us."

"Depth of water beneath us?" Bocharkov directed the question to the navigator.

"Still at the three-hundred-meter curve, sir," Tverdokhleb answered.

"Sir," Ignatova called from the fire control console. "Aft tubes one and two are ready in all respects, sir. Aft tubes three and four have decoys."

Bocharkov acknowledged, then ordered, "Make forward tubes one, two, three, and four ready in all respects." If he was going to fire two torpedoes, he might as well give the Americans four to worry about. He'd keep forward tubes three and four reserved for a quick shot. Forward tubes five and six would be the safety reserve while the torpedomen reloaded the empty tubes.

"COGHLAN, I say again, we are preparing to fire our over-the-sides torpedoes, if . . ." And the loss of synchronization caused the comms to drop out for a few seconds. "I say again," Burnham continued.

MacDonald stepped inside the bridge. "Give me a pad," he said to the quartermaster, snapping his fingers. He quickly wrote a note, and then handed it to Lieutenant Goldstein. "Sam, have the signalmen send this to the *Coghlan*."

Goldstein read it, then nodded. "Aye, sir." He turned to the boatswain mate of the watch and handed him the note. "Have the messenger take this to the signal bridge."

MacDonald raised his glasses and scanned the sea in front of him, hoping to detect a periscope. His glance at the chart on the way to the port bridge wing showed they were nearing the three-thousand-foot curve. With that much depth beneath them, the Echo most likely would elude and evade them.

"Understand, *Dale*. You are preparing to fire your torpedoes. We are in launch position and awaiting your orders," came an announcement from the *Coghlan*.

"CTF-Seventy on the bridge!" shouted the boatswain mate.

MacDonald stepped back inside. "Morning, Admiral."

"Morning, Danny," Green said, handing him a biscuit wrapped in a napkin. "Brought this back for you."

MacDonald set it on the small shelf running along the front of the bridge. "Thank you, sir."

"I listened to your watch officer pass the information to *Coghlan*. I'd be careful if I was you. I'm not fully convinced the *Coghlan* understands the orders. Comms are all screwed up."

"I'm sending them a signal now, sir."

"Very well. Do we know how far away the submarine is?" Green asked as the two men stepped onto the bridge wing.

"No, sir," MacDonald replied, "but we know it bears dead ahead of us."

Green rubbed his chin. "Then ten knots seems reasonable to me, but I was thinking as I walked from the mess hall to the bridge: There is no law against dropping a fourth grenade."

"It might confuse them enough to fire their torpedoes."

"And it might confuse them enough that they don't know what we are doing and they may hold up firing them."

"They might think they're under attack."

Green nodded. "And they should. So they will have two options. Surface or fight. From what I have heard, you have your surface action group prepared for fighting. Let's get this over with before we lose all of our communications due to Mr. Sun."

MacDonald swallowed. Green was right. He was taking too much time making his decisions. His orders were clear, so why did he not want to bring them to a conclusion?

"First time is always the hardest," Green said.

MacDonald stuck his head inside the bridge. "Officer of the Deck, bring us up to twelve knots, maintain course."

As Goldstein relayed the orders and the quartermaster made the log notations, MacDonald crossed the bridge to the starboard side and flicked the toggle switch. "Lieutenant Burnham, this is the captain. Work with the bridge to keep on course toward the submarine. I do not want to pass over it, but when we have steady contact, my intentions are to drop a fourth and final grenade. If the submarine fails to surface, then we are going to launch the over-the-sides." He paused, and then added, "But only at my command. Make sure *Coghlan* is aware."

MacDonald slapped the handset into the cradle and looked toward the port bridge wing. Admiral Green nodded. Mac-Donald turned to the sound-powered phone talker. "Tell Lieutenant Kelly to stand by for grenade."

He listened to communications internal and with the *Coghlan*, as both destroyers ramped up to attack the intruder. He hoped the Soviet captain would surface, but if the man was anything like him, he would launch his torpedoes almost instantaneously when he heard the high-speed blade rates of the torpedoes searching for them. What if the Soviet captain still had the two destroyers on his sonar? Then the *Dale* and the *Coghlan* were going to be at a disadvantage.

The first attack would be a double launch. He would fire one over-the-side torpedo off the port side of the ship and simultaneously another torpedo from the starboard over-the-side weapon system. He would order the *Coghlan* to bracket the *Dale* fore and aft with ASROC-launched torpedoes. The four torpedoes should make contact and zero in on the submarine. When the submarine responded, he would know its location. Then, and only then, would he launch his remaining four torpedoes and order the *Coghlan* to launch everything it had.

It would take three minutes to reload. He took a deep breath. Fighting an antisubmarine warfare operation was more than brawn and weapons. It meant outthinking his opponent. In the next few minutes the Soviet captain and he were going to play "war." Only this time it would have real consequences.

MACDONALD overheard the sound-powered phone talker relay to Lieutenant Goldstein that the *Dale* was one minute from the estimated location of the contact. He looked at the clock. The minute hand was seconds from zero five ten.

"Officer of the Deck, slow to ten knots."

"Aye, sir. Slowing to ten knots."

A humid breeze blew through the open port side hatch,

whiffing across the bridge as it found egress through the starboard hatchway. MacDonald pulled his handkerchief from his rear pocket, reached up, and wiped the sweat from his forehead, before jamming it back into his pocket. Olongapo wrapped you in its humidity with a dank humus smell, and covered everyone with matted sweat, like some gardener's dank woolen sweater permeated with the odors from a rich compost pile.

"Steady on two-seven-zero, speed ten knots," Goldstein shouted.

"I heard it, Officer of the Deck," MacDonald said from near the captain's chair on the starboard side of the bridge. He turned to the same sound-powered phone talker. "Tell the bow to throw over the fourth grenade." Then he flicked the toggle switch of the 12MC down and told Combat to be ready, the fourth grenade was going over.

MacDonald watched as Chief Benson drew back and threw the fourth grenade. A few seconds passed before he saw the slight spray of water as the grenade exploded.

Almost immediately the 12MC blared. "Sir, Sonar got detection off the submarine with the grenade. It is dead ahead of us, less than a thousand feet."

"WE'RE there!" Tverdokhleb shouted. "We're over the thousand-meter curve, sir," he said again, half-standing astraddle his chair.

"Status?" Bocharkov asked.

"Depth two hundred meters, speed ten knots, course two-seven-zero," Orlov replied.

"Take her down to three hundred fifty meters," Bocharkov ordered.

Ignatova and Orlov both looked at him. Bocharkov raised his eyebrows. "Three hundred fifty meters," he repeated.

The movement of Uvarova turning to look at him from the chief of the boat's position near the planesman drew his attention.

"Making my depth three hundred fifty meters, aye," Orlov repeated.

Fifty meters beneath the recommended maximum diving

limit would be all right. The K-122 could handle the depth. It had already shown it could. If the Americans had him, this should help lose them.

The explosion came from directly astern. It was a fourth grenade. The echo of the grenade off the skin of the submarine would act like a sonar pulse locating the K-122.

"Make your course two-niner-five!" Bocharkov shouted. "Make your speed twelve knots!"

"Making my course two-niner-five, speed twelve knots, aye!"

Bocharkov looked at Ignatova. "Prepare to fire at my command."

"WE got him!" The 12MC squawked with Lieutenant Burnham's voice. He's almost directly ahead of us. Shouting voices in the background interrupted Burnham. "Wait one," the lieutenant said.

A second passed. "Sir, the contact is accelerating and heading directly toward the *Coghlan*. Sir, its doors are open and it's lining up for a bow shot on the *Coghlan*. Orders?"

"Are there any sounds of it coming to the surface? Any clearing of the ballast tanks? Any sound the submarine is surfacing?"

"No, sir, nothing," Burnham immediately replied, his voice tight and high.

"Contact course?" The fourth grenade had failed. All it did was accelerate the rush to combat.

"Don't have it yet, sir, but he's in a right-hand turn, bringing his bow toward the *Coghlan*."

MacDonald turned to the sound-powered phone talker. "Tell Lieutenant Kelly to drop a fifth grenade."

Admiral Green walked over to where MacDonald stood. Their eyes met and the admiral nodded slightly. MacDonald knew where this was going, and was he delaying the inevitable?

He turned from Green to the 12MC. "Prepare for fifth grenade and prepare to go active on sonar."

The fifth grenade curved through the morning sky like some slow-pitched softball drifting through the rise of its path before falling. The slight waves of the incoming morning tide masked the moment when the grenade hit the water.

THE fifth grenade exploded slightly behind the K-122.

"Contact One is directly astern of us, sir!" Orlov said, his voice slightly higher.

He would fire two torpedoes from his aft tubes and two from his forward tubes at Contact Two, which was now less than a thousand meters in front of him.

"Prepare to initiate a targeting pulse. One pulse and one pulse only," Bocharkov said, holding up one finger.

He listened as Orlov told Sonar.

Bocharkov turned to Ignatova. "Pass the word along to the crew to prepare for imminent attack." He turned back to Orlov. "Be prepared for a quick left turn immediately after launch. I want you to bring the speed up to twenty knots in the turn, then immediately reduce it to ten. Understand?"

"Aye, sir."

Though it seemed to have heard his plans, the American sonar pulse still caught him by surprise. It hit the K-122, the deadly sound reverberating throughout the ship. If he had had any doubt the Americans were about to attack, the single pulse erased it. The Americans had a targeting solution.

"Active sonar, now! Single pulse!"

"SIR! You hear it?" Burnham shouted. "The contact has sent out a single sonar pulse. *Coghlan* reports the pulse did hit it."

The Soviet captain had a targeting solution.

"Our sonar?"

"Sir, we have a targeting solution. The contact is five hundred feet ahead of us, in a right-hand turn, crossing away from our bow. Depth estimated at eight hundred feet."

Admiral Green grunted. "If he is at eight hundred feet, then any torpedoes he fires are going to have to ascend to reach their target, and that ascent won't be straight up. You know what that means, Danny."

MacDonald nodded. The *Dale* was too close for the submarine to hit them. They were inside the torpedo range for a

Soviet torpedo to activate, lock on, and hit them, but not too close for the *Dale* torpedoes.

"Combat, this is the captain. Launch one port-side torpedo and one starboard-side torpedo. Execute the attack plan!"

"Aye, sir," came the quick retort.

"SIR! Sonar reports torpedoes in the water!" Orlov said, his voice loud, shattering the silence within the control room.

"Firing solutions Contact One and Contact Two!" Bocharkov said, his voice calm and forceful.

"Firing solutions gained on Contact Two. Contact One is aft, estimated range four hundred meters."

Contact One, the leader of these two American warships, was too close for his aft torpedoes, but maybe the captain of the warship would not know how deep they were. Active sonar had a reputation for giving erroneous information on submarine depth. It was a chance he would have to take.

"Launch decoys!"

A few seconds passed before Orlov reported, "Decoys away."

"Fire tubes one and two fore, tubes three and four aft."

He watched as Ignatova reached up. It seemed time had slowed down. He could fire tubes one and two aft. Put torpedoes in the water, but it would be a waste, though it might cause Contact One to take some sort of evasive action. Any evasive action might even open up an opportunity for one of the torpedoes to hit.

"Sonar reports the American torpedoes are circling; they are in a search mode."

It would not be long before that search mode took the torpedoes lower and lower, until they penetrated the layer above them.

"Left full rudder! Make your speed twenty knots!" Bocharkov shouted.

"COGHLAN reports two ASROC launched, sir," Burnham reported.

MacDonald looked to his right. The smoke trails of the

rocket-fired torpedoes separated from the canisters on the foredeck of the *Coghlan*. One was heading forward of the *Dale*. It should splash forward of the submarine.

"Officer of the Deck, left full rudder, all ahead full."

The *Dale* tilted to starboard as the destroyer cut a sharp left-hand turn.

The other contrail showed the second ASROC heading near the exact location of the submarine. So far, everything was going according to MacDonald's plan, but why hadn't the submarine fired? He would have launched by now.

"Bridge, Combat! We have torpedoes in the water." The 12MC switched off for a second and then Burnham came back on line. "Their torpedoes, not ours!" he clarified.

MacDonald leaned down to the 12MC. "Lieutenant Burnham, where is the contact now?"

"Sir, last contact had the—"

The Navy Red speaker squawked, the squeal drowning out Burnham. "*Dale*, this is *Coghlan*. We have torpedoes inbound. Taking evasive action."

MacDonald watched the other destroyer lean to starboard as Kennedy put the *Coghlan* into a hard left turn. MacDonald knew the *Coghlan* would be accelerating to maximum speed. The left turn was bringing the bow of the destroyer directly toward the inbound torpedoes. Puffs of smoke rose from amidships of the *Coghlan* as the destroyer deployed decoys port and starboard of itself. The bow of the *Coghlan* would reduce the noise of the propellers and allow the decoys to act more effectively. He hoped Kennedy was right.

"Combat, this is the captain. Fire remaining over-the-sides."

At that moment the *Dale* passed over the underwater obstacle the K-122 had hit earlier.

"Torpedoes launched."

Out the starboard side window, MacDonald saw the two over-the-sides splash into the water and disappear beneath the slight waves. His stomach tightened. This was the fear the instructors said came with an attack, but *ignore it*, they preached. *Stay to the plan.* You fight like you train. Do it by rote if you have to, but keep doing it. The tightness seemed to lessen for a moment.

* * *

"MULTIPLE torpedoes in the water. We have a splash ahead of us with fast blade rates!" Orlov reported.

"Come to course one-eight-zero, speed twenty-five knots!" Bocharkov commanded.

"Making my course one-eight-zero, aye." Orlov turned to the helmsman. "Left full rudder! Make your speed twenty-five knots."

Behind the K-122, two decoys filled the void as the Soviet Echo submarine sought to sprint away from between the two American destroyers.

"Depth three hundred fifty meters!"

"Where is the layer?" Bocharkov asked.

"Two hundred meters," Tverdokhleb answered, drawing Bocharkov's attention for a moment. Tverdokhleb leaned back in his chair, an unlit cigarette dangling from his lips. "Two hundred meters," he repeated.

"Make your speed five knots, come to course two-six-zero!"

"Aye, sir. Making my speed five knots, right turn to two-six-zero."

"Bring her up to two hundred meters once we are steady on course two-six-zero."

Taking the submarine up would reduce the noise signature of the shafts and propellers by pointing them downward away from the torpedoes.

"Sonar reports torpedo inbound off our starboard bow, Captain. It is heading our way, sir," Orlov reported.

"Very well," Bocharkov said.

The K-122 began to level off as it steadied on the new course.

"Steady on one-eight-zero," Orlov said.

Bocharkov looked at the gauge. The boat was still going too fast as it decelerated from twenty-five to five knots. He needed to reduce the cavitation the propellers were making in the water.

He had to show confidence. Behind him he had left two decoys and a huge knuckle in the water from the high-speed turn.

Behind the K-122 the two decoys sped aft from where they'd been launched. One ran directly into the sunken derelict K-122 had hit minutes earlier, lodging itself in what remained of a bridge area. The other sped under the *Dale*, continuing aft.

"SIR!" Lieutenant Burnham said. "We have the submarine behind us. Directly aft of us, sir!"

"How is that possible?" Admiral Green said.

"Left full rudder, speed fifteen knots!" MacDonald ordered. If the contact was behind them, then they would be its next target. He glanced out of the starboard-side hatch. The *Coghlan* was in a right-bearing drift down the beam of the *Dale*.

An explosion to the right side of the *Coghlan* caused everyone to stare out the starboard-bridge-wing side. Water spiraled upward, spreading apart its fingers like some Las Vegas display.

Seconds later the left decoy successfully pulled away the Soviet torpedo, and the explosion sent a similar water fountain display to accent the sound.

"*Dale, Coghlan*. Unless otherwise ordered intend to launch additional ASROCs!"

MacDonald grabbed the Navy Red handset. "Permission granted!"

That was good. He needed the other destroyer's ASROCs in the water. The *Dale* was too close to do any good with its rocket-fired torpedoes.

"Our torpedoes have locked on something, sir."

"Make sure they don't lock on us," MacDonald said quickly.

"No, sir, they are aft of us and heading toward the target."

THE Soviet torpedoes launched from the aft tubes changed course to follow the *Dale*. They locked onto the destroyer when it went into its sharp left turn at high speed.

The *Dale* and *Coghlan* torpedoes locked onto the decoy lodged in the derelict. They immediately changed course, chasing the decoy.

The first explosion was followed almost immediately by three near-instantaneous ones. MacDonald and Green dashed onto the starboard bridge wing. Water exploded skyward, arching out like some wet fireworks display from beneath the sea. The *Dale* shook and vibrated from being in the vicinity of the explosions.

"Damn," Green said.

Both officers gripped the top of the railing, holding their balance as the concussions rode through the ship.

MacDonald stuck his head back inside the bridge. "Right full rudder, speed six knots, steady up on reverse course."

The Navy Red speaker blared to life. "*Dale,* this is *Coghlan.* We have multiple explosions behind your position. Do you require any assistance? What is your status?"

"Coming to course zero-zero-zero."

The sounds of cheering on the topside joined those inside of Combat. MacDonald grinned. The *Dale* had done its mission.

"Continue left to course one-one-five," MacDonald corrected. He needed to be back on the reciprocal course they were on when they launched their torpedoes. Now he needed proof they had destroyed or seriously damaged the Soviet submarine.

"WE have explosions," Orlov said as the first concussion hit the K-122, rolling it right and left, sending the bow and stern undulating up and down as the nearby explosions pushed everything up, down, and away from the submarine's center.

A cheer went up within the control room.

"Quiet!" Bocharkov snapped. "There is still another American warship up there."

Heads hung down, but not without broad grins on them.

Bocharkov was proud. He took a deep breath. The K-122 had done its mission and escaped. His and Ignatova's eyes locked. The XO smiled and rendered a two-finger salute.

"Let's get out of here," Bocharkov said, then issued several orders, keeping the K-122 inside the layer as it slowly left Subic Bay and entered the deeper waters of the Pacific Ocean.

SEVENTEEN

MACDONALD walked down the gangplank, opened the door, and slid into the backseat alongside Admiral Green.

"How you doing, Danny?"

"I'm okay, Admiral."

"Over thirty dead and over one hundred wounded, according to the latest situation report."

"I can't believe this has happened."

"Must have been accidental. The USS *Liberty* is limping away from station. The SITREP says it was attacked by both Israeli fighter bombers and Israeli torpedo patrol boats."

"Where were our forces?"

Green shrugged. "I was told we launched phantoms toward them, but McNamara himself ordered them back. Rumors have it that President Johnson even got involved and ordered the aircraft back."

MacDonald shook his head. "Even if it was an unfortunate and accidental attack, I cannot see our navy turning its back on one of its own ships."

MacDonald caught a hint of moisture in the old warrior's eyes as the admiral turned away to stare out of the left rear window of the sedan. "Sometimes politicians view us as castaways for political expediency, even as they wave their fists in the air shouting their love for us boys in uniform."

"I heard the skipper was wounded in the attack, but stayed on the bridge and directed the response."

Green nodded. "Lots of confusion and conjectures going on right now on what has happened. Admiral Moorer, chief of the Joint Staff, has ordered all quiet on the subject until all the facts are known."

"I just don't understand how they could not see the American flag flying from the mast or—"

Green turned back to MacDonald. The glistening in the eyes was gone. "Let's change the subject, Danny. Lots of things on the *Liberty* attack don't add up yet, but I have full confidence in the ability of the United States Navy to lay all the facts out for all to see."

"Aye, sir."

"You know that I'm catching all kinds of shit on our torpedoes sinking an already sunken ship. Seems Subic Bay Operations knew about that vessel. Seems everyone who is stationed here has dived on her at one time or another. The only folks who expressed ignorance about it were our chart makers. Subic Bay Operations showed me their locally developed harbor charts. They even have it notated on those. Just seems they never got around to sending the data into Washington so the United States Coast and Geodetic Survey could incorporate it into our navigation charts."

The automobile picked up speed as it left the pier, heading along the coast road, toward the main area of the naval base.

MacDonald smiled. "If nothing else, all the Soviets did was sink the same sunken derelict as we did."

"On the positive side, we have explained to the Filipino Navy that we were conducting some shallow water ASW exercise. They believe it, but we have to explain why we were using live explosives." Green sighed. "I am meeting with Commodore Heracleo J. Alano, head of the Philippine Navy at Cavite Naval Base to explain about yesterday morning." Green held up a folder. "Our public affairs officer and Legal have given me my talking points."

"Glad I'm not going with you."

Green smiled. "Nope, this is why they pay me the big

bucks. To keep our country safe, secure, and explain why we do the things we have to do for national security."

"What is going on with the spooks?"

"What do you mean?" the admiral asked with a sly smile. "I have no idea what you are talking about, Danny, and besides . . . you don't want to know. Sometimes not knowing is safer than knowing."

"They have the warehouse side of the base roped off, guarded by marines, and my supply officer is unable to get our supplies. We're getting under way this evening for Operation Beacon Torch. It would be nice to top off our food and such."

"Won't be getting anything from the warehouses before we set sail, Danny. I have sent out some logistics requests for supply ships to meet us en route to Vietnam. We'll do an underway replenishment at sea."

MacDonald nodded. "Are we sure we are going to Vietnam, Admiral? Rumor is we are going to be diverted to the Middle East."

Green chuckled and shook his head. "I don't think the U.S. Navy is very excited over anything having to do with helping the Israelis, and right now, it looks as if the war is about over. Seems the surprise air attacks on Monday destroyed the fighting power of the Egyptian and Syrian air forces. Reaching the Suez Canal in forty-eight hours sent a little fear through the Arab armies."

"How about the Jordanians?"

Green nodded. "They are the only military I was concerned with. Probably the only one of concern to the Israelis. The Jordanians are well trained, well disciplined, and have the morale and confidence to be formidable foes. Fortunately for the Israelis, they are also the smallest of the forces they are fighting. From this morning's Naval Intelligence briefing, looks as if the Jordanians are limiting their fighting to Jerusalem and the West Bank. That was probably intentional on the part of Jordan."

"I read where the Israelis have overrun the Golan Heights and driven the Syrians off of it."

"That's what Naval Intelligence says. Plus, the Israelis are having tea on the banks of the Suez. They could cross it, if they wanted. The Egyptian Army is in full retreat."

MacDonald shook his head. "I thought Nasser would put up a fight commensurate with his bluster."

"I think Nasser thought his army would put up a fight commensurate with his bluster. Soviet tactics designed for the plains of Germany don't work well in the open desert with no air support."

The car slowed as it neared Subic Operations Center. The driver turned into the curved driveway of the main headquarters.

"Danny, this is where I drop you off. I'm off on my trip up the road to meet with Commodore Alano. We met in Washington a couple of years ago, so I suspect it will be a cordial meeting, but I have to give him enough information so he can report events up his chain of command."

"Seems the Philippines are changing."

"I'd be surprised if we are here ten years from now. I think the national identity of the Philippines is changing. Nearly seventy years as a colony of Spain or us, occupied by Japan, and used by the United States as a critical element of our Asian national security, one of these days the Philippines will want—no! they will demand—their right to stand on their own two feet and be responsible for their own security."

"We're helping them. We're their friends."

Green laughed. "Danny, you are still a naïve young man who believes there are things in this world like low-cost lawyers and the tooth fairy." Green sighed. "We're also using them. Eventually, all nations prefer to have foreign armies and navies on their own soil and not theirs. We need to do what we are doing now to make sure that when we part it is amiable—as friends and comrades."

"I would think Marcos would want us to stay."

"I'm sure he would. We are part of his power base, but even if he survives and remains in power, he will be forced to ask us to depart."

The car stopped in front of the door and MacDonald opened it. "I think we did well on Monday."

Admiral Green smiled as he nodded. He stuck his hand out. "Danny, you and your sailors along with the *Coghlan* did an outstanding job. Tell your men how proud I am of them.

Once we get under way and I have a little more free time, I will send a message to Washington detailing the professionalism displayed by both ships. The problem will be that what happened on Monday will disappear from history. The USS *Liberty* incident earlier today is the eraser that will ensure this near catastrophic event where the Soviet Navy and the United States Navy tried to sink each other will be forgotten. Between you and me, it is something that should be forgotten—like Operation Highjump in the Antarctica."

MacDonald looked questioning. "Operation Highjump?"

"In the navy as in the other military services, there are secrets, incidents between us and the Soviets that will never see the light of day. Sometimes it is better to shut up and forget something rather than be in the public position of losing face."

"More of an Asian phenomenon than Western, wouldn't you say?"

"What? Losing face?" Green shook his head. "Face is very important even if we don't use the term a lot in our own world. America is losing face in Vietnam. We can't afford to lose face in the eyes of the world, which is why this incident on Monday will go into the U.S. Navy's book of secrets, which the chief of naval operations keeps. Good-bye, Danny."

MacDonald shook the hand and stepped out. "Have fun, Admiral."

"At least I will have some good wine for my early dinner with the admiral. Enjoy your bug juice."

"See you later?" MacDonald asked.

Green leaned down, his head visible to MacDonald. "We sail at midnight, Skipper. Talk to you later."

"UP periscope," Bocharkov said.

He rode the scope as it ascended, flipping down the handles and watching the water cascade from the lens. He stepped clockwise, feeling the slight vibration of the hydraulics helping the periscope turn in its tube as he searched the horizon. Off to the east, clouds marked the landmass outlining the Philippine coast.

"Stream the wire," he commanded.

At the Christmas Tree, Lieutenant Kalugin, the underwater weapons officer, pushed the *Boyevaya Chast'* 4 button and relayed the order to the communicators to start trailing the long wire.

The wire was an antenna for both transmitting and receiving signals. Used primarily by the K-122 for receiving the continuous navy broadcast, right now Bocharkov was using it for his new mission. Lieutenant Dolinski would be in the radio compartment with Starshina Malenkov. The installation had yet to work, after three days on station, and no one knew why.

Bocharkov leaned away from the periscope. "Periscope down. All clear." He looked at Kalugin. "Sonar contacts?"

"Sonar reports all clear, sir, with exception of the fishing fleet returning for the night."

Bocharkov patted the message in his shirt pocket. He thought he had escaped further contact with the Americans, but the K-122 had been less than a hundred kilometers from Subic Bay when Moscow ordered them back. His mission now was to monitor the telephone conversations inside Subic Bay so Moscow could determine if the original plan of the American battle group to head to Vietnam was the true plan, or if they were going to head toward the Middle East to help their ally Israel.

Bocharkov did not want to think what the Americans would do if or when they detected the K-122. After all, even with no news being reported by the Americans, he knew he had at least damaged Contact One with his aft torpedoes. The Americans would not be so cautious in their next contact.

"CAPTAIN Norton!" Chief Welcher shouted from the doorway.

The marines patrolling the perimeter surrounding the telephone switching unit glanced toward the chief.

Norton raised his hand from where he paced outside the building, his pipe puffing small clouds of smoke, marking his presence and path like the stack on an old coal-driven train.

"You should come, sir."

Norton hurried toward the building. Welcher disappeared inside, and a moment later Norton crossed the threshold. Around the Soviet equipment a couple of sailors stood, monitoring meters on the face of a bay of equipment the operational deception team had installed late yesterday afternoon. Wires stretched from the system to the Soviet equipment, with several more multicolored wires running parallel to the thin antenna the adversary had run from the equipment through the wall of the building and up along the outside wires to the telephone pole. Then they had started their patient wait. Several small reel-to-reel tape recorders made up the remainder of the American OPDEC system. A system without a name, designed and put together by the technicians of OP-20G, the secretive technology department within the United States Navy.

"It just came to life, sir," Welcher said as Norton squeezed himself between the sailors and the chief.

It had taken the communications technicians from San Miguel about forty-eight hours to figure out how the system worked. They could have done it in less time if they had been allowed to disconnect it.

"Is it transmitting?"

"Not yet, sir," Welcher said, touching a small yellow bulb at the top of the system. "Someone is trying to get it to transmit, but we are still interrupting this every time in accordance with your orders, sir."

The first-class sitting on the floor of the building with headsets pressed against his ears shook his head. "I believe they are trying to run some sort of diagnostics program on the system, Captain."

"Are we ready?" Norton asked.

The first-class looked up and smiled. Welcher nodded, winked at Norton, and said, "Two minutes after we do it, sir, we can have this system dismantled and on its way to our foreign technology exploitation bubbas at Naval Intelligence. They're going to wet their pants when they get this."

"They are going have cataclysmic orgasms," the first-class petty officer added.

Norton took another puff. The sailor nearest him stepped away. Norton failed to see the man wince and fan away the smoke.

"Okay, let's do it, gents," Norton said.

"Hit it," Welcher said, leaning down, his finger nearly hitting the button.

The first-class pushed the forward button. The four reel-to-reel tapes began to roll. The whisper of the tape could be heard as everyone watched silently.

Behind the deception system, another sailor with headsets raised his finger. "It's on its way."

Norton pulled his pipe out of his mouth. "Great work, Chief. You, too, sailors." He chuckled. "Don't you just love it when a plan comes together?"

The fake conversations from the deception system rolled into the Soviet equipment, traveling up the lines to the antenna, and out into the airways, heading toward the Soviet operator who waited for the results of his work.

"Captain, have you heard any news from *Liberty*?" Welcher asked.

Everyone turned toward Norton.

"They haven't released any names of the dead or the wounded yet. They won't until the next of kin are notified."

"I had friends on board the *Liberty*. I was on the *Georgetown* before being transferred to San Miguel. My shipmate on the *Georgetown* got follow-on orders to the *Liberty*. I just . . ." Welcher choked.

Norton touched him on the shoulder. "We all have friends on the *Liberty*, Chief."

"Why in the hell did the Israelis attack us, sir?" the first-class asked.

Norton shrugged. "Probably a mistake. Mistakes happen in the fog of war."

BOCHARKOV looked at the watch. Hard to believe that a little over three days ago he was being fired upon by the Americans and now here he was less than fifty kilometers off Subic Bay watching them without being among them. Lot safer this way.

Lieutenant Kalugin listened to the internal communications report and turned to Bocharkov. "They have what they want, sir."

"Who?"

"Lieutenant Dolinski, sir."

"What is it they wanted?"

Kalugin looked confused. "I don't know, sir."

Bocharkov grunted. "Makes two of us. Tell Lieutenant Dolinski to come to the control room."

Kalugin quickly relayed the order.

Moments later the GRU Spetsnaz officer emerged through the forward hatch. His head was bandaged in the back. As he approached Bocharkov, he could see that the broken blood vessels in the man's right eye were beginning to fade from the incident with the fire extinguisher.

"How are you doing, Lieutenant?"

Dolinski nodded. "I am beginning to lose my double vision, sir," he said.

The anger was not well hidden. When the K-122 returned to Kamchatka, there was no doubt in Bocharkov's mind that he would be summoned to explain his actions before the Party officials. He was not too concerned. His record was sterling. On the other hand, he had little knowledge of how much political influence Dolinski welded. He knew the K-122 *zampolit* Golovastov was thought a buffoon by those who had served with him, but being thought that by the fleet was not necessarily a bad thing when it came to what Party officials might think.

"Have we gotten what we want?"

Dolinski nodded and winced.

"Got a nasty blow to the head, Lieutenant. It'll go away in a few days."

"I was told I slipped and fell against the fire extinguisher someone was holding."

"Things like that happen on a submarine." Bocharkov raised his hand out, palm down, and wriggled it back and forth, up and down. "Submarines are notorious for their sudden movements." The hand fell back to his side.

Dolinski's eyes glared. "So I have been told, sir."

Bocharkov pulled the message from his pocket. "Our orders are to discover if this Beacon Torch operation is for Vietnam or if the Americans intend to redirect it to the Israeli war of aggression in the Sinai."

Dolinski gave a weak smile. "Lieutenant Golovastov and I are writing the message to pass along what we have learned to Moscow, sir. Our quick analysis shows the *Kitty Hawk* carrier battle group along with the American amphibious carrier *Tripoli* will not go to Vietnam. They are going to join another American carrier battle group sailing from America, around the tip of South Africa, somewhere near the Gulf of Aden. From there the warships will enter the Red Sea."

Bocharkov shook his head, grunted, and then said, "We got all that in the short time we have been here? I thought the system was malfunctioning."

"It was, sir, but the diagnostics circuits appear to have corrected whatever was wrong, because we are able to hear the Americans for several minutes before it malfunctioned again."

"Were we able to tell when they are getting under way to go west?"

"Yes, sir. They are going to set sail tonight. Not sure what time."

"Does it seem strange to you that we just happened to find this information between bouts of malfunctions, Lieutenant?"

Dolinski let out a deep sigh. "Sometimes we wait long periods to gain our intelligence, sir; other times it just lands in our laps. This was a blue bird. It flew in the proverbial window just as we needed it."

"I would think we would get bits and pieces—"

Dolinski interrupted. "Sir, if they are leaving the American base tonight, if we can restore the system again, then for the next few hours we should get lots of information, from their ammo load out, to where their flag officers are going to be embarked . . ."

". . . even to what happened to the destroyer we hit Monday?"

"Yes, sir, even to that."

"Very well, Lieutenant. I want to see the SITREP before it is transmitted."

Dolinski's eyes widened, but before he could speak, Bocharkov added, "It is my boat, Lieutenant. I like to know what is being transmitted off it."

The Spetsnaz intelligence officer nodded once and stormed out of the control room, heading forward again to the radio compartment.

"IT'S gone, sir," Welcher said. "They are going to think we are massing forces to go help Israel."

Norton smiled. "I do truly love this work we do, Chief, even when we run the risks we do, such as what has happened to our shipmates on the USS *Liberty*."

He took a puff on his pipe, and then looked at the sailors. "For all of you, what we have done is given the Soviets information where they will think Beacon Torch is a secret American mission to provide military support to Israel. We were lucky to get Naval Security Group Command to approve it as soon as they did."

"What will the Soviets do, sir?" the first-class asked.

"Most likely they will redeploy their submarines to the Indian Ocean to track us. That will pull some away from the Gulf of Tonkin. Then they will give the information to the Arabs. Might even hasten a peace agreement to bring this Middle East war to a close, until the next one. Then again, it could backfire on us and the Soviets start airlifting troops into Egypt and Syria while deploying their air force. Then this little deception activity of ours would become a self-fulfilling-prophecy kind of a self-licking ice cream cone."

"What is Beacon Torch, Captain?" the sailor in back with the headphones asked.

Norton shrugged. "Right now, it's an operation to land the marines behind the lines in South Vietnam. Trap some North Vietnamese regulars with their pants down. Giving the Soviets this misdirection will help the success of the mission because they should also tell their North Vietnamese ally to relax, the American battle group is going elsewhere. Meanwhile Soviet Navy elements are going to sortie out along where they believe we'll transit and wait for us to pass. It's going to cost them some operational tempo and assets to track our ghost battle groups."

"Wow!" the young sailor in back of the OPDEC system gasped. "I'm glad they have never done that to us."

Norton looked at the sailor for a few seconds before he laughed. "Son, what we just did is something that militaries have been doing for centuries. All we did was use modern telecommunications technology to send the adversary galloping over the wrong hill."

"Or at least we hope we did," Welcher mumbled quietly.